ACCLAIM FOR *EM*

C000075746

Emergency Powers rockets 1
political intrigue in a way far
expect and enjoy. This high-speed thriller is thought-provoking, well-researched, and timely. Add McCrone's books to your shelves. — J.J. HENSLEY, author of *Resolve, Bolt Action Remedy* and *Record Scratch*

Emergency Powers brings the Faithless Elector trilogy to a nail-biting finale. A dynamic mix of political intrigue and high-stakes personal drama, ultimately offering keen portraits of true patriotism —its weight, its costs, and the courage that drives it. — ART TAYLOR, Edgar Award-winning author of *The Boy Detective & The Summer of '74*

"The seamless writing…multi-dimensional characters and depth and breadth of research here is a testament to McCrone's craftsmanship. Readers will enjoy discovering the strengths and flaws of good guys and bad guys alike. RECOMMENDED" – KATE ROBINSON, *US Review of Books*

"Three tough female characters steal the show: FBI agents Vega, Sartain, and Trager. Overall, the power dynamics of these women with the rest of the cast are something special to pay attention to." — T. LIEBERMAN, *Independent Book Review*

McCrone's knack for capturing the complexity of political vulnerability in an intelligent thriller is on full display here. As timely as it is compelling... — MYSTI BERRY, editor, the *LOW DOWN DIRTY VOTE* series

FBI Agent Imogen Trager is "a memorable protagonist—a 'bookish' and 'formal' intellectual who's as tough as she is smart. *Emergency Powers* "has a highly cinematic quality to it, with plenty of action along the way." —*KIRKUS REVIEW*

Emergency Powers
James McCrone

This is a work of fiction. All characters, organizations and events portrayed here are either products of the author's imagination or used fictitiously. Anyone seeing a resemblance to actual persons, living or dead, is paying the author an extravagant compliment.

ISBN—978-0-999-13772-7 (paperback)
ISBN—978-0-999-13773-4 (ebook)

Cover Art Design, Daniela Medina

Proofreading provided by the Hyper-Speller at wordrefiner.com

EMERGENCY POWERS

James McCrone

An Imogen Trager Novel

As always, for Lisa

I am deeply grateful to the following people during the preparation of this book for their support, insight, and kind, critical eye: Jim McCue, editor; my family—Lisa, Fiona, Annie and Jake, Don & Carole, Elmer & Lois; Judy Aks, Maura Mahoney, and the Table 25 Group – Matty Dalrymple, Jane Gorman, Lisa Regan and Jane Kelly.

To all of you, thank you.

"Three may keep a secret, if two of them are dead."
    -Benjamin Franklin, *Poor Richard's Almanac* (1735)

Friday, March 10
Seattle, Washington

1

Just before 5am, FBI Agent Imogen Trager gave a low growl and reached for the phone, buzzing officiously on the nightstand. She sat on the edge of the bed she shared with Duncan Calder, glowering at it as her eyes focused in the dark. Fixing a strand of red hair behind her ear, she scrolled through texts and posts from colleagues and friends. Her anger turned from dismay to sickening fear.

"Duncan!" She shook him awake and handed him the phone. He sat up and took it, scanning the news, instantly awake.

Imogen rose and picked her way to the living room in the dark where she turned on the television. The piercing glare of the screen stung the murky Northwest morning. Some 3,700 miles away, Vice President Robert Moore approached a phalanx of microphones, manfully fighting back tears:

"My fellow Americans," he said, "it is my sad duty to confirm that Diane Redmond, the President of the United States, is dead."

Bob Moore, a towering figure in person, looked small on screen, standing in the rain under a canopy of black umbrellas at the entrance to Walter Reed Medical Center. Duncan joined Imogen in the darkness, and she reached for his hand.

They stared, dumbfounded, as Moore continued: "Her doctors have informed me"—here he paused to clear his throat—"that the cause of death is believed to be a heart attack; that it was sudden and fatal. A full autopsy is underway, and it will give us a clearer picture. Our prayers go out to her family and loved ones.

"The Chief Justice has administered the Oath of Office to me here in the presence of cabinet members and hospital staff. The preservation of our great nation's interests, its security and the continuity of government are assured."

Duncan turned to Imogen: "Is it starting again?"

"I don't think it ever stopped," she brooded, her green eyes smoldering. "We failed. We didn't cut the head off the snake." Fury rose within her, sharp and raw like nausea.

Duncan handed her back the phone. It continued buzzing as reporters swarmed, asking for a quote from her as the public and photogenic face of the Faithless Elector investigation. She'd learned her lesson there and declined each call.

Their texted questions—the ones she bothered to read—were, as usual, off the mark: Would the Faithless Elector task force be revived to look into the President's death? Would unanswered questions from the investigation strengthen or weaken support for the new President? Regarding the first: the task force was alive, if not well, she thought, and at any rate, she'd be one of the last to know about any official changes or developments. As to the second: Take a fucking a poll.

None of them asked the real questions—the ones *she* needed answered: Was this the final move of the conspiracy she had chased madly into a blind alley? If so, how had the dark network assassinated a President inside the White House? Who was moving the pieces, and what were the next moves? Most pressing: How would she get herself back in the hunt? From her phone, she deleted the draft email bearing the resignation she had planned to send on Monday morning.

Dawn was still some two hours away as Calder sat down on the couch next to her. "So you won't be resigning, I take it," he observed.

"No," she said, not looking up from her notebook.

"How will you begin?"

She looked up. "We were digging in the wrong place. I'm going to go back over the associates and links we've established, see where or how any of them point at Bob Moore."

2

"So Moore digging, eh?" he quipped.

Imogen sighed. She loved him, but how was he able to have distance at a moment like this? she wondered. She eyed him wearily. "Duncan, I'm going to get stonewalling from Nettie at the office about this new direction. I'm—"

He held up a hand. "What will you do?" He looked at her notebook. "And who's Carla?"

"I'm going back to the data."

"You've gotten nowhere with that," said Calder acidly.

"Because we were looking at it in relation to other actors. Not Moore. And Carla's not a who, but a what—short for 'CARLA F BAD': Character, Associates, Reputation, Loyalty, Ability, Finances, Bias, Alcohol, Drugs. It's what you look at in a security clearance, among other things. It helps define spheres of influence and interaction. The disclosure dossiers on the men who've been working directly under Moore will have looked precisely at these CARLA factors. And I want to look at them, too. And his associates. So I'll go backward, this time with Moore in mind. I want to look at his campaign finances. Who funded him early on in the race? Who else was involved or associated? Maybe something jumps out at me. Maybe that'll point me in a direction."

"It's a lot of maybes, 'Gen." He scratched at his iron gray hair.

"It's where I'll start. There's always a gap in the armor somewhere. The really hard part is that I can't just request materials the regular way through regular channels without telegraphing what I'm trying to do."

"Or looking like you're still part of the Faithless Elector case."

She nodded and looked at him uncertainly. "And...I think I should cut this weekend short, if I can get a flight back to D.C."

"I'm wondering what you're still doing here," he said.

Imogen leaned in and kissed him.

On the East Coast it was early morning, but across much of the country the sun was still not up. In the darkness, the announcement of Redmond's death in office set off a series of moves seemingly unconnected and largely unremarked, as pawns were sacrificed and battle pieces were moved into place for the final gambit.

Rocky Mountains

Snow lit by headlights split the darkness, blinding the Highway patrolman who waited for the tow truck to pull out a car buried in the snow. Working in the dark about 14 miles west-by-southwest of Aspen, Colorado, the tow truck was having a difficult time dragging the car out. In what must have been whiteout conditions, the car had plunged through a guardrail and into the ravine.

As the patrolman stood at the side of the road waiting for the winch operator to do his work, he took off his right glove to read an alert on his phone. Speechless, he watched the news clip of now-President Moore at the hospital. Bewildered, numb—and not just from the cold—he stared over the still-dark, bleak expanse of mountains.

"Damn," said the winch operator, breaking the patrolman's reverie. The contorted steel shell of a car came into view and slowly ascended backwards up the steep hill. "You guys close Route 82 for more than half the year. Maybe you should think about closing this one, too."

"We serve and protect," the patrolman countered. "We can't protect them from their own stupidity."

Maricopa, California

Ninety-five miles northwest of Los Angeles, near Bakersfield, west of where the lush groves of San Emidio return to desert, police had responded to a call reporting shots fired.

The bodies of four men lay strewn around the living room and kitchen of a battered, double-wide trailer home, victims of an apparent drug deal gone bad. Even before forensics got to work, it was obvious the house had been used as a meth lab. An acrid stench burned the eyes and throats of the responding officers, who quickly backed out and awaited the Kern County forensics team.

As two officers sat in a squad car in the dark guarding the site, news reached them of the death of the president. They watched Moore at Walter Reed on the lieutenant's phone. The death of these four drug dealers now seemed even less important. Desultorily, they searched the onboard police computer for information about the four corpses. Two of them had arrest records, known agitators and members of a border vigilante group.

"Right," the lieutenant said to the patrolman. "Illegally funded law and order."

"For some," the officer added.

In Seattle, Imogen packed her bags, while fewer than six miles away but as blind to one another as opposite sides of the same coin, a sleek Eclipse 500 jet touched down at Boeing Field. The light jet taxied rapidly in the damp winter darkness, coming to an abrupt stop on a dimly lit portion of the tarmac at the north end of the field.

The hiss of its engines became a plaintive whistle as the doors popped open and two young men, Dan Cardoso and Eric Janssen, ran down the steps. They immediately turned round and helped close the stairs. But for this gesture of help, anyone witnessing their arrival—and no one did—might have mistaken them for two young executives returning from a casual outing.

Its doors sealed once more, the small jet in the tan-on-beige livery of Flintlock Industries, pushed on, the whistle of its engines discordantly climbing the scale as it taxied away. Cardoso and Janssen walked toward their cars parked just outside a chain link fence, fist-bumping as they separated at the gate.

"See you April 20," Janssen said.

Cardoso gave a thumbs-up as he turned away. Though the tarmac was deserted, the bravado exchange was a crucial performance. They had each been schooled in the need for watchfulness—especially of one another. Any sign of dissent, hint of doubt or fading spirit should be reported.

Alone for the first time in more than 24 hours, each man allowed himself to think about what had just happened. On orders, they'd dispatched the members of a cell near Bakersfield, California, much like their own, though a failing one according to their handler. Although they had kept their misgivings to themselves, each had arrived at the same conclusion: when given a list of people marked for death, the quickest way to get your name added to the list was to refuse or even question the job. Each ruminated on the final step to come, and whether they would receive their just, or their eternal, reward.

Before their cars were started, and as Imogen zipped her suitcase closed, the light jet was in the air, headed east to another rendezvous.

2

Reactions to the death of the President were swift across the nation and the political spectrum. Imogen, now waiting at the airport gate, had inadvertently seated herself between two television monitors, each tuned to a different 24-hour news channel. They faced each other, across her and the political divide. At times, they seemed to be arguing with each other, and she found herself glancing back and forth like someone watching a tennis match. Travelers congregated silently at screens large and small throughout the terminal.

The remarkable unanimity of official emotion on television and across social media made it seem that everyone in Washington had been issued the same talking points memo: Redmond was praised for her "integrity," her "dignity" and "strength," each promising to uphold the unity she had embodied and to deliver on her legacy while offering support to Moore. There were, Imogen noted, still a few unfilled cabinet positions left. Snapchat, she mused tartly, seemed like a better venue for all the disposable preening and jockeying.

The news was rife with speculation about what had befallen President Redmond, and what a new Moore administration might look like. Between the two televisions and along the political spectrum, while politicians hewed to their "unity in adversity" tropes, the talking heads seemed to be going through their own peculiar stages of grief: conservative hosts, when not in denial about the larger implications, presented with over-modulated anger; whereas mainstream pundits registered shock and dismay, their interviews with Democratic leaders manifesting pain, and above all bargaining. Only religious leaders seemed to have progressed to acceptance and hope, anointing Moore as one demonstrably chosen by Providence. In all cases, speculation was rampant, and there were no facts in evidence, save the obvious—Redmond was dead and Moore was president.

Bob Moore was taciturn by nature, the pundits opined. He had a reputation for bloodless pronouncements, heavy on procedure and mindful of every political angle, earning him the ironic nickname "ad lib Bob." But on the campaign trail, and during the contested fight for the Presidency, they noted, he had been a different man. All dispassion spent, he became a man of conviction. It remained to be seen, the pundits agreed, as to which version of Moore would prevail now that he was President.

Imogen left her center court seat and wheeled her suitcase to a deserted area where she could think and work. She texted her friend and colleague, the only person in the FBI she felt she could fully trust, Amanda Vega: *"Moore was the objective the whole time? Can't believe we were so blind,"* Imogen wrote.

"I can practically hear the bad guys getting away," Amanda replied.

They both could hear it.

Imogen cracked open her notebook and turned past the CARLA F BAD page, to a fresh sheet. At the top she wrote "Opportunity" and "Contingent."

Working closely with Duncan and Amanda, she had seemingly stopped the plot to steal the presidency, called the Faithless Elector plot in the press. But they had failed to expose or pierce the tight circle of leaders at the heart of the network or to catch at any loose threads.

Under the first two words, she wrote: "Provisional."

Despite risking her professional reputation and her life, she had only provisionally thwarted The Faithless Elector plot after the general election. The case she and Duncan had built about killing Electors and trying to manipulate the election outcome was compelling, though largely circumstantial. It had been enough to get the votes challenged and refused when Congress met back in January to certify the vote, but there had been no arrests and the three Faithless Electors were murdered before they could be questioned.

The refused votes had forced a Contingent Election in the House and Senate, and the conspiracy she was chasing had continued their clandestine efforts to get Diane Redmond's challenger elected. She had fought bitterly to get the Bureau to take the new threat seriously, but her work on the Faithless Elector plot, her use of outside experts like Duncan and leaks to the press, had made her simultaneously the public face of the investigation and a pariah within the Bureau. Finally, working with her new supervisor, Special Agent Amanda Vega and an FBI-IT specialist named Trey Kelly, she was able to break inside the network, though not to break it apart. Another provisional win.

There had been arrests, but the conspiracy was organized like terrorist cells, each with little knowledge of the bigger picture, or who the leaders were. Imogen and Amanda's investigation identified and implicated some high level operatives, and they had been close to taking down the head of the Senate Judiciary Committee, Senator Drew Eliot, when his aide was murdered. In death, all blame stuck to the aide. Eliot was still on the hot seat—provisionally—but it looked like he would survive. Imogen wasn't sanguine about her own prospects.

As much as she needed a win with no provisos—and for the full implications of her investigation to be taken seriously—she needed the dark network conspirators to lose even more. At best, her work so far had done no more than temporarily stall phases of a corrupt, opportunistic gambit. She had thought she knew what the goal was—defeat Redmond and install their own man. She had thought their man was the one at the top of the ticket. But had Vice President Robert Moore been the objective all along?

She'd written down nothing new. She was frantic to get back to D.C. and make a fresh start. She dialed Amanda, who was in Nebraska following up a tenuous lead on their main investigative target, Frank Reed.

The FBI had a phone trace from January when someone in the vicinity of Fairmont, Nebraska, ordered Reed to "go dark," which he had done, disappearing without a trace. The Omaha field office had investigated, but had turned up nothing. Amanda had decided to go herself and try again. A cop to her core, Amanda Vega wanted to crush the conspiracy, and bring those responsible to justice, redeeming the investigation, and her friend, Imogen.

Vega understood why many of her FBI colleagues disliked Imogen. She wasn't a cop. She could be bookish, formal, and her manner sometimes came off as superior—the very reasons Vega herself had disliked her when they first met. But Imogen was a keen investigator, animated and driven to search for the whole truth, wherever it led. Those qualities, as well as her personal and professional bravery endeared her to Vega, even if they hadn't to those at the top.

"Nothing here," Amanda answered dismally by way of greeting as she plowed along a service road north of Grafton, Nebraska. "And a whole lot of it," she added, gazing across the flat expanse.

"I'm at the Seattle airport now," said Imogen. "I'll be in D.C. this afternoon. You're not finding anything?"

"Well, I can tell you that Nebraska roads sure give it to you straight. North-south are numbered, and the ones running east-west all have letters. Each a little one-mile grid that lets me check off that there's absolutely nothing going on here or worth following up in a surprisingly ordered way."

"Well, at least it's tidy," she noted, smiling to herself. "But nothing?"

Amanda sighed. "Yeah, I've got coordinates, 'Gen, not places—and certainly not leads."

"And the areas Trey noted in his phone trace report?"

"*Vague* coordinates," she lamented. "The cell towers around here are farther apart than back east, which makes triangulating less accurate. And it was a short call that seemed to drop in and out. Trey said it could be a hardware issue—and Nebraska has terrible cell phone ratings, so that's a possibility. Or whoever was giving Reed his orders could've been going really fast...whatever that means. Or it could've just been a glitch." Then, in exasperation, she added: "Who ever thinks about the *Vice* President?"

Imogen gazed down at her blank page. Nothing in the Faithless Elector case related to Moore. He was a cipher, not so much in the background as the background itself. "OK," she sighed. "Looks like my flight's boarding now. Let's talk when we're both back in D.C." And she hung up. Amanda hung up and tossed the phone onto the passenger seat.

Special Agent Amanda Vega's day had begun in a Super 8 Motel just outside Lincoln, Nebraska. Stunned by news of the President's death, she nevertheless got down to work on the old case. With Imogen reassigned, she was the keeper of the no-longer-growing Faithless Elector file, and she re-read the FD-302 interview sheets compulsively, hoping against experience that some new insight would emerge.

If she and Imogen were right about Moore's involvement, Amanda thought, the new administration would move quickly to question or suppress her investigation. What little there was of it. It had been a difficult and politically contentious case from the beginning.

With facts thin on the ground, rumors and theories were rife, not the least being the counter-narrative in certain press and government circles that the moribund Faithless Elector investigation was nothing but a sham and a distraction. If the investigation continued in this fruitless vein, she worried, the case would be stamped RUC—"referred under completion"— FBI-speak for file closed, active in name only. And she would be reassigned, perhaps farther afield than poor Imogen had been.

Desperate to take the investigation forward and finish the job, she had wangled permission from Headquarters to come here to Nebraska on her own initiative and search for clues. Frank Reed, the only known investigative target still at large, might be the key to everything.

They knew he directed at least one of the cells they had captured. His last act, before he went dark and vanished

11

completely, had been to communicate with someone presumably higher up; and that someone had been travelling near Fairmont, Nebraska, when he got the call.

"You know Reed's probably dead," her boss Don Weir had noted as he paused before signing her travel request. "Given these guys MO, that's the move I'd expect."

"Maybe so, Don." She caught his skeptical look. "OK, *probably* so. But maybe the fact there's renewed FBI interest in the area will force an error, or provoke a reaction." Now, the loose end she was chasing from yesterday's case might be the best hope of solving today's assassination—for that's what it surely was. She was grasping at straws, and she knew it.

She had heard that central Nebraska had been unseasonably warm for March, with bright sun and temperatures in the fifties. But that had been the previous week. Now, as the sun struggled higher, freezing rain followed snow squalls, driven by heavy winds that seemed to grow stronger by the hour, rocketing in bursts out of a dark, insensible sky. There were few trees on the plains to whip and twist in sympathy, only winter-hardened corn stalks razored to an inch or two from the ground, indifferent as only the dead can be.

3

Just after 4pm, with the wind finally dying down, and having spent a frustratingly pointless day crisscrossing the plains, Agent Amanda Vega pulled to the side of the road and responded to Imogen's text letting her know she was back in D.C., and had there been any developments?

"*Nada*," Vega texted.

She headed south along Interstate 81—also designated Road 13—when she saw a sign for Fairmont State Airport and turned off onto Road H. The pavement quickly became gravel as she bounced along the road toward five Quonset huts looming out of the fields ahead. She slowed at the entrance and looked at the airport's historical information board, which told her that the base had been opened in 1942 as part of the war effort and "inactivated" in 1946, when it was given over to civilian control. She drove on slowly.

Seeing nothing official-looking, she went into the airport cafe.

It was difficult to give a homey touch to a Quonset hut, but the management of the little Fairmont Airport had tried. There was a counter, predominantly white, reminiscent of an old soda fountain shop, with a mirror behind. Glass shelves fixed to the mirror held dainty parfait glasses and stainless-steel milkshake cups. High in the top of the roof's curve was a clock, ringed with pink neon, below which "Coffee Time" was written in neon-tube cursive.

The stools at the counter, in keeping with the soda fountain motif, were chrome, topped with wine-colored plastic that had been stamped with a texture meant to suggest leather.

The illusion of having arrived at an oasis in time fell away as Vega's eye roved to the furniture that filled the rest of the room, oak and pine tables surrounded by mismatched chairs of varying styles, materials and levels of craftsmanship.

"You looking for someone, honey?" asked the waitress. "'Cause I think he mighta just left."

"Who did?" asked Vega.

"A pilot. He'd been sitting here for 'bout two hours. You mighta seen that little jet taking off?" She didn't so much wipe the heavy wood table as scrub it.

"No," said Vega. "I was looking for an administrative office."

"Did exactly the same thing about two weeks ago, too."

"Did what?" asked Vega.

"Landed and then hung around for an hour-and-a-half or more and then left again," she said, staring at the tabletop from different angles to catch the light. "Empty both ways except for some samples from across the road."

Vega shrugged. "He was probably waiting for it to load, right?"

"No," she said, satisfied the tabletop was clean. She began walking toward Vega. "That only took about two minutes. It wasn't but a little box, and he put it on board himself. Normally, I'd be glad of the company, but he"— jerking her thumb back toward the empty table—"wasn't much of a talker. What can I get you, honey?"

"Coffee please," said Amanda, "black. What kind of pie is that?"

"Peach," said the waitress, ruefully. "I've got a lovely German chocolate cake."

"That sounds better," Vega agreed as she settled herself on a stool.

"Did you hear what's happening?" the waitress asked as she put a monstrous slice of cake in front of Vega and poured a blistering hot cup of coffee.

The waitress was a head taller than Vega's five-foot-four, but like her, she was ample and sturdy. She had a round face and large brown eyes. Her pink smock said "Kirsten" in script

14

over her left breast. Vega guessed Kirsten was in her late-forties. Her hair was plainly cut, short, golden blond, but with grey showing at the roots where her hair parted. She had an open, pleasant face.

"The President?" asked Vega.

"Just awful." She shook her head sadly. "I didn't vote for her, but I certainly don't wish her any ill...didn't."

"Of course not," said Vega, taking a bite. She gestured with her fork at the cake, her mouth being full, to indicate how good it was.

The waitress smiled warmly. The smile slowly faded. "Of course," she said thoughtfully, "I don't feel like I voted for Moore either. I mean, I don't think you ever know all that much about Vice-Presidents, do you?"

"No," agreed Vega, delicately sipping at the coffee. "No, you don't." There was silence as both reflected on this truth, and the sense that now no one was getting what they had wanted.

"What brings you out here?" asked Kirsten at last.

"I'm with the FBI," said Vega. "I'm following up some leads."

"Something happened here?" the waitress asked, her tone a mixture of delight and incredulity.

"Not exactly. I can't talk about an open case, obviously, but it's nothing to be worried about. What was the pilot picking up?" Vega asked casually as she took another bite of cake.

"I don't know," said Kirsten, before adding, "He didn't say," as though it now seemed pretty suspicious, didn't it? She smiled and nodded, as though she and Vega shared a secret and she understood what the investigation was about, but that mum was the word.

"Coulda been anything," she allowed with a shrug. "They work on plastics over there, fertilizers, gasohol." She paused. "You know"—leaning forward on the counter conspirator-ially—"that pilot seemed odd to me last time, too."

Vega was about to protest that she had no interest in the pilot, but felt herself a little caught up in Kirsten's tone of intrigue. She tried to shake it off. She remembered how Imogen, ever the PhD even when she didn't want to be, had said the most dangerous moment for an investigator is when she's desperate to find something and correlation *is* causality.

It also occurred to her that whether the pilot was involved in anything, it might shake the tree a bit if folks round about knew that there was FBI interest in the area. All she would need to do to make sure that everyone knew was to impress upon the waitress the need for secrecy.

Vega raised her eyebrows. "In what way?" she asked.

"I mean, we already get regular courier service in here twice a week for FedEx and UPS and all," Kirsten was telling her. "Why send a jet just to pick up a little box?"

"Why indeed," Vega affirmed before putting another piece of cake in her mouth.

"*Unless* you're in some awful hurry. But, if you are, why're you hanging around after you've picked it up? He'd just sit there"—she pointed to the corner table—"looking at that clock, looking at the door, drinking more coffee; playing with his phone. He wasn't very friendly. Are all FBI agents as nice as you are?"

"Some," Vega allowed. "Most of us are probably a bit more like your pilot, though—all business."

"What's he done?" the waitress asked, a sly grin on her face.

"Maybe nothing," said Vega nebulously. "Truly. And the FBI can't discuss open investigations." She took out a business card and put it on the counter in front of Kirstin. "But I wonder," she said, bringing up a picture of Reed on her phone, "have you ever seen this man?"

Kirsten took Vega's phone and studied the picture. "No," she said forlornly.

"If you think of anything else, or something happens that seems strange, or if that man shows up, please contact me." Vega tapped the card and put money on the counter. "That's my cell number. And Kirstin, I must stress that you not tell anyone I was here."

Kirstin was absorbed in looking at Vega's card. Her big eyes sparkled. "Yes, yes," she said distantly, her eyes still on the card. "Special Agent in Charge," she said reverentially. "In charge of what?"

"Nice try," said Vega good-naturedly. "Maybe we should have you do some of our criminal interviews."

"Probably not," Kirstin sighed. "I've told you a lot, and you haven't told me a thing."

"Is there someone in the tower I could speak with?"

Kirstin looked at her, amused. "There's no tower here, Agent Vega."

"Call me Amanda. A main office?"

"Not really. But you can talk to Denny. He runs the gas station." Kirstin leaned in close. "He calls it the FBO," she said, rolling her eyes. As a Federal employee, Vega was well versed in acronyms, but that one eluded her. "Fixed base operation," Kirsten offered. She glanced at the clock behind her counter. "He should still be there."

Vega found Denny in his office, a drab, overheated space at the front of one of the Quonset huts. There were four calendars on the wall depicting various kinds of aircraft in flight. Neither the calendars nor the planes were current. The two-thirds of Denny's desk not covered with forms and loose paper were piled high with binders, logs and dog-eared catalogs. A large, overflowing plastic ashtray sat atop one of them.

As she approached the door, she could see Denny. He leaned back in a battered, faux-leather reclining office chair, his feet resting on the desk's only clear space. He quickly sat up and stubbed out his cigarette as Vega walked in. He squinted at her through the lingering smoke, his fingers squeezing the filter and pushing it firmly into the ashtray, as though he were drowning someone. His thumb rocked back and forth over the crushed filter, administering the coup de grace.

"Hello," she said, "are you Denny?"

"That's me," he said, wiping his hand on his trousers.

17

"I'm Special Agent Amanda Vega." She showed her ID. "Kirsten in the coffee shop told me where to find you."

Denny paused as he reached to shake her hand across the desk. "FBI?" he asked, startled and straightening up.

"Yes, I—"

"I don't wanna hear nothin' more about the Nebraska Indoor Clean Air Act!" He was dressed all in kelly green—matching work shirt and trousers. The heavy winter coat hanging on a hook on the wall next to the desk was the same color. He was in his late fifties, with a wizened face the color of mahogany and a shock of white hair, thistledown tinted with nicotine yellow. His forearms were dark and sinewy. "Did Kristen send you in here?" he demanded.

"No," said Vega, "she told me where to find you...and is it Kirsten or Kristen? She told me Kirsten."

Denny shrugged. "So whaddya want?"

"What can you tell me about the plane that left a little while ago, the light jet?"

"That asshole?"

"Yes. I'm assuming," said Vega.

"Name's Scott something, I think," he said. "I get the impression he's some executive type courier. When some big shot needs something quick, or needs to get somewhere quick, he takes care of it."

"Where's his base?" she asked.

"Don't know."

"Know where he was headed?"

"Nope."

"Did he file a flight plan?"

"Not with me," said Denny.

"Aviation isn't my area," said Vega, "but aren't they supposed to?"

"Yep. Most do, and they can do it online with the FAA and a bunch of others. What's he done?" He looked at her expectantly, as though he would be very pleased to hear something appalling about Scott.

"Maybe nothing," said Vega.

Denny's face fell slightly, his expression that of a man accustomed to people disappointing him.

"Probably nothing," she added. "But I'd sure like to get a look at where he's going and coming from. You don't have any logs pertaining to him?" she asked, looking around at all the papers lying about.

"You mean like his tail number?" Denny began. "I would, if that asshole'd ever got gas or paid a tie-down fee, or did anything other than land, hang out for a couple hours and then take off."

"I see," said Vega, now wondering how she would track him.

"It's not a law or anything," Denny explained, "but little airports like ours stay in business 'cause people buy fuel, or need maintenance or pay a tie-down fee when they stay overnight—sometimes even if they don't stay overnight. And when we do anything like that, we write down the tail number for reference." He shook his wizened head. "I mean, would it kill ya to buy something? And a couple cups of coffee don't cut it."

Vega sighed, sensing more defeat.

"Of course," Denny grinned, "I wrote it down anyway."

Vega smiled warmly back at him. He grinned, scratched the top of his white head and looked away with Midwestern modesty.

4

Seven hundred miles northeast of Nebraska, in the upper reaches of Lake Michigan, the March thaw was still an unsubstantiated rumor. On Beaver Island—official population, 657—clear days flirted with temperatures just above freezing, but nights still fell into the twenties. An austere languor hung over the countryside. Longtime residents could tell you things were changing, that the ice was beginning to thin on Fox Lake, in the middle of the island, even if the edges remained frozen solid. A battered aluminum rowboat, hauled partly ashore and forgotten there in October, lay stuck in the ice, as much a lesson in not leaving things undone as a testament to winter's fierce grip.

Tourists, the essence of the island's economy, would not arrive in any numbers until the end of May. Nevertheless, the island saw its small share of winter recluses who craved the island's bleak seclusion, taking solace in its deathly slumber and the frozen wind hissing across the landscape. One such had arrived in late January. That lone passenger had thrown his duffel bag on his back, tucked his arms inside the two looped straps and trudged off to his cabin along Sloptown Road. The crunch of his boots faded into the distance with the diminishing light.

Since that January day, glimpses of him had been rare— hiking along the frozen shores, ice-fishing on a few occasions, surfing the internet at the library—and they were noted and spoken of by locals at Carl's Island Coffee Shop in much the same way as sightings and movements of the island's wild turkeys. Anyone running into him, whether out in the wilds or in town buying supplies, found him pleasant enough, if reserved. His quiet, awkward demeanor and long-distance gazes were just what you'd expect of a guy who chose a remote island in the middle of winter. Not that folks weren't curious to know more, but a Midwestern distaste for being seen as nosy outweighed the desire to pry.

Frank Reed, now going by the name Ian Gerritt, had left Silver Spring, Maryland, by bus on January 19 nursing a gunshot wound in his arm. The deep graze blistered and wept. He had changed buses, bandages and his name in Cincinnati before starting north—first to Detroit, before continuing to Grand Rapids and then Charlevoix, where he waited a day to take the 25-minute flight to Beaver Island and the cabin he had owned in Gerritt's name for 20 years.

If he had looked out of place while in D.C., in his faded camouflage jacket and heavy boots, he fit in easily enough on Beaver Island. He carried no cell phone, and didn't have a landline, television or electricity in his cabin. His escape—and isolation—was complete. No one had followed him. Not even his superiors knew of his Ian Gerritt alias, a relic from another life. He was safe. On the morning the President's death was announced, he made some bitter coffee on his potbelly stove and walked into town for a day-old newspaper and a proper breakfast.

Reed had stayed on Beaver Island, deliberately missing a rendezvous in Fairmont, Nebraska, during the last week of February. On the day the President died, still safely anonymous on the island as he trudged through the snow to Carl's coffee shop for his breakfast, he looked at the date on his watch and noted that he was missing an extraction flight today, and that he'd have had to leave the island days earlier to have been in place to catch it. But before making contact there, he had to be sure of his reception; and until he could be sure, he wasn't going to risk traveling to the rendezvous or exposing himself to his colleagues.

When he arrived at Carl's, he stopped in the coffee shop's glass entry to stomp the snow off his boots. Through the door it seemed everyone was watching the television set behind the counter. Two customers near the door turned to him and stared. Reed felt a jolt. Through the window, on screen, he could see a reporter standing in front of the Capitol. Was this news about the plot? Had his picture been shown? For a moment, he lamented not having already escaped to Nebraska.

Rather than stare back at the customers sizing him up from inside, he calmed his nerves and focused on the screen. Still standing in the vestibule he saw the news crawl running below the reporter: "President Redmond is dead."

He took an empty stool at the counter and ordered steak and eggs. He would stare up at the news reports from time to time between bites. At first, he felt blank, stunned. The plan he had worked on for more than four years had come together, and the last moves had happened without him.

He was careful to adopt a mask of concern and shock for the benefit of his fellow diners, but relief and excitement flowed within him as he watched. He stopped in mid-chew, however, and listened with growing alarm, when the newscast cut to a reporter in Washington named Hugh Salter.

"As of now," Salter began, "we have no new information. The autopsy and toxicology reports on President Redmond are in process, and it will take time to do a faithful, thorough investigation.

"The government will continue, as President Moore noted earlier this morning, but the details of how it will continue, and what—if any—new directions a Moore Administration might undertake remain to be seen. It's probable that he will see his mandate as ensuring a continuation of Redmond's policies, in a sort of caretaker role, as Lyndon Johnson did after the death of President Kennedy.

"It will be interesting, though," Salter continued, "because he has majorities in both Houses, so whatever agenda he chooses to follow should be able to get through more easily than we might have expected from a Redmond Presidency."

Reed listened with heightened attention to the report, attuned to any hint that the FBI was closer to finding him. So far as Reed could make out, Salter had not found out the name of the source known to him only as "Patriot76." He watched the broadcast, listening intently for anything leading back to him.

His mouth twisted as he reflected on how it all ended, how his tactics had backfired, how his contacts and operatives had been blown. Far from destroying Imogen Trager, as he had been instructed, she had outmaneuvered him. He himself had become exposed, necessitating this tactical retreat to the upper reaches of Lake Michigan. He rubbed unconsciously at the spot near his right bicep where Imogen's bullet had hit him.

Yet despite his failures and blunders, the men he had put in place to carry it out had succeeded. Moore was in place and the final steps could begin.

* * *

In a sprawling office park outside Wichita, Kansas, a tall, spectral man rose and excused himself from a meeting he had been chairing to answer a call. Closing the door unobtrusively behind him, he asked: "Anything?" He listened, nodding. "So, your people are on her phone, and it's clear she's on the outside this time? She said 'Nada?'" He chuckled. "Good. But stay on it."

He listened again. "Yes, that's fine. I'm not worried he didn't show if you're not. As you say, he'd have found out only today. But we'll get him next time. The next potential rendezvous is in two weeks?" He listened. "Good. Presumably after today, when he sees that it's all worked out, he'll feel safe enough to come in. And yes, that's a good time-frame for Mr. Fisher, too."

Pause to listen. "I leave it with you. What about that business in California and Colorado? Meeting concluded?" He smiled as he listened. "Excellent," he said and hung up. A good end to this day of days.

5

March 15

As with everything else since the general election in November, Diane Redmond's funeral was provisional. Like President Kennedy, she had not made funeral arrangements. The observations and ceremony, like those for Kennedy when he died in office, were intended to follow those accorded Lincoln more than 150 years earlier. For 24 hours the "Old Guard," the 3rd Infantry, would attend the casket in the East Room. Then her remains would be moved from the White House to the Capitol Rotunda to lie in state during a national day of mourning.

It was to be a somber procession, the only sound along Pennsylvania Avenue that of the horses' hooves and muffled drums as her husband and their two college-age children preceded the caisson, walking hand-in-hand up Pennsylvania Avenue. After lying in state for two days, the casket was to be put on a train bound for her hometown of Evanston, Illinois, and her final resting place.

But now, four days after her death was announced and President Moore had taken the oath of office at the hospital, none of this had happened. Preparations had been made and put on hold. President Moore called for a national day of mourning on the following Monday, but there was no finality, no full stop.

Where the autopsies of Lincoln, FDR and JFK had been largely perfunctory, confirming the obvious for the sake of the record, there was no consensus about what had befallen President Redmond. She lay on a cold metal table under piercing halogen lights in a refrigerated room in the basement of Bethesda Naval Hospital, and in place of the reverence of the honor guard, she was being subjected to indignities perpetrated by masked inquisitors in pale green surgical garb.

News outlets crackled with speculation, and social media with the panorama of contradictory certainties. Some decried organized grief in the tradition of the Lincoln and Kennedy ceremonies as only befitting a president murdered in office. Many countered that it was self-evident that she *had* been murdered. Others, frustrated with the Electoral College debacle, the so-called Interregnum while the House and Senate deliberated during the contingency election, and now this further blow—wanted nothing more than for government to settle down to business.

With the death of their President, Democrats, a minority in both the House and Senate, were now bereft of all power except that of pontificating to the media. They fretted impotently over the uncertain direction of a Moore Administration. The minority leaders in both House and Senate continued to preen and pronounce, but they were actors playing to near-empty houses in a production that seemed about to close.

Imogen had returned to D.C. from Seattle. Behind her closed office door as she dug through disclosure dossiers, she found that a good many of the new players in the Moore administration—notably the cup bearer, Clayton Quantrelle, and the slippery Senator Eliot—had all worked together in one capacity or another with a series of ponderously christened, tenuously linked and plausibly deniable PAC's and charities with names like the Voter Veracity Project (V^3, for short), the Sovereign Caucus, Opportunity Initiative and even the think tank Forefathers Institute.

Far away from the inquest into the President's death or her former case, Imogen hoped that by backtracking through filings, audits, policy papers and the like, she might find that low, unlocked door leading to those in charge. Until now, the investigation had proceeded provisionally. Now was the time, she thought, to end it permanently.

She had seen steps—murdered Electors, interference in the Contingent Election—and had misread the objective each time. Now that she saw the end product clearly, she could track backward, could unearth who had been behind it from the start. And stop it going any further forward.

Though it had been some three months since she was forced into her new role, rarely a day went by where she didn't silently, angrily rehearse the Bureau's injustices to her. Staff had learned to steer clear when the storm of indignation was on her, and it was why today her door could remain safely closed with no interruptions or questions.

"Fucking time-serving morons," her silent catechism began. "Sure, I fed the press information, beyond my authority. But only because I couldn't trust the Bureau to act. 'Cause I couldn't trust that they wouldn't share information with moles like Kurtz. And I was right! Almost got me and Duncan killed."

At such times, she could hear the Director's portentous tone again in her head at the ill-named award ceremony:

"Agent Trager," he had said solemnly, "you are being promoted and given a new title, reflective of your background and talents."

At this, she might have felt herself elated, she remembered, anticipating the words "Special Agent in Charge," but the temperature of the room suggested otherwise and she had felt her breath coming short. Neither Amanda nor her boss would look at her. They stood next to her, yes, but facing straight ahead, polite, brittle smiles frozen like rictus.

"Director for Studies in Electoral Integrity," he had pronounced, and Imogen felt a bone chill settling on her, a kind of rigor mortis taking hold. The polite golf-clap applause when the Director had stopped speaking was as awkward as a "like" on a Facebook post announcing the death of a mutual friend.

Along with Imogen's new title and cubbyhole in surplus space at the Government Accountability Office building had come new responsibilities, for studies, for reports that no one would read, much less heed. She would attend conferences and "interface" with policy people engaged in equally abstruse work.

And it got worse. Her new superior, perhaps a little too eager not to be managing the FBI's problem child, had suggested she might enjoy a courtesy appointment in academia, away from the Bureau. They would happily arrange leave for her. "Many politicians and service staff do so, you know," he had said helpfully, "and their insights and experience are valuable teaching tools. With your PhD..."

"Well," she thought sitting in that barren office, "the best way to disguise what I'm doing will be to hide in plain sight." She grinned as she composed an email announcement to her superior about an exciting new study and direction for her working group. The title of the report, she thought, would be the key not only to making sure no one would ever read it, since it was a smokescreen, and to ensure she was given a wide berth.

After twenty minutes she came up with: "Study on the Effect of Super PAC's in the Post-*Citizens United* Context, and Differences in Spending Across Region and Party on Voter Mobilization and Suppression: A Structural Equation Model."

That ought to do it. She pressed "send."

If what's past is prologue, Imogen's experience taught her that no matter how well armored the foe, there was always a weak link—something overlooked, something not deemed important and therefore unguarded. A seeming strength could be turned into a weakness. She had ample experience in finding a way in by digging where others disdained to look.

Days into the new Administration, she was already hearing speculation that Moore would force the Attorney General out; and if successful, it seemed likely he would install Senator Eliot. As she contemplated what might lie ahead, she was by turns furious and sick with dread. If the conspirators could strengthen their grip on the levers of power, they would control all the systems meant to check them. They already had Congress and the Executive branch.

* * *

Richmond, Virginia

Mason Brandenberg stood in his kitchen, fixated on news of the lack of progress in the Redmond inquest. The former assistant co-chair for finance at the Forefathers' Institute, a Washington think tank, he was stout and nervously vigorous. His complexion tended toward robust pink, his small eyes improved by the thick, rimless lenses he wore. But today his eyes grew large and the color drained from his face when he caught sight of a former colleague, Clayton Quantrelle, standing just behind now-President Moore at a press conference. Even Brandenberg's thinning hair seemed to pale.

He set his coffee cup down absently, his gaze fixed on something either far off or not there at all. His wife—solid herself, with a museum-piece grandeur—looked at him with peevish concern. She had noticed Quantrelle, too.

"Looks like *he'll* have a place in the White House, now, doesn't it?" she stated, more than asked, her tone implying that her husband, too, might be preparing for loftier work had he stuck it out with Quantrelle and his coterie. After some moments, he broke from the trance, smiled weakly at her and walked into his study. He coaxed aside a closet door and dragged out a Bankers box.

He stared at it for a few moments, then lifted and carried it to the trunk of his car, leaving for work and neglecting to say goodbye to his wife.

FBI Executive Assistant Director Don Weir was at work, and like a great many Americans still wishing for some resolution, he wasn't getting any. In fact, it was the opposite. He leaned toward the speakerphone on his desk, trying to hear more clearly. Another task group was handling the investigation into the death of President Redmond, but the Attorney

General and FBI Director had wanted Weir, as head of the Faithless Elector task force, to be "conferenced in." He quickly lost track of what voice represented which agency, whether the Secret Service, the Surgeon General's office, the AG or the FBI Director.

"We'll have the full clinical toxicology report in a few hours," a voice was saying. "The forensic toxicology will take another week."

"A week!" a number of voices said in unison.

"Possibly longer," the beleaguered voice defended. "We're still examining what lasting damage there may have been in the Transient Ischemic attack she seems to have suffered some years back. Which will also take time."

"So, it's true?" asked another voice. "She did have a TI stroke?"

"We think so," said the first voice. "It was noted as 'probable' in her medical record. In the absence of obvious toxins—and doctors Menlo and Somers have been thorough, checking and re-checking each other's work—our hypothesis is that the TIA was the root cause, but we haven't found anything conclusive there yet either."

A new voice chimed in.

It was bland, in the particular way that the sonorous and stilted can be, yet assured:

"This is a very sad time in the life of our nation, and the President is not unaware of the cloud hanging over all these proceedings," it announced, as though dictating a newspaper leader to be printed with black edges, "particularly with so much unresolved." A portentous pause and then: "The death of any President, after the most regular of elections, would be enough to spark intrigue and notions of conspiracies. But with all that's happened up till now, it's vital that everything issuing from this working group be consistent. Everything needs to be coordinated through the White House, and my office particularly."

Weir leaned a little closer to the speakerphone, brow furrowed.

"Of course," continued the assured voice, "I'm by no means seeking to trespass on any agency's turf or prerogatives, but in times such as these, a clear message—or set of messages—issuing from a single source will serve to dampen an easily inflamed situation."

"This is Don Weir, FBI Faithless Elector Task Force. Who's speaking, please?"

"Chief of Staff, Clayton Quantrelle," said the voice. "I and President Redmond's former Chief have been working in tandem during the transition. I was Counselor to the Vice-President. I am now President Moore's Chief."

"I see," said Weir, unable to keep an uncertain tone out of his voice. "Welcome aboard," he added. A chief of staff didn't need Senate confirmation, it was true, but this abrupt appointment hadn't been made public, so far as he knew. Redmond wasn't even in the ground.

"The preeminent goal of this Administration, and certainly this transition, is continuity," Quantrelle continued, "but as you can imagine, President Moore will want to have his own people—those with whom he feels most comfortable—closest to him. This is not to do with policy but with effectiveness. Trust."

Weir sat back in his chair and scratched at the back of his head. "I suppose that's right," he said into the speakerphone, not at all sure that it was.

"And thank you for your kind welcome," said Quantrelle. "I never forget a friend."

Who is this creep? he wondered. Weir resettled his bulk in the chair and scratched again at his head. The blond, crewcut hair was so light that he appeared bald in certain lights. He jotted Quantrelle's name down on the pad next to the phone and circled it. He wanted to see the disclosures dossier that the FBI and Secret Service had put together.

"We're looking into everything," a Secret Service representative was saying on the conference call. "We've looked into what she ate the night before; we have a picture of the movements of everyone inside the Residence. We seized the B-12 ampoule she injected just before bed as the most probable cause, and it's been reviewed separately by Dr. Menlo and Dr. Somers—and by our own team. There are traces of cyanocobalamin, but that's exactly what should be in there…it's a man-made form of B-12. The injection site on her right thigh also shows trace amounts of it. There's nothing else."

"Could there have been an allergic reaction?" someone asked.

"There's nothing consistent with that, either, not on her skin, in her mouth, internally. And she'd been taking the supplements for months. Any reaction would have presented much earlier."

He paused a moment, and his tone changed to one of gloomy resignation: "We're sampling the air, pillow fibers. No detail is too small. Everything we learn, no matter how small, we're transmitting to Menlo and Somers, who are in charge of the medical inquest and are overseeing each detail, double-checking one another's work. Fortunately, Dr. Somers was on call at the hospital when the president arrived, so he was able to quickly take charge. We want to make sure that we either catch those responsible or we're able to give a clear, thorough report as to how and why this is just a terrible misfortune."

"Excellent," said Quantrelle, taking charge again. "Good work everyone. And I'll coordinate for the new White House Press Secretary, Anthony Marek."

6

Now also back in D.C., Special Agent Amanda Vega began going over her only lead, the identity and itineraries of the pilot in Nebraska. Evanescent at best.

"That's all you found?" asked Weir, fresh from the conference call, as he stood in the doorway to her office.

"It's something," she offered weakly. "So far, the bad guys work in plain sight. There's always a plausible cover for what they do," she said more assertively.

"Hmmm," Weir grunted.

"Don, they seem to count on people assuming there's a perfectly innocent reason for their actions; that their cover activity's just what it seems to be. Perfectly plausible every time. If Imogen hadn't followed *her* tenuous lead, we might never have caught the few people we did." She gestured toward the pictures on the crime board she'd erected.

"Yes, well don't follow her example too closely, Amanda. I'd hate to lose you too." He paused, clearly embarrassed at having offered praise, even if in a roundabout way. "Let me know what you've found by the end of the day, and we'll discuss next moves." He put his hand on the doorknob. "Open or closed?" he asked.

"Closed, please," said Vega. She would need quiet to stay focused. Her lead was barely something. Still, she remembered that when Trey Kelly at IT had suggested possible reasons why the phone call made by Reed had been so intermittent, he had also mentioned that the recipient of the call might have even been in a plane. And here was an airplane making mysterious stops.

She leaned back in her chair and looked at the crime board on the wall of her office, hoping to draw inspiration. Most agents now had all their info tidily onscreen, but she still found it best to have the big picture up there in all its provisional, low-tech suggestiveness. As she stared at the board, she pulled out the elastic band holding her raven hair in place. Twisting it round and round her fingers, she gazed over the board.

Special Agent Colls had headed the FBI/DC "cell." His picture, because he'd been killed, had an "X" drawn across it, as did the pictures of his network lieutenant, Agent Tom Kurtz and their flunkies. Beside each was the operator's real name and his "network" name—Colls was "Beadle," Kurtz was "Farmer."

Like Vega, the network had used a low-tech approach— no computers, no texting—and part of that approach was a simple, robust plain-language code that, like everything they did, could seem perfectly innocent if overheard. Network codenames were a piece of that. Alec Nash, codenamed "Fisher," was leader of the Boston cell.

There was a check mark across Nash's handsome photo because he was in custody, though not cooperating as yet. Vega wondered if the new administration would be so brazen as to pardon him. Perhaps later, she thought, after they'd thoroughly discredited her and her case. Frank Reed, codename "Cooper," was the only person in the Boston cell still at large. Vega had drawn a bull's eye onto his face.

Was this airport business worth anything at all? she wondered. As ever, they were elusively close, feeling around in the dark—either one step away, or, equally possible, straying purposefully in the wrong direction. Perhaps now that she'd told Kirsten how secret all this had to be kept, someone in the network would hear that the FBI was taking an active interest at Fairmont airport, and that might shake the tree a bit, might panic the bad guys into making some sort of mistake.

You never knew where a lead might take you. The FBI had started with the two dim-witted assassins killed in self-defense by Imogen's Professor Calder in the stairwell of an office building. They were getting nowhere until Imogen and Trey painstakingly created a trace combining and overlapping both the drop phones and their regular phones, which they sometimes forgot to switch off. That sphere had begot another, and it seemed to be leading up the command chain. Until it stopped dead.

The FBI had been tracking another cell, perhaps closer to leadership level, when Senator Drew Eliot's aide, Casey Hague was killed. Vega still had a picture of Senator Eliot on her board. There were also three code names pinned to the board, unattached to any faces—Postman, Tucker and Baker—which she presumed were the leaders of the network. Each cell on the board was still an island unto itself.

She knew from the cooperating witnesses that none of them knew anything about any other cells. But if this pilot was somehow involved, he might have a bird's eye view of the whole network. The view's good from up there.

Vega dialed a number at the FAA and after giving her credentials was put through to an inspector Sims. "Good morning, this is Special Agent Amanda Vega, and I'm looking for information on a very light jet. I've got its registration, and who owns it, but that's about it."

"OK," he said. "Go ahead and give me the tail number." His voice and accent were subtle. Vega couldn't quite place it, but thought maybe West Virginia, and he'd been gone a long time. "I can get you their base, owner, insurance carrier. And I can get you their flight plans, travel habits. I'm assuming it's a US aircraft? There'll be an 'N' at the beginning of the tail number if it is."

"Yes," said Vega, "it's N8977A, registered to Flintlock Industries."

"Looking for anything in particular?" There was a refreshingly languid quality to his questions, as though he had all the time in the world, tasting vowels, considering his words.

"I'd really like to understand how the plane operates," said Vega, "who the pilot or pilots are. And I'd really like to know where it's been going." She could hear him tapping away in the background as they spoke.

"Eight-nine-seven-seven-Alpha," he murmured as he typed. There was a pause. "All right," he said. "Says it's a personal jet, an Eclipse 500 . . . 'bout three years old. Owned by Flintlock Industries, like you say . . . based in Omaha. It's a corporate jet."

"Right," said Vega. She could still hear him tapping away.

"It's all pretty standard stuff. Good bit of activity, I'd say, but nothing out of the ordinary. Principal pilots...well, now that's gotta be a mistake."

"What?" asked Vega.

"For principal pilot it says Archie League. I think someone's messin' around here."

"I don't understand," she said.

"For these types of carriers, it's pretty standard either to list a whole bunch of pilots who're checked out on the equipment, or to do what they've done, which is just list their subcontractor and one name, often the chief pilot."

"OK."

"But they've gone and listed the main contact as Archie League. That's the name of the first ever signalman, back in the Twenties—kind of a folk hero around here at the FAA. Maybe folk hero's a bit strong, but I tell you, I hate stuff like this. No respect. I'm going to open an inquiry—"

"—Please don't," said Vega quickly. "Not yet. In fact, I'd like you not to mention anything about my call or what you've found. It's possible—hell, it's *probable*—that this is nothing more than an FAA matter. But it might be related to an open case we have, so please let me make some inquiries first. I'll keep you informed."

"Fine by me."

"Thank you," she said. "How do I call up their flight plans? Is it public record, or do I need authorization and access through you?"

"I can certainly help with that. ATC—Air Traffic Control—has everything, and if I make the request it'll all just go that bit faster," he offered.

"That'd be great. Could we go back two years? Maybe a bit more?"

"No, ma'am, I'm sorry. ATC records have everything, including radar. But the records are only kept for 45 days."

"That's it?" she asked, incredulous.

"Yeah," he said. "It used to be a space issue, but what with everything being digital nowadays, it's still a recordkeeping challenge."

"I see."

"Anyway, our investigations are usually about accidents and near-accidents: 45 days is ample for our purposes. I know DEA sometimes looks for patterns, but there you're dealing with international flights, and that's a whole different ballgame. I'm not seeing any international hops here." He paused. "Lot of diversions, though."

"What does that mean?"

"That they file a flight plan from one airport to another airport, and then en route they contact ATC and go somewhere else."

"You can just do that?" she asked.

"Sure."

"So where do they go?" Vega asked.

"Well, that's just it. Almost every time this aircraft deviates it's with a request to go VFR...visual flight rules. Which means flying low over uncontrolled airspace. They could be going anywhere, landing anywhere."

"Anywhere?" she asked.

"No. Sorry. Not *anywhere*. I'd say the aircraft's probably only got about a thousand-mile range...less at low altitudes. The Rocky Mountains would be a barrier." He seemed to be talking more to himself than her. "Not that he can't fly *over* the Rockies, mind you, just that he couldn't do so without climbing up into instrument range."

"So?"

"Well," said the inspector, "if he stayed mostly in the plain states, and stayed clear of controlled airspace—bigger airports like Omaha or St. Louis—he could come and go just about anywhere—Kansas, Nebraska, South Dakota, Oklahoma, huge parts of Illinois. Look, what's going on?" he asked her.

"That's what I intend to find out."

7

The Postman sat in his Kansas study peering at eight muted television screens along a wall. Taller than most postmen, he had the lank of a basketball player, which he had been in college some fifty years earlier. Even sitting down, he seemed outsized in relation to the room. But the face that had once radiated health and eagerness, and lively eyes that had scanned the world with alert curiosity, were now hollowed-out cheeks, and skeletal eyes wearied by the rankness of the world.

Five of the screens were tuned to local news, and two to the national. Bloomberg News clamored on the eighth. The news spooled across, over and over. The market was showing fluctuations, but no longer anything to be alarmed about. Its gyrations were to be expected and losses were less than the week's trading profits. Even with the ups and downs, the trend was now upward on all the indicators important to him.

As he often did when watching television in his study, he occupied his hands by cleaning one of the rare guns in his collection, displayed in a glass case at one side of the room. Today, he worked on his favorite, a Colt Thunderer, Sheriff's model, circa 1877; nickel-plated, with pearl grips, an anniversary present from his late wife. Short-barreled, fit for purpose, it was simultaneously workmanlike and exotic. He liked the feel of it in his hands, the weight, the concussive power and the feeling of connection it gave with those who wielded it before him.

The local news was his barometer of the country's mood. The goings-on in small-market America were inconsequential of course, but being close to their audiences, the local news had a more reflective-reactive loop than the national. The big-shot Washington correspondents could decipher and postulate all they liked, but so long as the locals stuck to missing children, sports and saccharine poignancies, he could rest assured that the nation was unperturbed about what was happening to it.

Known only to three people in the dark network, and then only as "the Postman," Rufus Hessel was also keeping track of the President he had created via updates from Quantrelle and Marek. By design, it was a remarkably small operation, with only the barest, necessary number of people knowing the plan that political leaders were now required to follow.

Quantrelle was in place stage-managing much of the work that was propelling the President, but Hessel didn't like Moore's caution. With so much achieved against long odds, many men might have eased off, but the Postman was avaricious, and vindictive. He was panting to get on with it.

Frank Reed and Alec Nash's strategy had been effective, he grudgingly admitted, but they had only a passing understanding of all the work that had gone into it before they were recruited. They'd barely been with the plan five years. The Postman had been working more than twenty years to gain control.

In that time, there had been near misses and reversals. He'd seen fiscal changes thwarted at the executive level in the states and in D.C. because his group had failed again and again to take control of the executive office. Yes, that pair had done well, but he resented having had to cede planning and operational control to them. Predecessors of theirs had pre-deceased them, necessarily. And now Hessel's patience was fraying again.

So tantalizingly close to his goal, he had nothing but contempt for what he saw as Moore's temporizing. It was one thing to say publicly that the administration would chart a go-slow course but quite another actually to go slow. Hessel hadn't seized the reins through his network to make petty rule changes, or enact new legislation, but to act valiantly, confidently, singly.

Moore's timidity and inability to think audaciously, he now worried, were either character flaws, a product of career politician indoctrination, or an early warning signal that he couldn't be trusted. The Postman had one final step that would cement his control, relieving the country of a messy, cumbersome establishment. Accelerating confirmation of Senator Drew Elliot—"Baker," to the dark network—as Attorney General would be the key to shoring up command before he made that final move.

The Postman saw his strategy in terms of a chess grandmaster. His opening moves had seized the initiative and the chaos surrounding those efforts had put his opponents on the defensive, made them reactive. He now controlled the center squares—House, Senate and the Presidency—and could move freely almost wherever he liked.

As soon as Eliot controlled the national police, he would be able to move at will. True, he had sacrificed some important pieces earlier than he'd have liked, but his gambit, gathering force even now, would play out like a lightning strike, sparking fear and awe, obliterating opposition and ushering in a new, permanent order. Checkmate.

* * *

Attorneys working for Drew Eliot, the senior Senator from South Carolina, had mounted a successfully convoluted fog of war defense, full of plausible deniability regarding their client's non-involvement in Interregnum chicanery, when Congress dithered over the vote for president and vice president.

His principal aide, Casey Hague, had been the subject of an FBI investigation concerning obstruction of justice and misconduct, and he had been murdered by co-conspirators just days before the historic Contingent vote. Nothing Hague had done, however, could be made to stick to Senator Eliot.

Hearings and interviews had not led to charges, even if Eliot's picture remained on Vega's conspiracy board.

On the day the Justice Department announced that it had insufficient evidence to proceed against him, Senator Eliot was home in Columbia, South Carolina, where he was meeting the Governor. There, on the first floor of the Capitol Building, the two gave an impromptu press conference. The Governor, grave and self-important, stood by Eliot, saying he "knew in his heart" that the voters of South Carolina would look past the error of judgment the Senator had made when he appointed Hague as his deputy.

For his part, the Senator looked the gracious, if weary, patrician. He gave a touching display of soul-searching about how he could have been so wrong about a man he regarded as a friend. Paraphrasing *Henry V,* he said in his affecting drawl that he had trusted Hague so completely that "his fall leaves a kind of blot which marks even the full-fraught man and best endued with some suspicion."

His remarks played well, even if those less charitably inclined thought it unseemly to shift blame to the blameless for being so. It was generally believed, however, that barring any further gaffes or renewed charges his Senate seat was safe, and he would handily win re-election some four years hence. His term as head of the Judicial Oversight Committee, however, was at an end. Some suggested that he would make a good Attorney General.

Hugh Salter sat at his newsroom desk, staring blankly at his bio on the network's website. He and his colleagues had received a directive stating that the network was updating its profiles page and taking "fresh" photos. Salter felt anything but fresh. He had made a name for himself as a keen, energetic reporter. "An award-winning Political Reporter whose experience, knowledge and expertise have established his reputation as one of the finest correspondents in the industry," his current bio read. Not the bio of a hungry investigative journalist, he sighed. More like the beginning of an obituary.

At 48, he didn't feel ready for pasture, for editing and producing, stuck in the studio. The photo on the profiles page was more than a year old, which didn't improve his mood. He was spending a fortune keeping his hair dark, with just a hint of distinguished gray. He still wanted to be the one out front, breaking the news, telling the story from tight-squeeze locations in the rain to brightly lit *haute couture* presenters in the studio.

In his head, he began composing an update to the bio: "Hugh Salter, once regarded as a keen investigative reporter, saw his status and reputation collapse during the wild days of the so-called Provisional Interregnum—the period after the tainted Faithless Elector votes were refused and the final Contingent vote for President." He rehearsed his many failures there, his naiveté, and his jaded acceptance of the salacious material that his informant, Patriot76, was peddling.

"His nose for news became suspect," he continued, "and his ability to look good in front of the camera drooped, along with his viewer ratings and other things…no, that's enough," he told himself. "Think positive." But as he scrolled through the photos of his colleagues, he saw perhaps it might be time to pitch for the elder statesman, safe-pair-of-hands, seen-it-all, good-in-a-crisis, reliable old Hugh. Not pasture, but anchor.

Then the phone rang.

It was the news director. "Hugh," he said, "There's going to be an off-camera press briefing at 2pm. A joint thing, with the out-going and in-coming press secretaries. I want you there. The new press secretary is named Anthony Marek. He was briefly on the Christopher campaign team, but we need to know more about him. There's also talk of a shortlist of candidates for VP. One: I want as much background as you can get on Marek. Jeanie's producing, so get with her. And two: I want you to work with her on as much background as you can get on the main VP contenders. I'd love to hear some handicapping."

"Got it." Salter sighed. Still holding the phone, he stood up and struggled into his jacket. It was the perfect riposte to his musings: he was doing off-camera reporting now.

"Your background on Marek will go on late in the three o'clock block or early in the four," said the news director, "but if you can come up with the VP short list, we'll lead with that."

Salter hustled out the door.

* * *

It had been six days since the death of President Redmond. Though her funeral had not yet happened, President Robert Moore was about to make his first speech to the nation. The Sergeant at Arms stood at the door of an overflowing House chamber and announced: "Mister Speaker, the President of the United States." To the customary applause, some of it perhaps a little too triumphant, Bob Moore, the President ordained by fate and fatalities, strode confidently into the chamber.

He was tall and robust, with sandy-gray hair. Lean and elegant, but not fashionable, in his dark grey suit, white shirt and burgundy tie, he looked accustomed already to the accoutrements of power. And he played perfectly, as the moment required, to an audience of exhausted onlookers seeking reassurance.

Though he stopped to shake hands and share a word with members of Congress as he passed down the aisle to the Speaker's rostrum, he did it without the swagger, jocular exchanges and backslapping that often precede a State of the Union address. This was solemn and direct—nothing like the entrance he and Diane Redmond had made that January day four months ago to tumultuous acclamation. As Moore processed to the rostrum now, there was a hint of doing reluctantly what had to be done.

Gripping the sides of the rostrum, he looked into the gallery, acknowledging his wife and children with a flicker of a smile. The applause died faster than usual on these occasions, and Moore nodded to the Senate President, who gaveled the House to order.

"Mr. President," said Moore, addressing the Senate President. "Mr. Speaker, members of the Senate, members of the House, my fellow Americans: Tumultuous, historic events have delivered us to this moment. As on the morning after a hurricane, we grieve for that which has been lost, give thanks for what has been spared, and with renewed purpose set ourselves to the task of building anew.

"We grieve with the family of President Diane Redmond. We grieve *as* a family. She was taken from us too soon, her many works left undone, many before they were even begun. I pledge myself today to do all in my power to fulfill her legislative intentions and fulfill her dream of America. Let us begin again, but in God's name, let us continue."

It was long, it was resonant, and it was just insincere enough to be comforting. At the end of it, he shook hands all around and processed back up the aisle. The feed that Imogen was watching turned to Hugh Salter, in front of the Capitol.

"President Moore stressed all the important points in his speech tonight," Salter began. He looked down at his notes. "He stressed 'continuity in sorrow' and 'fulfilling President Redmond's agenda.' Though a Republican, he pledged himself to the Democratic program that she laid out in her Inaugural address just three months ago. This is, as he said at the beginning of his speech, a most remarkable situation.

"Let's remember, Bob Moore was running mate last year to the Republican candidate, James Christopher, who *lost* the election last year to the Democrat Diane Redmond. And now, after the as-yet unexplained death of President Redmond, Bob Moore finds himself a Republican President pledging to follow a Democratic agenda. These are extraordinary times, and we have to ask ourselves, will the Republicans *allow* him to follow their opponents' program?

"In his speech, Bob Moore also spoke of stability at home and commitment abroad. Those points would have played well with our allies. He said that America honors its commitments and stands by its partners, and that would have reassured a good many people who have been worried about what he might do, particularly in Europe and the Middle East."

"So, Hugh," said the studio anchor, "he seems to have found the right tone at a difficult time for the nation, but there were some things left out, weren't there?"

"Indeed, John. This wasn't a speech about specifics, but about frameworks, broad strokes. Even so, those omissions will leave some people wondering how committed the new administration will be to issues concerning universal health care, student debt, environmental protections and a number of other points that were left out of this speech. We'll probably get some better framing from the new Press Secretary, Tony Marek, tomorrow."

"You've met Marek, haven't you, Hugh?"

"I did, John, earlier today when he was introduced for the first time."

"What do we know about him?"

"It's a bit of old home week," Salter chuckled. "Tony Marek was a deputy press secretary in Massachusetts when President Moore was Governor of that state. He later became communications director for the V-Three Project—or Voter Veracity Venture."

"So," said the anchor, "we've seen a new Chief of Staff in Clayton Quantrelle, and now a new press secretary—both in short order. Are you hearing whether there will be other shake-ups and changings of the guard?"

"That remains to be seen, John. Chief of staff and press secretary are not posts that require Senate confirmation. And it makes sense—even in an Administration that seeks to be one of continuity—that the President have his own people close. The confirmation process for Cabinet and other posts is long and often difficult. It's unlikely a continuity government would want to waste time putting their own people in place just for the sake of doing so.

"As I've reported elsewhere, Congressman David Carr of Pennsylvania looks to be the front-runner to get the nod for Vice-President. It was his tenacity and courage during the so-called Interregnum that brought down the conspiracy to steal

45

the Presidency, and his inclusion in this new Administration would go a long way toward repairing the scars of the past months." Salter paused for a moment. "That being said, the collegiality that was the hallmark of the first couple weeks of Redmond's term quickly faded. President Redmond faced an all-too typically intransigent opposition party.

"She actually quipped some weeks ago that the confirmation process had not just reverted *to* the mean, but— as she said—had 'reverted to *being* mean.'" He smiled wistfully, as though quality bon mots would now be in short supply in "Ad lib Bob's" administration. "Though unlikely, it's certainly possible that some of the currently unfilled posts would be switched to people Moore prefers. It all remains to be seen."

Duncan Calder, watching in Seattle, called Imogen as soon as the speech was over. "Well," he sighed, "what would we expect him to say? Moore's canny. His early actions seem perfectly in keeping with what an accidental President would do, slow, patient steps, calculated not to offend. And the way he seems to be holding out hope to the Democrats means they'll be slow to go on the offensive. But a shoe will drop. We need to be watching, and ready."

"Yes," she answered distantly. As she stared at the muted television in her Arlington apartment, she thought again of the investigation she and her staff had only just begun, trying to envision what shape and direction it might take. She loathed the need to disguise it as some abstruse, drowsy case study.

In Kansas, sitting in his study, cleaning one of his guns, the Postman nodded as he listened to Moore's speech. "Now we get to work," he said with smug satisfaction.

On Beaver Island, watching from Carl's Coffee Shop, the man known as Ian Gerritt also nodded in agreement as the speech ended. It had been a good week. Things were falling into place, and it might indeed be safe for him to come in from the very real cold on the next scheduled extraction flight, now little more than a week away.

* * *

Alec Nash lay deathly still on his prison cot, with its thin, hard, lumpy mattress. An arm laid across his face, the crook of the elbow shielding his eyes from the sunlight that was straining through the bars of the window and dazzling the sterile walls. The other arm propped the back of his head.

Out in the world, he had contrived a dashing, insouciant, unkempt air. A great deal of work had gone into keeping him looking casually indifferent. After two months in stir with no stylist to call on, however, his sculpted stubble beard had grown thick and matted, somewhere between a "vacation" beard and the Mountain Man anti-style in which his friend Frank Reed grew his. His closely cut, stylishly coiffed hair had also become unruly. The prison-issue orange jumpsuit did not flatter.

For all the outward changes, he didn't look defeated. His pale blue eyes shone with energy and intensity. He bore captivity with resigned hauteur, like someone who knew his confinement would not be long: just a necessary, if disagreeable, step. Right before he invoked his Fifth Amendment right and refused to testify or give evidence, he had bafflingly suggested that the false charges in the government's case against him somehow also managed to be illegally obtained.

The trial proceeded nevertheless, if slowly. The FBI had stopped trying to interrogate him, and his days fell into a routine of waking, eating, taking some exercise and lying on his back in the cell. It was a solitary cell, but technically not solitary confinement. He took meals in the canteen. But other prisoners shunned him, and he largely shunned them too. The real confinement was in his head, from which his only respite were newspapers and the occasional television report, which gave him glimmerings of satisfaction. The plan he and Frank Reed had contrived was working perfectly, he read. Things were going well—for everyone else.

He felt no rancor towards the others, though. They all knew what they were setting out to do, and each had accepted the risk. And his own part had been too important for him to be left to rot. He knew too much. His friend Bob Moore—*President* Moore—would find an excuse and an opportunity to pardon him after the final step, and life could begin anew. Nash's own first step, he mused, would be to show that buffoon Quantrelle the door.

A Justice Department agent appeared at the cell door, interrupting Nash's interminable ruminating. It was a welcome diversion, though it meant he had a court appearance, which signaled that the trial was progressing. Almost anything was welcome that broke the dreary routine. At such times, two FBI agents, stiffer than a pair of bookends, would attend, as he put on a prison-issued suit of clothes and ran a brush through his now unruly hair.

So, it was to be more of that. Nash sighed as he rolled off the bed and stood in front of the agent. The agent laid a pressed suit on the bed. Nash turned away modestly to face the window before unzipping his overalls.

It occurred to him as he struggled out of one arm that two agents, not one, always attended him. He was a high-value prisoner, and the standard operating procedure called for dual control in all aspects. Where was the other? Nash considered mentioning that he was hurt by their apparent downgrade of his importance, but Justice Department functionaries weren't known for their sense of humor.

He was just pulling his left arm out of the sleeve, his shoulder twisted awkwardly behind him, when the agent garroted him with a tie.

The sunlight through the cell window seemed to explode with colors that seared his brain. He tried to reach the tie constricting his neck, but couldn't get hold of it. He kicked his heel backward but missed. He tried again to rip the tie off his throat.

Unable to get a finger hold to loosen it, he swung his free arm wildly, but without finding the agent. He kicked out again, missing again. And again. Now his legs gave out and he fell forward toward the wall, his full weight suspended by the tie around his neck.

The colors were fading, turning to sunspots that spread like oil on the water, blotting out his vision. Somewhere an alarm sounded, far off, muffled. The assassin guided Nash's body gently, delicately to the ground. He stood over him for a full minute, with the tie cinched taut. Another alarm began, much closer, but the agent took no notice. He turned the corpse, hoisted it, and pinned it to the wall with his shoulder.

He fastened the ends of the tie in a knot to the window bars and let the body fall limp. He felt for a pulse and pushed back the head, looking into the dull, bloodshot bulging eyes. He checked the noose to be sure it held.

The agent checked his watch, examined his hands and smoothed his jacket. He straightened his own tie and walked quickly out of the cell, leaving the door slightly open. Some twenty minutes later, he would return, "discover" Nash's body and report the death.

At the inquest, he would be cited for dereliction of duty for leaving his post to respond to the alarm, the actions which allowed Nash to kill himself. However, since his arrival was instrumental in quelling the burgeoning riot said to have been the cause of the alarm, he was not further disciplined.

8

Seated once again in his customary spot at Carl's Cafe, in view of the television, Frank Reed ordered a big breakfast—chicken-fried steak, eggs up, hash browns and coffee. Meanwhile, he devoured as much information as the television could offer. He was peering at the mouth of an inverted ketchup bottle, willing it to deliver a massive dollop for his hash browns, when the news came that Alec Nash had committed suicide in his jail cell.

"The Justice Department's case against the conspirators was unfolding, but slowly," said the news anchor. "Alec Nash was standing trial for murder and conspiracy voter fraud, the highest-ranking conspirator to be arrested. There were hopes of an eventual plea bargain, which might have led to further arrests and convictions.

"However, he refused to cooperate with investigators or prosecutors, saying the charges against him were manufactured and politically motivated, and that he would not get a fair trial. Nevertheless, the evidence of his involvement in the plot to throw the election was substantial, and he was expected to be convicted on all charges, including ordering the murder of retired FBI Special Agent Andrew Colls, himself a suspect. For more, we go to Hugh Salter at FBI headquarters."

"This is a severe blow to the FBI's case, Phil," said Salter. "Justice Department officials were using the trial not just to prosecute Alec Nash, but to piece together more about what they believe to be a broader conspiracy."

"Do we have any details?" asked the anchor. "How can he have been left unguarded in jail for long enough to commit suicide?"

"The FBI has released a statement, Phil, saying that what looked like the beginnings of a prison riot broke out in the wing of the jail where Nash was being housed, and the officer guarding him was distracted. Apparently, the officer ran toward the alarm as Nash was changing into a suit for a court appearance, leaving Nash alone for some minutes, during which he hanged himself with a necktie."

Classic misdirection, Reed mused. Nice work. He wondered who had actually done the job. One of the late Special Agent Colls' bright young things, no doubt. Well, back in January, it was Nash who had ordered the hit on Colls. Strange how the dead hand can still pull a trigger.

Reed's philosophical distance didn't last long. He pushed his food away, suddenly sick to his stomach, his thoughts a toxic mixture, equal parts anger and fear. If Nash, the leader and architect of everything now playing out, was disposable, then he was, too. The rendezvous with the plane in Nebraska was a trap.

Was it cruel or ironic, he wondered, that one of his best contributions, Flintlock Air, was meant to be his downfall? When he and Nash had organized the network cells, Reed had worried about the operatives' ability to get where they needed to be quickly, particularly in the western states. Nash saw the difficulty, too, and through the Postman had made contact with Flintlock Industries. The corporate jets of the company's aviation division were perfect cover. They were small and could come and go pretty much anywhere.

Flintlock was a legitimate business, and it ferried its executives all over the country, operating primarily west of the Mississippi. They made legitimate trips, hauled legitimate cargo and made stops all over the West, often on an emergency basis.

And because they often made unscheduled stops or were diverted, and were small enough to fly easily under visual flight rules, they were perfect for the dark network's needs, keeping its operations opaque. Nash had recruited and briefed two new pilots, Menzies and Rosewood, and given them a dedicated frequency for communications, known only to the three of them.

Reed stared blankly ahead as he scratched absently at his auburn beard, envisioning himself being tossed out of a plane at 5,000 feet if he kept his appointment. If not that way, how *would* they do it? he wondered dispassionately. He saw that he wouldn't be going anywhere for a while, unless to meet his Maker.

He returned to the breakfast, which some moments before had seemed like a robust and fitting send-off from Beaver Island, but which now felt more like the last meal of a condemned man. And like many a condemned man, he reflected on the circumstances that had brought him to this point.

This era of Reed's life—now seemingly hastening to an end—had begun five years earlier, in Newton, New Jersey, in 2012. And it began with Alec Nash.

When Reed first left the navy and the tense game of military intelligence, he had retreated gratefully into the obscurity of a job as a state game warden. But his gratitude didn't last long. In military intelligence, he had seen the dangers in the broader world. He knew what it needed, but he had failed to get anyone to listen to him, failed to make his mark. As a civilian for the first time in over twenty years, as he had looked out from his Wildlife Management Area redoubt, he seethed at the feckless, demented idealism of America's leaders.

As a civilian, he was now free to work for a political party, to try to supercharge it with momentum, and by late summer 2012, he had volunteered for a role in the campaign to elect a Republican senator in New Jersey. Though he wouldn't be paid, it sounded like an influential post, where significant decisions were required and his experience would be respected.

Perhaps he would be noticed and invited to share his ideas at a higher level too. A few weeks in, though, he felt himself being marginalized—just as he had been in the military. The organizers didn't understand his proposals, and chastised him for his manner when talking to would-be voters. They couldn't see what was staring them in the face. The campaign *had* to be more aggressive.

He was thinking of quitting, when the campaign manager told him that Alec Nash, a public relations executive who had once been chief of staff to the Massachusetts Governor Bob Moore, wanted to meet him. Nash was running the Voter Veracity PAC at the time.

Late one evening he arrived to meet Reed for a private word. They took cups of lukewarm coffee into the office of the campaign manager, who had vacated it for them. The campaign manager left for the night, hoping Nash wanted to recruit his stroppy, problem volunteer, and that he might be seeing the back of Reed and his belligerent self-importance.

Reed and Nash faced each other on metal folding chairs. Reed wore what he always wore, work boots and Carhartt dungarees, drab fatigue jacket, work shirt, and a suspicious, beleaguered scowl. Nash's manicured crispness was in sharp contrast, though by this hour he had loosened his tie.

"You said something to the campaign manager the other day about going after supporters of the rival candidate," Nash began, "and you're quite right we need to do more of that."

"Uh huh," Reed grunted.

"But what did you mean by 'going after?'"

"I meant, clear them out of our path. I meant, make sure that New Jersey gets the Senator it needs, and then that America gets a President with some balls. We have a duty to do it. Whatever it takes."

"Whatever it takes?" mused Nash.

"Yeah. We have to be realistic...for once."

"I don't doubt the efficacy of that, but I'm sure you see why a campaign staffer can't be seen to be involved."

"Is that why you're here?" Reed asked, "to tell me to dial it back?" He spoke in low growls, making statements he didn't expect to be contradicted. "You want to win or not?"

"Yes, we do. And no, I'm not here to tell you to dial it back."

"Then what? Fire me? How do you fire a volunteer?"

"I'm here to ascertain whether you're just someone who likes to bitch and gripe and feel superior. Someone who sees the big picture but in the end isn't prepared—or equipped—to do what's necessary."

"You don't know me at all," Reed growled.

"Not as well as I hope to soon," Nash countered, brightly. "Which is why we're here right now." He frowned at the Styrofoam coffee cup.

"I don't have to work for the party, you know. I'm a private citizen. I can—"

"—Yes, yes," said Nash impatiently. "That's why you could be so useful. But do you want to be *effective*? Because that's what I'm here to offer."

"You asked if I'm capable of doing what's necessary," Reed replied. "Sure I am."

Nash contemplated another draught of the unpalatable coffee, decided against it, and left it on the desk. A suitable present for a campaign manager who was rather too luke-warm himself.

"I've looked into your background a bit, of course, and seen your service record."

Reed was jolted. What was this? And why? Perhaps someone was taking him seriously after all.

"Deployed in Baghdad, Kandahar Province; an early Distinguished Service medal," said Nash, proving his point. "A good intelligence officer. Precise. Keen. You're an impressive guy...but with mixed overall ratings from your CO's. Very capable, but not always *liked*, it seems.

"What I see is an officer who could have gone further, and should have done. Would it interest you to know that a Commander Snyder put a note in your file that says he felt your attitude put you dangerously high on the MICE compromise index, but that Rear Admiral Fleming dismissed it?"

Reed grunted. Damn that bastard Snyder. But those files were secret: the very fact he'd been a naval intelligence officer was classified. Nash must have advanced clearance, or a mole somewhere. He had known, though, that some people in the service regarded him as clever enough to be dangerous. That was no great revelation, but this was a strange time to have it all come up again.

A moment passed as Reed contemplated Nash. He was as smooth and groomed as any of those commanders. Was he any more honorable?

"Yes," Nash continued, a smile spreading warmly across his face. "Fleming's note in reply said you were arrogant and egotistical because you were good at your job. He said as far as the Money-Ideology-Compromise-Ego index was concerned, you couldn't be bought, couldn't be compromised and were ideologically sound."

"Timid as mice," Reed murmured to himself in a moment of loathing. "Mice and moles—what a fucking combination."

"And yet you left the service," Nash observed. "At only forty-four years old."

"Listen. I've done more than most in the name of what's necessary," Reed said, eyes fixed on Nash, estimating him. "I've done things for my country because they had to be done. Ugly things—despicable, even—but I don't lose sleep over them because I did them for the greater good" (Nash nodded) "—or thought I did. That greater good turned out to be bullshit, but my motives were true and my conscience is clear."

Nash summed up for him: "Dirty hands, clean conscience."

"Sure, whatever," Reed batted, suddenly a little defensive. Had he said too much? What else did Nash know from those files? Some of those things he didn't like to think about really *had* been ugly, and he wouldn't want other people thinking about them either.

"Where's this going?" Reed demanded.

"You've said you were willing to do what it takes; that you've done what it takes...but you didn't stick with it. I'd like to know if you're *still* willing to do what it takes. And if you'll stick with it to the end."

"For whom?" Reed asked. "You?" he sneered.

"I don't act alone. We have powerful friends in and out of government."

"Some kind of coup?" Reed's face twisted scornfully. "You're talking to the wrong guy. Admiral Fleming didn't lie. I love my country." He stood up.

Nash waved at him to sit down. "Which is precisely why I wanted to talk with you. Frank, we both know the real threats to this country, don't we? Worst, they're from within: patsies content to leave our borders wide open...invaded by hoards looking to suck up all our resources. Elites with no stomach for a fight anymore.

"The stuff they're taught in college? Faculty spouting well-meaning, dim-witted, idealistic bullshit that demoralizes youth, undermines initiative: we're full of limp, ineffective, anti-competitive, anti-capitalist, un-American..." here emotion overwhelmed him.

He sighed. "If we can't right this ship, we might as well just ask the Russians or the Chinese to run the place for us. Frankly, that'd at least be more honest than the slouching socialism and pandering, slack-jawed pabulum we're being force-fed now." Nash paused. He meant it all, but he also knew it was what Reed wanted to hear.

"But the infection can be excised," he went on, now leaning in towards Reed. "Eradicated. If a small, dedicated group could get the right kind of man elected President."

Reed resettled his camouflaged bulk on the chair. "I see."

"As I said: the enemy, regrettably, is within. So, that dedicated group would be required to operate in secret, a fiefdom of its own, probably separate from the parties. And their activities would be under threat of exposure at all times. They would have to trust each other implicitly. We think you could lead that group. We'd look to you to help recruit that group."

56

"How do you know I'll play ball?"

"I think you're wise enough." The words were calm and confident, but not flattering or reassuring. "Anyhow, I didn't drive five hours to let you waste this chance. We're going to do whatever it takes to get a presidential candidate elected. No coup: *elected*. A President who will champion the true values of America...and I think you want in."

"Hmm," Reed muttered, unsure about what he was hearing.

"This is politics, Frank. Not a coup. But let's be clear: the stakes are very high, and it'll be bare-knuckle. The service to the nation that your group will provide might never be known. They'll be anonymous, but their job will be crucial: to put the right people in positions where they can do the most good.

"There's a plan, Frank," he continued, "and I need good men. I need *you* to find them. We're going to need a network across the country, but most of them will be single operators covering a large area...maybe even a number of states. Ready to travel at a moment's notice, and to put themselves on the line for a greater good. We'll give you all the backup you need. And money." Sardonically, then, as if to himself, he added: "Any currency you like."

The building was now dark except for this floor, with its fluorescent pall. "It's late," said Nash, suddenly affable. "I've got a long drive ahead, and you've done a great day's work. It's good to have you on the team. We need more like you."

Reed found himself ushered toward the front door, and the two men parted with promises to be in touch soon.

For a few minutes, Reed sat in his car without turning on the lights. "I think you're wise enough." Those had been the words, and there had been a curl to them that conveyed all the threat that was required. An offer he couldn't refuse. Whoever they were, they knew all about him, and they were prepared to be ruthless. And so, he realized, was he.

9

Trey Kelly stopped by Imogen's office.

"Trey!" Imogen exclaimed as she stood up and hugged him. After a moment, she stood back, looking at him quizzically, wondering to what she owed this pleasant surprise. "I was actually thinking about coming to see you," she said cautiously.

"Probably better that you didn't," he said.

Imogen felt an inward twinge. Maybe, like so many of her colleagues, he too needed to keep distance from her, the FBI's problem child. She worried that he might also have been promoted out of a job.

Kelly, an FBI IT specialist ("a Fitbit specialist," he would say drolly), had been instrumental in expanding the phone traces that had led to their uncovering two of the conspiracy cells during the Interregnum. He worked out of an unassuming, hiding-in-plain-sight building near the D.C. Armory, part of the shuttered, largely derelict D.C. General Hospital complex. Tucked discreetly among emergency psychiatric service offices, mental health and substance abuse clinics, his office was marked only by a small sign reading "Bus Rentals," next to three buzzer buttons, only one of which worked.

His oversized designer eyeglasses were the pair he'd had for years, and looked it. The lenses were cloudy and smeared, as though he'd dropped them in a puddle and not bothered to wipe them off thoroughly. He wore a dark blue pea coat topped with a lavishly orange scarf. He unwound the scarf as he stood in front of her.

The only change was his hair, which two months earlier had been tightly clipped. Now, it was blossoming into a sculpted Afro. He was slender, gangly, and he walked with a bounce in his step. He had a ready smile, not as a means of ingratiating, but because he seemed prepared to find things funny. Imogen had always found his affable, non-FBI goofiness appealing.

"Everything all right?" she asked. More quietly, she added, "Has Nash's suicide catalyzed any activity?"

"No," said Trey. "There hasn't been a peep on the network. But there is one thing I need to talk with you about." Here he closed the door before continuing: "I tried to get my buddy Mike at NSA to help me screen out some of the noise on that final phone call Reed made to Nebraska back in December—maybe get something more definite. Vega's been trying to follow it up."

"Was he able to?" Imogen asked.

"He said he couldn't. That he'd been told *only* to communicate via approved channels, meaning his boss would talk to my boss."

Imogen nodded. "Yeah," she allowed, "there's a lot of that going around. I guess even if NSA was pivotal in bringing down some of the gang, some department head there got shirty about not being in the loop. Mike's not going to lose his job or anything, is he?"

"No, not at all," said Trey.

"Or you?"

"No," he said. "I'm fine, too. But here's the thing: when I called Mike, I was going to be asking him about phone traces, so I had all my detection and surveillance programs up and running." He paused, frowning.

"It turns out someone's running a highly sophisticated surveillance on him . . . and on me. They're using what looks like some cloning tech or a shadow, switching link. I don't really recognize it. On screen, it registers two phones with the same number and plots both their movements."

"Can you trace them? Can you block it?"

"I think maybe I could block it," he said, "but I haven't tried yet. I thought you and I should talk first face-to-face. It might be better *not* to try and block it, 'cause if I start trying to trace them back, it might alert them."

Imogen nodded.

"Also," he hesitated, "they're tracking you, too."

* * *

Through Inspector Sims at the FAA, Agent Vega had been able to find two pilots who were still active but no longer flying for the executive air service arm of Flintlock Industries. She had traveled back to Omaha to talk to them, or rather, to get them to talk to her and give her some background for her investigation. Omaha's Eppley Field was a sprawling complex, but there was no FAA field office and Vega didn't want to use official premises at this stage. Sims pulled some strings and found her a vacant office to use in among the car rental agencies.

The first pilot, Taylor Percy was a 52-year-old Georgian with courtly manners, meticulously tailored uniform, and a head of salt-and-pepper hair, cut "high and tight" under his captain's hat. As he walked across the lot toward her, Vega thought she saw him growing taller with each stride. Six-foot-two could hardly be comfortable in cockpits.

They shook hands briskly as she thanked him for coming and conducted him to the office to sit him down. Apologizing for the Spartan surroundings, she referred to him as "Captain Percy" at just the moment she wanted to assure him that this was an informal talk. "We're really only fact-finding at the moment. Background." (Now that they were seated, she could at least look him in the eye.) "And I'd like what we discuss to stay with us."

"Very good, ma'am," he said.

"It may be that from our discussions today we find no reason to pursue our line of inquiry any further. Or we may find there's more digging to do. I must stress that you *not* discuss this conversation with anyone." She turned to a fresh sheet of notepaper and pushed an errant strand of black hair behind her ear.

"Understood, ma'am," he said smiling. "And in exchange for this testimony do I get immunity from prosecution for any crimes I may have committed?"

Vega wasn't sure whether she'd understood. "You're not giving testimony here, Captain. This is a voluntary interview. But since you've brought it up: *have* you committed any crimes the FBI should know about?"

"No," he laughed self-consciously. "I mean, maybe some parking tickets." His face reddened. "I've just never been interrogated by the FBI before. I'm sorry if I seemed glib."

"We call them interviews, Captain Percy." She stared at him for a little longer, her dark eyes impassive, letting him sweat. "What can you tell me about your time with Flintlock Industries?" she said finally

"Did they say something about me?"

"No," she said. "What would they say?"

"I don't know. I worked for them for seven years. Things really picked up in late 2015, and they hired some new people, mostly young guys. But since the New Year, business has dropped again. They let me go about three months ago, right at the beginning of 2017."

"Just a standard layoff?"

"Yep. Not a bad severance packet, honestly. Still, I thought I might have a shot at claiming age-discrimination." He shrugged. "But then I didn't want to mess up my chances with another outfit by being labeled that kind of guy."

"What did you do for Flintlock?"

"What *didn't* I do would make for a shorter answer, Agent Vega."

"Such as what?" she prompted.

"I was pilot-on-call, so I had to do all kinds of things. I'd take executives to meetings, I'd haul cargo. Execs to their retreats, special parties. We have to clean the aircraft in between flights, carry bags. We aren't glamor boys."

"I see," said Vega.

"I've brought girls to meetings who didn't exactly look like they were there for their business acumen, if you get my meaning."

Vega's face registered no emotion.

"I don't know it for a fact, obviously," he added quickly, coloring again. "They may have been CPA's, for all I know. I didn't ask. Once, I flew some businessmen and politicians to The Bahamas for a long, weekend party. We got there. I'd put the aircraft to bed and was just getting to my hotel room, when the call comes in: they need some live Maine lobsters—could I just pop up and get some? Crucial for the party, you see."

"Pop up to Maine?" Vega asked incredulously. "From The Bahamas?"

"Only to Boston," he said, smiling and rolling his eyes. "Still, it's over twenty-four hundred miles round trip."

"And do all pilots end up doing that kind of thing?"

"Oh, we've all got a story or two. The Bahamas one's not the worst. You're dealing with a very wealthy clientele," he added wearily, "and they're not used to hearing people say 'no.'"

Vega nodded, thinking. "Given that there's no normal, walk me through what's typical. You were based—?"

"—Here in Omaha."

"OK, and you're just sitting around on call?" she asked.

"Not typically. You're scheduled four days on, and three days off. At the start of your four days, you're given an itinerary for your first two days, sometimes the whole four: places to go, things to deliver, people to pick up. But you also have to be prepared and available for deviations. We had an informal protocol sheet—'Hoyle's Rules,' we called it—that ranked requests."

"Hoyle's Rules?" she asked.

"You know, Hoyle's puts out those rulebooks for card games, and it lists what hand beats what? You know, flush beats a straight, full house beats a flush. If a passenger, some big man on my list asks me to deviate for some reason, I do it, unless, you know, there's a fuel issue or some genuine obstacle.

"And sometimes, you get a company request to deviate, but you've already got a passenger who tells you *not* to deviate, to disregard. So, you check your list: whose direction are you gonna follow? Is your passenger a royal flush, or just two-pair?"

"That could get ugly," Vega allowed.

"Actually, it's not so bad. You can put it off on the company, and the guy who's being inconvenienced usually works for the company himself, so he gets it."

"Under what circumstances would you deviate?"

"Could be anything. They need a factory part, and you're near the plant. Samples are ready for some presentation and need to get where they're going fast. Might be delivering parts for another aircraft that's broken down miles from anywhere."

"Were you ever sent to Fairmont Airport in Nebraska?" she asked.

"Once or twice, to pick something up from a research facility near there. Never on a deviation."

"When was the last time you were there?"

"Fairmont?" he asked. "It's gotta be close to a year. Maybe more. It's not somewhere we'd go very much. It's tiny."

"Nothing scheduled there?" she asked.

"No, there's nothing there except the research facility," he said.

"When you deviate, how often do you go with Visual Flight Rules?"

"VFR? Just about never," he said. "Why would I?"

"That's part of what I'm trying to understand."

Her second interview that day confirmed much of what she had learned from Percy. But the second pilot, Jacob Wilder, added that while most communications about destinations or deviations came over the company's dedicated radio frequency, he'd discovered a second company frequency by accident. Wilder said he thought there was maybe some kind of corporate espionage going on. He couldn't be sure. It seemed to him that the newer hires were more keyed in to whatever it was. She wrote down the frequency and made a note to check on new hires.

Perhaps her long shot was paying some dividends after all, and she was proud to be the one who kept panning where no one else had thought to look. She was eager to get back to Washington, and the trip back was a chance to think. For the second time in her life, though, the thrill of chasing down clues was accompanied by a rising dread of what lay behind them.

Until she had begun working on the Faithless Elector plot her experience of casework had been decidedly one-sided. She had known only the righteous, powerful sensation of drawing ever closer to the truth, the hunter pursuing the hunted.

But this conspiracy was different, more like war. The prey fought back. Strikes at these guys were met not with capitulation—or even retreat—but by counterattacks, flanking maneuvers, rearguard actions. Her friend Imogen, she felt certain, was the latest casualty.

Was it worse than that? she wondered. Did her notion of this investigation as a war extend to espionage and double agents? As she flew home, staring out of the window at the country unrolling below, she wondered if the killing had only seemed to stop. Had it just gone under the radar? And what was the meaning of Imogen's note inviting to her to a meeting but warning not to use a cell phone?

10

When they began working together five years earlier, Reed and Nash became an unlikely couple. Nash had the vision, strategy and access to funding. Reed was tactics and implementation. Initially, both worked on recruitment. The first stage had been to agree a hierarchy of command and control, modeled on espionage organizations. Nash would be the equivalent of Station Chief, managing all activities, payments and reporting to a superior, referred to only as "the Postman."

Nash's sub-field specialty, issuing from his PR background, would be fabricating dis- and misinformation, where he excelled. He stuck to the basics—divisions and fractures within factions, "whatabout-ism," and amplifying tincture tempests, sowing with the seeds of truth, and only the cherry-picked pits. His strongest suit was pre-emptive blame, though he would never have called it that himself, where the trick was to accuse an opponent of something you're doing, thereby insulating against attack on that very issue.

The malevolent genius of pre-emptive blame was that if evidence of one's own true illegal activity were uncovered, it could be glossed by noting that the other side was just trying to shift attention away from what they were doing: moreover, it could be pointed out that the other side hadn't properly answered the earlier accusation—even though there was nothing to the initial allegation. Reed's tour de force would be the Illinois vote-rigging scandal at the heart of the Faithless Elector case.

He foresaw that the contest for the presidency would in many ways be an asymmetric clash. The parties were big, well funded and well run. Their fuel, however, was public sentiment, and the mixture might be adulterated or even siphoned off.

"Like eating an elephant," he had said early on with a wry grin, "and with my sincere apologies to St. Francis, you begin with what's necessary; then do what's possible—"

"—And suddenly you're doing the impossible," Reed had chimed in.

"Exactly," Nash rejoined, relieved to have been understood. "A little at a time."

The first step in conquering was to divide. If the groups that might be expected to coalesce could be riven by infighting and suspicion, their small group, led by Reed, might flow into the gaps. Nash would prove indefatigable in sowing enmity, stoking hostility and dividing already highly-charged fringe groups. He hinted at "foreign" help.

Reed handled the delicate business of recruiting, as well as training. They saw quickly that the 2012 cycle would not be theirs to win. It was a weak field of candidates against a popular incumbent, but they knew that the presidential election circus would draw committed people to the fore, and among them would be the ultra-committed. By working at the edges of a number of campaigns, Reed and Nash were able to spot and recruit other HWITs, as they began to call them. Have What It Takes.

Reed took easily to Nash's vision and ruthless drive. He reveled in the slow-burn intelligence gathering, the strategy, the long game. Here, for once, he saw himself using his talents on a vital platform. They created, or like any good hostile takeover, usurped and cannibalized, a number of non-profit shell organizations, PACs and Super-PACs with demure names.

"Opportunity Initiative" and "Sovereign Caucus" became useful places to wash money. Through the Postman and his moneyed connections, Nash had easily got a foothold in the venerable Forefathers' Institute think-tank, first by disrupting its ranks and later by collecting allies and freezing out opponents. Useful idiots sprang out in the academy and the media: an embarrassment of idiots, in fact.

"Opportunity" became the umbrella organization for the Voter Veracity Venture PAC and the byword for their efforts. Though Forefathers' was effectively subsumed, its facade was swept, buffed and polished to maintain the perception of independence. Adding Mason Brandenburg to the Board on the audit committee was part of the effort. And anyone from the Institute who was invited to join one of the other PACs resigned promptly from the think-tank.

Early on, Reed had impressed upon Nash (and through him, on his superiors) the complexity of what they were attempting. As well as patient, with 2012 being virtually a dummy run, they would need to remain flexible in their planning and learn to capitalize on chance opportunities.

"Remember," he told Nash, when discussing the need for flexibility: "no battle plan survives contact with the enemy." And the real battle wouldn't take place until 2016.

The Opportunity Initiative campaign, working in the background for their preferred candidates, performed surprisingly well in 2012, winning ten House and four Senate seats. Fully vetted alumni of the Forefathers Institute were recruited to staff their offices. These staff immediately set about placing the politicians in key committees. And with these appointments, alliances and infiltrations, Opportunity brought in more associates, secured more funding and studied what it would take to win in 2016. It was these associates and funding that Imogen and her staff were now scrutinizing, desperately trying to catch up.

During the 2012 election, Reed and Nash met or spoke every week. The keys to discreet communications, they agreed, were keeping the operation low-tech, with *no* computers or email; using disposable burner phones that would be changed each month; no texting; and the use of a simple but robust, plain-language code.

It was crucial to keep the number of operatives to a minimum, even as they expanded the dark operation in preparation for 2016. The two debated the optimal number, with Nash initially advocating fewer than Reed.

"He that would keep a secret," said Nash as they sat in a Waffle Café restaurant near the airport at Portsmouth, New Hampshire, "must first keep secret he hath a secret to keep." He leaned forward, his fingertips pressed together, smiling urbanely across the Formica tabletop at Reed, who stared at him somberly. "And the fewer people who know a secret, the simpler it is to keep."

Reed stared at Nash flatly, shaking his head. "Unless, due to insufficient manpower, thy mission *faileth*, exposing all to the slings and arrows of outrageous fortune."

"Thou hast most kindly hit it," Nash observed.

"Can we cut the crap?"

"By your leave," said Nash, looking suddenly gloomy.

Reed smiled despite himself. "You know Squids and Jarheads say that?"

"What?"

"'By your leave.' At least they used to. I thought maybe you knew, and that's why you just said it."

"No," said Nash. "I didn't. *Really*?" he seemed genuinely pleased. "Why?"

Reed ignored him. "Six cells," he said. "'Chapters' in plain language. Four men per chapter. That's twenty-four operatives, plus ourselves, plus maybe another ten as sleepers or listeners in other groups. Now we're up to thirty-six. The four-per-chapter's a good number." He paused a moment. "And I assume the Postman—whoever he is—has his own little squad?"

"His palace guard?" Nash murmured.

"Right. Let's hope for our sake it's not a Praetorian Guard."

"Indeed," he mused. He stared past Reed. After a moment, he recollected himself and leaned forward. "I see that," Nash agreed. "Thirty-six total...irrespective of what the Postman's doing."

"I feel confident about the strength and responsiveness of the chapters in the North and Northeast," said Reed, "but the area and distances we need to cover in the Midwest and West are a concern."

"Oh?"

"For instance, what if we have to respond to a situation in California—Sacramento, let's say?" He pushed his plate of half-eaten steak and eggs aside and turned the paper placemat around. On it was a cartoon map of Waffle Cafés throughout the US. Reed pulled out a Sharpie pen.

"We could deploy LA, Seattle or Denver to take care of it," he said triangulating them on the map, "but how do we deliver them quickly and quietly? Commercial air travel's fraught with dangerous recordkeeping, and charters keep records, too. We could expand the number of chapters, I suppose, but I'd like to figure out how to avoid it."

Nash stared at the map, nodding his head. "I think I see a way," he had said. "Let me talk with the Postman, see if we can't fashion a workaround."

"I'd be happy to speak with him," Reed offered.

"No," Nash had ruminated, "I'll take care of it."

It had been the first time Reed wondered how close he and Nash really were, and whether there were other things going on he wasn't being let in on. He began a dossier on his interactions with Nash that very night, not to burn him, necessarily, but to keep a record for protection.

He realized he would need that dossier now, and the others he had kept, if he ever hoped to survive the coming days.

* * *

President Moore, his Chief of Staff, Clayton Quantrelle, and Press Secretary, Tony Marek, sat on the Oval Office couches around the coffee table in the middle of the room. Moore was distracted and choleric, though his scorn for Quantrelle seemed fixed enough. Despite public claims of "needing his own people close" during the transition, the job of White House Chief of Staff was to have been filled by his close friend Alec Nash, smooth, affable, urbane—not Quantrelle, a bellicose, swaggering, transparently partisan political hack. The Postman had pushed Quantrelle up the pecking order, and it was he who had brought in Marek.

As Diane Redmond's few weeks as President had been taken up, mostly, with appointments, the Moore administration—if it could rightly be called that—began its first weeks by undoing any appointments already in process, irrespective of promises to keep to her agenda.

"Mr. President," Quantrelle began, eagerly drawing his attention, and sweltering gaze, away from himself and to the papers on the table, "I suggest we leak details of the memo report stating that Redmond had been considering replacing the Attorney General, and that Senator Eliot's name was on the list of possible replacements. Then, we condemn the leak while confirming its veracity at the same time. Now that it's public, when we make the change, we'll say we're just following through on one of her initiatives. And it moves our timeframe forward."

"They only put Eliot's name on to placate me," said Moore, a sour look on his face. "The whole thing was a farce. They never intended to make any changes."

"Then the joke's on them, Mr. President," Marek interjected. "Because they did the work, the backgrounder report exists. All we're doing is taking them at their word. What're they going to do now—say they were lying, trying to make you look foolish?"

Moore nodded, but he was clearly thinking of something else.

Selected—though, again, not by Moore—for his loyalty rather than for any strong abilities, Marek radiated a sticky, ingratiating anxiety. Like the Flintlock pilots, who would consult their "Hoyle's Rules" sheets to decide whose direction to follow, Marek seemed preternaturally able to sort out who played the higher hand and orient himself accordingly.

Though of average height, he looked small and a bit podgy standing next to Quantrelle or President Moore, and this added a fawning quality to his wet-behind-the-ears, eager-to-please, new-boy appearance. His thinning brown hair had no natural part but swooped toward his brow in a manner last seen on a Roman statue.

"We need Eliot as the final piece, Mr. President," he continued. "He's been cleared, and this leaked list inoculates you against any claim that you're deviating from Redmond's legacy," said Marek.

"Still..." Moore objected.

"Yes, sir," Quantrelle affirmed. "There *will* be pushback. There will be people saying you're covering up. They'd say that no matter what you did, sir. He's the final piece we need before our big move, and this document we'll leak moves us forward just that much quicker."

Moore nodded, taking it all in. "I want to talk about Alec," he said.

The deferential smile dimmed on Marek's face, and he exchanged a chastened glance with Quantrelle.

"Well?" he demanded, looking at each in turn. "How the fuck did that happen?"

Still the others remained silent, staring at their papers. Moore looked from one to the other. No one met his gaze.

"Alec Nash was the architect of this thing, for Chrissake!" Moore bellowed. "He put the structure in place. *Us* in place. We owed him!"

"I wish it could've been different, sir," said Quantrelle superciliously. "I know he was also your friend. I have a friend, too, Mason Brandenburg, who used to work with me at Forefathers' Institute. He quit in the fall, before the election. We've been watching him ever since."

"Why is he still walking around if you're worried about him?" Moore demanded.

"It seems that his stated reason for leaving, that he'd had a better offer, closer to home, was true. But we're still on him. And I swear to you, sir, if he gives any indication that he knows something, or that he's going to talk, we'll...deal with it."

"Nash wasn't cooperating," Moore stressed.

Quantrelle sighed resignedly, shaking his head. "The evidence against him was too strong, sir—him *and* Reed," he explained with weary forbearance.

"We owed him! I told you to find a way," Moore stated again. "After April 20, we could've spun it that he'd been falsely accused to cover up what the FBI was supposedly really doing—maybe even pin it on that redhead."

Quantrelle sighed. "The order'd already been given, sir."

Moore's features, which had been growing florid as he contemplated the fate of his friend and confidant, turned ashen as he rose to his feet. "Already given?" he screamed at them. "*I'm* the fucking President!" he sputtered.

Outside the White House, Hugh Salter spoke to camera about how the extraordinary circumstances leading to Moore's accidental presidency "have led the President and his team to proceed only very slowly with changes to the administration's agenda, out of respect for his predecessor."

11

Paranoia had crept back into Imogen's life. She found herself looking over her shoulder again, and searching the faces of people she worked with for signs that they might betray her. She couldn't be entirely sure of her own staff, though the chances of any one of them being involved with the dark network were miniscule. As she set about articulating the new investigative priorities for her team, she felt as though she were putting a group of grad students to work on a new academic project without much hope of success.

She would have to rely on Nettie, the analyst turned FBI Agent, to keep it all moving, to help her look deeper for clues she hoped might pry open a window on who was behind the dark network. Annette ("Nettie") Sartain was a demographer with a Master's from the University of Maryland, a black woman with inquisitive, chestnut eyes.

She was petite and youthful, her thick, natural hair fashioned into short twist-outs. She had joined the FBI as an analyst in her early twenties, and then reapplied to become an agent after getting her Master's Degree. Now, at thirty, she was on her third squad.

It was clear she regarded her assignment to Imogen's Studies in Electoral Integrity team as something less than a step up on the career ladder. She had spent her first weeks making phone calls to and taking lunches with anyone who might have been able to get her reassigned. She was the senior member of the group in age, experience and rank, yet in many ways she seemed its most youthful and aware, even if her sharpness had been somewhat blunted by running into this dead-end posting.

The analysts gathered round Imogen's desk, her cheerless office brightened by their eager faces—three young women and one young man in their late twenties, all in their own ways intelligent, ambitious, energetic and polished. Nettie sat slightly apart from the group, leaning back in her chair, legs crossed, watchful.

In contrast with Agent Sartain's jaded view, the analysts saw Imogen as having created a new mode of data-driven investigation. Each one of them had jumped at the chance to work for her, though had they known the depth of doubt and self-loathing in which she held herself, as damaged goods humiliatingly dispatched to the FBI's naughty step, they might have reconsidered their placement requests. In the light of their beaming enthusiasm, she felt only lethargy and the bleakness of having been forced to the periphery. Again.

But there was work to do.

"The beginnings of this kind of investigation are slow and monotonous," she was saying, attempting to manage expectations—theirs and hers.

Having identified targets through their initial work, she now described how she wanted them to proceed, beginning with gathering Federal Election Committee reports and audits and then turning to the audits of the various lobbying groups and charitable organizations she believed were involved.

And then they would go deeper.

"We will first establish and understand the pattern of normal behavior and accounting in these groups; and when we have that, we'll go back through the data and start looking for patterns that don't fit the norm. It'll take time. It's a bit like an archeological dig—slow and methodical. You investigate, sift, evaluate and record evidence. You define boundaries, establish patterns, create and test theories as to what is—or *was* in this case—going on.

"Some days there's nothing. Other days, what you find only raises more questions. Sometimes what you find contradicts what you thought you'd find before you began digging. And that's OK," she added. "But these are the discrepancies I want you to investigate. If something doesn't fit ordinary data patterns, let's find out why not."

She paused and looked at them. "It may also be that, like in a dig, you see the shape of something—a bone fragment, say—but you can't take it out of the ground right away for fear of breaking it, or ruining something it's attached to, something you might not see yet. Patience, caution and silence will be our watchwords."

She had figured this would be a difficult little pep talk, with her team wondering where it was all leading. But as she talked about the monotony, the inevitable false leads and the frustration, perversely, she saw a new eagerness in the faces. They seemed to welcome the task.

Well, they would need to. There were masses of data to sift through—public and otherwise—of the various PACs and grassroots 501c-4 organizations; and they would be going back five years—more where they could. They would look at where and how projects interacted with others on their list, like Sovereign Caucus or the Opportunity Initiative.

They would look at the delegation of authority framework, the reward structure; they would look at budgets, policy papers, where and how they spent their money; whom they employed. And Nettie, as the sole agent in the group, would start by scrutinizing Flintlock Industries.

She hung back as the group dispersed to begin their tasks.

"OK, so you've tasked me with finding out more about this Flintlock Industries," Nettie began. "I get that the analysts are looking for patterns in the various PAC's that might suggest problems, but if I'm going to be effective, I need to understand how you think a plastics and energy company is impacting electoral integrity."

Imogen had grown used to her laconic manner, but she asked probing and precise questions about framing and patterns. Well, that's what a good staff was for, irrespective of tone. Imogen found she couldn't blame Nettie for her misgivings about this unit, since she shared many of them. It was a shame, she thought, because she also felt some kinship.

They were both graduate-level wonks who wanted to do more; both had started as analysts before graduating again as agents. She could see herself and Nettie getting into long discussions about applications of FBI Enterprise Theory, or going further down the rabbit hole of Path Dependence, Counter-factuals and Multi-structural Equation Models as applied to investigations.

"I'd like you to look particularly at their executive air division," Imogen said. "Cross-reference with the analysts and find out if Flintlock has any links to the PAC's we're examining—whether the main company, or the air division. I'd like to know what the overall corporate structure is—again, with particular attention to the air division: names, titles, duties and responsibilities, payroll. See if they've been audited, too."

"What is it you think they've done?" asked Sartain.

"There may be nothing at all. I'm sorry to ask you to fly blind here..." She smiled, thinking that Nettie would pick up and enjoy her wordplay about Flintlock Air and flying blind, but Imogen's weak quip either went over her head, or—more likely—was beneath her notice. She stood impassively in front of the desk.

Imogen cleared her throat: "Yes, well...at any rate, I'm betting that if there *is* something it'll jump out at you."

"I could be of more use if you read me in, Agent Trager."

"Call me Imogen," she said. "It's more about not coloring or limiting your approach than with not taking you into confidence."

Sartain nodded and turned to go out, but it was clear she didn't regard Imogen's response as satisfactory.

With her charges now set to work, each examining and sharing their findings, Imogen left the office for her meeting with Amanda. She gave herself lots of time, and went first to an outside café with tables spread across a broad square with shadows of bright, chilly light. She chose a chair with a view of the direction from which she had just come. There was something pleasing about the cold, she thought, as she

76

rearranged her plum scarf and turned up the lapels of her pear-green overcoat.

Not many people were about, and so far, she didn't see anyone obviously tailing her. She drank her espresso quickly, left payment on the table and walked briskly to a Metro stop. She bounded down the stairs and stopped in a broad causeway. As she scanned the sparse group of commuters, instinctively distinguishing men who might be tailing her from men interested for other reasons, she thought that if "they" were tracking her movements, they would also be tracking her phone, just as she had so effectively tracked theirs. Her hand closed around the phone in her coat pocket. Well, people often lose their signal underground in the Metro. She switched it off.

Riding the Red Line from Judiciary Square to Dupont Circle, Imogen found herself preoccupied. This constant studying of faces and body language was having predictable negative consequences. Before the train reached Gallery Place, she had politely rebuffed two unsuitable suitors and retreated into the feigned obliviousness that many women adopt on public transportation.

The tea and coffee shop a few blocks west of Dupont Circle was dark but warm, its ochre colored walls painted with murals made to look like graffiti. Amanda waved to her from a table beside a broad pillar. They embraced warmly and got down to business among the *caffeinati*.

"Why can't I call you?" Vega asked, her dark eyes smoldering.

Imogen related what Trey had told her about being tracked. "I feel so helpless," she said. "They've chucked me out with the garbage. I've been stripped of Bureau access . . . sent to fucking Siberia. The one person on my team that I should be able to confide in resents me. It's making me paranoid. If I'm being spied on, it's probably by our own damn people."

Vega's standard-issue FBI stare was unblinking. Finally, she said: "Which makes you the perfect person to break this all wide open. Stop feeling sorry for yourself. You've got a team, don't you? And you all can follow leads I'd have to report on."

If I had any, she thought, clinging to her resentment. "What have *you* got?" she demanded.

A smile broke over Amanda's face. "I'm having a really interesting thought right now," she said.

12

It was ironic that the dark network conspirators had turned the tables and were using phone traces, just as she and Trey had done so effectively to bring down two of the cells. Talking with Amanda, Imogen realized that they could possibly turn the tables yet again.

She turned her cell phone back on as she climbed out of the Metro at Gallery Place. It was best, she and Vega had agreed, that her dropped signal appear to be caused by subway interference. She spent 40 minutes nosing through shops and grabbing a bite to eat, establishing her whereabouts and a routine. So far as she could tell, no one was tailing her. She withdrew cash—$500—before shutting off her phone and descending again into the Metro's digestive system, taking the Green Line to Congress Heights.

The dampness of the morning was gone, and a dazzling spring sun invigorated the eight-block walk from the Congress Heights station to the corner where Jimmy May "shaped up" for work. He was a courier of sorts, involved in all kinds of things. She and Vega had arrested him three months ago as part of their investigation into the dark network. They had identified him by a thumbprint left on a Ziploc baggie Imogen had retrieved at the site of the conspirators' last known drop.

It turned out that May was just what he had claimed, an entrepreneurial courier for hire, with no knowledge of what he carried or why he carried it—only that he got paid. They had let him go, but Imogen had worried at the time about his safety. The network was leaving bodies everywhere.

Jimmy had impressed Imogen. He was sharp, enterprising and lively, and within the scope of his illicit vocation, honorable. As the song said, to live outside the law you must be honest. She wondered how he would react when she showed up, whether there was a way to signal to him that she'd like to talk privately. It couldn't be good for his reputation be seen with an FBI agent.

In the breeze along Alabama Avenue Southeast, stray hair came loose from her smart bun. She donned her green aviator sunglasses against the glare, and looped the red tendrils behind her ears when they drifted across her vision. She breathed the sweet air deeply, enjoying the tidy houses and small, well-kept lawns.

From Jimmy's description of "his" corner and what she'd seen of the derelict house in which they arrested him—squalor, no heat, electricity or running water—she'd expected a rough area. This was nothing of the kind, and she began to worry that she had walked the wrong way out of the station. She couldn't turn on her phone for a map, so it wasn't until she neared the corner that she knew she was in the right place. It was both lively and languid in front of McDonalds at the corner, clearly a neighborhood hangout.

Any thought of stealth was lost long before she reached the corner of Mellon and MLK. Eight or more young black men were peering curiously in her direction. Jimmy May spotted her, too, detached himself from the crowd and sauntered across the street to meet her. He pointed north along MLK.

"That's where you want to go, lady," he called as he paused in the middle of the road to let a car pass. "The school's just up there, about three blocks."

"That way?" she asked, taking the hint.

"Yeah," he shouted, still in the middle of the road. "Past the Chinese kitchen." Then more quietly, "wait in front; I'll be by." He looked at her quizzically and took a quick look up and down the street. He turned back to the other side of the street shaking his head.

"Thanks!" she called brightly, and started off north.

Some drivers slowed to examine her in front of the black metal schoolyard fence, hands deep in her overcoat pockets. Not quite sure how to stand, she took out her dormant phone and pretended to be engrossed. A couple of boys about ten years old strolled past and looked doubtful.

After twenty minutes of alternately checking the phone and street, she began to think Jimmy was just getting rid of her and giving himself time to get away. As she wondered what more she could do, he walked up behind her from the school side of the fence, startling her. "What the hell you doing here?" he asked from inside the fence.

Imogen turned quickly. His dreadlocks had grown out more since she'd last seen him. His cultivated long-distance stare, like that of her FBI colleagues, was meant to convey a seen-it-all indifference, but there was too much happening behind those dark brown eyes, too much interest and curiosity.

"I'm sorry," she said. "I needed to speak with you."

"Doesn't the FBI know *anything* about undercover? Damn! They send the whitest, ginger-top white lady I ever saw over here for some confab? Y'all're about as subtle as a Batman searchlight."

"It's me that wants the help," she said. "Not strictly FBI."

He stared at her flatly. "I take enough risks. I'm not about to get mixed up in some governmental bullshit. Don't come round here again." He started to turn and Imogen put a hand on his arm. He looked at her, then contemptuously at the hand. She didn't let go.

"You saw it immediately," she said, a pleading tone creeping into her voice. "We were investigating ourselves. You said so in interrogation."

"Yeah," he said. "I did. And I wanted clear of it."

"It isn't over, Jimmy. The bad guys've been putting people down. You're already involved, and you might be next."

"You offering me protection?" he scoffed.

"No. I can't protect you," she said ruefully. "Not now. The only way to make us all safe—me included—is to find out who's pulling the strings. We have leads,"—she wished—"but we don't know who we can trust."

"Who's 'we?' You and that fierce Mexican girl?"

"Guatemalan, actually," she replied pointlessly. "Her parents. Amanda's an American, of course."

He looked again at the hand on his arm. "What do you want from me? How's me getting involved in shit that ain't my business supposed to help me be safe? More likely it'll bring a bunch more down on me."

"It's simple," she said bluntly. "I need four burner phones that can't be traced back to me," she said.

His eyes roved the street.

"I think you're the guy who can get them for me," she continued. "I don't know if it's the bad guys, or the FBI, or if the FBI *is* the bad guys. But someone's tapping my phone, tracing where I go—don't worry," she added quickly, patting her coat pocket, "it's turned off right now."

"That's it?" he asked, his gaze finally returning to her.

"Can you do it?"

"Yeah, but it ain't cheap," he said.

"How much?"

"Hmm," he deliberated, his eyes once more flicking up and down the street. "Forty for each burner, that's a hundred sixty dollars—call it one-seventy-five. My overhead." He looked at her pointedly. "Another fifty dollars to me for delivery."

"Can you get me four extra SIM cards in case we have to switch 'em up?"

"Four hundred dollars," he said.

"Four hundred?" she said.

He nodded. "For everything. And they'll be clean, not recycled, not tied to anyone already on the radar. Take it or leave it."

"Sold," she said.

13

On March 20 the Senate and the House voted with strong majorities, confirming David Carr as Moore's new Vice-President, just ten days after Redmond died in office and Moore was elevated to president.

It was good news for newsman Hugh Salter, drawing a line under an ugly and dangerous time, both professionally and for the life of the nation. His connections with Carr went back some years, and were paying dividends in terms of access. He had been on-air constantly in the past week. Adding to his growing prestige, many in press circles in D.C. believed that it had been Salter's call to Carr about rumored threats to members of Congress, back in January, that had spurred then-Congressman Carr to call the Capitol Police.

That call from Salter had indeed been the prompt, Carr himself had said, because it told him that the strong-arm tactics of men such as Nash and the threats to his own Pennsylvania delegation weren't exclusive to his state, but were widespread and apparently coordinated.

It was Carr's resistance and testimony before the full Congress that ultimately led to the unanimous consent vote in the House, which saw Diane Redmond elected President, bringing an end to the Interregnum. A nation rocked by scandal, intrigue and murder had been relieved by the statesmanship of that vote. And it found a hero in David Carr.

Prior to January and his call to the Capitol Police, Carr had been notable only for his age—a youthful 42—in an environment where fully half his colleagues were past average retirement age. Otherwise, he was conventional, unremarkable. He was conventionally earnest, conventionally featured, and conventionally conservative, believing in guns and butter more than bread and circuses. Though not athletic, he was trim and firm.

There was no single feature that led, and his chin, like his haircut, appeared to be preparing for a recession. His wife Susan was pleasant and attractive and, like her husband, unremarkably so. In public appearances, she favored skirt suits in too-bright pastels. Taken together with her loyal, chirrupy smile, her aspect seemed stranded in an imagined, revisionist time.

Carr wasn't to be discounted, though, especially now he had caught the eye of the public. He was energetic, canny and had risen quickly. He'd shown a grasp of budget fundamentals and had learned the legislative ropes. Many said privately that the smart money was on his making a run for the Presidency in the near future. Everything, including time, seemed to be on his side, although Salter noted pessimistically that time tries idealism, and youth never comes twice.

Salter continued to file news reports, but increasingly he was being asked to comment on a range of things. Despite his personal and professional satisfaction, grim, dark divisions loomed: the unsatisfactory election result in Illinois and the quashed inquiry into it remained the subject of bitter dispute; and as voters had learned how much the election may have been manipulated, they had become ever more suspicious and reluctant to accept anything as straightforward truth. Even so, Carr—and Salter too—kept emphasizing that despite the rancor, the nation was whole because its systems and institutions had ultimately worked. The United States was a nation of laws, and all were subject to the rule of law.

But the Illinois vote-scandal was deathless as a zombie, and the urgency of calls to replace the Attorney General was increasing. She had first missed and then mishandled the threat to the integrity of the voting process there. Because of the irregularities in Illinois, there was now a movement to implement the best practices called for in the Voter Veracity

Venture's playbook, measures which opponents claimed would restrict certain kinds of voters and actually increase the system's vulnerability to fraud. The Justice Department was delaying these measures as it conducted studies, but it looked as though some form of voter verification would be introduced. Additionally, a number of congressmen were asking for a special counsel with a wide-ranging brief. Such an investigation, they noted, would not be able to operate unless the Attorney General recused herself or stepped down.

At the fringes of the debate, though getting ample play in a number of sectors, was the contention that the whole Faithless Elector plot and the turmoil of the Interregnum had been a Democratic false flag operation designed to spread chaos and to discredit leading conservatives. Senator Drew Eliot, former chair of the Senate Judicial Oversight Committee was often portrayed as the injured party, though he declined to wade into the fray.

Privately, Salter worried about Carr's ability to maintain his independence from those around him now that he had been catapulted so close to the center of power. He worried that Carr's winning forthrightness might erode. It was one thing to risk all and seize the high ground. The real difficulty lay in holding it when tactical waves and the tide of opinion eroded it piece by piece.

Salter himself knew it all too well. He still felt the sting of conscience for the role he had played in propagating scandal, innuendo and false news that he'd been fed. The reward structure was not on the side of the angels.

At the FBI, Don Weir also found himself buffeted by swelling tides. He was uneasy about new transfer requests to join the moribund Faithless Elector Task Group. The eager young men making the requests didn't say outright that they wanted to rake through the ashes of the investigation in the hope of finding compromising details to leak about its legality and findings, but it was pretty clear to Weir that it was all part of a "cleaning house" initiative. But whose? The Bureau was not immune from the strife and rancor taking hold of the nation. There were definite camps, and even some willing to step outside the confines of their straight-laced anonymity to make pronouncements on the direction and conduct of the Faithless Elector investigation.

He and the Deputy Director had thus far been able to forestall the transfer requests and to tamp down the smoldering discontent within their ranks, arguing that manpower was appropriately assigned and that other active cases took precedence "for the good of the Bureau." It was clear to him, however, that the good of the Bureau had itself become a contentious proposition. He wished he could be certain of where the pressure was coming from.

That afternoon, Clayton Quantrelle pulled his silver Mercedes into a parking space in front of a series of squat, brick buildings in an industrial park on the outskirts of Springfield, Virginia, ten miles southwest of D.C. Most of the area's action—off-loading and shipping—happened in the wee hours of the morning. Mid-afternoon was a slow time of day. The area looked abandoned in a chilly, gently falling rain. The parking lot was empty. He pulled out a flip phone and dialed a number.

"This is Bannister," he said into the phone, using his work name. "Update report." He frowned as he listened, the thin lips on his small mouth twisting in disappointment. "All right, I'll check at the next regular time." He hung up, shut the phone off and put it in the glove compartment of his car. A moment later, he stepped out of the car and jogged up the stairs to an empty shipping office rifling through his key ring for the front door key.

The glass door had an aluminum frame and led into a darkened room. Once inside, he flipped a switch, illuminating one of the dim, overhead fluorescent lights. It cast a feeble bronze haze over the room. As the glass door closed behind him the frame made a metal-on-metal scraping sound. He could see no one outside as he pulled the door shut and locked it.

A beige filing cabinet was shoved against the left-hand wall with a Steelcase desk next to it and missing a leg. Stained acoustic tiling hung precariously from the ceiling grid where there was any tile at all. The rest of the ceiling was a lattice of metal squares and dangling wires. He strode across a tattered indoor-outdoor carpet to a door at the back that led to the truck bays, taking care not to trip over the phone on the floor. Through another locked door and he was in the warehouse.

The juxtaposition was stark. The truck bay resembled a high-tech clean room. Quantrelle quickly closed the door, sealing in the light. Ryan Campbell and Adam Tudor, the two operatives on shift, looked up and acknowledged him with a nod as he trotted down a set of concrete stairs to join them.

Quantrelle had nicknamed them "Tweedledum" and "Tweedledim" because they seemed so interchangeable, and he never saw one without the other. Tweedledim's shift was over at 4pm, but he did seem to hang around.

Both young men seemed on uncertain terms with the concept of grooming. They were slovenly and snarky, immature and latitudinarian. They dressed appallingly for work, as though it were perpetually a rainy laundry day and they had overslept their alarms, their hair, by turns lumpy or spiky.

Though the network Nash and Reed created was characterized by the decidedly low-tech traces it left, even they acknowledged that some cyber-fluent contingency was necessary. But only for surveillance.

The day after the House vote in the historic contingent election, with their boss Alec Nash in jail, Quantrelle had reassigned the Tweedles and set them up here in what was quickly becoming their private dorm room at the end of a row of loading bays, out of sight, in an area and a place used to comings-and-goings at odd hours.

'Dum and 'Dim belonged to a special group of recruits talent-spotted and trained by Reed but run by Nash. In contrast to the campus nihilists Reed had recruited, these two were difficult to pigeonhole. Their idealism, if it could be called such, was fluid. It seemed to him that so long as access to the proper toys was on offer, they'd work for anyone.

Quantrelle was used to idealists, true believers and chancers. He knew how to motivate such men, and he knew how far to trust them. But these two seemed barely in it even for the money and more for the chance to stretch their technical prowess. He wondered how close to Nash and Reed they were, and where their loyalties lay, if they had any.

"Anything to report?" he asked, dropping into one of the rolling desk chairs. He kept his coat on, as did both young men. The room was cold for the benefit of the servers. "Did she turn off her phone again?"

"Yeah, about that," said 'Dum. "We've had a chance to analyze it?" he said.

Tudor, or Tweedledum, was an "up-talker," his statements often sounding like questions, or as though pausing at odd moments to make sure his listeners were with him or approved of what he said. He also had the habit of tossing his mop of dirty blond hair with the distressing regularity of a physical tic. "And we looked at her movements a bit more carefully? Her phone went dark when she went into the Metro, and the signal reappeared when she came back out of the subway? We don't think she turned it off now."

"That's good news, isn't it?" said Quantrelle, his face brightening.

"Yes," they both agreed.

"What've you got on the others?"

"They're as boring as she is. At least they don't go shopping as much as she seems to."

Tweedledum chuckled as he shoved an energy bar into his mouth.

"What've you heard on their calls?" Quantrelle asked.

"Here's the transcripts," said 'Dum, handing him a folder, his mouth still full. "But there's nothing to tell. Trey Kelly called his girlfriend. They're having Thai tonight, even though according to her, they've had it like twice already this month. Mike at NSA's gonna hang at home and play GTA ...again. Trager's going to Seattle this weekend to be with her professor." He handed over the transcripts. "We're still on the professor's phones from back in December. Nothing interesting there either."

"They don't even talk dirty to each other," lamented 'Dim scratching at his shaggy head. "It's just 'honey' this, 'boo' that, 'whaddayou wanna eat?—I dunno, whattayou wanna eat?' I hadn't realized, ya know? just how banal existence could be 'til we started snooping on these guys."

"There is one thing," said Tweedledum, grabbing a sheet he had been working on. "We've also been analyzing Professor Calder's email, but we don't know what to make of it. For the most part, what's there is exactly what you'd expect—grade complaints, faculty correspondence and bullshit whining from other professors."

"Course demands, papers from overseas," added 'Dim.

"Right," said 'Dum, still studying the paper, "but he's also sending a lot of emails around talking about 'crossover voting' and 'party defection,' 'down ballot roll off.' Things like that, so we opened some of the files, but it's encrypted."

"Well," Dim chuckled, "Not *encrypted*, really. Just dense. Even when we looked at it through this Open Sesame program, it didn't read." He caught Quantrelle's icy stare and his smile evaporated. "It all seems to be coming from something called American National Election Studies?" he said.

"What does?" Quantrelle asked.

"The data? We're pretty sure it's just part of his work, but the coding—which looks like encryption—makes us wonder. There could be messages inside the data. Ya think it's something we should worry about?"

Quantrelle stood up, his vulpine face white with rage. His blistering gaze took in both young men. "I don't come here to answer questions," he hissed. "I come here—we pay you—to give *us* answers," he spat.

"We'll have something for you tomorrow, sir," said Dim. "It's just—"

"—Yes?" asked Quantrelle.

"Well, it's likely that it's something to do with his work. But obviously we need to check it out," he added quickly. "I don't have a Ph.D., though. I have no idea what I'm looking at, much less what it means. Is there someone in our group who could help? Someone with this kind of training?"

"No one like that on our payroll," said Quantrelle. "Work it out."

* * *

Amanda Vega had been monitoring Flintlock's second company frequency, but there had been no chatter whatsoever. She was beginning to worry that she had reached another dead end. She monitored the main company radio channel, hoping for clues as to how the two were given instructions to switch to the private channel, but she hadn't learned anything. Something was going on, she felt, even if she didn't know what.

She and Imogen met Jimmy May at a Starbucks across from Gallery Place, where he gave them the untraceable "burner" phones in a small gift bag and collected the remainder of his money.

"Thank you," said Imogen. "Do you want anything? A coffee or something?"

"Nah," he said, his eyes roving over the coffee shop. "I need to keep moving. Go see my auntie up north."

"Oh?" said Imogen brightly. "Where does she live?"

"With respect to you agents of the law—whatever that even means nowadays—it's none of your damn business where she lives, and she might not be my aunt." He stood up. "Stay safe," he said with indeterminate irony as he turned.

Imogen and Vega watched him heading to the door.

"You think he knows anything more than he's letting on?" Vega asked.

"Doubtful," Imogen mused. "He's been pretty straightforward with us so far."

Vega nodded. "Still: how do we know 'they' didn't get to him? If they did, they'll be listening in to everything we do. Is there a way Trey can test these quickly before we use them?"

"Good idea," said Imogen, her eyes following Jimmy May as he walked out through the double doors. She noticed that the eyes of two security guards also followed him out.

"I have some follow-up to do with Trey," said Vega. "It won't raise any red flags with the dark network if I pay him a visit. I'll take these over. Meet back here tomorrow for lunch at 12.30?"

* * *

Quantrelle dropped in at the shipping office a little earlier than usual the next evening for an update. Tweedledum and Tweedledim handed over their intercept transcripts. There was nothing new. "Trey and his girl are getting Mexican tonight," said Dum. "Trager goes shopping every lunchtime. She really likes that Gallery Place. Basically, radio silence from Mike at NSA. My money's on a *Matrix* marathon," he snarked.

"And what about Calder's communications?" Quantrelle wanted to know.

The two young men exchanged a glance. "It's all just poli-sci gobbledy-gook? No hidden messages or anything. Like we thought," said Dim. "Nothing to worry about."

"Yeah," Dum chimed in, "we did a deep dive, and the whole thing's related to his research, stuff he's asking his graduate students to look at and work on. Not an issue for us. Also, you'd asked us to look a little deeper on that Mason Brandenburg? Nothing. He's more boring than our other targets."

'Dum chuckled. "I mean he *is* an accountant."

14

When he realized he would be delivering himself for execution if he met the next scheduled extraction flight in Fairmont, Nebraska, Frank Reed changed his plans and retraced the steps that had brought him to Beaver Island three months earlier. This time, though, he stopped in Cincinnati. On his first morning there, he presented himself as Ian Gerritt at a bank on East Fourth Street and asked to be let into his safe deposit box.

It was the largest box the bank had. The bank manager left him alone while he opened it and withdrew the dossiers on each member of each cell and chapter he and Nash had set up. He stuffed the files into his satchel and went back to the row house he was renting through Airbnb on Orchard Street in the Pendleton neighborhood.

As he sat there at the kitchen counter turning over the pages, Reed was nostalgic for the time when he and Nash felt they were building something lasting, a time when his own prospects seemed so bright: Nash was to have been Chief of Staff, not that skeletal, pompous ghoul Quantrelle; Colls, now dead, should have been FBI Director, and he himself the Director of National Intelligence. There would be a firm, clear-eyed hand on the wheel, the right people, making the right decisions for the nation.

The lead-up to the 2016 election had been a heady time for him, and he delighted in the work. He had burnished the recruits' sense of their own importance by proclaiming to them that they were the vanguard for a reclaimed America. The enthusiasm in them for the work and what they were learning was exciting to be a part of, he remembered.

He had schooled the recruits in tradecraft—word codes in plain language, the proper method for effecting hand-to-hands and arranging dead drops; how to engage in surveillance without giving themselves away; how to test if they were being followed, how to gather evidence, how to face interrogation. How to get away with murder. He had also inculcated the need for watchfulness—foremost of one another. Each was to report on the others. Each must accept this as a matter of self-preservation. In his arrogance, Reed had never suspected that it would be he who needed preserving.

The records on each one were meticulous, detailing their crimes—the damning evidence which could be used later for leverage, should the need arise. The Postman, or one of his Palace Guard, even held a dossier on him and Nash.

* * *

Duncan Calder sat in his Gowen Hall office on the UW campus, staring at lines of figures from the American National Election Studies database. Grim Seattle light seeped through his window, chilling everything it touched. He had been working through the morning. Every half hour or so he would stand, stretch, and walk up and down in front of the desk, rotating his injured right arm to relieve the stiffness and get the blood moving. More than just pain, the sensation was disquieting, disconnected. At one end, his shoulder burned ferociously, yet the pulses of pain radiating from there to his injured hand were like the creep of damp cold through bone. It was now only a little after eleven in the morning, and he'd already taken more than half of the recommended maximum dosage of ibuprofen.

Though Tweedledum and Tweedledim couldn't know it, because they'd lied and hadn't actually bothered to review Calder's work, much less done "a deep dive" on any of his election research, they were right. Duncan Calder was indeed carrying on with his work, and the communications regarding "crossover voting, "down ballot roll off," and a great many other factors he was asking his graduate students to examine were exactly the esoteric study they purported it to be.

ANES only published every two years, and it was important data. Calder had thrown himself back into work and was directing two promising graduate students and assisting two others in how to use it for their research. The work kept his mind occupied; kept at bay the recognition that the initiative in the larger battle was slipping away. Pain and bouts of depression, however, seemed to dampen his higher faculties, to steal focus from the task before him, making slow going of the scaling and "integerizing" that he was directing. Having to break roughly every half hour didn't help either.

At such times, as he paced in front of the desk, grimacing each time his arm came to the high point of its arc, thoughts about what was happening in Washington intruded. Inevitably, he found himself thinking again of Matthew Yamashita, his promising student and rising star, who had first discovered the Faithless Elector plot and had been murdered for it.

Calder was stoic about physical pain, but whenever thoughts of Matthew's death burst in on him, the guilt and anguish were so raw and violent that the edifice of himself seemed to collapse, leaving him shattered and desolate. He saw again in his mind's eye the spot where Matthew had died; felt again the cold solitude of death. The bone chill in his arm and in the dead fingers of his hand seemed to resonate in sympathy. The numbness and pain felt like a clue he was staring right at but hadn't the wit to understand.

Why hadn't he believed Matthew from the beginning? his catechism began. Could it have all been different— Matthew not crushed at the roadside but still alive, with his incandescent mind and precocious spirit still dazzling? Or would he have been dead along with Matthew, with whatever was now happening in the conspiracy farther along?

There was a knock at the door as the shell of Duncan Calder rested on the edge of his desk, massaging his shoulder. "Yes?" he said.

A man in his mid-thirties entered. He smiled at Calder, who returned a quizzical smile. It was normal not to recognize undergraduates; but this man looked familiar, a former graduate student? His brown hair was full and wavy, almost a pompadour in front but with a short ponytail at the back.

"You don't remember me," he said, the smile ebbing from his face.

"I do know you," said Calder staring into the man's face. "I'm sorry, but I just don't know how."

He was tall and sturdy. Although his clothing was old, his hair was tidy, and he wore a fastidious moustache and soul patch beard. He had an expensive looking diamond stud earring in his left ear. Calder worried that this was the moment the Pirate King pulled out a gun and shot him. He wondered if he'd seen too many movies.

"Professor," said the man, extending his hand, "I'm not sure you ever got my name, but me and you, we took the scariest fuckin' cab ride of my life."

"The cab driver!" Calder exclaimed. Relieved and pleased, he took the driver's hand warmly.

"Rich Lamberti," he said, introducing himself.

"I'm so glad you looked me up!" said Calder. "Really glad to see you're OK. How've you been?"

"Not so good, professor. I heard on the news you got pretty dinged up too."

"Yeah," said Calder, automatically beginning to massage his shoulder.

"I had my hack license suspended 'til about three weeks ago."

"You? But the other guy—"

"—Yeah, that's what I told 'em. I even got an attorney. Somehow it all got blamed on me. I gotta tell you, even as the whole inquest was happening, it felt like the fix was in. Like they wanted this to go away."

95

Back in December, as Calder had headed for the airport in Lamberti's taxi, a network operative had tried to force the cab off the road and into incoming traffic just as they had started across the First Avenue South Bridge. It was only by brilliant driving, split-second timing and luck that they had escaped. The moment flashed through Calder's mind. He felt again the sliding of the car and the weightlessness; saw the headlights of the oncoming traffic.

"After hearing what you went through, professor—the people behind it—I knew that they—*someone*—had fixed me. Anyway, I figured the safest thing I could do was keep my head down, just go ahead and swallow the shit they were shoveling at me, take the deferred jail sentence; take the license suspension, crawl in my little fucking hole, ya know?"

"But you're back at work now?"

"Yeah. I'm a week shy of ending my probationary period."

"That's good," said Calder.

"Yeah, I guess," he said, not sounding convinced. "Listen, I came here today because I wanted to tell you something: a couple days ago I saw the guy who tried to kill us."

"What?"

"I got a glimpse of him during the crash, but I got a real good look at him at that bullshit hearing. Not that he was *at* my hearing," Lamberti added bitterly. He trailed off, lost for a moment in thought. "I gotta ask: aren't you supposed to be able to confront your accuser? Isn't that like common law jurisprudence or something?"

"I suppose it depends," said Calder equably, falling back into a professorial tone, "on whether it was a trial or a hearing. I'm afraid it's not my area."

Lamberti waved off his explanation. "I saw him in the lobby of the courthouse. My attorney pointed him out. He looked pretty chummy with the cops, standing there bullshitting with them. After what happened at the hearing and seeing that...And one of the guys looked Federal—FBI, Secret Service, I dunno. Crisp, arrogant. Beefy. Stuffed in his expensive suit like a fucking sausage. Sunglasses. Not Seattle PD for sure."

Calder was so lost in thought, he forgot the pain in his shoulder.

"So, after the trial I suddenly had a lot of time on my hands," Lamberti continued, "no job, nowhere to go, and it starts to bug me. Really bug me, like when you're not supposed to pick at a scab but you do anyway. I look up the 'complainant,' Tim Hayward."

"You went to confront him?" Calder asked.

"Hardly. I went to stake out his house in White Center. Turns out, it's for sale again. Empty. No one lives there. The guy who did live there killed his girlfriend and himself. Hayward was dead four years before he tried to run us off the road," said Lamberti, shaking his head, "and when I got a copy of the final police report, all mention of another driver was gone. All it had was an account of a single-car crash with the divider. We never hit that divider: he did."

"Shit," said Calder. "I'm sorry. I had no idea what I was involving you in."

"I'm not mad at you. Not at all."

"You could be in real danger. They killed my student, Matthew. They tried to kill me in your cab. They tried to kill me twice in D.C." Calder felt sick at the thought he had led yet another innocent to potential slaughter.

But Rich was sanguine. "I'd been thinking, I'm fucked here. Maybe I need to move someplace else. Then, two days ago, I saw him again getting into someone else's taxi."

"Did he see you?"

"No," said Lamberti. "Fortunately, the little prick was in a hurry. But I watched him get in, and I wondered about following. I even did a U-turn, but then I thought about what happened to you and me." He sighed. "I kinda chickened out and pulled over. I just saw myself getting crushed and rolled over by the judicial system again. . . or worse. But Professor, I've had a lot of time to think. I'm done taking shit. I want to burn them back. I figured there had to be a smarter way, and I thought of you."

"You don't want to go to the police?" Calder asked.

"Hardly," Lamberti scoffed. "Even if they're not in on it, they'll get waved off by the Feds."

"Right, and we'd alert them—the bad guys—that we were on to something."

Lamberti smiled. "We?"

15

Frank Reed sat up late into the night with the dossiers on his recruits. His adopted street, in the Pendleton neighborhood was tranquil and well-tended. Durable row houses crowded amiably together in a jumble of styles, reflecting the different stages of renovation each owner had undertaken. If any of the neighbors or passing dog-walkers had noticed the kitchen light burning late through the tasteful, arched windows and had glanced inside, they'd have seen a stern, middle-aged man poring over papers with a mixture of disdain and resignation, like someone doing his taxes.

The files were incomplete by design, a fact he now regretted. Alec Nash had held some of them. Due to Reed's forced winter seclusion, even those he had were out of date. He arranged the piles across the marble countertop in a pattern relating to their location and took stock. There were six so-called "chapters," based in Seattle, Los Angeles, Denver; Springfield, Illinois, Boston and D.C. Each was strategically located in Democratic-controlled or –leaning states, with responsibility for the broader region surrounding their base.

He had the records for Agent Colls' FBI/DC chapter, which were useless now they were all dead. He had the papers relating to his own Northeast network-chapter, around Boston—also irrelevant because Alec Nash was dead and the other three operatives were now being held in safety as cooperating witnesses. Fortunately for Reed's plans, each member's knowledge beyond his own cell was miniscule. The FBI needed him to help join the dots.

But he was missing information on a number of chapters. Nash had held the Colorado and Illinois chapter files, leaving California and the Seattle chapters to Reed. He would need to set about remaking the files on Colorado and Illinois, as best he could. He had recruited every one of them, and knew their names and backgrounds, but he didn't know the specifics of what they had been tasked with after he had handed command of them to Nash.

Even so, their names and his scant notes on their recruiting would give the FBI something to follow. He also held the dossiers on the two pilots flying for Flintlock, the men, presumably, who would collect and kill him. Unfortunately for Reed, Alec Nash had held the "insurance" files on the Postman, Tucker and Baker. To get all this to stick, Reed thought, and have a chance of living, he had to get to those.

He considered how best to pay out the information and win a deal from the FBI. Like a high-stakes poker game in which he held a winning hand, he would need to raise the stakes slowly to keep the FBI in the game. He was already looking over the piles of folders, wondering what his best opening bid might be. To survive, it wasn't enough to win a deal: he'd have to persuade the FBI to bid big so that he could scoop the whole pot.

He would Bid confidently but not big, he decided, opening with some scrap of intel. If he gave them everything at once, he'd lose his ability to bargain for real protection and sentence reduction. Presumably, they would Call, probably with some scrap themselves, like a vague offer about sentencing recommendations.

He would Raise, and they would See. He would have to establish his insider status with some low-level burns, and then move up the ranks. If he played it well, when he finally went All In, and let it be known he could identify and incriminate the sinister fairy tale characters Postman, Tucker and Baker as well as give them the doctors who forged President Redmond's test results, the Justice Department would have to bet big, too.

He stared at the files he had. The LA and Denver chapters weren't particularly useful, he noted. They'd seen little activity in the years before the election, and the men there were a little too eager for self-promotion. He'd never fully trusted those chapters to get the difficult jobs done, he reflected.

In fact, though one of the Faithless Electors had come from Colorado, it had been the Seattle chapter that had done the work in turning her. The California chapter, too, was sound only in theory. Each chapter member there talked big but seemed reticent to get his hands dirty. They had been of no real use to him, and now that he needed something to trade with the FBI they were even less so.

Giving up either of those two moribund chapters first might backfire. The press, and possibly the FBI itself, would see those members as he himself had reluctantly come to view them—as narcissistic, ineffectual cranks; stupid, deplorable, and criminal, certainly, but about as much a threat to the nation as the various US-Mexico border vigilante groups. The resulting string of arrests would look like the sideshow of a laughably ill-conceived and pathetic witch-hunt.

It would bring the Justice Department no nearer the real operatives, and it would alert the network that the FBI had someone cooperating on the inside. The right-wing echo chamber he and Nash had so faithfully nurtured would have an easy time linking any further activity to this first, dubious series of arrests. It was possible, he allowed, that California and Colorado had already been eliminated. That's what he'd have done. He pushed those piles to the side.

Reed wished he had a full dossier on the Illinois chapter, though, which had proved an effective, cohesive group. They were responsible for the Illinois voting scandal, which still had life; the murders of two Illinois Judges of Election, the blackmailing of a county clerk; the murder of an Elector in Iowa City and producing one of the Faithless Electors outside Minneapolis. It was fortunate, he allowed, that no one knew his own current location, because Cincinnati was within the Illinois chapter's "jurisdiction," and he didn't fancy his odds going up against them alone, particularly now that he had made up his mind to burn them.

This meant that after his chickenfeed Ante, he could raise the stakes by bidding the Seattle chapter on the next round of betting. He could deliver them signed and sealed. Quietly and effectively, the Northwest chapter had killed two Electors—one in Seattle, the other in Yamhill, Oregon; had murdered Matthew Yamashita, the graduate student who first stumbled on the Faithless Elector plot, and they had come within inches of eliminating the professor. They had even turned one of the Electors in Colorado, and then killed her when that became necessary.

Reed was most proud of the Northwest chapter members, and though he didn't feel any qualms about burning them to save himself, he did feel a profound sorrow when he contemplated tearing down a structure he'd worked so earnestly to bring into being. The Northwest chapter had thoroughly fulfilled the need for flexibility and effectiveness, despite there being fewer of them in place than he had originally projected.

As Reed leafed through all the dossiers, arranging them for action or further review, he placed the folder about the crown jewel to one side. In it was the background data he had collected to blackmail the doctors who examined President Redmond's remains. It wouldn't be as clear and damning as the full dossier that Nash held, but it would probably get the job done.

He turned to the recruitment notes. He thoroughly vetted each potential operative to ensure that the recruit was both ideologically sound and ruthless. It also helped, they found, if the recruit was nursing some anger or resentment for past and present failures. The individual didn't need to be particularly intelligent. He needed to do what he was told, when he was told, with just enough wits about him to think on his feet should that become necessary.

The key was that he should be someone looking to make a score. Loyalty was a cardinal virtue in these men, but Reed and Nash knew that choosing men for loyalty alone, as perhaps the Postman did not, was fraught with danger. Better to get those who were good at their jobs and then seal their loyalty through grooming, payment and, if necessary, blackmail. Failed policemen, and disillusioned or dishonourably discharged ex-military men made up most of the early operational recruits, along with small-time hoods and petty grifters—not ideal candidates for a war of ideas, but perfect for working in the dark. ("Well, one works with what one can get," Nash had been fond of saying.)

He wished his recruitment files on the "sleepers" in the various PACs were as detailed and explicit as those he had supervised directly, such as those embedded in the Opportunity Initiative, Sovereign Caucus and V3. The sleepers' recruitment had been Nash's area, and again, access to the dossiers may have died with Nash.

For their moles in the various PACs, Nash had found that the fringes of campus-based university clubs offered any number of overconfident, anti-social narcissists eager to put their amoral and outsized ambitions into action, however clandestine. Reed had found them distasteful, motivated more by power and vindictiveness than patriotism. He'd been happy to leave the recruitment and training in Nash's hands. Now, he wished he'd paid closer attention. It would actually be fun to burn those little fucks, he thought.

The paper trail he had implicating the Postman, he noted ruefully, was circumstantial at best. In order to be truly safe, and to get the best deal from the FBI, he would need to burn the whole thing to the ground and somehow draw the Postman out. Without Nash's intel to corroborate, he didn't immediately see a way to do it. He knew where Nash had hidden his half of the dossiers, but possibly so did his bosses, and he didn't much like the potential for exposure involved in going there to get it. And how would he gain access? He stared at the files spread across the countertop.

The craziest part of it all was that now there was only one person he thought he could trust.

* * *

103

Calder sat with Rich Lamberti in the Husky Union Building cafeteria, in the corner reserved for faculty, with their papers spread across a table.

"What do we know?" Calder asked.

"His real name is Dan Cardoso...or at least that's the name on the mailbox outside his house up in Maple Leaf. He lives just off 82nd near the reservoir. I tracked down the cabbie from the day I saw him, and he told me where he'd dropped his fare off. So, I went there. Tiny place, but a big compound. Cardoso may not be his real name, though. The name he used on that piece-of-shit accident report was Tim Hayward, who lives in White Center. Well, lived. Hayward's dead. He was a murder-suicide back in 2012."

"What happened?"

Lamberti rifled through his pages. "I found this article in the Seattle Times from November that year." Lamberti passed Calder the printout. "He killed his girlfriend and then himself one drunken night. It was pretty bare bones. I guess the coroner was able to confirm that Hayward and his girlfriend had been drinking heavily."

Calder frowned as he looked over the article. Bare bones was right, he thought—seven concise sentences:

> November 15, 2012. Police believe the shooting death of a couple in their White Center home is a murder-suicide case. King County Authorities say a neighbor, 62-year-old James Snyder, became concerned when he hadn't seen either Tim Hayward or Samantha Banks for some time.
> There was no response in the house at the front or back door, though Mr. Snyder said he could see through curtains that someone was in the bedroom.
> Police entered and found Hayward, 45, and Banks, 38, dead from gunshot wounds. Samantha Banks was a stylist and Tim Hayward had recently

retired from working security at the Port of Seattle.

There is no information about surviving relatives.

"And do you think Cardoso—or whatever his name is—is the only one?" asked Calder.

"Probably. I don't know," said Lamberti. "Why?"

"Well, Imogen and the FBI were able to unravel two of these groups—if that's what we're even looking at here—on the East Coast. Both of those groups were made up of three to four people—two low-level foot soldiers, directed by one guy, who reported and took orders from someone else, like a case officer or something in a spy network."

"So, we may not have the whole picture," said Lamberti.

"We definitely don't," Calder rejoined.

"What I mean is, if we only know one of the people in the group—Cardoso, or whatever his real name is—it could be that while we're watching one of them, the others are watching us and we'd never know." said Lamberti.

Reflexively, Calder looked around, but saw only faculty and students.

16

"May I have your office?" the Postman asked the CEO of one his companies as they peeled off from a meeting. A knot of dark-suited executives bustled behind them. The CEO was a well-fed sexagenarian, with a simple, untroubled face, bland and soft like a baby's. His thinning hair and pink complexion completed the impression. He blinked myopically and summoned a dim smile as he held out his hand offering the office: "Of course." His grandiloquent gesture went unseen by the tall man who had already turned his back and stalked into the office without waiting for reply. The Postman closed the door, leaving the CEO alone in the passage.

The Postman dialed a number. "Nothing?" he said by way of greeting. He listened a moment. "He didn't show? Hmm. I'm worried that dismissing Fisher might have tipped our hand," he said, using Alec Nash's codename. "Could Cooper be on the run now?" he asked, using Reed's codename.

He listened.

"Christ! What *do* you know? What's our liability?" he demanded. "How much does he really know? What can he prove? What trouble could he make?"

He listened again.

"No, that's too many 'ifs.' They were close, those two. Who knows what each told the other—regardless of protocol. Start looking for Pete Snyder, if you haven't already. That's one of his other work names, isn't it? You've got the exposure assessment. Look at it again with this possibility in mind. For instance, which of our people did he train? Whose dossiers does he have? I want a draft plan of action for my review by the end of the day."

He hung up and leaned back on the desk, staring at but not seeing the skyline outside the baby executive's window. Perhaps, he considered, they were inventing things to worry about. It wasn't clear yet that Reed was on the run. He merely hadn't checked in.

And if he'd been waiting for Moore to assume the Presidency before coming out of hiding, he'd only missed two extraction flights—one of which occurred the very day the new President was installed. Reed was bound to radio silence until he made contact with the pilot in Nebraska during one of the scheduled extraction flights. Perhaps he was biding his time and would soon be back in the fold.

This line of thinking did little to reduce the Postman's rising anger and wounded sense of justice delayed. Quantrelle, he mused, wasn't even second best when weighed against Alec Nash. He deeply regretted the necessity of killing him, brought about by his arrest, but he was impatient to eliminate Reed.

As the Postman stood staring out the window, he found it touching to think of Frank Reed, out there somewhere, waiting for the right opportunity to come in from the cold, to be received as a hero. Only to meet his death. Unlike Alec Nash, Reed was merely an instrument. His continued service had never been part of the overall plan. Even Nash had known it.

Frank Reed had sealed his fate when he argued vigorously and passionately against the final step: staging a false terrorist attack in Washington that would allow the president to assert emergency powers.

Reed had pointed out that with one-party control of the Executive and both Houses, there was practically nothing they couldn't get done for the good of the nation. What Reed failed to see, in the Postman's estimation—the only one that mattered—was that what democratically elected governments do can be undone. Elected power is fleeting.

He picked up the phone and dialed the same number. "Focus on Cincinnati," he said. "That used to be his base before, wasn't it? Well, you've got his dossier, haven't you? Look for habits, places he used for drops . . . friends. Start in Cincinnati." He hung up.

The Postman's journey, now two steps from becoming reality, began in the 1980's. The decade had been an expensive lesson in ingratitude, and his single-minded, rancorous pursuit of this ultimate solution now was stoked by the obstructions and slights of those early years. First, as a candidate himself, he had difficulty shaking the popular perception that he was a boutique, vanity candidate, which frankly he was.

Later, when it should have become clear that he and his message was not one to which the voters were receptive, rather than examine his own shortcomings as a candidate or the unsuitability of the message, he ascribed the repeated failures to a rigged system. Well, two could play at that game. He found that funding candidates and surrogates was more effective, though it came at a cost. He rewarded those who agreed to toe his line. After which they would do his bidding.

Except when they wouldn't.

He was impatient with the messiness of government and politics, and he was used to people he had bought *staying* bought, held in check by the fear of termination or reprisal. In those early years he was dismayed to find that a great number of politicians were willing to lie even to him. They said the right things, of course, supported the right positions in principle, but in the end they didn't see the grand vision, saw only his money and a way to win an election. They paid homage only at re-election.

So, in the mid-90's, he started again. He started small, with innocuously named interest groups and charitable organizations, creating single issue, "non-connected" PAC's and duplicitous grassroots campaigns—so called (though not by him) Astroturf groups.

Through them, he found equally aggrieved men within his own rarefied circles, men who were also tired of having

108

their hands tied and bank accounts emptied by a credulous, pandering government; men who were willing to open their check books. Through these suddenly well-funded groups, he found and promoted eager, loyal young men—men proven to be ideologically sound—from the ranks of his Astroturf organizations.

Such men, it happily became clear, owed more to him and his organizations than to any party; and because they were so closely allied to his groups, they were unlikely to win elections any other way. Those who won their races through him certainly understood which way the wind blew. In that sense, because they were beholden less to a party—because they had no other option—they stayed bought and did as they were told. Over the years, as those candidates rose, Hessel gained a measure of control, but still nothing like what he was used to having in the business world.

As he continued to stare out the baby executive's window, he thought petulantly—not for the first time—that after gaining ownership or a controlling stake in a company, he would begin immediately disposing of it and its assets as he saw fit, making it leaner or breaking it into profitable pieces, rewarding those who had helped in the effort, punishing those who had opposed it. It was the natural order of things: to the victor belong the spoils.

First, though, he had to eliminate Frank Reed. He knew too much about the operation and its ultimate aims. He had opposed the terrorist gambit as unnecessary and un-American. Second, install and confirm Drew Eliot as Attorney General to frustrate and wind down the Faithless Elector and Interregnum investigations. As part of that pretense, Eliot would also subpoena (and then destroy) the damaging information in the dossiers Nash had kept, now sitting anonymously in a safe deposit box in suburban Boston.

Finally, with Eliot as the government's "designated survivor," there would be an attack as President Moore gave a State of the Union address on April 20, after which, Congress and the public would demand that Moore assert Presidential Authority in the face of these attacks—aided from within. It

109

would be inescapable, and irrevocable. It was also fitting that succinylcholine would play its individually deadly, nationally paralyzing part again, as it had on the soon-to-be interred President Redmond.

17

Hugh Salter flopped into his office chair, causing it to roll. He raised his feet and swiveled in it as it rolled, his joy in the moment belonging to a younger self. The chair came to rest gently against his desk. He smiled as he called up his email.

The smile disappeared when he saw the message from "Patriot76," with the subject line "more for you." Breath would not come. A wave of panic and nausea passed over Salter as he stared at the unopened message. His right index finger wavered above the mouse.

During the Interregnum, this Patriot76 had tendered fake news, salacious stories and disinformation. With eyes only for a scoop, Salter had negligently reported what Patriot76 peddled to him. Now, once more, he accused himself of having contributed to the circus atmosphere in US politics, of having departed from or undermined basic journalistic rules, with hideous results. He saw himself as a kind of antithesis of Woodward and Bernstein. Instead of bringing down a corrupt President, his reporting had abetted a conspiracy to steal the Presidency—a conspiracy that had almost prevailed. Patriot76 had probably been working directly with Nash.

David Carr's resistance had saved the integrity of the nation when he galvanized the House, leading to the unanimous acclamation vote that handed the Presidency to Diane Redmond. Carr had said publicly that it was Salter's investigating that had spurred him on, and that tribute had protected Salter against any charges of complicity, naiveté or outright wrongdoing that might have been hurled during the heady days of the new Administration. But it didn't put any halt to his self-accusation.

His finger was still frozen over the mouse. A wave of frigid sickness surged over him. It broke and passed, leaving him in a sweat, finger still poised to click. Dread and self-loathing clung to him, orphans of the storm. Was there a way to redeem himself? he wondered, or would he just be handing Patriot76 a final nail to seal the coffin of his career? His options were limited. Certainly, there was no going back. He could either repair his reputation, or live with his shame. He opened the email.

* * *

Amanda Vega had been sifting what little data she had for any insight into Flintlock Industries when she received a message from the field office in Omaha, Nebraska. "Contact," it read.

The field office had been monitoring the company's second private frequency since she learned about it from her furloughed pilot interviews at Eppley Field in Omaha. The frequency had been silent until now. Amanda was accustomed to receiving a no-contact report from Omaha at 10am and 6pm each day. Today's email had an audio attachment with a four-second message from 4:07pm local time: "This is FL-One," said an unidentified voice, "Cooper negative. Resuming." Then dead. No reply.

Vega's chest grew tight. For a moment she felt deathly cold. She replayed the message: "This is FL-One; Cooper negative. Resuming."

"Hell, yes!" she shouted, standing involuntarily. She turned to the conspiracy board on her right, and punched the picture of Frank Reed. She smiled at the photo. "My dear Mr. Cooper," she said with a patronizing tone to the photo, "so good of you still to be alive...you motherfucker. We can't wait to make you sing!"

She picked up the phone and called the Coffee Shop at Fairmont Airport.

"Kirsten? This is Special Agent Am—"

"—He was just here!" she hissed.

112

Vega heard the excitement in Kirsten's voice, felt the bloodlust rising in herself and thought she should tap the brakes. "Are you in a safe place at the moment, Kirsten? Are you able to speak freely?" she said, hoping that a professional tone would help ground both her and Kirsten.

"Yes," said Kirsten, her voice becoming calmer. "Yes, I am."

"Is the person you're discussing still on the premises?"

"No, he's not. He left. Took off not ten minutes ago."

"Was it the same pilot as before?" Amanda asked.

"Yes. Same plane and all, that bitty Eclipse-500: 'N-8977-Alpha.' Denny over at the FBO told me."

"Thank you, Kirsten. Just to confirm for my notes, the pilot stayed in your cafe for approximately two hours today, from two p.m. to four p.m. approximately."

"Yes."

"And he is the pilot you were telling me about when I was there two weeks ago on 10 March when he also stayed for two hours, at the same time in the afternoon. Is that correct?"

"Yes," said Kirsten.

"And the same pilot was there a month ago on 24 February, and also stayed in your cafe at the same times and for the same duration?"

"Right. It's always been him, always those times."

"Are those the only times you've seen him? Did he have contact with anyone else, or interact with anyone?"

"No, he just played with his phone and ignored everyone. I've only seen him the three times."

"Do you recall the photo I showed you when I was there?" Vega asked, referring to the picture of Frank Reed.

"That mean-looking guy with the beard?"

"Yes, has he been in?"

"No. I've never seen him."

"So, just the pilot," said Vega. "And he's only been there the three times?"

"It's possible he's landed here before but didn't come in the coffee shop. I could ask Denny."

113

"No, that's fine. I'll call him directly. Thank you, Kirsten. This is a big help."

"Should I send you his photo, Agent Vega?"

"What?"

"I took a picture of him," Kirsten said. "The pilot."

"That was very dangerous, Kirsten."

"Oh, I don't know about that. He just looks like some stuck-up college boy type," Kirsten said. "I was just about to call you when you called me. See, we had some nice folks in here passing through on their way to a basketball game while that boy-pilot was sulking in the back. I asked if I could take their picture for our travelers' album. We don't actually have a travelers' album, Agent Vega," she said conspiratorially, "but now I think maybe we should have one. It's a nice idea, don't ya think? Something for the wall maybe?

"Anyways, I took two pictures—one of them, and one just of him. 'Course, I pretended it was just another angle on them so he wouldn't catch on. It's not great, but you can see his face. Should I send it along?"

"Yes, definitely, Kirsten. Thank you. Please send it."

And within moments Vega had it.

"Kirsten," she continued, "you've really helped us out here, and I'm very grateful, but I'm duty-bound to tell you that what you did was dangerous. He might not look like much, but we think he's part of an organization you wouldn't want to mix with. I can't say any more, but it's best if you just make him his coffee."

"Don't worry about me, Amanda. I divorced my drunk of a husband and raised three boys on my own here. I'm not afraid of a kid like that."

Yes, Vega had to admit, looking at the young pilot's photo, if it were just Kirsten against this boy, her money would be on Kirstin. But it wasn't just this boy-pilot. Reed and a host of assassins were lurking somewhere behind him. Out of shot, no doubt, but perhaps not out of shooting range. And Vega hated to think of Kirsten getting hurt.

Her personal mind-map of the US looked like a Washingtonian version of Saul Steinberg's "New Yorker's

View of the World" cartoon: the eastern seaboard was alight with bright spots, from friends in Boston and New York, down to her home and childhood friends in Maryland and D.C., and on into Northern Virginia. West of the Appalachians, she had no fond memory or physical connection—except for a happy tryst years ago in Denver, which was both. And now, standing out against the dun-colored monotony of the American plains was this no-nonsense waitress in the heart of the heart of the country.

Amanda called Denny. If Kirsten was the warmth of that beating American heart, Denny was its acid reflux. She imagined him sitting at his desk in the airport's service station, as he spoke gruffly between puffs on his cigarette.

She felt she could see him drawing mightily on it, the smoke stinging his eyes and making him squint as he rifled through his notes. He confirmed what Kirsten had just imparted. He was also able to confirm that the plane had indeed been there on 7 January, matching with data she already had from Trey Kelly about the last phone call Frank Reed had made before he vanished.

She gathered up her notes and headed to meet Imogen at Gallery Place.

18

The House Judiciary Committee had yet to say anything publicly about its investigation into the Justice Department's handling of the Faithless Elector plot. Unofficially, though, there had been harsh words aplenty for the Attorney General's lack of progress and lack of prosecutions. Her standing was further undermined by a failure to identify and indict those responsible for the offenses during the Interregnum, who were quite possibly the same criminals.

Everyone known to be associated with the plots was now either dead or co-operating as a material witness, but ever since the Government's key witness, Alec Nash, had refused to cooperate and killed himself in prison, the investigation had been becalmed. The Attorney General's energy seemed to go more into denying that things were drifting than prosecuting cases. The Attorney General had kept her job when Diane Redmond became President specifically to keep the focus on uncovering the cabal. With Moore now in the White House, her hold on the job was becoming tenuous.

Worse for the Bureau—and Attorney General Judith Welco—a list and backgrounder report had leaked the previous day showing that Senator Drew Eliot of South Carolina, Moore's leading potential candidate for Attorney General, had been vetted by the Redmond administration. On Capitol Hill, there was talk—never for attribution—that Eliot's name had been included on the list only to placate then-Vice President Moore, but no one in the Democratic Party or in the former Administration would admit it.

Senator Eliot of South Carolina, lately of the Senate Judiciary Committee, made the rounds of the Sunday political programs.

"Senator," a pundit on one of the Sunday programs began, "the question on everyone's mind is not *whether* you'll be the next Attorney General, but when?"

Amid the open antipathy between the White House and the Attorney General's office, together with the revelation of his inclusion as a possible replacement in Redmond's own Administration, it did seem only a matter of time before there was a big change at Justice, and Eliot was the front-runner for the job.

He had a strong pedigree, as former District Attorney of Columbia, South Carolina, as the State Attorney General and as Senator. The whiff of Interregnum scandal had all but dispersed. While it might have seemed odd to regard a man in his late sixties as the best bet to inject new vitality into the Justice Department, momentum for his candidacy was growing.

"Forgive me, Chet," Senator Eliot began with patrician forbearance, smiling diffidently, "but the only information I have is that the media are working themselves up into a speculative frenzy. There have been no overtures, no discussions." He smiled and looked thoughtfully past the camera.

"The Attorney General and the FBI Director are pursuing a devilishly difficult and important investigation," he continued. "One with far-reaching implications. It's clear that whatever happened during the Faithless Elector plot is a tangled knot, and the men and women of the FBI have to untie it before we start lending credence to any of those who're second-guessing their motives."

"You're speaking of the Interregnum, Senator, and the charges that some of your House and Senate colleagues have leveled saying that the FBI's linking of the two—the Faithless Elector plot and the attempted coercion of House representatives—is just politics."

"Chet, I'm sure the Justice Department investigation is painstaking and comprehensive. I'm no longer privy to what's going on there, but I'm confident they're moving forward." He stared off again as he considered his next remarks. "Having said that," he intoned, "the danger—even under the best circumstances and with the best intentions—is that in trying to catch something elusive in your net, you venture farther and farther out to sea, where you can lose your bearings."

"You're worried this is all just a fishing expedition, then?"

"I did not say that, Chet."

"Are you saying you feel that your Chief of Staff, Casey Hague, is being maligned?" the interviewer asked.

"I'm sick at heart about what the FBI alleges against Casey, may he rest in peace. But the overwhelming evidence is that Casey was guilty. He used his position in my office to his own ends, he got mixed up with bad characters, and it cost him his life. I don't know what drove him to do it, or why he did what he did. All answers died with him. I only wish I'd known, or had a chance to stop him." He shook his head sadly, moved almost to crocodile tears by the thought of that lost opportunity.

From the sofa in his Federal study, the Postman nodded approval. From Cincinnati, Reed looked on and knew his time was growing short. Eliot, it was clear, would be the new AG, and he'd quash the investigation, so the conspirators could murder him with impunity and bury him next to Jimmy Hoffa. In Seattle, Calder shut off the television in disgust.

* * *

A black, four-door Ford F-150 pickup hurtled through the night past sleeping farmland—a panther streak, glimpsed only when a streetlight flashed off its sleek sides. The engine growled menacingly, low, guttural and insistent, its oversize wheels devouring the miles between Springfield, Illinois and

Cincinnati, Ohio, a five-hour journey. Three men rode in the cab, two of them sleeping, heads pressed against the windows. Though just 40, their leader, Kelsey Brandt, was a veteran political foot soldier and fixer, and older by a decade than the pair he had helped mold into a deadly efficient criminal gang. He glanced at them as they slept, the truck relentlessly closing to meet the sunrise.

They knew Frank Reed as "Mr. Cooper," and it would be a reunion of sorts, if they could find him. He had recruited them and given them their basic training, and they referred to him affectionately and admiringly as "Coop." Now he was an enemy, reportedly working against them. On Bannister's orders, he was to be eliminated.

* * *

"This is Hugh Salter at the White House, where President Moore has just told a press conference that he has asked for the Attorney General's resignation." The news report cut to Moore at a press conference, flanked by Marek, Quantrelle, Senator Drew Eliot and the new Vice President, David Carr.

"I have today received the resignation of Attorney General Judith Welco. While I have every confidence in her integrity and zeal, I have been disappointed," he noted disingenuously, "by the lack of progress in both the Faithless Elector investigation and the Interregnum scandal, which the nation badly needs to see resolved.

"Attorney General Welco has seen the FBI not only through a difficult election, but also through the subsequent death of a President and an unprecedented change of administration, and has maintained the continuity and integrity of those investigations.

"But it is that integrity which is at issue now—not hers, but that of the investigation she has led. So, I am appointing Senator Drew Eliot of South Carolina to be Attorney General with a brief to bring these investigations to a swift conclusion. I'd like to thank Judith Welco for her service." And with that he was gone, and so was she.

* * *

Imogen and Amanda sat down to their tacos.

"I have confirmation that the pilot who's been waiting around at Fairmont Airport—this guy," she said, showing the photo Kirsten had sent of the pilot—"is showing up on some pre-arranged schedule every two weeks, waiting to pick up Frank Reed."

"How do you know that?" asked Imogen.

"We're monitoring a secret third frequency some of the Flintlock pilots use for internal communications. When the pilot left Fairmont last night, he noted that he had *not* made a rendezvous with 'Cooper.'" Here she grinned widely. "Weir should be back this afternoon. He and I'll huddle, and I'll let you know about next steps. I think we're going to have to move quickly, now that Welco's out. Eliot's not going to want this investigation to continue."

"Hand-picked not to, I'dve thought."

"So, what've you got?"

"Nothing," said Imogen with a frank shake of her head. "I had a call from Hugh Salter. He asked me to call him back, but I don't want to get sucked into that circus again."

"What'd he say?"

"It was just a message," Imogen replied. "I was in a non-progress report meeting with my staff and didn't pick up. All he said was that he had some follow-up for me, and he'd like to meet."

"Bloodsucker," Vega hissed, remembering all that Salter had done to expose and defame Imogen. "Tell him to kiss your alabaster ass."

"You're right. Fuck him. I won't call back."

"You're gone this weekend, right?" asked Vega.

"Yeah. It'll be a nice break, and I'll give Duncan his phone."

"Good," said Vega. "And come back ready to get to work."

Vega ate lustily, while Imogen picked at her food, feeling herself shrinking in comparison with her friend. They finished their lunch in silence and parted, Imogen to her dreary cell of an office, while Vega went to see Trey.

As Imogen approached the 'H' Street entrance to her building, a man who had been leaning against one of the metal bollards straightened up and walked toward her and waved. It was Salter, and she turned purposefully toward a different door.

"Agent Trager," he called. "I left you a message. I need to speak with you."

"I got your message," Imogen spat. "I don't think there's anything you and I have to talk about."

Salter stepped in front of her. "Yes, there is."

Imogen paused.

"Could we talk somewhere away from here?" he asked.

"You'll get nothing for attribution. I will not speak on the record."

"Agent Trager, I'm not here about a story."

"Then what?" she asked.

"There's a coffee shop up at the corner. You go first. I'll make sure you're not being followed and then I'll meet you there," he said.

Imogen looked at him, disbelieving.

"Please," he said. "I'm not going to say I was as much a victim as you, but I *was* duped. I think I see a way to make it right."

Despite the claxon sound of her internal alarm, curiosity got the better of her. She nodded agreement, turned on her heel and walked up the block. Salter walked the opposite way, looking for anyone who might have been following her or watching their conversation. The street was clear, but he walked all the way around the GAO Building. Imogen had composed herself by the time he arrived at the coffee shop, deciding just how little she would say.

19

Her back was to the wall and she stared into an oversized mug of coffee. Perhaps caffeine hadn't been a good idea at all: she felt her heart knocking in her chest, as though it wanted out of there. She looked up as Salter sat down heavily, shoulder bag between his feet. He reached into his jacket and put two burner phones on the table.

"For most of the stories I filed during the Interregnum," he began, "I was getting information from an anonymous source calling himself 'Patriot Seventy-six.' I figured he was FBI—or former FBI—because he had access to everything. Those pictures of you and Kurtz, the internal emails about the Illinois results—everything."

Imogen stared at her cup.

"He also fed me information—damaging information—about some of the Congressmen and women in the run-up to the House contingency election vote. I checked some of it out, but by that point I'd realized he was probably an agent for whoever was trying to steal the Presidency, and I stopped running his stuff."

Imogen looked up, but still said nothing.

"My news director would kill me if he knew I'd spiked some of those things."

"You want me to understand your sacrifices? Is that what this is about?" she demanded, her face coming into high color. "Are you here to apologize, or something?" Her face contorted, unbelieving.

"I suppose so. Yes. But that's not what this is about. That same source emailed me yesterday with new information."

"I haven't fucked anyone else and taken pictures of it, if you're here to verify something he sent you," said Imogen acidly.

"No. No, I don't suppose you have. I wouldn't be touching any of this if I didn't feel like maybe I could make things a bit more right."

Imogen was still silent, her green eyes burning at him from across the table.

"He said he has information about other 'chapters,' as he calls them," Salter continued. "He said you'd know what that meant. He said you were the only one he could trust, and that I was to speak only with you. He said he knew you were for real and couldn't be bought off or scared off. I printed out his email. He says you'll know what it all means, and it'll prove to you that he's who he says he is."

"Who does he say he is?" Imogen asked.

"Frank Reed." Salter reached into his bag and pulled out a sheet of paper. He looked around the empty café and then placed it on the table between them.

Imogen stared at the paper, not seeing it, the blood draining from her face.

"He tried to murder me, you know," she said. "We have him on tape. He called his handler to report that Nash was blown and that he might be compromised, too. His handler, whoever that is, told him to cut and run, but he said he had one last thing to do. That turned out to be killing me."

"He says you're probably being watched," said Salter. "That you're probably being bugged or at least being tracked. He says Nash was murdered."

"Now he's my protector? What's he supposed to want? Or maybe he or someone from one of these chapters is watching us right now? Maybe you're the lure, a dupe all over again, and I walk out of here and right into a bullet the moment we leave. Maybe he has a spare one for you."

"I don't know. This whole thing is beyond any story I've ever covered before. I'm going to take my cues from you.

Here," he said, rapping one of the phones with his finger. "He said you should get a drop phone for communication. So, I got you one." He pushed one of the phones toward her. "And I have this one." He put the other in his jacket pocket.

"A simple way for him to track me," she said. "So he can have another try?"

Imogen sat back in her chair. She looked past Salter, trying to scan the street outside, but from her vantage at the back wall she could not see well. Her first thought was that it was a trick, that for Reed the dark network's operation was personal and he wanted her dead.

That realization brought a kind of clarity. She found herself stepping back from the puzzle; saw that while she was frightened, she was not undone by fear. If there were any truth in what Salter was telling her, then Reed must be equally vulnerable and frightened. He hadn't turned up to his rendezvous in Fairmont, she'd just learned. Could she turn that to her advantage?

As she continued to stare across the table at Salter, she wondered whether he was a co-conspirator, some kind of "useful idiot," or just an asshole reporter. As she searched his face for clues as to which, she admitted that none of those inspired much confidence in her.

If he was a conspirator and she waded in now, she could only further muddy the waters and further discredit herself— or worse; and if he was just a reporter, he had already, by his own admission, been a useful idiot. No matter what he was, his involvement could potentially lead her further astray and put her in danger. But for now, he was the intermediary.

She folded the paper he had handed her and put it in an inside pocket of her coat. "Have you already loaded your number into this phone?" she asked, reaching for it.

"Yes," said Salter. "It's all ready to go."

"I'm switching it off. When I know what I'm going to do—tomorrow or the next day—I'll switch it back on to get in touch. *I* will make the next contact. You will do nothing with the information you've gleaned so far. You know Reed as a treacherous agent provocateur and a traitor. I know him as that and worse. We're both in danger—even if we can believe him. Even if I believe you."

* * *

Calder and Lamberti disagreed. They had been watching Cardoso for some time now, but he hadn't led them to anyone else. How long should they wait?

"See," Lamberti began pulling at his goatee, "I think we're looking at this the wrong way. We've *got* the guy, right? We know who he is. Let's give him up to the Feds and be done with it. You've got a contact there, right?"

"Yes and no," Calder began patiently. "If he's arrested, the FBI would only have our testimony, and I'm sure his handlers have worked out an alibi, so he goes free . . . only to die in some bizarre accident a month or two later, and any further evidence is destroyed.

"Or if we just tip off the Feds about who he is, we still risk blowing up everything because they'd just sit on him . . . like we're doing, waiting for him to do something they could arrest him for...or for something else to happen. And while they sit and wait and build a non-case, they dither long enough for the Administration to appoint someone new at the top who kills the investigation. Let's not kid ourselves about what this Eliot appointment will mean. And we'dve just exposed ourselves as knowing something, which brings the shit down on us."

"We're in it already," said Lamberti.

* * *

Back in her cloister, Imogen stared at the array of telephone technology in front of her shaking her head. Three burners: the two Jimmy May had procured — one for her, one to pass on to Duncan — plus the one Salter had just given her, and her personal smart phone. What a cluster fuck, she thought. Phones 'R' Me.

She pushed them aside and took up Salter's message from Reed. It detailed the two chapters already known to her—Boston and D.C.—the 'chapter' moniker being known to her from details provided by the cooperating witnesses. He claimed to have information about all of the chapters. He was "willing to trade," he said, and could supply information and evidence if they "could come to some agreement."

"Agreement?" said Imogen to the paper in front of her. "Fuck you."

"Sorry?" said Nettie, standing in the doorway over Imogen's right shoulder.

Imogen looked up. Either Nettie hadn't knocked or she hadn't heard the knock. Either way, Imogen felt exposed. "Yes?" she said, turning around.

"I was just checking in," said Nettie, her dark brown, almond eyes taking in everything at once. "I'm about halfway through the latest data you gave me," she reported, her eyes falling on the four phones on the corner of Imogen's desk. "But...but I'm coming up with a lot of questions." She paused. She now clearly had questions about the four phones as well. "You'd said to check with you before making requests for follow-up data . . . that we're flying under the radar."

"Yes," said Imogen. "We are. I'm in the middle of something just at the moment. Could we circle back Monday morning maybe?"

"Of course. Sure. Absolutely." Her eyes fell again on the phones. "Is there anything I could help with?" Then, mischievously: "Burn some phones for you, maybe?"

Primly: "Not at the moment, *thank you*. Keep going, write up the questions, and we'll deal with them together on Monday. All right?"

"Sure, sure," said Nettie, backing down. This should have been her exit line, but she lingered. Imogen looked into her inquiring eyes. Nettie obviously sensed a special project in the offing—maybe there was finally something interesting in this detail.

"Please close the door on your way out," said Imogen.

Exit Nettie. Imogen took up the burner Jimmy May had told her to use, and dialed Amanda Vega.

"I've just had a trade offer from Frank Reed," she said to Vega. "Yes, his name seems to be coming up a lot today," she added wryly. "That reporter, Hugh Salter, brought it to me. I think you and I should sit down with Weir. Could you two come to my office? They're still tracking me, and I don't want to be seen going into Headquarters just yet."

Nettie didn't miss a thing. A good quality in an investigator, but a little unnerving. When Vega and Weir filed past her desk half an hour later on their way into Imogen's office, she watched them closely. Vega didn't greet or introduce her, though their eyes met. She continued to watch as Vega closed the door, her expression by turns perplexed and then furious.

Inside the office, Weir smiled as he sat down. "Well," he exclaimed, "if the bosses thought they were getting you out of the way by sending you here, they didn't send you far enough, did they?" He pulled off a black FBI baseball cap and rubbed his blond crew cut.

Imogen smiled stiffly.

"You've been at the heart of two cases," he went on, "either one of which would've made any other agent's career, but they send you here 'cause you pissed them off." He shook his head. "Now you've got Public Enemy Number One on speed-dial. Jesus!"

"What's he want?" asked Vega.

"I haven't initiated contact yet. I wanted you two in on it before I did anything."

"Maybe your time in Siberia's taught you a few things," Weir quipped.

"You said he wanted to trade," Vega added helpfully. "Obviously, he wants a deal."

"What kind of deal does he think he can get?" demanded Weir. "We know he's committed at least one murder. We've dealt Deptford, who killed Agent Colls, twenty-to-life. With sentencing recommendations, time-served and so on, he might be out in eight to ten, but unless Reed can deliver

127

someone significant — whoever's pulling the levers — he can't expect much in the way of clemency, can he? It's not the Mercy Department, you know, it's Justice."

"And if he gives us his boss and all the networks?" Imogen suggested.

Weir threw up his hands and sighed. "Well, yeah. That's it. Usually we make deals with the grunts to get at the bosses, but he's clearly one of the bosses. It feels like a very flat hierarchy." He paused, drew a deep breath. "I don't know," he sighed. "I'll have to bring the Deputy and the Director in on this. I'd rather not deal with this piece of shit at all. Christ, what would the media make of it?"

He shifted in his chair and his meaty lips twisted bitterly. He frowned toward the opposite wall. Finally, he turned his gaze on Vega. "How close are we to the two pilots who seem to be making all the diversion flights?" he asked her.

"I've got the picture of one of them I told you about. The waitress took it. We have pretty good confirmation that he's waiting for Reed, Mr. Cooper as they call him. We're trying to locate Wilder, the pilot who put me on to the private radio frequency, so he can give me a name to go with the face of the pilot," she said. "I'm doing this a little bit backwards. I don't want to go barging in at Flintlock and let everyone know there's FBI interest just yet."

Weir nodded his agreement.

"Unfortunately, the nature of their work makes them hard to pin down, and for the same reasons that I'm not just contacting Flintlock straight out, I don't like the idea of leaving messages all over the place."

"Meanwhile, don't contact Reed," Weir said to Imogen. "I want him to sweat a bit that we're not getting right back to him. Before we talk to him, I want to be in a stronger position, maybe by flipping the pilots so we have some new intelligence. He's afraid of us, right, but we're not killers. He's more afraid of his own bosses."

"Which is about the only reason we can trust him," said Imogen.

"It's a strong motivation, though," said Vega, "knowing that if he doesn't bring them all down, he'll end up like Nash, dead in his cell."

"*If* we can trust him," said Weir. "I'm not convinced this isn't just some attempt at disinformation—a plausible contact with a plausible reason for wanting to help us; and he has precisely the information we need just when we need it?"

He paused, seeming to consider it from multiple angles. Finally, he said: "Work on the pilots first. Then we'll see about talking with Reed. We're the God-damned FBI, but somehow I still feel like he holds all the cards."

* * *

In his West Wing office, Quantrelle was feeling the heat of the Postman's impatience and displeasure. As was usual when he became frightened, Quantrelle grew bellicose and lashed out:

"You're the Senate majority leader, for fuck's sake!" he screamed into the phone. His secretary, her desk in the next room, stood up and closed the door to his office, giving him an indulgent, we've-talked-about-this-before smile as she did so. He stared for a moment at the closed door as he listened to the Majority Leader's excuses, wondering if he should fire her. Listening on the phone, he shook his head with exasperated impatience.

"Not my problem!" he said finally. "Schedule the vote for no later than April 19. The president's said he needs a new broom. Let's show the American people we can give it to them."

He paused to listen. "I don't care how long confirmation normally takes. We're forging a new normal. And let me be clear: whatever problems you think you have now, they'll be much bigger and much worse if you don't deliver on or before the 19th." He hung up.

He stared a moment longer at the shut office door, then checked his watch. It was 3:12pm. He reached into an inner pocket of his suit jacket and pulled out a flip phone.

"Checking in," he said. "We're still on for the 20th. Any issues I need to know about?" He listened. "Very good."

In Cincinnati, Reed fretted about his money running out. He had three weeks, a month if he was frugal, which he wasn't inclined to be if he was marked for death. To be pinching pennies while hiding in some bleak, cold-water flat eating beans and rice and canned soup on the day you died was a particularly dismal ending to look forward to. Better to meet the bullet with a bellyful of briny oysters and aged NY strip steak, a good Burgundy still resonating on the palate.

He could extend his time with another month's worth of funds he had under the alias Pete Snyder, but that name was known to the network, and probably to the FBI. For the moment, his bosses could regard his absence as innocent, merely maintaining radio silence, but if a credit card charge or a cash withdrawal was made in Snyder's name and he didn't then turn up, they'd know he was no longer their man. If they didn't know it already.

He resolved to run his funds down as slowly as his appetites would allow. Then he would draw down the Snyder-alias money and replenish the accounts he had in Ian Gerritt's name. That might buy him another few weeks.

That evening outside Wichita, just fourteen days after the death of President Redmond, the Postman lay the phone down with a peevish snap, having received the news that there was still no sign of Reed in Cincinnati or anywhere else.

Salter sat in his office for just a few more minutes staring at the phone before turning the light off and going out. At Dulles Airport, Imogen boarded a plane for Seattle. And at a Brazilian steakhouse in Washington, D.C.—just the sort of place Reed was dreaming about—Special Agent Amanda Vega and Don Weir met with FAA Inspector Rawley Sims and his immediate superior.

"Good to meet you in person," Vega said to Sims. He nodded, and they sat across from one another. A few yards away, by an unoccupied table, Weir and the technical

130

operations administrator spoke without sitting down. Having come to an understanding and exchanging sets of papers, they shook hands. Each nodded toward his respective agent, before they parted.

"Thank you for meeting with me," Vega began as she watched her boss leaving.

"I'm to give you every courtesy," said Sims in his pleasant drawl, "and I'm pleased to do it. It does seem a little cloak-and-dagger, though."

"It is," Vega admitted. "Though we're trying to avoid the daggers."

Sims was a serious but amiable bureaucrat. At 44, he was old enough to know Washington's hazards, but not so long tenured that he'd internalized its inertia. As far as she could tell from her dealings with him, he cared as much about doing good work as about advancing his career, which was refreshing. He sat, his hands clasped, his face bearing expectant. In his bomber-style leather jacket, he reminded her of Taylor Percy, the pilot she'd interviewed in Omaha. Same courtly Southern manners, too.

"You're OK with this?" she asked.

"'Deed I am. What little I know of it. I'm given to understand that this has to do with national security. For the time being, my brief is to give priority to any and all requests from you or your office, and not to divulge anything I learn to anyone—except to you, assistant deputy-director Weir, or my boss."

"In fact," said Vega, "it would be best if Weir communicated directly with your boss."

"Is there a spy in Justice, Agent Vega?"

"We're part of the Faithless Elector Task Group. We're trying to ascertain the movements and activities of a shadowy group who crop up all over the country. You may have heard the press speculation that Special Agent Tom Kurtz, who was killed, had tried to murder another agent."

"Right, that redheaded woman," he said.

"Well, the speculation is correct, but it didn't end there. Agent Kurtz's boss was also involved—Andrew Colls—now also dead. We don't know if they were the only ones, but we'd be foolish to act as though the threat was contained."

Sims was staring blankly at the tabletop, nodding his head. "I see," he said. "You've got FBI killing other FBI?"

"And it's more complicated than that," Vega responded. "Colls was murdered by the people he was doing extra-curricular work for; and he was killed because we were getting close to exposing him. Don Weir's predecessor, Doug Pollack, killed Kurtz in self-defense. And Pollack himself was lucky to get away with his life."

"I see," said Sims, who still hadn't looked up. "Well, now, that's a little more than I bargained for . . ."

"Yes, you've been thrown in at the deep end," she said, allowing him a moment to grasp the kind of thing she might be asking of him.

"We have an offer of service from a confidential informant," she continued, leaving Reed's name out for the time being, "but you and I need to move quickly because frankly, we don't want to use this guy. He's implicated, and we don't trust him. We'd rather arrest and try him, and not have to deal with him at all. But even if we do hold our noses and work with him, we'll need to be able to corroborate anything he says. The more we know, and from various angles, the stronger our case."

"And you think Flintlock Industries is involved?" asked Sims.

"Yes. I think they're the linchpin," said Vega.

"Well, there's definitely something going on there," he offered, casting off his reserve and leaning forward. "After we talked last time, I retrieved the flight logs for 8977-Alpha on my own initiative. We got lucky. You know how I told you we only kept records for 45 days?"

"Yeah?"

"Well, clearing the decks is itself an onerous task, and it doesn't always happen in a timely manner. There were 67 days' worth of records for 8977-Alpha—back to January 15, and a range of dates for all the other aircraft in the stable. I downloaded them all."

Vega sat forward in her chair.

"Which was just as well," he continued, "because I checked again just before coming to see you, and they've been erased now."

"So, someone got at them?" she asked. "They're covering their tracks."

"No," said Sims. "No, I don't think so. I think admin finally got around to doing the job is all. Part of their normal purge cycle. There's nothing nefarious at the FAA, Agent Vega."

20

Calder and Rich Lamberti had driven by Cardoso's house in the Maple Leaf neighborhood on a number of occasions. They had photographed it from the front (not much to see but a tall, wood fence) and from the back while cruising through the service alley (not much there either). Just a small house, set back from the street, with a high, decorative fence with Japanese motif running around the whole perimeter. If Cardoso had hoped a decorative wooden fence would make the grounds look less like a compound, he'd been mistaken.

Calder and Lamberti had taken turns following him, but his movements seemed calculated to put everyone to sleep. Leave the house at 6:38; number 63 bus toward the South Lake Union/Cascade neighborhood, then walk the few blocks to work; a latte, a banana, and he would disappear into one of the interchangeable, shimmering office buildings by 7:30; lunch presumably within the building because he never ventured out; return home at 5:30 each evening. Various take-out shops delivered to his bungalow-fortress and were buzzed in through the gate.

It would be impossible to sneak in without being noticed. There was at least one camera at the front gate, they surmised, which was how he vetted the delivery drivers, and presumably more cameras were placed around the perimeter fence.

Japanese motif or not, it had a feeling of mild paranoia. Though it was difficult to see clearly, he seemed to set a house alarm as he left each morning, and he set a second gate alarm at the fence. Even though they rarely go off at the right time, it was too much of a risk.

Equally difficult for their purposes, the South Lake Union neighborhood, the "commons," where his office was located, for all its seeming openness, was a heavily controlled patch of ground under intimate surveillance and requiring key-card access—even to get into some of the cafes.

So far, there'd been no sign of a partner—or anyone else, for that matter. Cardoso seemed to be a lonely, austere worker-bee. Calder had imagined a young man (Cardoso was in his early thirties) living high, perhaps beyond, his means off the spoils of murder. Instead, there was just banality.

Cardoso didn't seem to have a life outside of work. He didn't acknowledge his neighbors if they happened to be coming home at the same time. He seemed to have no interactions whatsoever, with the presumable exception of whatever happened at work. Cardoso just wasn't doing anything that might lead to a slip.

Worse, for Calder and Lamberti's purposes, they were known to him, and so had to do their surveillance from a great remove. Calder began to worry that Cardoso knew they were watching him; that they might already have missed their chance. But they needed proof that it was Cardoso, alone, who had killed Matthew. There had to be a reckoning. Professor Calder didn't explain it to Lamberti, but he needed to be sure, because he intended to kill whoever had murdered his student Matthew Yamashita.

That revenge was now his purpose filled him with dismay, not because he doubted the justice of it, but because as he turned it over in his mind it seemed less a decision than a realization. Far from weighing on him, the thought had become a driving force, lifting the weight of depression and anger, flip sides of the same debased coin, giving direction to all he did. It was taking him step by step toward an inevitable outcome.

He had tried to go back to his old life, where he measured and tested, theorized and discussed, but he'd felt leaden and empty. He saw that what others called the "real" world was no better. Imogen's FBI was riddled with dysfunction, intrigue and infighting. He knew from long study of bureaucracies, not to mention the personal infuriations they inflict on everyone, that they care more for their own internal structure and prerogatives than about their ostensible functions. There had been no breaks in the case so far as he knew. Imogen's humiliation-promotion told him all he needed to know about the Justice Department's priorities. Their piddling inertia was content to leave Cardoso to his empty life while Matthew putrefied in his grave.

No. A life for a life. That should be the way.

The previous week, when Calder had bought a used gun at a pawnshop not far from his apartment along First Avenue, he'd walked there, worried he might give himself away. But on arrival, having said he was looking for a good home security weapon, he was surprised to find he wasn't anxious at all. As he chatted with the salesman about the merits and drawbacks of the various weapons in the shop's large inventory, he was struck by how unremarkable it all felt. Like buying a used car.

After almost half an hour of discussion, and some haggling, Calder walked out with a ticket that would allow him to pick up his 9mm Beretta M9A1 five days later, once he'd passed the background check. The next day, though he didn't yet have the gun in his possession, he bought bullets for it at Wal-Mart. That Friday, background check complete, he picked it up. He scheduled a beginner appointment at a range out in Bellevue for Monday morning, after he and Rich Lamberti had watched Cardoso safely into his hive. Imogen would have gone back to D.C. by then.

* * *

Calder picked Imogen up at SeaTac airport late Friday night. He double-parked, blocking another car, jumped out and kissed her passionately before taking her suitcase and throwing it in the trunk. He kissed her again when they got into the car, ignoring the bellowing horn from the blocked car.

"God, you look scrumptious!" he exclaimed, the horn sounding again. His hazel eyes flashed devilishly. "How am I supposed to keep my eyes on the road?" Imogen grinned demurely as they sped off toward his Pike Place Market flat.

Imogen was excited by the greeting, and hoped there was more to come. Her concerns about the weekend retreated a step. She had felt odd about seeing Duncan with so much on her mind. As the plane had begun its descent into SeaTac, her thoughts had been a jumble, her emotions conflicted. She was looking forward to seeing him, but also felt the weight of the things she'd decided not to tell him—Reed having made contact, for instance, and how they were closing in on the Flintlock pilots.

Lovely as he was, and as committed as she was to him, an unattractive sourness had crept into him. In their discussions about the investigation, he no longer seemed the devoted researcher, probing, problem-solving, loving the puzzle. He would often become impatient, dismissive, clearly angry and bitter at the lack of results. He tried to mask it, but in those ugly, revealing moments she glimpsed a harsh, seething undifferentiated anger. Worse, in their calls the previous week, she had begun to sense there was something he wasn't telling *her*.

His hand was on her knee as they rushed along the freeway through a misting Seattle rain, and caressingly it found its way up to her thigh. This was a rejuvenated Duncan. She wondered what had changed, but didn't want to break the spell of whatever had gotten into him. She had been tired as she trudged off the plane, but now she felt she could rally.

Conveniently, they avoided the subject of the investigation until breakfast was over. While Duncan refreshed the coffee, Imogen handed him one of the clean burner phones she'd procured from Jimmy May. He stared at it. Imogen walked to the window to look out over the Market and Elliott Bay.

"It's definitely still on," she said, not turning round. "And someone's watching us. Trey confirmed it, and he's the one who checked out these phones and passed them as clean. We should keep our regular phones on, and use them from time to time, so the network doesn't know we're on to them, but we should only use them for things that don't pertain to all this."

"Has there been any movement?" he asked mordantly. "*Any* change?"

"I've got my team working on PACs and Astroturf organizations," she offered. "But so far, no leads there. I'm still hopeful there'll be some crossover, some payment, or something that'll give us a link to another chapter, or link us back to Senator Eliot or even Moore himself."

Behind her, Calder said nothing, and Imogen couldn't bring herself to face his expression. She worried she would see in it more of his disappointment and anger, what seemed to have become his resting state. Despite his amorous greeting at the airport and the vigorous lovemaking, there was something missing between them.

It wasn't a lack of trust on her part, but she feared that in this state of mind, he might try to persuade her that they should take matters into their own hands again as they had to expose the Faithless Elector plot. She would not do it again. Whatever was taking shape now that Moore had become President was too big for two people. She was dismayed that, preoccupied as he was with Matthew, he didn't see that bigger picture. Was she letting him down? she wondered.

Each longed to tell all. As wonderful as the sex was, they were still more exhilarated to have found in one another a mind equal in depth and substance. It was miserable to be holding back, yet each did, and each sensed that the other was too, so quiet moments became empty, questioning moments. Imogen felt that Duncan's anger left no room for hers. And Duncan worried that if Imogen wasn't telling him everything it was because the FBI was bungling the investigation again—or they were making deals that would let a shit like Cardoso walk.

Outwardly, the weekend was tranquil. They shopped in the Market for dinner that night, picking up salmon, scallops, fresh pasta, and a crisp bottle of Ken Wright Cellars Oregon Pinot Blanc. After dinner, they lay in each other's arms on the couch while a wet wind gusted against the windows, watching a movie about the life of Stephan Zweig that Imogen had wanted to see. They spent early Sunday morning walking through a chilly, shifting fog along the waterfront up through Myrtle Edwards Park and then crossed to Lower Queen Anne for a bite before rushing Imogen back to the airport.

As they kissed in the passenger drop-off area at the airport, Calder's mind was already on target practice at the gun range the next day. Where he was going, she couldn't follow. Imogen, for her part, had her mind on getting back to work on the pilots and flushing Reed into the open. As he got back into the car, she waved, pulled the extending handle on her small suitcase and walked toward her flight. He was ready for her to go.

21

In Cincinnati, Reed stood at his kitchen counter and "refreshed" his email for the fourth time that Sunday, still without result unless more spam email about fat burning counted as a result. He hadn't felt as isolated as this even on Beaver Island, he reflected, and the silence and solitude were getting to him. Didn't these idiots work over the weekend? he pondered as he stalked back into the living room where the news droned on. It was no wonder defeating them had been so easy if they worked only weekdays 9 to 5. Who was minding the damn store? It was probable, he allowed, that they were letting him sweat before making contact. He further allowed that their tactic was working.

Happily, he had found a good French restaurant on Vine Street near where he was staying, so his seclusion wasn't absolute. He'd taken to visiting it regularly for lunch, which he ate at the bar. It was warm and casual, with first-rate food. He had even visited occasionally for dinner. The staff liked to chat—he had most favored customer status now—and he could eat well while spinning his cover story more and more intricately each time. He'd met the chef. Earlier in the evening, he had taken himself out there to get away from staring at his laptop and refreshing email, hoping that by going out he might make *them* wait a bit. The warm glow of salade lyonnaise and duck breast with roasted root vegetables faded, however, the moment he returned to no news.

His chief concern now was that the FBI had intelligence from some other channel and didn't need him at all. If so, they could lure him in and potentially capture him, and then their only concession would be to agree to keep him safe. He would be sentenced to life in a federal prison and would be lucky to get only one life sentence. That was if his bosses didn't kill him first.

It was galling that someone of his caliber and professionalism —and his obvious patriotism—was in this position at all. He worried that he had misread Trager and her colleagues. Could it be that for them this was personal?

Not knowing how Trager and the FBI had uncovered the cells was the source of his growing unease. His operatives had kept to their protocols; they'd changed their burner phones every month, so they should have been untraceable. And information had flowed only one way—by design— down the hierarchy. Their identities, he had believed, were secure because although the operatives kept their phones on constantly, their chiefs turned theirs on only long enough to convey instructions. And yet, the FBI had found them.

Trager and her partner at IT, Trey Kelly, had pried open the D.C. and Boston chapters. The FBI had found the late Agent Andrew Colls through the courier Jimmy May. But how had they found May? As Reed reviewed the details of the protocols he and Nash had put in place, he could find only one weakness—the operatives' personal phones. Agent Kurtz couldn't turn his off, for fear of raising suspicions. The same was true for Colls. It was probable that their underlings, Trebor and Covington, kept theirs on too, not because they were otherwise important but because they were stupid. If tracking their personal phones was how the FBI had done it, it was a nice piece of work. And a colossal blunder on his part.

Fortunately, Reed mused, there had been no further cross-contamination. If he was broadly right about how they'd cracked the two cells, his system had bent but not broken. There'd be no way to get at the remaining chapter members without his help. He hoped. His operatives were below the radar—innocuous, seemingly innocent people. The FBI needed him.

A news anchor introduced the Press Secretary, Antony Marek, who introduced Doctors Menlo and Somers. Reed looked up and sneered.

"Our initial hypothesis concerning the death of President Diane Redmond has proved to be correct," Dr. Menlo was saying. "A thorough macroscopic and microscopic investigation revealed underlying dysfunction as a result of—or at least related to—her Transient-Ischemic Attack some years back. It is still not known whether pulmonary blockage or some other underlying cause was the precipitator . . ."

What followed was a series of slides pointing out all kinds of possible contributing factors. Reed wondered whether they were photos from Diane Redmond at all. He admitted it was excellent work, and he wished Nash were alive to see it. It had worked perfectly. The two doctors took press questions, but Reed muted the sound.

When the original Faithless Elector plot failed, Alec Nash had salved Reed's disappointment by reminding him that the goal had always been to get Bob Moore into the White House—and, he said, there was still a way forward. Certainly, achieving a Moore Presidency became simpler if James Christopher, Moore's running mate, was elected. Removing Christopher would be simpler with their own people around, true. But there were always means, Nash had indicated.

After the failure in the Electoral College, they had set to work on the contingency vote in the Senate and House. Since the Senate voted on the Vice-President, it was vital that Moore win there. The vote in the House for President was actually less important, because whoever won would be having a very short tenure. Reed had complained that it was all fine and good to say such things, but it would be impossible to assassinate a President inside the White House without leaving a trace. It was too tall an order for any operative.

Nash had agreed. "You're absolutely right. Impossible," he said. "Unless"—and here he beamed mischievously—"unless you do it so discreetly that the cause of death isn't clear, and you choose the doctor in charge of the autopsy and he falsifies the findings. Then, you also own the doctor in charge of reviewing the first doctor's work, who signs off the bogus findings."

Reed could see Nash in his mind's eye, smiling broadly. "And, as far as FBI forensics is concerned," he shrugged, "you don't even need them to collude. Our bought-and-paid-for-MDs simply give them false samples, and they dutifully report their investigation, which back up the White House conclusions—that the TIA episode we planted in her medical files was probably the culprit, or at least a contributing factor. All tidy, all natural causes. With a little help from our friends...and a dose of succinylcholine."

Reed looked back toward the files on the kitchen counter. One thin file contained the incriminating evidence the network had to blackmail Menlo and Somers if need be. They had been paid handsomely, but the families had been blackmailed for good measure. The drug habits of Dr. Menlo's elder daughter were unknown outside the network, and the violent predilections of Dr. Somers' son had not yet come to light either. And now, perhaps, they never would.

* * *

Jacob Wilder, the second furloughed pilot interviewed in Omaha by Amanda Vega, had identified Kirsten's Fairmont pilot as Scott Rosewood. Vega, Sims, and a spare FBI pilot, along with her handpicked lieutenant Gus Davies, arrived by FBI jet at Theodore Roosevelt Regional Airport in Dickinson, North Dakota, hoping that Rosewood would keep to his flight plan today and not be diverted. They arrived an hour ahead of his scheduled touch down.

Rising low across a flat expanse, three squat buildings—the FBO—erupted from the landscape. Set apart from the main terminal, one was a Quonset hut, indistinguishable from the one at Fairmont, next to which sat two, squat, cinderblock bunkers: the charter airlines' building, with the pilot lounge, and the fire brigade garage and office. Davies made his way to the pilot lounge, while Vega and the others made their way to the airport manager's office.

The pilot lounge was a small, dingy room with yellowing walls. Everything felt handed down, from the frayed rug, below, to the brittle ceiling tiles and old fluorescent lights, above. The vending machines along one wall, the coffee maker and the bulletin board had all seen better days—but not for some years. Outside the dusty hanging blinds, a frigid gray light loomed outside like a fog. Three pilots sat at a table playing cards.

Davies told them he was a Flintlock Industries executive and that he been called to an emergency meeting. He'd been told there was a flight out that day soon, and he asked if there were any company pilots around. No, was the cursory answer. Were any expected soon? he asked tetchily.

One of the three pushed heavily away from the table and walked indolently to a clipboard on the far wall. Yes, a Flintlock pilot was due imminently—the only such flight that day. "Unless he gets diverted to pick up another one of you guys for a different emergency meeting," said the pilot with barely concealed disdain as he dropped the clipboard and returned to his game.

"If he doesn't show up," another called, not bothering to look at Davies, "we could fly you via charter."

With his thick, cropped, black hair making him look a little like a Royal Foot Guard in his busby, Davies patrolled the hallway monotonously. As he did so, he took to looking impatiently at his watch. Occasionally, one of the pilots would give him a glance and shake his head, pitying Rosewood for having to deal with these executive pricks.

Vega, Sims and the second pilot had gone straight to the FBO manager's office. Chipper, eager Chadwick Marshall, 32, fairly gleamed with pompous efficiency. "FAA *and* FBI?" he blurted as he examined their credentials, and his manner switched abruptly from helpful to damage-control reticence.

"We're certainly here to help," he said cautiously, as he ushered them into the back office.

Marshall wore middle-management livery—white, short-sleeved, button-down collared shirt and navy blue tie, sensible charcoal slacks and black shoes. Like everyone else Vega had encountered in the airways business, Marshall wore his thinning brown hair military short.

"What can you tell me about Flintlock Industries courier planes?" Vega asked as she and Sims sat down. The second pilot stood behind them. He remained standing, stone-faced, mechanical, his affect like that of a soldier "at ease" among superiors, and with his eyes, behind aviator sunglasses, not seeming to see or register anything.

"Not much," Marshall allowed, nervously scanning the faces of his inquisitors. "*Seems* like a good outfit," he pronounced after a moment of reflection. "Their pilots are sound, the company pays its bills. No issues, no problems. Nothing we could have noticed," he added, putting in an early bid on his—and the airport's—innocence. "The company maintains a common locker here for its pilots to use. They use our repair facilities from time to time as needed, just like everyone else. We're not their hub, of course. I think that's in Omaha."

"May we see your records for 8977-Alpha, please?" asked Sims.

"Do you need a warrant for that?" He glanced nervously between Vega and Sims.

"No," Vega answered nebulously. "No, not if you're cooperating with us. There's no reason you wouldn't." She smiled pleasantly. Sims stared straight into him.

Marshall returned a weak smile. "I can get you what we have through here." He drew a keyboard toward him and squinted at the screen as he clicked through his database. "I can't completely disaggregate all the planes. I'll just give you everything we've got for Flintlock, if that's OK."

"That'd be mighty fine," said Sims. "Thank you."

Marshall nodded and clicked "print," sending 15 pages to a printer at the far end of the room. He stood up from his desk and retrieved them.

"Two more things, if you wouldn't mind," Vega said, as Sims took the papers from Marshall and examined them quickly.

"While we don't need a court order for those records," she began, indicating the papers Sims had just tucked away, "I'll need a warrant to inspect that company locker you just mentioned. While I'm waiting for it, can I get you to seal the locker? Will that be a problem? Nothing grand; no yellow tape or anything. Just change the lock, maybe?"

Marshall nodded. "We could do that."

"Wonderful," she said. "And, if somehow it came up, you could note that there had been a problem with the billing. I'll have someone here with the warrant from the Minneapolis field office before the end of the day."

He nodded his understanding. "Um, you said two things?"

"Yes," said Vega. "We're trying to do this quietly. This is a national security matter, and we're going to arrest a Flintlock pilot when he lands, but I'd rather it wasn't known we'd done it. I'm told," she said, casting a glance back at the stone-faced pilot, "that pilots have a pretty chatty network?"

"Yes, I think that's true." Once again, he looked at each of them, searching for something that might tell him if he was in trouble personally. "I...I'm not sure how to help you," Marshall said carefully.

"I noticed slot Three-B open next to two other planes," said Sims, "in the row facing the pilot lounge. Is that probably where 8977-Alpha will tie down?"

"That sounds right. I'd have to check. Ground control would handle that."

"Of course. Why not ask them to direct him there?" said Sims. "Tell them you're a little perturbed at the sloppy way some of the aircraft are being parked.

"Yeah, I could do that."

"Which, by the way, Mr. Marshall, they are. Sloppy. Which isn't a violation, but it might indicate deeper problems. It was just a cursory glance across the tarmac as I walked in here—"

The point was made. Vega held up her hand, the gesture communicating that they needed to stay focused. Sims nodded and asked the manager, "That's the fire brigade, over there?"

"Yes."

Rosewood's tan-on-beige plane touched down 25 minutes later. Ground control directed it to tie down at 3-B. Davies' phone pinged and he read the message. He waited just inside the glass doors giving onto the tarmac, as the plane's stairs were let down and the sole passenger disembarked, a man in his mid-fifties dressed business casual. Davies took his picture.

A moment later, a black limousine from the local country club glided to a stop next to him. As the driver got out and trotted around to open the car door, Davies snapped more pictures on his phone. Passenger, driver, license plate

As the car swept away, a fire brigade truck sped across the tarmac and came to a stop in front of the plane, holding as though waiting for something in front of it to pass. In doing so, it blocked the view of the plane from the pilot lounge windows. On the truck's passenger side, away from prying eyes, Sims, Vega and the stony FBI pilot stepped out of the truck and walked briskly into the plane. The tanker truck moved on, and Davies climbed the stairs into the plane.

22

For all his determination and resolution as he fired six rounds into a target seven meters away, Calder found he had qualms. It was one thing to believe a man should die, to see him dead in your imagination, and another to train to make it happen.

The logistics began to grow complicated. The fact of the gun carried its own gravity. The 9mm Beretta M9A1 weighed just under a kilo, about the same as the pink dumbbells he struggled with every morning. It felt potent in his hands, freighted with purpose. But how, for instance, to carry it and not give away that he was carrying it? He couldn't just put it in a pocket of his sport jacket.

His aim at this distance was improving, and his shots this round were nicely grouped. He frowned nevertheless, as he reeled in the target for inspection. Raggedly it came fluttering toward him like laundry damaged in a hurricane. He was annoyed with the instructor, who kept using the term "squeeze" for "fire."

In the instructor's view—a strident, self-assured gun apostle—shooting was a detached operation, natural, clean, direct, the trigger squeezed and the bullets burst from the gun barrel as simply as an orange seed popped between thumb and forefinger. The nerve damage in Calder's right hand made that just a bit more difficult. Calder might have also noted, if he'd thought the instructor would hear it, that an orange pit didn't "pop" out at 1,700 feet per second. One didn't generally speak of a seed's "stopping power."

Calder had heard that men who took up shooting were often awed by the power they held. But he was accustomed to power being associated with freedom, a loosening of bonds. This was the opposite: he felt constrained, heavier. It was not conscience that weighed on him, but the burden of the weapon itself.

* * *

Nettie Sartain had worked over the weekend and had been waiting for Imogen since seven that morning. She followed Imogen into her office as soon as she arrived.

"I'm glad we're talking today and not on Friday," she said, dumping a group of files on Imogen's desk. Imogen put down her coffee cup, hung up her purse and jacket in the corner and slowly walked back to the desk.

Nettie sat on the other side, leaning across the files, her eyes burning. "Because I kept going," she said, "after our talk on Friday—do you mind if I just close the door?" she asked, interrupting herself and jumping up to shut the door. Resettled, she began again: "After our talk on Friday, I kept at it."

"What've you found?" asked Imogen.

"These Astroturf groups? I started sifting through what the team's been working on for commonalities—they didn't find any, by the way. I looked at their registered bank accounts, and they're all different. I looked at their disbursement reports. Nothing. I looked to see if I could match treasurers from one PAC to another. I can't. All of us were looking for something to tie them together—names of operatives, employees, volunteers who might have worked for both. Nothing."

"And yet you found something," said Imogen.

"Yes," said Nettie, her eyes sparkling with joy. "So, I went back to the beginning. This time, I started sifting through their original Federal Election Commission filings. I thought it might be helpful to look at their specific organization matrix. I pulled the FEC-Form One, Statement

149

of Organization for each PAC and started writing out the names and addresses they provided on a grid—physical address, PAC email address, treasurer name and contact info; custodian name and info, designated agent info. I was hoping I could find a match somewhere, like maybe they were using different names but the same email. Again, though, nobody turned up twice on any of the forms."

"OK . . ."

"Well, I was getting a little punchy from working late when I wrote down the Forefathers Institute PACs custodian—Francis Trebor."

"Holy shit," Imogen whispered.

"I know, right?" said Nettie, giddy with triumph. "He was one of the guys your professor killed in that stairwell."

Imogen nodded mutely.

"So, then I was focusing on custodians, and there, for the Opportunity PAC, the custodian name was Allen Covington, the other guy he killed."

Imogen started reaching for the papers.

"Wait," said Nettie. "When I got to the Sovereign Caucus PAC Statement of Organization, the name of their custodian didn't jump out at me. But they list their 'agent' as Peter Snyder. Isn't that one of Frank Reed's aliases? It was in your background notes."

"Amazing work, Nettie. This is great!" said Imogen as she gathered in the papers.

She beamed. "So, over the weekend, I went back over every name I had and scrutinized each of them as best as I could. None of them—except Trebor, Covington and Reed/Snyder—are in the FBI database, so I resorted to Googling. I'd put in addresses to see if they were real places. They all are. I Googled the names of each person listed on each Organization form. Most don't have much of an online presence. One has no presence at all—he's been dead since 2012. Tim Hayward. Does that name mean anything to you?"

"No," said Imogen, "I'm afraid it doesn't. How did he die?"

"Murder-suicide. He killed his girlfriend and then himself. I've got the *Seattle Times* article here."

Imogen nodded and went back to scanning the report.

"Until now, there were no red flags, nothing strange about any of these organizations. They were just what they seemed to be. But this proves there's something fishy." Here she paused for a moment.

"I thought you and I—together—might take a closer look. And if I bring you personnel lists for those three PACs, you might recognize some more names. It could be faster if we work together. It would mean bringing me totally inside, though."

Imogen was trapped. This was Nettie's work, and it couldn't be taken from her. Imogen knew she had to recommend to Weir that Nettie be brought in and given higher clearance. And by doing that, Imogen would be putting her in jeopardy. She stared at Nettie. Fresh, young, eager—effective. Imogen felt the circle of those in harm's way growing. And there had already been losses.

Insistently, Nettie said, "But I need you to tell me all you know about what's going on."

Imogen nodded. "I don't make that decision, but I will make a very strong recommendation to Don Weir. Mostly, though,"—here she patted the files—"I'll let your work do the talking."

* * *

Davies pulled the airplane steps up behind him and secured the door. There was a final hiss and clunk as the door sealed. The FBI pilot was waiting with Sims in the co-pilot's seat. As the engines started up, they were engrossed in a checklist.

"I'm familiar with the glass cockpit of the Cirrus," Sims was saying to the pilot. "This looks like pretty much the same thing."

"Good. This is gonna be fun," the pilot was saying. "This thing's powerful. I'm gonna have to stay on the pitch to avoid any altitude excursions."

"Autopilot should help," Sims was saying.

The pilot scoffed. Sims shook his head good-naturedly.

Davies turned away from them. Though it was all one cabin, they were clearly in their own world. Of the five seats in the aircraft, three were for passengers, one in mid-cabin, leaving a passage to the two at the back. Rosewood and Vega sat in the back, Vega placidly looking out of the window. Rosewood looked frightened. He was ashen, sweating. He looked as though he couldn't wait to tell his side of the story. While the plane taxied, Vega was content to let him fret. It would make the interrogation that much simpler once they were in the air.

In the middle seat, Davies heard Sims say to the pilot, "Yeah, here it is: 'saved routes.' He was on his way to Great Falls, Montana."

"I think I'm gonna be sick," said Rosewood from the back.

"Don't you fucking dare," said Vega and turned back to her window.

22

Still at his Airbnb in Cincinnati, Reed was staring down the long end of a week. How had he become so blind? In the years leading up the 2016 election, he had received weekly—sometimes daily—updates from his operatives and from Nash. He had felt preternaturally aware, attuned to every shift and tremor, like a spider feeling the vibrations of her web, extending her consciousness beyond physical limits. Reflexively, like Vega with her FD-302's, he turned to the files again. Re-reading them, he rebuilt the network in his mind.

He started with Seattle. That chapter had seen the first early test, almost five years earlier, on the night of the November 2012 general election. He had debriefed them afterward himself, and now he read over his summary.

The three cell members—Tim Hayward, Eric Janssen and Dan Cardoso—together with Hayward's live-in girlfriend Samantha Banks, were having what turned out to be a commiseration drink in a Pioneer Square pub as the election results were announced. The mood at their table was sour, a silent rebuke to the self-congratulation of most people in the bar. Hayward and Banks had arrived earlier than Janssen and Cardoso and they had been drinking for some time.

Hayward was a retired security guard at the Port of Seattle docks. He looked shabby and hounded; and the harrying he perceived was real. Only 45 years old, he had bounced from job to job all along the west coast, from Long

Beach to Seattle and back, with the alcoholic's premonition of danger generally keeping him just ahead of being fired. His girlfriend Samantha had the hollow bearing of someone who had never done anything in particular for long. She was a few years younger, vital and attractive, if no longer quite youthful.

The hard set of her mouth, the frayed rasp of her voice and the tubercular rattle when she laughed, pointed to a hard-bitten future as she tried to hold on to what was slipping away. For now, it was difficult to guess why she stayed with the brooding, mercurial Hayward. As Reed reviewed the document, he wondered how he had ever tapped that lout Hayward for a leadership role. What had he seen in him, either?

Janssen and Cardoso had spotted the couple at the back of the Pioneer Square pub and joined them, the file read.

"You picked the wrong side," said Samantha, as one-by-one the networks began officially announcing that Barack Obama had won a second term, "that's all. Wrong side. S'okay," she offered equitably, raising her head to look at Hayward. She finished her drink and sat back, slouching in her chair, her gaze still drunkenly fixed on him. She drew her black hair into a ponytail, but let it go, having nothing to tie it with.

There was something sarcastic in her words, like a woman taunting a flaccid lover by telling him it didn't matter. The subtext was certainly what Hayward seemed to hear. His flushed face grew redder.

"Shut the fuck up!" he hissed, leaning toward her across the marble tabletop, the color showing through his thinning brown hair.

"What'd I say?" she wondered aloud, looking innocently at Cardoso and Janssen, who looked concerned and abashed in equal measure. They remained silent, watchful. Hayward had more than a decade on them, and was their ostensible leader, the go-between for instructions from Reed.

They looked crisp and fresh—especially by contrast with Hayward—and could have been mistaken for junior salesmen, but for their air of unexpressive coldness and austerity. They were groomed, unlovable petulants, for whom salvation meant immunity and authority. Cardoso and Janssen both wore "hard part" haircuts, razored high up the sides, like an Army Ranger (which neither had been), but longer on top. The effect on Cardoso was a golden blond pompadour, while Janssen's thin black lanks pasted on his skull suggested he might be an actor auditioning to be Master of Ceremonies in a Weimar-era Berlin nightclub.

"You'll see! We're building something, we are," Hayward yelled at Samantha, implicating Cardoso and Janssen. "Something big. Lasting. I tell people. I tell people all the time"—the two young men exchanged a look—"but you," he said, pointing accusingly at her, "you don't do shit. You sit there—"

"—Talk, talk. That's all you do...all you fucking *can* do."

Hayward lunged across the table at her, but Cardoso was quick and snatched his wrist. In a deft movement, he bent Hayward's arm behind him and they both stood up, Cardoso knocking over his own chair, kicking Hayward's chair out of the way and propelling his sodden bulk toward the front door.

At the same time, Janssen was surprised to see Samantha—no shrinking violet—launch herself at Hayward. Less tactically graceful than his compatriot and aware that if no one had noticed them before they were certainly watching now, he grabbed her around the waist as gently as he could to slow her down, and put a hand on her shoulder. "Just wait a moment," he said in her ear.

The waitress was walking quickly toward them.

"How much do we owe?" he asked, digging his fingers into Samantha's shoulder and watching as Cardoso and Hayward reached the door.

The waitress looked uncertainly at him. "I don't know, I haven't—"

Janssen reached into his pocket. He fanned out six $20 bills. "More than this?" he demanded.

"Oh, no," said the waitress. "More like—"

"—Keep the change," he said stuffing the bills into her hand. "Sorry about the trouble."

Out on the sidewalk, Samantha announced loudly that she wanted another fucking drink. Seeing that Cardoso was dragging Hayward towards South Washington Street, Janssen elected to head in the opposite direction with her. They found another bar on Yesler Way.

Cardoso hoped the damp, chilly November night might clear Hayward's head, but in vain. Hayward stalked morosely in front as the two of them headed south along First Avenue.

"Timmy's sweet, mostly," Samantha began, sipping a Cosmopolitan at the new watering hole. "Don't be mad at him 'bout tonight."

"Yes," said Janssen, non-committedly.

"Is your friend gonna hurt him?"

"No. Not at all. We're just letting you both cool off."

"I am cooled off!" she barked.

"Yes, I see that," he replied without irony. "But what about him?"

"Him," she said. "Him. He's just useless. Always talking about whatever it is you guys are doing for the government."

"Always talking?"

"Yeah," she said. "How super secret it is. How important it is. How important *he* is." She drained her Cosmo and signaled for another. "Boring. I never see him do anything. He tells me they're paying you guys a lot . . . maybe they are, but *we're* still living in that shitty, little house."

Three blocks away, at the far end of Occidental Square, Hayward was sitting in the trolley station shelter. "No," Cardoso was saying. "No, I don't think you're cooled off."

"Oh, come on!" Hayward pleaded.

Cardoso stepped away from Hayward and took out his phone as he crossed the street.

"You calling her?" he asked.

"I'm calling our friend," said Cardoso. "Who's waiting with her."

"Tell her from me to fuck off!" he yelled.

Cardoso turned and stared at Hayward. "Does that sound like you've cooled off? Now be quiet. I have to make a call." Hayward nodded and laid his head against the wall of the station. He closed his eyes. Cardoso crossed to the other side of the street.

Frank Reed picked up on the second ring. "This is Mr. Cooper," Reed said evenly, giving his network codename.

"This is Mr. Sawyer," said Cardoso, all but snapping to attention as he addressed his superior.

"I wasn't expecting a call, Mr. Sawyer," said Reed.

"No," said Cardoso. "But we've run into a problem with Mr. Cobbler and his girlfriend. It's pretty clear he's been giving away samples."

"Flooding the market?" asked Reed.

"Doubtful. But it seems only a matter of time before he does."

"Do I need to meet with him?" asked Reed.

"No, sir, I don't think so. It's still a local matter, and should be handled that way," said Cardoso. He paused. "We can take the meeting."

"Can Mr. Cartwright corroborate that he's giving away samples?" Reed asked, referring to Janssen.

"He can, sir. He's with the other person in all this right now at a separate location."

"I'd like to speak with him," said Reed. "Do nothing until you've heard back from me."

"Very good, sir. They seem distraught—both of them. I'd like to see them home."

"Wait for my call."

Cardoso closed his flip phone and looked across at Hayward, dozing against the shelter wall.

Despite the seriousness of the problem, Reed was impressed with Cardoso. His protocol had been sound, and the plain-language code had worked effectively. Reed understood that Hayward was talking too much. When Reed mentioned a "meeting," it was ominous indeed for Hayward, and Cardoso's use of the word "distraught" was a coded recommendation of murder made to look like a suicide. Cardoso was taking the responsibility himself.

Reed dialed Janssen's number. "This is Mr. Cartwright," Janssen answered.

"Pretend you're talking to Mr. Sawyer," said Reed.

There was a pause. "Yes, everything's fine. We're here, cooling off." He stood up and walked toward the back of the dive, making a signal for Samantha to wait at the table. To make sure she did, he waved to the bartender for another Cosmo.

"I hear Cobbler's been giving away samples. Can you confirm that?"

"Yes, I can, Mr. Cooper."

"I see. Mr. Sawyer seems to think it requires a full meeting."

There was a pause at Janssen's end. "I concur," he said finally.

"Mr. Sawyer seems to think he hasn't yet saturated the market, and that if you two were to conduct the meeting, you might be able to keep this misunderstanding all in the family, before it spreads."

"We conduct the meeting?" Janssen asked.

"That's what Sawyer's suggesting. Do you have any problem with that?"

"No, sir," Janssen said finally.

"Good. If you can do it today or tomorrow, there would be no need to involve head office. I would drop by in the next few days, just as a status-check."

"Yes," said Janssen.

"You're sure you're on board with this, Cartwright?"

"Totally, sir. I've just never had to plan a meeting."

"Would the *Citizen Kane* scenario make the most sense in this case? Do you know what I'm referring to?"

"I do," said Janssen quietly.

"Good. And then, obviously, Cobbler would be particularly distraught."

"Yes! Yes, I see. I understand. Will you communicate the meeting details to Mr. Sawyer?"

Reed hung up, impressed with Janssen now, too. His first kills. He wasn't looking forward to it, but he wasn't shirking it either.

Now, re-reading the file, Reed reflected for a moment on how well he had trained them, glossing that it was also his fault that an oaf like Hayward was involved in the first place.

Reed had called Cardoso back and relayed the choice of plan. Early in the film, Kane tells his news editor to accuse the husband of a missing woman of her murder: "But we don't *know* that," the editor pleads. "Of course he killed her," says Kane, surprised at the editor's naiveté. "The husband always does it."

And in Reed's training, the "Citizen Kane scenario" was part of a larger strategy of following the line-of-least-resistance. For any action, the operatives had been instructed, they should make the case easy—obviously solvable—so the police wouldn't dig too far. If you commit a murder, plant evidence on the brother or business partner of the dear departed; if it's a woman, her lover and/or husband. Always preferable, of course, to make it look like an accident, but Cardoso and Janssen didn't have time for that.

It was a cheerless, two-bedroom, post-war bungalow that Janssen and Cardoso took their two distraught charges home to. The very end of a dead-end street in White Center, just south of the city line. They arrived separately. Hayward was dozing in Cardoso's car; Janssen drove Samantha there some twenty minutes behind. Each of the small houses along the street was set back, with substantial property around it.

Even in the dark, it was clear that Hayward's home was the least desirable on the block. The sky-blue paint was scarred and peeling. Like most of the others, the property was surrounded by a four-foot high chain link fence, and it too needed maintenance. The grass in the front yard was overgrown, with fountains of weeds erupting here and there. Far behind the house, Cardoso noticed, there was a service alley for garbage pickup, running down the spine of the block between the streets.

Cardoso and Hayward arrived first. Cardoso had been dosing him with liquor since receiving the go-ahead for the "meeting" from Reed. Hayward had fallen asleep on the

159

drive, and Cardoso had to help him into the house. As they approached the gate, Cardoso asked: "Do you have a dog?"

"Nah, no dog. Thinkin' about gettin' one though."

Cardoso got a better grip under Hayward's arm, hoisted him with some difficulty against himself and pushed the gate open. "What about your neighbors?"

"What about 'em?"

"Dogs?"

"Nah. Lady about three houses down has one of those tiny, yippy things...fucking little rat, if you ask me. You scared?"

"No," said Cardoso, "not scared so much as I don't want something running at me in the dark, waking the neighbors; and then everyone knows your business. We're supposed be keeping a low profile."

"Right," said Hayward, breathing heavily. "Thanks, buddy. Yer a prince." He could barely hold his eyes open.

"Don't thank me," said Cardoso grimly as he unlocked the front door.

They stumbled as they picked their way heavily through the living room in the dark. "Which bedroom?" asked Cardoso. Hayward indicated the one on the right with a heavy swing of his head. They paused at the door, and while Cardoso searched for the light switch, Hayward launched himself at the bed. He was asleep instantly.

Cardoso surveyed the room. It was filthy. Clothes and dirty glasses were piled on the floor. There was an overflowing ashtray by the bed, empty beer bottles. The bed was a mattress and box spring resting on the floor, unmade. The fitted sheet drew away from the top left corner. A glass and an empty bottle of vodka stood on the nightstand on the near side of the bed. On the shelf below was Hayward's Smith & Wesson Shield.

Cardoso picked it up. It was loaded. He checked the safety and put it in his jacket pocket. Then, he reached down to the slumbering form on the bed, and took the network flip phone out of Hayward's jacket. He pocketed it and walked out to the darkened kitchen where he dialed Janssen with his own.

"Cobbler's asleep," he told him. "I'm leaving in a moment. Drop the girl at the house. See her in, I guess, and then meet me at the Seven-Eleven over on South 112th Street. I saw it on the way here. I'll wait for you there."

Cardoso unlocked the back door and unfastened the latch on the aluminum storm door. He took out a handkerchief and wiped down everything he could remember touching as he went out, using the front door. Once in the car, he drove to the end of the street, but doubled back to check the service alley running behind the houses to make sure it was clear.

By the time they met at the Seven-Eleven, it was almost 3am.

"We're agreed on this?" Cardoso asked as they sat in his battered Ford Taurus.

"Yeah."

"Was she asleep when you left?" Cardoso asked.

Janssen nodded. "I helped her into bed. She was getting frisky, but she was about to pass out. And besides . . ."

"Frisky? Like what?"

"Like rubbing up against me, stroking my face, telling me how much she'd always liked me. I think she was about to reach for my cock," Janssen added, visibly shaken.

"You're kidding."

"I'm not," he said shaking his head. "But then she passed out."

They sat in silence for some minutes, staring into the brightly lit store. Cardoso sipped coffee, while Janssen took delicate pulls on the straw stuck in his massive "Big Gulp." A passer-by would more likely have taken them for a couple of young men unwilling to concede that their night on the town has been a bust than for a ruthless pair of assassins.

"We're definitely doing the right thing," Janssen said finally, staring straight ahead. "He's weak and stupid—a danger to all of us. And it's his fault we have to do her too."

Cardoso nodded. "That's right."

"I'm ready, if you are," said Janssen quietly.

161

"A job well done must rattle," said Cardoso, quoting an old Prussian military proverb as he started the car. "I've got his gun," he added.

They approached the house from the back, along the alleyway, coasting with headlights off for the last 60 yards before coming to a stop at the back gate. Both looked left and right for any trace of movement, or hint of anyone awake in the other houses. All were dark and quiet. They paused to put on their gloves, then moved quickly across the yard to the backdoor. Janssen winced as the springs on the storm door creaked.

A moment in the kitchen to hear if anyone was awake. Heavy snoring from the bedroom. They padded across the living room toward the open bedroom door. Cardoso tapped Janssen's shoulder, signaling him to wait a moment while he fetched a bath towel. At the threshold to the bedroom, they could make out both Hayward and Samantha on the mattress. The stale smell of the room had grown sharp and rank.

Cardoso handed Hayward's gun to Janssen, who walked to Hayward's side of the bed.

Janssen paused and looked toward the ceiling. Both men drew deep breaths and nodded to one another in the darkness. Then Janssen nodded one, two, three...

Cardoso fell onto Hayward, pinning him to the bed. Janssen slapped the gun onto Hayward's hand and fired two shots into Samantha's head. Hayward bleared and startled, eyes wide, face covered with her blood. He stared wildly, his arms flailing, not seeming to know whether he was awake or asleep.

A scream erupted from Hayward's mouth as Janssen grabbed his hand again, put the gun to his head and pulled the trigger. For a moment, there was silence. The living stood rigid and alert beside the dead. Cardoso handed Janssen the towel. Even in the low light, he could see that Janssen was splattered with the shrapnel of Hayward's head.

It was more of a mess than either of them had anticipated. There wasn't time to rehearse how it could have gone better—or to retch. Janssen flicked gobbets off his clothes onto the bed and the floor. In turn, they wiped at their shoes and the bottoms of their feet. Cardoso clicked on a penlight and they examined one another quickly. "I'll get the doors," Cardoso whispered.

Next day, Reed had arrived, anxious to tidy this episode away into his dossier.

The full Seattle Chapter dossier contained the account of their "meeting" with Hayward and Banks, transcribed by Reed in their own words. There was nothing of further note added to the file but brief updates and ready-status reports for the next four years, when Cardoso and Janssen's mettle would be proved again.

Reed had a lot to trade in this file. Picking up again on November 12, 2016, after something of a hiatus, Cardoso and Janssen had drowned the Elector in Seattle who wouldn't sell his vote, documented well; two days later there was an entry regarding the winemaker in Yamhill, Oregon, they had murdered; and below that was their December 9th report on the murder of Matthew Yamashita in the Arboretum.

But to trade you had to have a partner, Reed mused, and no one was getting back to him. He exhaled heavily to calm his fraying nerves. No one knew anything, he reassured himself. He had the bird's eye view.

He closed the file. He had been pleased with their initiative; and though he might have been less so had he witnessed the murder scene (they didn't describe it too closely), he took an almost literary pride in the report he composed. He'd even rounded off by asking the young men to sign the document.

Their very own death warrant.

23

"So," Vega began as the plane leveled off, "you're a courier not just for Flintlock Industries, but for a conspiracy to subvert the government. You have a private radio frequency in addition to the company frequency, used only by you and one other pilot, John Menzies, to communicate with your handler. By the way, Menzies will also be in custody shortly." The western United States drifted by underneath them.

"We know," she continued, "that you've been seeking a rendezvous with a Mr. Cooper at the same time and place in Fairmont, Nebraska, every other Friday. We know you were there on January 7 and that you've been hanging about waiting for someone on February 24, on March 10, and again on the 24th. You may or may not know that his real name is Frank Reed."

Sims handed Davies a piece of paper, which Davies passed to Vega. She read it and nodded. "This aircraft," she said, "will begin flying to your next scheduled destination, Great Falls, but before we get there we'll divert and head to Pocatello, Idaho. That means we have roughly four hours until I have to surrender you to the head of the FBI Resident Agency there—four hours until your bosses know we've picked you up. You will be formally charged as an accessory to four counts of first-degree murder, aiding and abetting a known terrorist—Reed/Cooper—and obstruction of justice. The FAA has some charges for you, too.

"If," she continued, "prior to touching down in Idaho, I hear nothing useful from you, I will hand you over and you can take your chances. And I'd be careful if I were you about letting your bosses supply the defense lawyer. If he were to get you acquitted somehow, or even out on bail, you'd be dead within the week. Unless you help us, Scott, you're going away for a long time. Or worse. What are you, 28? 30? That's a lot of life to throw away, but if you do this right, you might never see the inside of a jail."

"What do you want from me?"

"Information, testimony," said Vega. "Will you cooperate and be taken into protective custody?"

"Yes," he said, unhesitatingly.

"Good."

"Please sign this form waiving your right to counsel," said Davies, handing Rosewood a sheet of paper. Rosewood signed without reading it.

"Thank you," said Vega, as she handed it back to Davies. "Agent Davies will take down what you say. From time to time, we'll pause and you will read what he's written and initial it as correct."

Rosewood nodded pitifully.

"First, what or who are you picking up in Great Falls?"

"Some factory samples, I think," said Rosewood.

"Part of your 'extra-curricular' work?" asked Vega, making it sound like a student helping out in a soup kitchen or a secretary performing little favors for her boss.

"No," he said. "Regular business."

"I see. Are you known to the delivery guy?"

"No, not really. We hardly meet. They hand me a box, or a bunch of boxes, and I take off again. Though I was planning on staying there overnight."

"Do you know people in Great Falls?"

"No. I was going to veg out at the motel and get an early start to get the samples to Minnesota by mid-to-late morning."

"You're due at Fairmont in two days. What was your plan?"

"After delivering tomorrow, I'd do the next thing on the list. Friday morning I'd radio the company saying I had a VIP diversion, meaning a special pick-up, off the books, as it were. They'd know I wasn't available for anything else until I radioed back in."

"Is your dispatcher an accomplice?"

"No. We're piggybacking on an existing company thing. Some of the VIPs do have special requests, and we're supposed to honor them. It's not that they're illegal, just anonymous, ya know? Maybe the company's thinking about a merger or an acquisition, so the company rep goes VIP-divert so as not to let anyone know they're in negotiations. It's also why we go VFR sometimes. That Flight Aware app has pretty good tracking information on routes in real time, so we need to go dark."

"With Visual Flight Rules?" she asked.

"Right."

"And the fleet captain knows nothing?"

"Not unless he's been told to contact us and reschedule us for one of these diversions," said Rosewood. "Generally, as far as the fleet captain knows or cares, I've been privately contacted by someone from the company and I'm taking some executive around, and he has to figure out a way to pick up my slack," he added.

"What's the fleet captain's name?" Vega asked, "and why is Archie League listed as the chief pilot?"

"That was just some messing around. No one ever checks that stuff," said Rosewood defensively.

"We did. The Fleet Captain's name?" she said again. "Is he distinct from the Chief Pilot?"

"No," he said. "Same guy. Larry Acosta."

Behind him, Davies duly noted the name. "OK," she said. "Who's your contact in Fairmont?"

"A Mr. Cooper," he said.

"You've been in contact with him?"

"No. I don't even know what he looks like. If he's there at the airport in Fairmont, he's supposed to introduce himself as Cooper and tell me he has something for the Postman."

"So, he didn't recruit you?"

"No, I was recruited by a Mr. Fisher," he said, referring to Alec Nash. "My standing orders are to wait at the rendezvous from 2pm to 4pm every other Friday until Cooper shows up. I can describe Fisher to you."

"We know who he is," said Vega. "Or was. He was murdered." She let that sink in a moment. "If the same thing's happened to Reed, you could have wasted a lot of Fridays."

Rosewood blanched.

"Where are you supposed to take Cooper?"

"I don't know," he said, urgently. "He'll tell me where we're going."

Vega sat back in the cushioned seat, believing him. The design of this operation was good. It was exasperating. No one knew much of anything beyond his own instructions. Finally, she said: "We'll keep to your schedule. No diversion," she said to Davies, indicating that he should communicate that to the pilots up front. "We'll stay overnight in Great Falls and fly to Minnesota in the morning. En route to...?

"St. Paul," Rosewood said.

"Very good. En route to St. Paul you will tell them that after delivery you have a VIP diversion."

24

In D.C., Imogen and Nettie were waiting for Weir when Imogen received a text from Amanda Vega. *"Got Rosewood at airport. Quietly so no one else knows. Not sure how far we'll get with him, or how much he really knows."*

"Understood," she replied. *"One more piece."*

"Asking him for timeline of so-called VIP diversions to match with any known acts."

Weir arrived, knocking and entering in one movement. "What've you got?"

"I'll let Agent Sartain explain," said Imogen.

"Proceed," Weir said to her.

Nettie detailed what she had found on the FEC forms, how Trebor, Covington and Frank Reed, using his alias Pete Snyder, were all listed as either custodians or agents of the various PACs.

Weir nodded, "That's good," he said and scratched at his head. "Do you have any suggestions as to how to proceed?"

"Yes," said Nettie. "Imogen, er, Agent Trager and I thought I should delve deeper. Start looking at payments and activities of those particular PACs. For instance, we could ask for a Federal Election Committee audit, but we'd need the FEC to be the front for us so as not to tip off the targets that we're getting closer."

"Are we getting closer?" Weir asked jadedly.

"Yes, Don, I think we are," said Imogen. "Tonight and tomorrow, Amanda will be getting as much intel as she can from the pilots about their movements and contacts. That will give us a better framework, and we can start sticking other things we know to it. It would be ideal if any of the PACs we're looking at were currently being audited, so all we had to do was request the files from FEC..."

"Let me look into that," said Weir.

* * *

That night in Great Falls, Vega and Davies met two local colleagues from Pocatello at a squat, brick-faced motel along Central Avenue. In Room 4, wedged between drab sofas, was a hand-me-down coffee table of heavy plywood, covered with vinyl to approximate a wood grain. Room 6 was the same, but the sofas were drabber.

Davies was interrogating John Menzies, the second Flintlock pilot, in 4. Down a hallway which seemed to undulate under a thick, brown carpet, around a corner and up a half-flight of stairs, Vega was doing the same honors for Rosewood in 6. The local men stood at the doors.

"How long have you been doing this?" Vega pressed Rosewood.

"End of September last year," said Rosewood, sitting on one of the loveseats, knees pressed against the coffee table.

"All right," she said from her perch directly across from him, one foot resting on the table, "we're going to go over each of your deviation flights. I want as detailed a picture as you can give since joining Flintlock." She turned over a new leaf of her yellow legal pad. "To start with, how were you contacted, what did your training entail, and who were your contacts?" she asked. "Where did they get you from?"

"I've been flying for years. I was working for Cargota, a little cargo airline in South Dakota," he began, "flying into little airports that the big boys don't service."

"You're ex-military?"

"No. I was pretty wild in high school, and the air force wouldn't touch me as a pilot," he said, his face settling into a sullen, smoldering anger. "Navy either. I went to a flight school in Florida. Got my license in 2002. I was building time to try to get on with one of the majors."

"Building time?" she asked.

"Flight time," he said. "Hours, pilot-in-command hours." He indicated the pilot's log next to her on the sofa, his record of all his flights. As he deviated into a self-pitying monologue about how hard it was to break in with the "bigs," Vega flipped through his leather-bound pilot's log, which reminded her of a small photo album. "You need three thousand hours—a thousand pilot-in-command hours even to be considered, and even then . . . " he was saying.

"How did they contact you?" she asked, interrupting him.

"Mr. Fisher—"

"Alec Nash, or just Nash, please," she said. "Let's keep this factual. Stop pretending."

"Fine. Alec Nash showed up at my motel room in Kalispell, Montana."

"Alone?"

"No," he said. "There was another guy, from the company."

"What was his name?"

"Jardine," said Rosewood.

"Is that 'Mr. Jardine'," asked Vega, "or is that his real name?"

"I don't know," he replied, obviously truthfully.

"So . . . ?" she sighed.

"I'd applied to Flintlock months earlier, but hadn't heard anything. They said they'd been thinking over my resume."

"They just turned up at your room and offered you a job?" she asked incredulously. "What was the date?"

"October 15, last year. Yeah, they offered to hire me at the regular salary, but I could tell there was something else about it. They said I could make some extra money, too. Jardine said that after a year or so he could help move me up the ladder, get me a trial with one of the majors—it would be pilot-in-command time on a jet. It was an amazing, really excellent deal." He grinned at Vega, but she stared at him impassively.

"What did they say about what you'd have to do for the extra money?" she asked, jotting a few notes.

"My first thought was drugs, right? And I was super bummed that I'd probably have to pass on the chance. I didn't want to get involved with that...obviously. Too dangerous. But they said it wasn't that."

"You didn't ask more questions?"

"I was desperate," he pleaded. "I was going nowhere as a pilot. They were pushing all the right buttons: hours—*jet* hours—some prestige. I mean, it's a good gig with a good outfit."

"What did they say they wanted you to do for the extra money?"

"Fly people around. That was it. Really. No drugs. Just people, but on the QT."

"Did you ask why?" she said, flipping to a new page.

"Not really my business. But they told me it was mostly corporate stuff—potential mergers they didn't want anyone to know about, other things maybe they didn't want anyone to know about. That didn't sound so bad. Didn't sound like it was breaking the law. Maybe a little shady, but hey." He shrugged. "You do what you gotta do, am I right?"

Vega didn't look up.

"Also, they needed someone who knew the little airfields in the Midwest and West. And I did. They needed someone they could trust."

"Sounds like they needed someone they could own," said Vega.

"When you're both getting something you want, it's called a transaction," he replied defensively.

"How did they communicate with you?" she asked.

"Via the second company frequency, and it's not a strong signal, so it really only operated within about a hundred-mile radius of Rapid City. Menzies or I would cross through that airspace at least a couple times a week, usually more."

"When did you realize it wasn't all corporate skulduggery or ferrying whores to down-low parties?"

"I..." he said, faltering. "I had...*inklings*, I guess, after about six weeks that it wasn't corporate stuff they were having me do. There were two very quick in and out flights—

171

Seattle to Boulder, drop off two guys; wait, turn around to take them back West, to McMinnville airfield in Oregon. Then back to Boeing Field."

"Why was that suspicious?"

"Well, at first, it wasn't suspicious. Just annoying. I'd have to fly to Seattle from Omaha, then from Seattle to Boulder, wait for the guys to come back, then take them to Oregon; wait for them again, and then back to Seattle. Meanwhile, I was given this convoluted diverting protocol— all this stuff about where and when I was supposed to go VFR."

"Had you ever done anything like that before?"

"Not like that," he said emphatically.

"What made it suspicious instead of annoying?"

"The guys themselves. Most of the corporate guys I take around are older—fifties and more. They dress in business suits, wear their ties tight even during the trip. They carry briefcases and work on their laptops the whole time."

"But these guys were different?" she asked.

"Yeah, the two I picked up in Seattle were these young, scrubbed-looking guys, barely thirty. Maybe not even that. Fresh-faced, eager, Ivy League maybe. Not my type."

"OK," she said

"But not like executives' rich-kids on a jaunt either. Too straight arrow, not fucked up enough, you know?"

"Not really," she said, "but go on."

"They looked nervous. They said hello when they got in, confirmed the route, and then they didn't say anything more to me the whole trip."

"You didn't get their names?"

"Yeah, I did, but I'm pretty sure they were fake, which was also kind of a red flag."

"Why?"

"I said 'Cartwright?' to one of them as they both climbed on board 'cause that's the name I'd been given. The guy I asked looks at me blankly, like he had to think for a second, and then he points at the other guy, and says 'I'm Sawyer.' Like I'm supposed to know that, or maybe he wasn't too sure.

They talked to each other pretty much the whole time in these low whispers—like I can hear anything with my headset on! It seemed like they were rehearsing a play, or fine-tuning a sales pitch. They looked really nervous."

"You said that. There's no listing in your log," said Vega flipping its pages.

"I stopped writing down any of my diversions."

"So, holes in the timeline mean something?" she asked, putting down the log and turning to a reference file sitting next to her on the cushion. "When would this have been, November what?"

"Thirteen or fourteen, I think," he said.

Vega nodded, looking at her notes. She was finally getting something like a bird's eye view, but there were still massive gaps. Rosewood's testimony was largely confirmational.

Throughout the fall of 2016, the dark network had lain seemingly dormant, unlooked for in their denning places around the country. Beginning on November 12—four days after the general election—the network roused; and it had struck with cold-blooded efficiency and stealth. The FBI saw traces, knew overt acts—the murders of the Electors who refused to switch their votes, the subsequent murders of the Faithless Electors who had; yet it remained blind to many of the details.

For Vega, much like Imogen and Nettie digging through the PAC history, putting the pieces of her case together was like reassembling a bomb after a blast. She saw the results, could guess at motives; but she didn't know who'd lit the fuse, whether he'd strike again, or what the endgame was.

Rosewood, for instance, could tell Vega that he picked up two code-named men at Boeing Field on November 14 and delivered them to Boulder and then to Oregon. He could also note that as Janssen and Cardoso left Boulder aboard Rosewood's plane, Janssen had called someone and confirmed that they'd "closed the sale," and they were confident about "selling" someone else when they arrived in Oregon.

But having delivered them, Rosewood couldn't say what his passengers did upon arrival. Vega knew the outcome from her notes on gathered evidence: they had turned the Elector in Boulder and had murdered the Elector who wouldn't switch in Oregon.

In Oregon, Cardoso and Janssen met Don Meadows, a widower, at his vineyard, just outside Yamhill. He was a garrulous, affable man in his late sixties, with thinning white hair and a milkweed-down moustache. He had seemed genuinely pleased to have company, even at that hour of the night, and had accepted them unquestionably in their unspecified, quasi-governmental role. He showed them around his "cave," where he was perfecting his own *methode champenoise* for the Pinot Noir and Chardonnay grapes he grew, a process where the wine is fermented a second time in the bottle.

The bottles were arranged in racks of twenty, placed in their slots with the necks pointing down, so that sediment and spent yeast could sink down to be drained before the final bottling. The orderliness and serenity, the somber, church-like atmosphere impressed the visitors. As though by instinct, all three men spoke in whispers. Meadows had shown them the goggles and the leather apron with neck guard he wore whenever he turned the bottles to help settle the sediment.

"Why protective clothing?" Cardoso asked.

"Because the bottles are under pressure," said Meadows. "They can explode. And when they do, glass goes flying everywhere. Sometimes it sets the others around it off too, and now you've got multiple bottles exploding in all directions. It doesn't happen very often, young man," he offered reassuringly, patting Cardoso on the forearm, "but as you can imagine, the consequences of not being prepared on one of those rare occasions are pretty stark."

They talked good-naturedly for close to an hour. When they broached the subject of buying his Electoral vote, however, Meadows was initially dismissive, regarding it almost as a joke. When he realized they were serious, he grew angry.

"You're talking about something . . ." he searched for the word, "something Goddamn near *sacred*," he said, incredulous. "Who the hell are you?" he demanded. "We're talking about the Constitution!"

No amount of money would alter his perspective, no threat would unsettle him.

"Fuck you!" he shouted, still standing amid his bottles. "Do your fucking worst! You're not with the government! Who do you work for?"

Cardoso turned to Janssen, his expression that of someone who is genuinely sorry it's come to this. Janssen took Meadows by the shoulder. "Listen, Mr. Meadows," he said kindly.

But before he could say more, Meadows shrugged his shoulder and batted Janssen's hand away. He was surprisingly strong for one his age, but while he was distracted by Janssen, Cardoso calmly took out a stun gun and shocked him.

Meadows recoiled and contorted with the force of 50,000 volts of electricity. Gasping, he took a half step backward and fell over. Janssen picked up an empty champagne bottle and smashed it on the ground. It shattered, but the bottom of the bottle broke away in one piece. The jagged piece sat right by his foot.

Cardoso picked up Meadows and dragged him in front of the racks of full bottles. Clutching the bottom of the broken bottle in a gloved hand, Janssen stepped in and jagged it across Meadows' neck, just to the right of the Adam's apple. Blood erupted as the shard sliced across his carotid and jugular. Janssen pushed harder and then stepped back.

Meadows' eyes grew dimmer, and the geyser of purple blood from his neck gradually abated. On his way out the door, Janssen grabbed a full bottle from a table near the door—the bottle Meadows had offered to share with them after their tour. Cardoso stood at the door ready to shut it quickly. Janssen paused in the narrow opening and tossed the full bottle at the rack of patiently maturing sparkling wine. He dodged away from the open doorway as Cardoso slammed the door. The sound from inside was alarming as bottle after bottle exploded in a kind of chain reaction.

When the noise had stopped, Cardoso opened the door carefully and both men looked in. There was a heady, biting smell of yeast and wine. A hissing sound—the only sound in the room—issued from the walls and the floor as the bubbles subsided. Meadows had been cut to shreds. They closed the door and headed back to the little airport, where Rosewood waited.

"So, I got scared," was the only information Rosewood could relate to Vega, "when they came back. They'd left the plane with that transparent swagger guys have when they're eager but nervous, ya know? But they came back pumped up—I mean *jacked*—like they'd just won a championship game or something. And I'd swear there was blood spattered on Cartwright's shirt." He paused and looked down, his eyes seeming to see it all clearly. Then, in a far-off voice, he began again. "And it got really scary," Rosewood related, "about a month later, I'd say."

"What date?" Vega asked. "Can you be precise?"

"No," he said.

"I think you can," she rejoined.

"December 18," he mumbled, eyes still directed downward.

"The day before the Electoral College met for their official vote on December 19," Vega offered. "When the Electors who had switched their votes were murdered."

"But I didn't put it together until afterwards," he entreated.

"What *did* you put together?"

"That my passengers were involved somehow; that they might've done the killing. But I had no idea why I was taking people anywhere. I swear."

"Tell me what happened," Vega said gently.

"I went to Boeing Field again and picked up the same two guys there to take them back to Boulder. I left them there overnight while I flew on to Springfield, Illinois, where I picked up three guys. I took them up to St. Paul and dropped them there, where I think Johnnie—"

"You mean the second pilot cleared on the frequency, John Menzies?" interjected Vega.

"Yeah. He picked them up, and then took them to Chicago; waiting again, and then he dropped them back in Springfield while I took the two from Seattle home."

"And so: What did you do when you did put it together?" Vega asked. "Will Menzies confirm?"

He nodded, unsure how to begin. "Yeah. If he's cooperating, I'm sure he can confirm those dates. 'Cause that's when we realized something serious was going on."

"You two discussed this at the time?" she asked.

"Later we did. But then we didn't get called for any VIP diversions for a while, and we thought maybe that was it. But last month we each did a VIP-divert on March 10th, me to this little field southwest of Bakersfield in California, then back to Seattle...and as you know, on to Fairmont; and Menzies went to Aspen. Apart from that and waiting to pick up Cooper," he said, "there's been nothing going on."

Vega furrowed her brow as she wrote the date. What had happened in Southern California and Aspen? she wondered. And to whom? She underlined the date and places twice.

"These guys we were flying," he continued, "they weren't involved in secret merger talks, and they sure as shit weren't corporate types." He took a deep breath before continuing. "The guys on that trip from Seattle had looked nervous and green—like I said—that first time I picked them up, but there was something different about them when I picked them up that second time. They looked flat, dull-eyed, but *stoked*, like they couldn't wait for something. I don't know. They just seemed really different.

"And those guys from Illinois? All business. And they were armed. I saw a rifle and a handgun in their duffel when they unzipped it to get something. That's all I know," he said.

"That's all I've done...just take people where they need to go."

"That's all you know?" she asked.

"I do know that I'm supposed to be back in Seattle on April 19."

"And you didn't think to report any of this?" asked Vega.

"What would I be reporting? What would I say? And what good would it do? The murders of those Electors or whatever was all over the news. Johnnie and I could put two and two together. We'd be implicated. Maybe the next flight brings someone who kills *me*."

"Yeah," said Vega. "That's what I meant about being owned." She closed up her pad and went to Room 6 to confer with Davies and corroborate dates with Menzies.

25

Despite a stated go-slow approach, President Moore had wasted no time in some areas. He had nominated, and the Senate had subsequently quickly approved, a record number of judges and there were more the way. There were whispers that through his Chief of Staff Quantrelle, Moore was creating a private "kitchen" cabinet of appointments operating outside normal channels. The FBI background checks and vetting had turned up nothing on Eliot. Senate hearings would begin soon, but they were expected to be perfunctory. Eliot was a Senate colleague, and therefore unlikely to be pressed. Even if he were, the Senate had the votes to confirm.

The investigation, Imogen was sure, would be the next victim of these ruthless people. Crueler still, an Eliot regime would probably institute reviews which would expose all the work the three unmasketeers had done over the past six months. Their informants, their leads and all that they knew would be revealed to the dark network, allowing them to clean house and spin the investigation as something other than it was.

Far from the tumult, Imogen and Nettie sat facing one another at either end of a table set up at the far side of Imogen's office. They stared at one another over grubby piles of Faithless Elector Task Group files, FEC audits and background files for Sovereign Caucus, the Opportunity Initiative, V^3 and the Forefathers Institute—17 full Bankers boxes. Like Vega, she and Nettie were reconstructing fragments. Once again, Imogen wasn't just looking for a needle in a haystack; she was trying to find out who had put it there.

* * *

It was like driving around with a body in the trunk, he thought. The box full of documents he'd taken as insurance rested disquietingly under a blanket in the trunk of his car, an ominous pressure. And like a dead body, he wondered how to get rid of it. Since leaving the Forefathers Institute in the fall before the election, Mason Brandenburg had been frightened.

His hope and fear lay in uncertainty. His previous bosses couldn't be sure his resignation was for anything other than his stated reason of wanting to work closer to home. He had been part of their window dressing as a legitimate enterprise, their Mr. Clean. He hoped they still regarded him as the dupe who blithely signed off on everything Quantrelle had put in front of him. He had tumbled onto what the dark network was doing, through Forefathers Institute, because he was a meticulous accountant. He had also been meticulous in covering up the fact that he had found anything, but he couldn't be sure he'd been successful.

What had seemed like security for him and his family in the fall felt like a liability now that some of the very men he worried about *were* the government. The box of documents stayed in his car, travelling with him from work, to home, to meetings. It seemed probable that his former bosses were watching him, looking for anything that might point to his knowing more than he had let on. It was probable that in addition to being watched, his phone was tapped, so "dumping the body," as he had come to think of it, presented great difficulty. Now that Senator Eliot was to be the Attorney General, if he reached out to the FBI, they'd know. If he went to an attorney, or opened a safe deposit box account, they'd know. He was afraid of what might happen to him or to his wife. He wasn't even sure if the car was the best place for them, but so long as there were no official inquiries into goings on at Forefathers, his somnambulant normalcy was his best protection.

* * *

Don Weir sat down with Deputy Director Bill Dyer in his office. "I think it's time to reach out to Reed," he said, uncomfortable in his tight collar. "I don't like it, but I see no alternative. We will need names, and we'll need testimony."

"Mmm," Dyer grunted as he leafed again through Weir's report from Vega.

"We have testimony that a pair of Seattle-based contractors is responsible for turning the Elector in Colorado, and subsequently killing her," Weir continued. "We also have information that that same pair is responsible for killing the Elector in Oregon. They're probably responsible for the murder of that grad student, and the attempt to kill his Professor too—Calder."

Dyer nodded but said nothing.

"We know less about another probable group based in Springfield which turned the Elector in Minnesota and killed him; and they probably murdered the Elector in Iowa City and those two Judges of Election in Chicago."

"But we still don't know who gave the orders."

"Well, it seems that Reed and Nash gave the orders. What we need to know is: who were *they* working for?"

"And we're no nearer cracking that," said Dyer, laying down the report and looking up at Weir.

"Not without Reed," he said. "And we know something's planned for April 19 or 20. The pilots have told us they're on alert for the 19th."

"Do you think Reed knows what's happening on April 19?"

"There's only one way to find out, sir."

"But if we make a deal with him, having made plea deals with their low-level operatives, and still can't get anyone higher or stop whatever's going to happen on April 20, we'll have failed the Bureau and the nation. Whoever's really running all this will control the country for the next four years."

"We'll've dismantled the network," Weir offered.

"Is that enough, Don?" said Dyer, presuming the answer No.

* * *

In Washington's Eisenhower Executive Building, in the Vice President's Ceremonial Office, the principal executive, Vice President David Carr, was feeling all-too ceremonial. Though himself a product of government, he was accustomed to action and progress in his professional life. Coming young to Congress, he had spent his life in politics, climbing from member of the local Pennsylvania School Board at just 22, to Township council at 26, State Representative and then Congressman. Now, at just 42 years old, he was Vice President of the United States; but far from power and influence flowing to him, he felt as impotent as if he'd run headlong into a filibuster.

He stalked the room's perimeter like a truculent prisoner in a cell. His wife Susan reclined on one of the office couches, bare feet tucked under her as though she were kneeling on the cushion. After another turn around the cramped room, he finally perched himself opposite her on the edge of another sofa.

"Some of this inaction's just the nature of being Vice President, I suppose. Right?" he said, giving voice to his interminable rumination.

"But it's not as though you're biding your time, waiting your turn. It's worrying you," said Susan. They had married right out of college, and she had been with him the entire journey. "You think there's something more going on, don't you?"

"I do," he said, staring into her blue eyes.

Historically, Vice President was probably the simplest, most boring job in the United States. Will Rogers had once quipped that, "All the Vice President has to do is get up every

182

morning and ask, 'How is the president?'" Recent administrations, though, starting with Clinton-Gore, had begun carving out a more robust policy role for the VP: Cheney had been active for Bush, as had Biden for Obama. When accepting the Veep's office, Carr had made it clear he was open and willing to take an active role in the Moore Administration.

But their seemingly enthusiastic embrace of his offer was really a way of smothering it. Perhaps they were just insincere—not unknown among politicians—or they didn't know what to do with him. Or it was something different. The internal alarms he was hearing had him wondering what lay behind the uncomfortable silences whenever he was together with Quantrelle and Marek and President Moore. It was as though they were filling the time until he left and the real work could begin. And there was a waft of caution among the members of Moore's private cabinet whenever Carr spoke with them, as though they were afraid of letting something slip or betraying a confidence.

"I know I said it before," he said as much to himself as to Susan, "but it's like there're two administrations," he said, "and I'm barely part of one of them. I can't believe there's been nothing in the papers about it, but there hasn't."

Susan pursed her lips and frowned. Finally, she said, "Is it possible you're getting caught up in the intrigue and conspiracy theories that *are* in the news?"

He nodded, as though he were just getting to that point. "I wish that was all," he said. "But just because there's a conspiracy theory, doesn't mean they're not conspiring against you."

His instincts and his wife's insight, had served him well down the years. He always knew when the mic was live, which camera to speak to, and which way the wind blew; and he knew how to stay composed when the wind howled. He could sense the difference between calm and becalmed; and he was attuned to things going on out of earshot.

"It can't be that they don't want you on the ticket next time," she said. "For God's sake, we're the ones pulling Mr.

Spontaneous' poll numbers up. You've made it clear you're a team player; that you're not going to run against him at the next election. What do you think they're up to?" she asked.

"There's just too much maneuvering," he said as he fell back into the couch. "Quantrelle and Marek are the keys. Bringing in a lot of new faces. Moore, I just don't know."

"Well, if they are fucking around and hiding stuff," she said, "they'll get caught. The press is into everything. Phones, emails, cameras everywhere. And if Quantrelle and Marek are hustling, no one'll believe we didn't also know what was happening. And down we go. These assholes can get lobbying jobs, or go to work for some rich wing nut. But we're out on a limb." She uncurled and sat forward on the couch, stockinged feet on the floor. "You need Salter," she said.

He nodded. "How do we speak with him without raising suspicions, without Secret Service and whoever else knowing about it?"

"I'm thinking," she said.

* * *

Rosewood was released to continue under cover as an FBI informant. He now carried a phone that recorded and transmitted his every word. He flew that Friday on his scheduled unscheduled diversion to Fairmont. Reed didn't show, and the little Elite 500 took off. On the second company frequency (and across his FBI phone) Rosewood squawked: "This is FL-1. Cooper negative. Resuming," and the plane had flown directly to Omaha, ending that week's work shift.

When the Postman took the call that told him Reed had not come in for a third time—now six weeks after Moore had been installed as President—he pounded the heavy desk in his study so hard the Tiffany lamp rattled in its base. "Do you have *any* leads?" he asked when he finally calmed down. "Whoever took care of Fisher," he said, using Nash's work name, "really fucked us." He paused to listen. "I know what I *said!*" he shouted. "I guess I just thought the people who worked for me had some Goddamn sense, that's all."

He sat back in his severe, high-backed leather chair, staring at his antique gun collection on the far wall. As he listened, he closed his eyes and massaged his left temple. "Right," he said finally, his eyes still closed. "So, if he's running—and we should assume he is—his only play is with the Feds. You're tracking the redhead and the black kid from IT, right? And you're on that professor's email and phone. Anything?" He made a sour face.

"Look," he said, "Cooper's only play is to Trager and her crew. He'd know, or at least be pretty sure, that we're watching her; so he'd know that he had to make contact outside our sightlines somehow." He was silent for a moment, listening, then blurted: "I don't know! I'm thinking out loud! Feel free to jump in any time," he sneered. "How else could Cooper get a message out?"

He closed his eyes again and smoothed his thinning, gray hair with a massive hand. Suddenly, his eyes darted open: "That reporter!" he said triumphantly. "Salter—Hugh Salter. Cooper used him before. They have a back channel. Cooper could get word to Salter, and *he* could get a message to Trager." He listened once more. "Do you have any other ideas?" he asked. "Are we watching Salter? Then *start* watching him. We're coming down to the wire, and we can't have this hanging over us!" As he hung up, his face changed from a mixture of curdled disappointment and disgust to one of triumphal satisfaction.

* * *

Imogen and Nettie had spent two days among audit files for the Sovereign Caucus, Opportunity Initiative, V^3, and the Forefathers Institute PAC, as well as a host of Super PACs and Leadership PACs associated with them. The rest of the team were examining less obviously related PACs, looking for patterns among the directors and sponsors, collaborations, cash flow, use of media and agencies. They knew from

Nettie's earlier data-mining that Francis Trebor, one of the assassins Calder killed in the stairwell, was listed as Forefathers' "custodian," and Frank Reed, using the alias Peter Snyder, was the "agent" for Sovereign. Allen Covington, another dead conspirator, was listed as Opportunity's "custodian," and the suspicious murder-suicide Tim Hayward was listed for V^3. Except Forefathers Institute, each PAC had come into being sometime in early to mid-2012, and each had been audited every year up to 2017. They had generated a staggering amount of paper.

The amount of money churning through the PACs was staggering, too. Money flowed in, and then it flowed out to cover all manner of things, from travel to consultants, administrative expenses, fundraising, polling, issue or attack ads, rallies and—of course—small payments to candidates. Modest, that is, so that there was no question of influencing politics with sheer cash. The travel, administration and consultants became the focus for Imogen's team. Every PAC—even their legitimate, above-board "control" files—had audit findings, but they were relatively trivial, and were dealt with in the published Final Audit Reports.

The Final Audit Reports online, they found, were not a good window onto what was really occurring. They were public documents, and much of the background was absent, which was where the musty boxes came in. As Nettie and Imogen began digging, some of the findings called out in the audits were clearly miscalculations or negligence—easily remedied.

But even when a finding rose above the threshold of an oversight, or a seemingly honest mistake, the summary note to the final filing would read something like, "in response to the draft interim audit report, the PAC has amended its reports to disclose misstatement of accounts..." or its "...inadequate disclosure of expenditures or missing information." A do-over. All of which could be further finessed. Because much of the staff was on a merry-go-round, there would also often be a note in the detail stating that "current committee representatives were not involved in this activity and were unable to provide any specific detail."

Reading this purblind oversight, Nettie would look across the stack of files and sigh to Imogen, "Well, isn't *that* convenient?"

Full undisclosure, they named it.

Going through the physical notes leading up to the creation of a "draft interim audit" often gave the best leads, but they were also the most time-consuming. It was remarkable how many "findings" dropped away as a report was drafted, redrafted in committee, reviewed and redrafted again by the Office of General Counsel, and again when presented to the PAC's attorneys in preparation for the Final Audit Report. Audits typically lasted two to three weeks if all the documents were available. But they could run to months in chaotic PACs, like Sovereign Caucus.

Late in the first day, Nettie slammed a report on the table and stood up. "It's like the FEC's their accountant, not their auditor," she said pacing back and forth.

"What do you mean?" asked Imogen, looking up from her own dismal pile.

"An accountant looks over your books, tells you what you did wrong and how to fix it so that the auditor will pass you. The accountant works *for* you and *with* you to make sure your books are clean. I'm looking at the back-and-forth between the FEC audit committee, the OGC and PAC counsel, and it's like exchanges you'd see with an accountant. I have yet to see *anything* where auditors flagged something for investigation."

* * *

"I think it's time to reach out to Reed and offer him something," Dyer told Vega and Weir.

"Offer him what?" asked Vega warily.

"This is going to be a long process," he replied. "To open, we can tell him that if he works with us, we'll protect him from the death threats these guys will have issued. But he has to give us something to start with—and we have to confirm it first, so we know it's in good faith."

"And if he produces?" asked Vega.

"Then we'll talk about plea deals." He paused. "There's something else. He wants to go through Imogen Trager. What're your thoughts?"

"I think she should only talk with him with me present—or you," Vega said. "It's not that I don't trust her—"

"—Of course not."

"But I've conducted fifteen, maybe twenty interviews where we needed to get something from the perp, but nothing like this. *I'd* be a little intimidated, and she doesn't have anything like as much experience."

"But Reed has to feel comfortable," said Dyer. "I want you with her during any communications with Reed, but she takes the lead."

"Understood, sir."

Vega caught Imogen just outside her office. "You ready?" she asked.

They walked into Imogen's office together.

"Agent Annette Sartain," Vega said with a smile. "You've been seconded to the Faithless Elector Task Force. Welcome aboard. Here's the authorization. Signed by Dyer. You need to sign the order below, accepting the transfer."

Nettie couldn't find a pen fast enough.

"Annette," said Vega kindly. "Nettie, if I may. Before you sign, you need to understand that this isn't just deskwork now. It'll be dangerous, too. These guys have killed ten Electors, a grad student, a reporter, a Senator's aide—and a handful of their own people, one of them while he was in FBI custody. We don't know who we can trust in our own Bureau. They've killed an FBI Special Agent. They've tried to kill Imogen twice. One of the people we'll potentially be dealing with is the guy who tried to kill her earlier this year."

She paused, looking straight into Nettie. "They probably killed the President, though we don't have proof of that...yet.

They're not sentimental about the sanctity of human life. Least of all, mine or yours."

Nettie looked between Imogen and Amanda, standing expectantly in front of her. "Isn't this what we're here for?" she asked.

"Yes," said Imogen.

Nettie signed and handed over the form. It was like any other employment contract, but it could also be her death warrant.

"We keep Dyer in the loop," said Vega. "Agents Guthrie and Davies also work with us, reporting to me. You'll meet them later when I can arrange it. And Rawley Sims from the FAA. But as far as anyone else is concerned—even within the Bureau—you're still working on a special election project with Imogen, and she and I have no professional connection. OK?"

"Will there be field work?"

"Yes," said Vega, "field work and file work both. We have to nail the case as many ways as we can, and make it stick. If we fail, not only will the country be run by a group of murderous thugs, but you'll be lucky only to be out of a job." She glanced at Imogen. "And if Imogen's experience is anything to go by, even if we succeed, we'll all be lucky to *keep* our jobs."

* * *

Hugh Salter picked up. The network's chief producer, Jeanne Hammond, was brisk. Though she was calling from two floors above, he sat to attention and quickly stuffed away the burner phone he'd bought to talk to Imogen Trager.

"Call from the White House," she said. "The Vice President's social secretary."

Salter started.

"Asked for you particularly. She said Mrs. Carr might join the call." She gave him the number and rang off.

Salter made the call, hoping against experience that it was a lead somewhere.

"This is Deputy Assistant to the Vice President, Georgia Desmond," she informed him when he called back. "And Communications Director to the Second Lady," she added. Desmond spoke rapidly, familiarly. It was to be "an inside look," she called it, at life at Number One Observatory Circle, the Vice President's official residence.

Not a political story. No beans would be spilled. No on-the-spot scoops to camera for the indefatigable Hugh Salter. More like a high-end celebrity feature for another part of the network. Lots of coverage of the immaculate wife amid the 18th-century furnishings. Might work for an Easter slot, perhaps?

The network producer had made it down the two floors in remarkably quick time, and was loitering by his door. He turned on the speakerphone so she could hear.

Georgia managed to be both brusque and fawning down the line. She was just telling him how graciously the Vice President was offering this exclusive access when Susan Carr joined the call.

"Hugh," she said, "I really hope you can make this happen."

Muttering the occasional "uh huh," Salter signaled to his director.

"I've been thinking about asking you to do something like this since that first time David and I met you here at Number One. Such a lovely afternoon."

"Yes," he said standing up. "When you were just moving in, I think."

"Yes," said Mrs. Carr. "Seems years ago already."

Salter scribbled on a pad. He was about to show what he'd written to his producer, but tore it off and wadded it up instead. He'd never been to the VP's house. He had no idea what they were talking about or why they were lying.

Thinking on his feet now, Salter said, "I think it's a great idea," he said with the initial enthusiasm that reporters always show, however unpromising the story. "Yes, absolutely . . . of course," he vamped. "I'd really like to come and talk about this before I go on vacation Monday, but it might . . ."

"That would be lovely," Mrs. Carr interrupted. "Georgia, can you book Mr. Salter in tomorrow for tea?"

"Well, you have . . ." Georgia began.

"—Good, I'll see you then, Hugh." And Mrs. Carr was gone.

"Excellent," said Georgia. "Four o'clock." And that was that.

Next day, as he reached the house, Georgia walked out to meet him and shook his hand warmly. Like her employer and friend, Susan Carr, she was in her early forties and favored smart pastel suits. She also sported the kind of deep tan attainable only by those who spent inordinate amounts of time at tennis in the Florida sunshine.

There was a disarming intimacy about the way she spoke that put him on his guard. She held his hand a moment longer than he expected as she turned him toward the house and ushered him inside past the Secret Service agents. She'd only been in the job for six weeks, but already this doyenne of Mifflin County had acclimatized. She was sturdy, loyal and intelligent, bristling with Bryn Mawr intensity.

"What we have in mind is a profile first of the house—its history, previous occupants—and then something about the family. I would start your tour on the beautiful, wraparound porch, but it *is* a bit chilly today," she said, leaning close to him. "You can see that by many standards, this house is rather cozy. We'll just go through to the dining room.

"Billy," she trilled brightly, addressing one of the Secret Service agents, "I'm just going to show Mr. Salter the house. Anywhere off limits?"

"Just the study, ma'am," he replied mechanically.

"Of course," and, almost whispering to Salter, "that's off-limits even to me, so don't feel you're being singled out."

He smiled.

As they passed from the dining room back into the reception hall, Susan Carr called from the balcony above. "Hugh!" she said. "So good to see you! I'll join you in the Garden Room."

David Carr stood up from the sofa as Desmond and Salter entered the Garden Room. "Hugh, great to see you!" the Vice President said. "Can we get you anything?"

"Not unless you . . ."

"Let's have some tea. Georgia, you'll join us?"

Susan Carr walked in, and they all sat down in front of the large windows, a cold light bleaching the room.

"It's good of you to think of me for this," Salter began, but Carr held up a hand.

"We can speak freely," he said. "We're among friends."

Georgia smiled.

"Yes, of course," Salter said, putting away his notepad. "How're you settling in? Looks as though the opulence suits you very well."

Carr looked doubtful. Characteristically, he began in mid-thought: "It's not the house, it's the Administration. I'm getting the cold shoulder."

"An old story with Vice Presidents, isn't it?" Salter offered.

"I don't have proof."

"Of what?" asked Salter.

"Of anything. Obviously, there's been some press speculation about the appointments. But sometimes that's the first I hear of them."

"Vice Presidents are often . . ."

"Yes, but it's more than that."

"He's pleased with some of the initiatives," Susan Carr bright-sided.

"Yes, *some*, but most of the time I'm being systematically excluded."

Nothing more was said as tea arrived and was poured.

"So there's a lot going on, Mr. Vice President?" he asked skeptically when the steward had gone out and closed the door.

"And none of it thanks to me. Whenever I'm in the Oval Office or meeting with the President, I get the feeling they're just waiting for me to leave. Like there's this whole agenda they need to get to, but I can't hear it."

"What *do* you hear?"

"If I hear anything at all, it's questions. Practically interrogation. The other day, Chief of Staff Quantrelle heard I'd had lunch with William Sims—Bill and I were freshman Congressmen the same year, both from Pennsylvania—and Quantrelle wanted to know *why* I was meeting with a Democrat. When I said he was a friend, Quantrelle looked genuinely perplexed."

"Well . . ." Salter began.

"He demanded to know what we talked about. Aggressively, almost threatening. What the hell business is it of his? I said we did some catching up, as friends do—wives, kids, a bit about some of the newer Pennsylvania delegates, how I was adjusting to being VP."

"And what did Quantrelle say?" asked Salter.

"He warned me about 'back-channel communications.' When I protested and called him out for his presumption, he shut me down. He says: 'Everything goes through me. Got it?' He actually poked me in the chest with his finger, the fuck. Then he walked away into the Oval Office, shutting the door behind him, presumably to tell teacher."

"Jeez . . ."

"And if I protested, I know which one of us Moore would back."

"Has he ever acted like that before?"

"No," Susan Carr answered. "He usually puts on this fake, solicitous air, the kind people use when they're having to deal with some senile, imbecilic great-uncle at a family event. It's that knowing look that says two things at the same time: 'I want you all to see that I'm showing proper respect' *and* 'I want you to understand that this whole charade is as wasted and distasteful to me as it is to you.'"

"Hugh," she continued, "you don't know how much this means to us, to find a friend in the press."

Salter sat back in his chair, his brow knitted. He ran a hand through his well-kept hair. "So how can I help?" he asked.

And so the conversation ebbed, until Georgia Desmond broke the silence. "There's nothing we can really point to, but"—here she glanced at the Vice-President and Mrs. Carr before proceeding—"we think they're keeping tabs on David. That there's a special detail tracking him. It's as though they're waiting for a slip. We think they're doing more in the background than anyone knows or is being reported. We think Quantrelle's concern about back-channels might be the key. It's possible that Quantrelle's worried that if David established something on his own—which he wasn't with Bill—it might draw attention to his, Marek's and Moore's *sub rosa* activities. Because that's their triumvirate.

"Moreover, David's noticed that there are a lot of deputy- and under-secretaries with direct access to the President and Quantrelle. Not Cabinet secretaries—most of whom were put in place by President Redmond as presidential appointees. And even some Schedule C staff." She looked back at the Carrs to see if she was leaving anything out.

"I see," said Salter.

"Hugh," Desmond appealed, "it could very well be that there's nothing nefarious going on, but little things are piling up."

"Why not take your concerns to the FBI?" asked Salter, immediately feeling the naivety of the question.

Desmond looked at him dubiously. "We don't know that they've cleaned house properly yet."

"And Hugh," said Mrs. Carr, "we so trust you and your investigations."

"OK," he said, unsure how to take the compliment. "I'll start poking around, see what I can come up with. But you'll have to tell me about the 'little things' first. And we need to cover the business of my life-of-the-veep-and-family piece. I'll have to tell my producer something. She'll be wanting to send in a crew as soon as possible, so I'll have to stall. Either you have to withdraw—we fall out over some technicality of permissions—or we bring her in on this, let her know that it's an investigation, and allow me the time to follow up. We've worked together a long time, she trusts me."

"If you say," replied the Vice President.

"Ms. Desmond," said Salter, "can we schedule a couple more background visits for cover? Just to talk about the filming—and you can tell me about the 'little things'."

As he made his way back to the office, south along Mass Avenue, Salter wondered whether he was being played again. "We *so* trust you and your reporting"? The lady doth protest so much. Can any Vice President be that frank with a journalist? Well, it seemed he just had. All off the record, of course—Salter still had an empty notebook, and no proof that any of this conversation had ever taken place—but they were playing a dangerous game.

If he chose, he could dig a series of scoops out of this. One report and the Veep's team would have to respond, which would strengthen the credibility of the original story and snowball nicely. But then, if the tone of the meeting had been extraordinary, the Administration was extraordinary too. And they were right about Quantrelle: he was a shit. Anyone could see that. Way too much influence, too assured for a stand-in Chief to an accidental President.

But still. Were they playing him? Getting him to dig for information where they couldn't? Were the Carrs above deceiving him for some purpose of their own? Probably not. Did they have a grudge against him personally? Something in one of his reports? Were they part of some dark scheme as well?

And yet, if there really was despair amongst the exquisite chairs and sideboards—perhaps even afraid for their lives as they smiled and took their toast and tea—then what? What would they do? They would need an outsider on the trail—and they'd give him as much help as they could.

26

"This is Hugh."

"Hugh, it's Imogen. Listen, we need to contact Reed. He's sweated long enough, don't you think?"

"We all have," he said.

"Can I dictate a message to you?" she asked. Vega and Nettie were beside her, a team within a team within a team. "You know the address to send to."

"OK," he said, as though used to sending messages on behalf of the FBI. "Go ahead." He typed:

From: Agent Imogen Trager.

We have considered your offer and are potentially open to a plea deal in exchange for information and testimony. This will be under the terms laid out in the legal charter of the FBI. The terms offered, at our discretion, will be confidential and subject to revocation in case of breach, perjury or secondary convictions.
Before making any plea deal, we shall require a show of goodwill from you. We need to know how many of your associates you are able to name, and that you will be willing to testify.
Before any deal is struck, you will be required to tell us the names and precise locations of your associates in either Springfield, IL, or Seattle, WA. Only if they are successfully apprehended, will we discuss terms for a deal in detail. You may signal me via the cell number discussed.

Salter clicked send, just as the network producer knocked on the door.

"Anything?" she asked about his meeting with the Vice President and family.

"I'm not sure," he responded, minimizing the email screen. "Nothing we can run with right now, but there may be some potential leads. There might be more than just a routine puff piece. I sensed real tension between their camp and the President. I've set it up to go back for more background on this puff piece, but don't arrange anything formally yet."

Ever the newswoman, Jeanne wanted to know more: "What do you think's going on?" she asked.

"Let me look into a few things before we talk to the news team or anyone else. So far, we could only run with 'new VP at odds with Moore Administration,' but I think there's more. Give me a few days?"

* * *

Quantrelle stood in the converted shipping bay, listening to the daily non-report on Imogen, Calder, Trey Kelly and his friend Mason. The clean-room sheen with which the project began two months earlier had dulled. Dirt and dust had crept back into the corners of the bay. Spent energy bar wrappers, empty cans of Red Bull and takeout containers littered the area.

"We have a new target," he said to them. "We're going to stay on these four, but we're adding Hugh Salter, the reporter. I want to know who calls him, where he goes, who he sees."

"OK," said Tweedledum.

"Here's his cell phone number and main email account." Quantrelle handed over a small slip of paper.

"Want us to do a little spear-phishing on his email? See if we can get in there?"

"Walk me through it," said Quantrelle. "What's the risk of exposure?"

"Well," began 'Dim, "we'll have to look at the protocols in place for the news org's mail system and then probe a bit."

"Who does he work for?" 'Dum asked.

"What?" said Quantrelle.

"What news org?" Dim, added helpfully.

"Jesus," said Quantrelle. "He's on TV giving a report most nights. He's one of CNN's lead correspondents and he's been reporting on the presidency for years." He looked at them incredulously. "I mean, I fucking hate him, but I know who the fuck he is!"

"Huh," said Tweedledum, tearing an energy bar in half and stuffing it into his mouth. "OK. I'd guess CNN has a pretty good firewall defense, and good detectors." He turned to Dim: "We might be able to do like a clone-phishing expedition, but it'd be best if we had someone on the inside." He turned back to Quantrelle. "Do we have anyone?"

Quantrelle shook his head, no.

Tweedledum jumped in: "Let us get to work on his phone right away, and we'll look into the admin structure of the place. Maybe there's some low-level guy somewhere who emails everyone; or someone careless in HR."

"Could they trace it back to you?" Quantrelle asked.

"Not a chance—between the VPN and the proxies, we're ghosts. That's the good news and the bad news. If they see traffic that's untraceable, they'll think it's suspicious, ya know? Just cause they can't get us, doesn't mean they can't figure out what we're trying to do." He picked up the uneaten portion of Dim's energy bar and popped it into his mouth.

* * *

Safe behind his own Virtual Private Network and his army of proxy servers, Frank Reed sat in the kitchen of his Airbnb in Cincinnati and read Salter's email. It was going as planned. It had taken longer than he'd predicted, but his was still the first move, and he still held all the cards.

Or did he? He re-read the email: *"you will be required to tell us the names and precise locations of your associates in either Springfield, IL, or Seattle, WA."*

198

"How do they know about those guys?" he asked aloud. He stared for a moment at his stacks of report files and reached for the Seattle folder. Out of habit, he began skimming through, nodding to no one as he looked them over. Finally, he reached for the drop phone lying on the granite countertop.

"This is Imogen Trager," she answered, as she flicked a switch that put the phone through a speaker so that she, Vega and Nettie could all hear.

"This is Frank Reed," he began. "I've read the email. I can give you the Seattle names, and dossiers on them."

"And the Illinois group?" she asked.

"You made it clear it was my choice. This is it."

"But you *could* give us Illinois if you wanted—if you wanted better terms...*if* we start to deal with you?"

"You've asked for evidence of my *bona fides* and my faith in you. I give you something you want, and then you offer something I require. Let's stick to the script."

"I just need to know what else you will or won't be able to deliver," she said. "I'd like to do my best for you, but you have to do your best for me."

"We have a long road ahead. It's cathouse rules, Agent. I'll show you some tit, and then we can talk about what you think it's worth. And if you wanna see more, or you wanna do more, you're gonna have to pay."

All three women looked at one another with disgust. Vega mimed removing her gun from its holster and executing the speakerphone.

Imogen shook her head, swallowing against the sourness rising in her throat. "All right, Frank," she said finally, "show us some tit: names, addresses and phone numbers for the Seattle group. How many do you have there?"

"Two."

"I need names, dates and activities."

There was a long pause. Finally, he said: "you're looking for Eric Janssen and Dan Cardoso—"

"—Codenames Cartwright and Sawyer?" she interrupted.

"Um, yes."

"Which is which?" she asked quickly.

"Janssen is Cartwright, and Cardoso is Sawyer."

"Good. Are they responsible for the murder-suicide of Timothy Hayward and Samantha Banks back in 2012?"

How did she know this? She knew code names, she knew the operation had been going on years. What else? Reed was ruffled.

"You said—" he began

"—*You* said you'd give us the skinny on the Seattle op. Will you or won't you?" Across from Imogen, Nettie looked on in admiration. She turned to register her astonishment with Vega, who was smiling and nodding her approval. "And I'm still waiting to hear about Hayward and his girl."

"I'm trying," he said, "but I have to look things up."

"Fine," she said calmly. "You have files? That's promising. Useful to us. The more you can give us... Let's take it at your pace, then. Slow as you like."

"First, well...this is the best information I have." His tone was now resigned, even apologetic. "I've been hibernating for a couple of months. My information may be eight, ten weeks out of date."

"We'll see how good it is soon enough," Imogen rejoined. "What's the last known address of Eric Janssen?" Reed gave it, and the last phone number he had, along with where they picked up their monthly SIM card replacements.

Despite having said he could take his time, Imogen made a habit of asking the next question before he was quite done answering the previous one. Cardoso's address, yes. The murder-suicide in 2012 had been Janssen and Cardoso's work, yes. No one else with them? They'd been taken on in early 2012. Reed had himself recruited them?

When they were done, Imogen concluded: "If this pans out, we'll be in touch." She held her hand poised over the disconnect button.

"It will," said Reed, sounding like he wanted to reassert himself. "Listen, I'm curious how you know so much."

"Let's stick to the script, Frank—cathouse rules: your rules. And a working girl doesn't give a shit how the guy who's fucking her made his money." And she hung up.

* * *

"I don't think we have anything to worry about with Imogen," Vega was telling Weir. "She was great. Confused him and left him worried that we knew *way* more than we're letting on. She never let him get on the front foot."

"Did she tell him about the pilots?"

"Nope," said Vega, "but he might be able to guess at this stage."

"Right. Well, good. Keep him guessing," he said, scanning the report of the interview.

"I'm leaving for Seattle tonight," she said. "Is there anyone known to you personally that we can trust to begin surveillance out there?" she asked.

"I think so, I'll get you their contacts and begin the authorizations for them to liaise with us. You'll have it by the time you get there."

"Thank you. Before I leave, I'm going to get Trey over at IT to begin running a historical trace of the last known numbers the Seattle guys were using. Reed also gave us the location where they picked up their new SIM cards, so we should be able to go backward and create a timeline and map of their movements, the way he and Gen did with the East Coast guys. But we need NSA for that part, don't we?"

"Yeah," he nodded. "I'll clear it with NSA . . . quietly."

* * *

Reed was seething about how his opening bid had gone. The redheaded bitch had seen to it that he never held the initiative. It was infuriating that the only person he could trust was someone who hated him, and he was particularly worried that he had to put his trust in her. He had envisioned a counter-scenario in which emotion would play no part.

His vision, decidedly unrealized, had been a meeting of minds, one of mutual respect and understanding between professionals. He realized that his error had been in crediting Trager with the wit to understand that there were soldiers, and there were civilians in all this. Soldiers—operatives—knew the game, knew you were sometimes up, sometimes down, but that it wasn't personal because in the end there wasn't much difference between you and the guys you were fighting. Both sides would take losses.

Civilians were another matter, and they should stay on the sidelines or they might get hurt. Civilians looked at right and wrong, took things personally. Imogen's cohort was unambiguously rooted in the civilian camp. Worse, they didn't see the combatants, clandestine or otherwise, for what they were: professionals engaged in an honorable struggle. This business, he thought, should have been about professionals reckoning accounts, effecting swaps—like Rudolph Abel for Francis Gary Powers.

The FBI clearly knew far more than they were letting on. There was a real chance they were just stringing him along, hoping to bring him in with no plea deal. They didn't seem to have any sense of honor, so why should he trust the bastards? He'd rot or be found dead in a federal penitentiary, and the bitch would gloat over it.

* * *

Vega couldn't sleep on the Dulles-Seattle shuttle. She never could sleep on planes, though she really needed the rest. The in-flight entertainment wasn't entertaining, so she flipped through the airline magazine. Was there anything that wasn't advertising, dressed up one way or the other? She put it aside and gazed out the window at the cloud tops.

A search of newspapers and police databases had found four men who had been murdered in what looked like a drug deal gone bad in Maricopa, California, on March 10. There were as yet no suspects, and the timing coincided with the date Rosewood had delivered Cardoso and Janssen to the area. The FBI knew that his colleague Menzies had delivered three men from Springfield to Aspen, Colorado, on the same day. Four men, driving drunk through the mountains there had plunged to their deaths.

She had directed agents from the Denver and Los Angeles field offices to delve into the backgrounds of all eight dead men. She had asked them to go over the dead men's personal effects, to look particularly for drop phones and seeming "gift" debit cards. If they each carried those, it would strongly confirm that the dead men were dark network operators.

She had been worried the network would begin rolling up its foot soldiers, and here was strong circumstantial proof that they were doing so. She wondered if the Seattle boys were next on the hit list. She fretted that she might arrive too late. She was also anxious about letting the pilots Rosewood and Menzies go free, albeit "turned" as FBI informants. There was still something in store, something undone, and it would happen on April 19 or 20.

* * *

Imogen's staff had identified a pattern of questionable PAC practices, which she and Nettie began applying to their targets. When they dug deep, it was astonishing how sloppy the targets were, particularly when juxtaposed with the meticulous operational protocols for the network cells they were investigating. In the non-target PACs, which they used more or less as norms or "controls" for their targets, Imogen and Nettie found that invoices were generally detailed and specific.

For all payments, whether for travel, polling, fundraising or consulting, the invoices were a true window into the work done and fees paid for services rendered. They didn't come cheap, for sure—charging $600 a day wasn't uncommon—but at least the expenses were detailed in full. And the banks clearing the funds were well known and US-based.

Not so for the target PACs: the paper trail quickly petered out, and what there was could seem laughably juvenile. Most telling, the payments often settled via offshore banks in Panama, Cayman Islands, Cyprus or UAE.

"It's like they think they can't be caught!" Imogen exclaimed as she turned over a set of bogus invoices.

"And they've been right all this time," said Nettie. "They might still be right."

Imogen had only a portion of the invoices for the audits she was wading through, and many lacked invoice numbers or any of the required details. Only a foreign settlement bank. One was handwritten.

She clutched a sheaf of papers and held it out to Nettie. "Would you call these people, please? Use the phone on my desk. Do you know how to dial so that your outgoing number is masked?"

Nettie nodded and took the sheets.

Imogen continued sorting. Without looking up, she added, "Tell them you're from an accounting firm representing whichever PAC and that you're trying to clear some open items. Then ask them if the invoice was ever paid."

"You're not afraid of this getting back to our targets?" Nettie asked.

Imogen sighed deeply and lifted her head. "There's that chance, I guess. But I'm betting these companies never heard of Forefathers Institute or V^3 PAC. I'm betting our guys just figured that as long as there was a slip of paper and an amount, and as long as the arithmetic was correct, no one would look any further. Do you think I should run it by Weir first, though?"

"No," said Nettie after a moment, "that makes sense. I think you're right. But what if they want me to send a copy? My phone number'll be masked, but I don't have a dummy email."

Imogen grabbed one of the phones she'd bought from Jimmy May and called Trey Kelly. In a matter of minutes, he had set Nettie up with a dummy caller ID, "Anacostia Acct Svc", and an email, nettie@anacostiaacctg.com.

Nettie plopped herself pertly in Imogen's desk chair and put on her best office-phone voice as she dialed the first number.

"Hi," she said, winking at Imogen as she added a little Valley Girl lilt to her delivery, "this is Nettie from Anacostia Accounting in Washington? Yeah, hi. Could I speak with someone in your Accounts Payable? Super. No problem! I'll hold." She grinned at Imogen, who smiled in return before going back to her papers. Something had caught Imogen's eye.

After forty-five minutes of chirrupy office chat, Nettie turned over the last piece of paper and laid it on the "done" pile. "Any more?" she asked, "I need coffee—you want some?"

"Definitely. But what have you got?"

"Exactly what you thought we'd get. Most haven't heard of whichever PAC claimed to have paid them. Some have a record of one little thing they did, but it's been paid to an account at a US bank. That's probably how the bad guys were able to make these bogus payments look legit."

Imogen nodded. "Would you check something else for me? I've got a copy of an internal memo from someone with the initials 'CQ' at Forefathers Institute. He mentions a memo from a Mason Brandenberg. I think he's their lead accountant—I've seen his name on a couple of things, but I don't see any memo from him. Will you check to see if he's still at the firm? And no sugar."

27

How to be surreptitiously nosy without drawing notice from a bunch of professional noses? This was Hugh Salter's quandary as he set about looking into David Carr's claim that a lot of under-secretaries and kitchen cabinet staff were bypassing Cabinet appointees and working under the radar with the President. He had been making informal calls to colleagues and trolling press-pool watering holes without success. It was tricky, he reflected, to ask the kinds of questions he wanted answers to without alerting fellow reporters that there might be a story.

He stalked well-known, high-traffic reporters' bars near the Capitol. Stopping into the third in as many days, he surveyed the alcoholiscape, wondering where to begin.

"Hi, Bledsoe" he said, dumping himself into a banquette. "How're things?"

"Hugh," said Tiffany Bledsoe matter-of-factly. "What brings you? I thought you'd be off giving your opinion or hobnobbing the VP."

"It's not all glamor, hon," he responded, "and if you're feeling envious, wait'll you hear why I've condescended to tread among you peons. What're you drinking?"

"Vodka-tonic," she said. He signaled to the bar for another round for her. "Same for me," he said to the bartender.

"You were going to tell me about the muck and mire, Hugh, and why I shouldn't envy you...though certainly I don't."

"Right," he said, as their drinks arrived. He drank deeply. "So, I have to do a puff piece on Carr and family. Goddamned Jeanie ok'd it. Whatever the fuck next, I wonder: voice-overs for state funerals and New Year's eve?"

"Oh, you'll be perfect for it, Hugh," she said. "My pal the VP." She leaned heavily on the table, extracting the straw from her drink delicately, her expression determined, as if she'd found a hair in her food but decided to eat it anyway. She looked sideways at him. "Oh, don't act hurt, Sweetums. It'll be all right." He noticed for the first time that she was very drunk.

"Just do what you always do," she continued sweetly. "Pretend there aren't any standards anymore; that we're not supposed to ask the hard questions, and just shill for them . . . buff out their *hard* edges"—here she started miming something that would have looked like fellatio if she hadn't been so drunk—"so they're happy with you. So they look nice, so respectable . . . so *electable*."

"That's a bit harsh, even from you, Tiff."

She flashed him a look of drunken menace, but it passed quickly from her face and she looked as though she was going to be sick. She lunged out of the banquet and staggered to the toilet. Salter stared after her.

"That's pretty much what the news director said to her today," said a voice behind him. "Not in so many words, mind you. And minus the blowjob."

Salter turned to see Anna Harding, a producer at another network. She sat down next to him thrusting him toward the center of the banquet with her ample hips. "The asshole was just repeating words from the dressing down he'd gotten from Quantrelle about a story we were working on about backdoor Oval Office meetings."

"Now I feel really small. I was just hoping to get some background on Carr, something that might give my puff piece some baby teeth." He sighed. "What do you mean backdoor meetings, and how come your news director's retreating?"

"It's the new normal, isn't it? Ever since Moore and his crew descended. Or is it that they've ascended? Difficult to tell up from down these days. Redmond's staff and press secretary were old normal. They spun, they hedged, and we read between the lines and tried to make sense of it. But they kind of left us alone. These guys . . ." she let the thought trail off, shaking her head.

"Had Tiffany found out something?"

"No, that's just it," Harding said. "She was just wondering why the President had so few Cabinet level meetings, as though he was busy somewhere else. When she looked, she found that he was spending more of his time with under-secretaries and deputy secretaries instead. She wondered why."

"Sounds like a good question."

"It is. But when she asked it, they stonewalled. OK, you'd kind of expect that. But when she asked to see the White House worker and visitor entry logs, that's when all hell broke loose."

"I don't get it," Salter said.

"Neither do I, Hugh. They said they'd stop sharing the visitor log, effective immediately, and that national security— can you fucking believe it?—*national security* was at stake. What's he doing, then, having tea with Kim Jong-un? That national security bullshit was all from the new Press Secretary, Marek. But then this morning Quantrelle got involved, and he doubled-down. He called our news director and ripped him a new one."

"Over that? Just for asking?"

She nodded as she took a sip of her drink. "I was there when the call came in. I couldn't actually hear the harangue, but he threatened our press credentials. Not in so many words, but there was a lot of 'unwelcome' and 'not invited to share,' that sort of stuff."

"Doesn't that make you more curious?" Salter asked. "More determined?"

"We're going to have to be careful not to escalate it. He was serious. We'd get solidarity from other networks, I guess, and they'd share their feeds (at a cost), and the *Times* would have think pieces and leaders. But we'd be stuck. Either we spend our airtime protesting that we haven't got the news or we shut up about it and cover politics without the White House."

"So," Salter began warily, "*are* there a lot of backdoor meetings going on?"

Harding shrugged. "Maybe, but we don't have confirmation. That place has a hell of a lot of back doors."

"Well Quantrelle obviously doesn't want you to know what they're up to in there."

She shook her head. "What we've got is just anecdotal from Tiff." She looked toward the bathroom. "I should check on her." She stood up and straightened her blouse. She looked at Salter and said: "No one's talking, on or off the record."

Must be a first for Washington, he thought as she walked away.

* * *

As Imogen and Nettie studied the Forefathers Institute paperwork, they noted that the 2015 Board of Directors list read like a Who's Who of the Moore Administration's kitchen cabinet, not just those they had already known about like Marek and Quantrelle. A number of them were also in key positions at V^3 and Sovereign Caucus.

Name after name; and the list of conflicts of interest was even longer. Conflicting with the interests of America, mostly. She sent the updated investigative target list, along with what she had of the PACs financial dealings, to Weir. He would forward them to the forensic accountants from the Treasury Department who had been working since December on isolating how the dark network operatives were being paid, with little result.

The chief investigator on the Treasury team established the outlines of the "gift card" payment-withdrawal structure as funneling through various offshore private banks. Ironic term, really, since so many of them are on the shores of the world's most expensive islands. Those leads, however, were going nowhere and Imogen and Nettie's additions only added to the mess. The Treasury Department investigators had run not into a dead end but a hall of mirrors.

Payments, when they could be traced at all, led back through a labyrinth of banks linked to a network of Special Purpose Entities: orphan and limited liability companies, whose owners were further shielded by another layer of SPEs, who had custodians and shell corporations (metaphorically speaking) of their own. Treasury had peeled back enough to secure a lifting order for a set of accounts linked with some of the payments through some of the private banks, but rather than revealing who was behind the curtain, it only showed more drapery.

Imogen had hoped that having a list of banks used by the network would give the Treasury Department investigators more to go on. She had found an accountant who was no longer with the PAC, Mason Brandenberg. She wondered if he could shed any light. Maybe, like the furloughed pilots Vega had interviewed, he could illuminate what was going on, even if he didn't have the whole picture himself. Nettie Sartain had the name of the company he now worked for, Statesman Accounting, in Richmond, Virginia.

Still in the parking garage across from his wife's office where he had dropped her moments earlier after their lunch together, the phone in Mason Brandenburg's car rang. He touched the hands-free button.

"Hello?"

"Mr. Brandenburg, I'm FBI Agent Annette Sartain, and I have some questions about Fore –"

"Dammit!" he swore as he hung up.

He paused on the down-ramp of the garage, his hands trembling, all color gone from his face. Sweat soaked instantly through his shirt. His former friends would have to silence him now whether they thought he knew anything or not.

In Imogen's office, Nettie looked at her phone. "I think we just hit pay dirt," she said.

A moment later, in the parking garage, Brandenburg reversed up the down ramp, to the level where he'd left his wife. She heard the car, turned, and looked quizzically toward her husband's beige Lexus backing toward her rapidly. The back end swung wildly as it accelerated, twice almost hitting a parked car before he came to a screeching halt next to where she was standing. The trunk popped open and Brandenburg jumped out of the car.

"Ellen, I'm sorry."

Shaken by the look on her husband's face, Ellen Brandenburg could only stare.

"That business with Clayton...I had to get out. They're into some very bad things."

"What's happened?" she demanded.

"I hoped it wouldn't come to anything, that it would all just blow over..."

"Mason, what's happened?"

"The FBI just called me. Clayton's goons are—"

"Clayton's *goons*?"

"Yes. I know what they're into. I know what they've been doing. They've been watching me ever since I left...probably tapping my phone. I wanted to keep you out of it, but I don't know what's going to happen next."

"If it's the FBI, let's call Adam. As your attorney—"

"We're way beyond that." He glanced at his phone and scribbled down Nettie's number on the back of his business card and handed it to her. "Open your trunk," he said, taking a quick look around the parking garage. He grabbed the box of documents and put it in her car, covering it with the same blanket he'd used. "Whatever you do, don't go home. Go to your sister's—anywhere but home. Promise?"

"Of course, Mason. What are you going to do?"

"I'm going to get as far away as I can. I need you to get in touch with that agent, and get her the box." He slammed the trunk closed. "Ellen, I'm sorry. I wanted to protect you, but...I can't."

The phone rang again. Brandenburg looked it. "It's her again."

"What's her name?"

"I didn't get that. I hung up too quickly. But that's her number. Forgive me. I've always loved you."

"In God's name, what's going to happen, Mason?"

"Don't even go back to work. Come out right after me and head somewhere—anywhere. Then call that agent. Get that box to her. It's the only way you'll be safe." He kissed her and jumped into his car.

* * *

Hugh Salter dialed the personal number of the Administrator of the Environmental Protection Agency, obtained through his producer, Jeanne. Georgia Desmond had tipped him off that the call might be worthwhile: the Vice President reckoned that the Administrator too was furious about seeing policy driven by unrecorded conversations between his under-secretary and the President, while he was never given access.

Salter had compiled what he guessed was a pretty thorough log of White House visitors from what was archived in different files on the news network's database, supplemented by what had been pieced together by an online freedom of information site. Before dialing, he looked at this patchwork to see the last time the EPA Administrator had met with President Moore. It had been the day after President Redmond died.

"This is Leslie Fortier," said a sonorous voice.

"Mr. Fortier, Hugh Salter at CNN. I'm wondering if you'd care to comment on what seems to be an end-run around you and other Cabinet members in favor of under-secretaries and even some Schedule C appointments."

There was a long pause before the director responded. "I'm not sure what you're talking about," he said carefully.

"Sir, we're hearing that the respectful, go-slow-approach narrative the Moore Administration has signaled might just be cover for what may prove to be a rapid series of moves."

"Who's saying this, Hugh?"

"Well," he began, peering at the log, "it seems your under-secretary has met with the President on several occasions—March 14, March 22 and possibly again yesterday. We don't know officially, because as you know the White House visitor logs are no longer open to the public." Salter paused, trying to give Fortier somewhere to jump in. Since that didn't seem to be happening, he continued:

"The full cabinet met with the President on March 11, the day after President Redmond's death, but so far as I can divine, you haven't met since, and it's been just over a month now. Are my notes in error, sir?"

"The new Administration is taking a go-slow approach," Fortier began. "We were told that nothing would happen quickly—"

"—Yes, sir, but *something* seems to be happening quickly, only nobody knows what it is."

"Why, what have you heard?"

"I'm interested in your perspective, sir. Are you and your staff working on something? Is there a reason under-secretaries are carrying the water for their departments?"

"I'm going to have to get back to you," said Fortier, and he hung up.

* * *

Weir had been better than his word. There were two agents in Seattle, Elmer Reyes and Jim Cleary, whom he had worked with during his drug war days. Under cover of liaising with DEA, the two had begun surveillance on Janssen and Cardoso that afternoon, while Vega failed to get any sleep on the plane. By the time she met them next morning, they had details and she had red eyes. She met Agent Reyes in the seventh-floor conference room in the FBI building downtown. Agent Cleary was still in the field.

Reyes already had a suspect board for his show-and-tell. He was young, energetic and clearly wanted to impress someone from Headquarters. "At the Exec's request," he began officiously, handing her a thin file, "Agent Cleary and I began surveillance of the targets, Target Cartwright and

Target Sawyer. Those names were given to us by Executive Assistant Director Weir."

Vega nodded as she moved to the other side of the conference table to study the photographs of Janssen (a.k.a. Cartwright) and Cardoso (a.k.a. Sawyer). It was her first look at them, and she understood now what the pilot Rosewood had meant about them looking severe and straight-arrow, even if really they were bent as a bow.

Except for Rosewood, who was in way over his head, Vega's experience of the dark network cell operatives was of hardened ex-military, accustomed to adversity. Janssen and Cardoso weren't that; they looked like what their covers said they were: tech geeks toiling in Reddit-thread obscurity. Though they were young and fashionably turned out, there was still a strange hardness, a blankness about them.

"Um, before I go any further," Reyes began uncertainly, "I've gotta ask: is there anyone else on this detail?"

"What do you mean?"

"Well, the Exec did say this is supposed to be on the QT—which we've done—but I'm wondering if there's any possibility that some other arm of the Bureau or another agency is also working this angle."

"I don't think so," said Vega. "We've only just gotten the intel on them ourselves."

He pulled two photographs out of the file and placed them on the table—Professor Duncan Calder and the cab driver, Rich Lamberti. "So, you don't have any idea who these two are?"

* * *

Ellen Brandenburg made the call to Nettie and pulled out of the parking garage about five minutes behind Mason, arranging to meet her and Imogen in Fredericksburg, Virginia, halfway between Washington and Richmond. Before she reached the Interstate, she saw Mason's car, abandoned in an alley across from South 14th Street and East Canal, the driver's door and trunk open. Was that part of his plan to disappear, or had Clayton Quantrelle's goons already taken him? Would he go to jail? She shuddered at the meaning behind his words "or worse."

She had no idea what was in the box, but it seemed that getting whatever it was to Agent Sartain and her colleague Agent Trager was the best way to save him. She felt sick to her stomach, frightened for Mason as she drove shaken and distracted up I-95.

They'd had a nice, comfortable life together, she told herself, and now it was time for her to prove her mettle. God help Quantrelle, she thought, if Mason were harmed. She'd fight whatever came next with every ounce of her not inconsiderable being and every cent they had. As the miles rolled on she fought the urge to pull over and check what was in the box. Better to get there.

The rendezvous was a poky, little restaurant along Caroline Street. Imogen's eyes adjusted slowly to the dark, and Nettie spotted her first, in a booth at the very back. She looked up, and beckoned.

"Thank you for meeting with us," Imogen began.

"Do you have Mason?" Ellen asked before they'd sat down.

"No," said Nettie, "we want to interview him, but we didn't arrest him."

"Then he's been taken. I saw his car empty in an alley as I drove here."

Nettie and Imogen exchanged a look.

"He said he was worried about Clayton Quantrelle's goons," she said. "Is that who has him?"

"We don't know, ma'am."

"You have to get him back!"

"We'll do everything we can. Where did you see the car? We'll get on to the local police, too."

Ellen told them while Imogen texted Agent Davies the information about where their target had gone missing. She told them how Mason had been afraid for months. "Afraid of what would happen if anyone found out what was going on at the Institute. Things he might be blamed for. And I never knew...never realized what he was going through."

"The Institute? Forefathers Institute?" asked Nettie, poised to write on her yellow pad.

"Yes."

"You mentioned a box of documents, ma'am," said Nettie. "Do you have them now?"

Ellen Brandendburg drew aside the wine colored tablecloth, to reveal the box under the table. "I guess this is what it's all about."

Imogen reached for it. "Thank you, Mrs. Brandenburg."

"What do you think's happened to my husband?"

"I don't know, ma'am," said Nettie. "We've begun looking for him already."

"Do I have your assurance that for the assistance we're giving you that he'll be given consideration either at trial or during sentencing...if it comes to that."

"You have our word, ma'am" said Imogen. She quickly looked down and examined the box's contents. She didn't want to meet Ellen Brandenburg's gaze, didn't want to let on that her husband was probably already dead.

Imogen and Nettie walked to the car, guns at the ready, assessing threat points. But it seemed Ellen Brandenburg hadn't been followed. Imogen's phone rang. It was Amanda Vega.

"We've got a situation in Seattle," she said. "Lover boy's gone rogue."

"Wait, what? Duncan?"

"Is there someone else? Yes, Duncan, and yeah, you need to get here. There's a 5:30 flight out of Dulles. Can you get to the airport in time?"

Imogen glanced at her watch. It'd be tight. "Yes, I can," she said, "but—"

"—You're going to get here and talk him down, or I'm going to run him in for withholding evidence, obstructing justice and anything else I can find to throw at him."

"I . . . What's happened?"

216

"Did you know?" Vega demanded.

"Know what?"

"That him and some other guy've been sitting on Cardoso and Janssen for God-knows how long. We're getting ready to make our move and he's in the way. He might fuck it all up!"

"Duncan's been—?"

"—I'm doing you a favor. I haven't told Weir yet."

"I'll be there," said Imogen.

"Call me when you're getting on the plane. I'll be there to pick you up. In the meantime, call him and tell him Mom's coming and she's spitting nails." And Vega hung up.

Imogen blinked at the phone. She hoped that Amanda was casting herself as "mom" in that scenario. She asked Nettie to drive and hopped in the passenger seat.

"You're going to need to take this back to headquarters," she said as they pulled out of the parking lot. "Weir's forensic accounting guy at Treasury will meet you there. We need to run by my apartment and then make a detour to Dulles, though. I'm heading to Seattle. There's an anomaly."

As Nettie accelerated, Imogen booked her flight on the phone. Then, about to phone Calder, she turned to Nettie. "I'm sorry about this. I need to make a call: it's personal *and* business. I won't put you into a tricky position by asking you not divulge it, but you might do me the favor of not volunteering anything you may hear."

Nettie frowned, her eyes on the road.

"Imogen, you can always trust me."

28

The three assassins had rolled into Cincinnati five days earlier. They knew that Reed had used Cincinnati as a base in the past; that he'd mentioned it once as an out-of-the-way place he liked to go for "a bit of R & R." While it was unlikely he would stay there, the fact he had chosen Cincinnati as his first stop before he had disappeared back in January meant the city held something for him. If they could find out what, it might point them toward where he'd gone.

The Springfield crew knew Reed's handwriting and habits because he'd recruited and trained them. The Springfield crew also knew intimately the kind of danger he—and they—were in. They knew that this was the home stretch, the time when operatives like them received either their just or their eternal reward.

On their most recent deployment to "mop up" and "tie off" loose network threads they gleaned from the pilot who brought them to Colorado that a colleague of his had recently ferried another team to somewhere near Barstow in the California desert—for what purpose they could easily guess, even if the pilot chose to play dumb.

They'd been sent on the Colorado job by a new contact, who'd been supervising them since Nash's unfortunate retirement from living. The new man had been direct about what needed to be done: the Denver outfit was "flabby," he had pointed out; and it was "not meeting sales expectations." Worse, it seemed possible that it might soon start "giving away samples." The Springfield crew was commanded to stage an unannounced "snap inspection" of the Denver operations and then conduct a "meeting" with the "sales force."

The Springfield guys were not so naive as to believe they were above elimination themselves, though they were anything but flabby; and when tasked with killing their chief, the Springfield people would consider the matter from several angles. But the dossiers they themselves had helped draw up and the admonishment to be ever "watchful" of each other meant it would be folly to discuss any misgivings.

From his desk in the carpeted section of the lobby of a small, independent bank on East Fourth Street in downtown Cincinnati, across a wide expanse of marble floor, the bank manager looked up as the door opened. A tall and powerfully-built man in an expensive but ill-fitting suit was striding across the glossy stone floor toward him.

As the click of his heels rapped and reported from the walls like far off gunshots, the manager saw a similarly dressed man take up a position outside the glass door, his back to the bank. The manager scooted his chair in closer to the desk and ran the fingers of his left hand over the alarm button for reassurance.

"Mr. Aidan Collingswood?" the tall man asked.

"Yes," he said.

"I'm with CID - Criminal Investigative Division. Secret Service." He drew an identification card from his breast pocket as though drawing a revolver and showed it to Collingswood. "My name's Brandt."

Collingswood was himself tall, and had once been powerfully built, but years behind a desk, working lunches, Rotary club dinners, Chamber of Commerce banquets and job insecurity at the bank had left their mark. His equator now required special tailoring. Despite his bulk, the bank manager rose spritely from his desk to shake the Secret Service Agent's hand. He took the badge and card and examined them.

"How can I help?" he asked, sitting down again with the Agent. The badge still in his hand, Collingswood looked at

Brandt's ID, wrote down his name and badge number and then passed it back. "You're not from the Cincinnati office, I think?"

"No," said Brandt, "Chicago. We're trying to track someone down, a counterfeit ringleader, and we're pretty sure he was in this area."

"I haven't seen any alerts about counterfeit money."

"No. No sir, you wouldn't have. This part of the investigation focuses on places where counterfeit currency *isn't* being passed around. It's kind of a 'don't foul the nest' scenario."

"I see," said the manager, not really seeing at all but anxious to keep his nest unfouled. "How can I help?"

"We have a couple aliases he's been using," he said, reaching into his pocket, "and I'm hoping you might recognize him."

"I'm sure we'd have known if anyone was depositing fake bills—"

"—I'm thinking he might've kept a safe deposit box," Brandt interrupted. "Have you seen this man? He has gone by the names Snyder, Reed, possibly Cooper—perhaps another name altogether."

The manager examined the photo.

"If you'd seen him it'd probably be mid- or maybe late January. We're behind the curve here, but we've just got some new intelligence."

"Yes, I know him. He's been a customer for years, with a joint checking-savings account and a deposit box. I'll have to think of the name."

"Good, thank you," said Brandt. "That's a great help. Is it any of those aliases?"

"No…" said the manager in far-off voice. "Gerritt," he said finally. "Yes. Ian Gerritt."

"You're sure?"

"Positive. Gerritt: double-r, double-t. I've known him a long time. Twenty years. Friendly enough, though I don't know anything about him." He shook his head sadly, mourning what now seemed the impending loss of yet another depositor.

"Do you have an address or phone number?"

"Yes, of course, but . . ."

"Of course," said Brandt as he stood up hurriedly. "I'll be back with a warrant to search the deposit box. Excellent. Thank you."

"And it's not as long ago as January that we saw Mr. Gerritt. He came in a couple of weeks ago and emptied his safe deposit box. I let him in myself."

* * *

Imogen had left two messages for Calder but received no reply. As she stalked through SeaTac airport pulling her suitcase, she listened to a series of messages from Vega giving progress reports. First, no progress: no further sighting of Calder or his accomplice. Second, Trey Kelly had synchronized phone traces from the Seattle operatives, confirming that they were just what Reed said they were. Third, Vega and her team had the go-ahead to make their move on Janssen and Cardoso, and Imogen should get a taxi.

Frantically, Imogen tried Calder again: "Duncan, it's Imogen. I'm in Seattle now. Just landed. Amanda's—"

Another call on the phone interrupted her. It was Calder.

"Duncan! What the hell are you doing? Amanda's getting ready to move. Where are you?"

"I can't tell you that, Gen."

"Fucking hell, Duncan! This is serious. Amanda says you knew about this guy but didn't tell us! That's withholding information, probably obstruction. If you're anywhere nearby when they make the arrests she's going to arrest you too."

"Right. They'll *arrest* them. Probably bargain with them, lighter sentences, maybe even immunity for some of their crimes in exchange for testimony."

"Duncan," she said, hoping he would hear sense.

"And how does that help Matthew?" he hissed. "This is betrayal."

"Matthew's dead, Duncan. We can't help him; we can only stand up for what he died for. He wanted to catch these guys."

"He needs to be revenged."

"Revenged? What the hell does that mean? How does *that* help Matthew—whatever it is you're planning? We're getting to the bottom of this, Duncan. *Finally*. That's what we wanted. Justice, not revenge."

"And they killed him for it, Gen. Left him crushed by the road like some animal. There has to be a reckoning."

Imogen felt she was going insane. She felt lightheaded, buffeted by some delayed trauma storm. She heard, or imagined she heard, gunshots echoing inside her head; she relived the chaos, the random, abject fear of a gunfight. In the middle of the SeaTac concourse, she stopped still and stared at the people walking briskly by, secure, oblivious. "A reckoning?" she hissed incredulously into the phone.

"I'd kill them with my bare hands!"

"With your one good arm?"

"I'd hoped you'd understand, Gen, but I don't require you to." And he hung up.

Imogen walked to a seat, feeling she might faint. Her phone rang again, but it wasn't Duncan, it was Nettie, to tell her that Mason Brandenburg had been found hanged in his Richmond home, an apparent suicide. Ellen had found him.

* * *

Back in the truck bay in Springfield, Virginia, Tweedledum and Tweedledim stopped their surveillance on Brandenburg. Had they been paying attention, they'd have noticed that Imogen was unexpectedly in Seattle and made a report, but instead they'd been fully involved in finding any mention of Frank Reed's new alias, Ian Gerritt. And it had paid off.

"Yeah," Dum was saying into the phone in his halting, uptalking whine, "he wasn't really being careful with the Ian Gerritt alias? Yeah, clues all over. Your best bet, I guess, is what looks like an open-ended stay he booked at an Airbnb in

Cincinnati." He gave the Orchard Street address. "Yeah, course we will. We'll get back on Hugh Salter and...hello?" He shrugged and laid the handset on the desk in front of him. "Maestro!" he called regally, pointing at Dim, who pushed a button, flooding the garage with Speed Metal at maximum volume. Dum tossed his friend a Monster energy drink.

* * *

Next day at the bank, Aidan Collingswood was concerned that Secret Service Agent Brandt hadn't returned. Brandt had made it seem so urgent yesterday, yet there had been no follow up; and second, while waiting for him to reappear with the warrant, Collingswood had missed lunch, the one part of his day he really looked forward to. He was beginning to have misgivings, and he was particularly glad he hadn't given the Agent anything more than the customer's name.

He was angry with himself that he had done that much. He should have acknowledged that the photo indeed looked like a customer, but that he'd have to wait for a warrant of some kind before proceeding. It's what he should have done, and yet he hadn't. He accused himself bitterly now, fearing that he might have embroiled the bank in something tawdry.

Collingswood was an anachronism, and he liked it that way. So did most of the bank's aging, dwindling customer base. He was exactly what he claimed to be, a discreet and "personal" banker. He was affable, gregarious, often greeting depositors as they stood in line, calling them by name, wondering if he could help them further in any way.

He conducted business with handshakes over lunch or drinks and then handed off details for others to type up and sign. He recalled some detail about most of the people he met or did business with so that he could drop it into conversation, relying upon notes about families and jobs entered in a battered, tottering Rolodex file on his desk. When he retired at the end of the year, it would leave with him, possibly bound for a museum.

223

At just after one o'clock that afternoon, he drew the Rolodex toward him, his fingers passing quickly across the bent tops of the cards as he looked for the number of a Secret Service agent he knew in the Cincinnati Field Office. When he found what he was looking for, he took a breath and dialed.

"Tom!" he cried jovially, "It's Aidan at East Fourth Bank. Yes, quite a while. You never come to see us...which, all things being equal isn't such a bad thing, eh?" He chuckled. "How's Wendy? Wonderful. Listen, I'm hoping you can help with something..."

* * *

At SeaTac Airport, Imogen sat at gate N-12, bewildered and numb at yet another death—stung by Duncan's accusation of betrayal. She wondered whether to call him back. Whatever he had in mind, why hadn't he told her? If he didn't trust her, it was because he knew she wouldn't agree to it—knew she'd object because what he was doing was wrong. Which was why he'd kept it secret. Or did he think she was somehow implicated in whatever these plotting bastards were doing? Did he think she'd been co-opted? Was that what he meant when he implied her betrayal? If she couldn't trust Duncan, was there anyone she could trust?

Two blocks from Janssen's house in Seattle's Maple Leaf district, Amanda Vega was parked with the engine running, waiting for status reports from her two teams. They had reconnoitered their respective targets, and both had confirmed that the targets were inside.

She got the "ready" status from Agent Cleary, stationed near Cardoso's house in the Cedar Park neighborhood, a couple of miles away. Agent Reyes, up near the top of Janssen's street, also reported his team was in place and ready.

Vega dialed Trey Kelly in Washington, who was monitoring both targets' cell phones. "Ready to block anything coming from either phone?"

"Ready," said Kelly. "But Calder's phone is off. I have no idea where he is right now."

"Let's hope Imogen talked some sense into him," she said.

"The street is clear," Agent Cleary reported. "Team Two is in position. Go/No Go?"

"Area's clear," said Agent Reyes, who had originally brought Calder's moonlighting to her attention. "Team One is in position. Go/No Go?"

Vega put her truck in drive and began rolling forward slowly. "Team one—go. Team two—go," she said into the radio as she accelerated toward the intersection.

"Mr. Gerritt?" he said, when Reed answered. "This is Aidan Collingswood at East Fourth Street bank." As he spoke, he scribbled next to the name on the Rolodex card: "Government Agent?"

"I'm not sure what to make of it, but I thought I should let you know: we had someone in here looking for you late yesterday. He had a photograph, and of course I recognized you. He claimed to be a Secret Service agent on the trail of a counterfeiter, but when I checked his credentials they turn out to be false. I'm afraid he has your name now, and I thought it prudent to alert you. I don't know why he came to the bank, but—"

Reed spoke.

Then: "Yes, sir. Yes, quite tall. You're very welcome, sir."

Duncan Calder had hidden himself behind a four-foot high solid wooden fence opposite Janssen's house. He had been crouching for more than two hours, and it was not good for the knees. His shoulder burned. He had watched as the FBI took up positions at either end of the street and behind their target's house.

Duncan's gun was tucked into the waistband of his trousers at the small of his back. It felt heavy with purpose. He had seen Janssen go into his house, stepping quickly out of an Uber ride and passing through the front gate, but it had been too quick for Calder to get him in his gun sights. He still wasn't sure that Janssen was Matthew's assassin, but he was certainly responsible for some of the carnage. In killing him Calder had a 50/50 chance of being right.

He knew from long inspection that there was no way he could get through the gate and door without giving himself away. He hoped Janssen would put up some resistance and the FBI would kill him, fulfilling his objective for him. But if they didn't do the job, if they took him alive, Calder would kill him. He massaged each knee in turn to keep the blood flowing.

In Cincinnati, Reed gathered his files and threw them into a leather satchel, along with his laptop. He pulled open a drawer and grabbed the last envelope of cash he had—$1,200. He ran to the upstairs bathroom, which had a window with a good vantage on the alley behind the house. If the Illinois clowns were coming for him, they would cover every exit. But there was nothing out of the ordinary in the alley, nor in the street at the front of the house.

Now, go.

Reed buttoned his jacket and launched himself out of the front door. Once out of sight down the alleyway, he began running. Forty yards along, and as close to a sprint as his bulk would allow, he heard a truck screech to a halt behind him and turned to glimpse two of his former charges jump out and rush the house. As he fled along East Liberty Street, he heard glass breaking as they broke through the front door.

At the same moment, in North Seattle, at addresses two miles apart, teams of black FBI SUVs converged on their respective targets' houses from front and back. In the Maple Leaf neighborhood, Calder spied as two black trucks arrived at high speed from the north and south ends of the street.

The truck from the north turned suddenly and stopped at the curb, while the other accelerated. It turned hard just in front of the other truck, leapt the curb, crossed the sidewalk and smashed through the high fence. Prefabricated sections of Japanese-themed fence exploded and splintered, bursting across the yard and against the front of the house.

Before the battering ram truck had come to rest, agents in full riot gear from the other truck were pouring through the hole in the fence, guns drawn, one brandishing a handheld battering ram. He hoisted it as he trotted up the front steps and bashed in the front door. In two minutes it was over.

The scene was much the same in Cedar Park: trucks on the sidewalk, black-clad enforcers swarming, and young assassins—coincidentally shoeless—struggling as they were led in handcuffs through their demolished front doors.

But in Maple Leaf there was a difference.

As Special Agent Vega congratulated Cleary and the rest of Team Two over headset on a job well done in Cedar Park, her truck was arriving beside the others from Team One in Maple Leaf. Trey Kelly had already confirmed to her that no cell phone transmissions had been made.

The operation hadn't been as sneaky and quiet as her capture of Rosewood in North Dakota, she reflected, surveying the carnage, but it had got the job done, and the dark network didn't know it had happened. The local press would hear it was a drugs raid—names pending, and that would be that.

As the truck pulled up and she was about to congratulate Reyes and his team, she caught something from the corner of her eye. Duncan Calder. Standing in the front yard of a house directly opposite, gun drawn and aiming directly at Janssen who was flanked by FBI agents. Calder's legs were shoulder distance apart, the left hand supporting the shooting hand, just as he'd been taught.

Agent Reyes's team saw him too, and they did just as trained. As Calder fired— missing Janssen's head by two inches—three of them opened fire, two hitting his chest and one his head. Simultaneously, the two agents supporting Janssen shoved him to the ground and fell on top of him. Calder reeled backwards.

"No: no, no, no, no!" cried Vega as she sprinted from the truck toward him.

29

Reed had a return ticket to Silver Spring, Maryland, and he activated it now for the bus leaving at 2:25 a.m., but he didn't board. Instead, he bought a ticket for Roanoke, Virginia, his boyhood home, under yet another name.

It was a dangerous move. His connection with the area was something his pursuers would certainly be aware of, and on its face, this was a classic "going to ground" blunder. He couldn't stay in Roanoke, no matter what he called himself. So, he would stop 90 miles short, in Princeton, West Virginia. One of his boyhood friends, Sam Hedrick, had a hunting camp in the hills to the north and surely wouldn't begrudge him the cabin. No one would be up there at this time of year.

Reed knew the area well, having spent time both at Hedrick's and his own family's camp nearby throughout his childhood. For a moment, as his bus travelled deeper into the West Virginia hills, he found himself growing calm, feeling almost nostalgic. He found comfort in the hills' confining embrace, was lulled and beguiled by the ethereal mists as they rose, winding from the hollows. But only for a moment.

Quickly his mind returned to the problem at hand: how had the Illinois squad found him? Had one of the idiots at the FBI let slip something? Or had he just trained his men too well? If so, his days at Hedrick's camp were numbered. They were bound to make a connection. But how long did he have? The new Attorney General might be in place within a week.

* * *

Imogen was still pulling her heavy suitcase when she arrived at Harborview Medical Center, where Vega told her to meet. Vega had said only that Imogen should get there, and that she couldn't talk right then. Imogen feared the worst. Harborview, she knew from her time in Seattle, was where all the tough trauma cases were seen.

Though Vega didn't say so, it meant Duncan had been shot, and he was either dead or dying. Imogen moved quickly, deliberately and fearfully through the labyrinth of the hospital, her spirit seeming to drip out of her with each step, each wrong turn. When she finally found the right wing and paused to check in with a nurse, she was conscious of emotions swelling and seething, as though a wave of anguish had been following just a little behind her and had broken over her the moment she stopped.

Ever-present was fear and the frank knowledge that her life was in constant danger. Added to that was the uncertainty—about her status at the Bureau and about the importance and value of her work. The one thing she'd been sure of was Duncan, and now that was devastated. Worst, for the second time in four brief months, the man she loved had been shot; and for the second time, no one would tell her whether he was dead or alive.

She sat down on the bench the nurse indicated. Presently, Amanda Vega walked in. Though she'd done well to remove the traces, it was obvious that she had been crying. Imogen stared.

"How is he?" she asked.

"I'm sorry, Gen. He's gone."

Imogen stared at the wall. She nodded. Everything seemed to be falling away from her, as though the whole building was a poorly designed stage, collapsing. She felt light, floating. Amanda sat down next to her and put her arms around Imogen's shoulders. The pressure, the weight, was the first real thing she could remember feeling since Duncan had hung up on her in the airport.

"I'm so sorry," Amanda murmured again.

Imogen put her hand on Amanda's forearm. She patted it absently, grateful that Amanda's embrace located her in space, told her where she was. Finally, she asked: "Can I see him?"

"No," said Amanda.

* * *

The East Fourth Bank manager was incensed that he'd been used. It wasn't financial fraud—wouldn't show in the books—but it was identity fraud and a breach of trust. He went to lunch by himself and ate an enormous meal. When he returned, content in many ways, and satisfied at least that he was not acting rashly or compounding his earlier error, he called his contact Tom at the Cincinnati Secret Service Field Office, who immediately put him in touch with the FBI.

Collingswood was ready when they showed up. He supplied them with CCTV footage of "Agent Brandt" inside the bank, and footage from outside showing Brandt's accomplice as well as their vehicle, a black, four-door Ford F-150 pickup.

The FBI had showed up with a warrant in hand—"much more like it!" he thought—and he had opened Ian Gerritt's safe deposit box. It was empty, but fingerprints they lifted would later confirm that Gerritt was Frank Reed. The same FBI detail also took charge of an investigation into a break-in at a row house along Orchard Street, where a truck matching their bank suspects' description was involved.

They issued an All-Points Bulletin for the truck and its passengers. Better still for the team, it seemed Reed had activated the return bus ticket he had in Pete Snyder's name to Silver Spring, Maryland. Vega's lieutenants, Agents Davies and Guthrie were put on alert—Guthrie to cover the bus station and Davies dispatched to Cincinnati to liaise with the field office there.

* * *

Nettie Sartain had wasted no time getting back to work among the boxes in Imogen's office: this time with Brandenberg's files as her key. The Treasury Department's forensic accountant, Abel Gardiner, joined her, at Weir's request.

Gardiner's investigation had been stymied thus far by complicated layers of shell corporations. Now with a key in hand, he and Nettie Sartain quickly pieced together a very criminal conspiracy. Draws from a number of target banks coincided directly with known Network activity, and he was now seeing which banks were behind the veil he had so far failed to pierce. What was more, it was becoming clear that far from being independent of one another, the Forefathers Institute, Sovereign Caucus, Opportunity Initiative and V^3 acted in concert, were centrally controlled, and it wasn't by Nash or Reed.

* * *

"I dunno," Tweedledim was saying into the phone, "we're on his cell phone, but we can't get access to Salter's office phone. Well, for starters, it's a landline? Second, it's bundled. He has one of those office phones, we think, that has four lines he can call out on, but it's not limited to just four lines. There's a program that's part of the system and it hunts for *any* open line whenever he or anyone in the office picks up to dial out." A pause to listen. "Yeah, so I guess I'm saying we don't know much." Another pause. "Well, see, that's the point: he's a politics reporter, so everything he's talking about could be relevant. Well, I *can* tell you he's a bit of a lush. He's at a bar almost every day. He's at one now."

Salter was early for his lunchtime meeting, at a bar in Adams-Morgan, well outside the usual government power-lunch circuit, but he had barely sat down when the Energy Secretary arrived looking haggard and not particularly energetic. His pinstriped suit might have been more appropriate for the

Treasury or the Commerce Secretary, the plum jobs—Salter remembered—that the Energy Secretary had hoped for.

He settled opposite Salter and began wearily: "I hear you've been speaking to some of my cabinet colleagues."

"Yes, yes I have."

"What have you found out?"

"Why don't you tell me why you called me, Mr. Secretary? What's got everyone so skittish?" The Energy Secretary was in his late forties, and he might well end up at Treasury or State under a different administration. Most days he had the self-assured bearing of one who has been party to important and delicate conversations his whole life and takes it all in stride as his proper métier. Today, however, he had a harried, indignant air about him, less like someone competent and well-trained confronting a thorny problem, and more like one incensed that circumstances have reduced him to this chicanery.

"We took the President at his word," the Secretary began, his eyes roving over the bar patrons, "when he said he wanted to be slow, methodical, respectful of President Redmond's agenda and legacy. To be fair, he did say he might not get done all that she had wanted, political realities being what they are. We understood that. This is all unprecedented, uncharted—we're the appointees of a Democratic President serving a Republican. He told us that given the realities of taking on the new job, he'd have to come at all this slowly."

"OK," said Salter.

"And that sounded reasonable. And frankly, it was as much as we could hope for from anyone—particularly given the new ground we're breaking. He stressed that he was unprepared, and he asked that we allow him to get up to speed."

"Yes, that's all been reported and discussed."

"Only, they weren't learning the ropes; they weren't going slow: they were completely prepared and moving fast, particularly once they started filling the under-secretary posts."

"What do you mean?" asked Salter.

233

"At first, all I was able to glean was that they seemed to be making preparations regarding rule changes throughout the Cabinet departments. And not just mine."

"Preparations?"

"I've found out that my under-secretary has been meeting with Quantrelle and Marek in the White House. And I've heard that my little department mole—fucking rat, more like—isn't unique. It's coordinated, Mr. Salter."

"What is? Who's coordinating it?"

"We're none of us sure what they're up to. But I think it's coming from the top—from the President." Here again, he looked about the room. "And these PAs and Schedule C appointees planted in our departments have been chipping away at the departments from inside."

"And you think—?"

"—Look this over," he said, passing some paper across the table to Salter. "It started with the director of the Office of Personnel Management. The director agreed to resign." The Secretary looked pointedly at Salter. "By firing him, they've begun a reorganization of the federal civil service. It's clear they'll consolidate and concentrate their power over the Departments by making hiring, firing and promotion a partisan issue. They're looking to bring the Personnel Department under the direct ambit of the White House."

"Yes, but—"

"Don't you *read* press releases?" Here, he removed a new sheet of paper from his inside jacket pocket and read: "...will today merge many OPM functions with the General Services Administration. Its policymaking responsibilities will be transferred to the Executive Office of the President at the White House."

Salter was scribbling furiously, but the Secretary shoved the new paper toward him with the dejected air of an instructor dealing with a bright student who isn't applying himself.

"At first we thought they were preparing clandestine rule changes to spring on us. But I think we were wrong. I don't know it for a fact, but the rule changes may be a smoke screen. They may or may not go into effect. The point is that the changes they're calling for are like litmus tests. I think they—whoever 'they' really are—are using these to vet my and other department staff; like they want to know who they can count on."

"You have proof of this?" Salter asked.

"No. But here's what I think will happen," he continued: "the White House will at the very least leak these new policy announcements and begin implementing interpretive rules—"

"—Wait," said Salter. "Isn't there a time frame? They can't just *do* it, can they?"

"Of course not," said the Secretary, wondering just how much he had to spoon feed this reporter. "The rule changes are *proposed*," he began patiently. "Then they're published in the Federal Register, but they don't go into effect for at least 90 days during the comment period. And then they can be held up by appeals and lawsuits...et cetera. Look, they could enact new legislation faster than that, if they really wanted to make changes. They have the votes to do pretty much anything they want."

"So why—?"

"—That's what I don't get. Except, it does make everybody lay their cards on the table. When the new rules are announced, it'll force us—the Cabinet Secretaries—to make a stand for our respective departments. If we refuse to comply with the new announcements or hedge about implementing the rule changes, the President will demand our resignations."

"Right," said Salter.

"And in the resulting furor within each Department, they'll get a better sense of who is and is not with the White House's program...and they're already compiling lists. If we refuse to resign, which we could—it's becoming more common—we'll be forcing him to fire us. Which, frankly, we think he'll do."

"This is nuts. If you resign, the world will know why," Salter pointed out.

"Look over the paper," he said tapping it. "If we're ousted—"

"—There'd be a vacuum at the top."

"No! That's the point," said the Secretary, "because the people who would become interim Department heads would be the very under-secretaries who've been working in the shadows to bring this all about."

"The whole Administration undermined," Salter whispered.

"And then—obviously—the new head will be the under-secretary or some other handpicked guy, and he'll fall right into line and probably accelerate the process of remaking each Cabinet Department. Which will be easy now that Personnel's role has been taken over by the Executive Office.

"We could try to be proactive, I suppose," he continued, "and start firing these new appointments," he continued, "but under the new OPM reorganization, we might not have the authority to do it. In the resulting frenzy, the White House would refuse the terminations and—again—ask us to resign."

"And if you all resigned together?" asked Salter.

"Checkmate, us. Since that's what they want anyway."

* * *

Reed had used his friend's name, Sam Hedrick, when introducing himself to the man he'd hitched a ride with from the camping supply store in Princeton up into the hills. His dossiers, a bedroll, a blanket, some tinned meat, a lantern, a powerful flashlight and a SIG Sauer M17 handgun, bought without a waiting period, were all he had. He lied to the driver that he'd been in New York City for the past three years and needed to unplug completely, up in the hills where he could get his head right again. The driver nodded, and said it was the perfect antidote to what the big city was shoveling.

"No huntin' though, I expect," he added.

"No, not this time of year," Reed replied sadly, falling quickly back into his hills cadence. "But might be I'll get to reconnoiter for later. Might do a little stalking of trails whilst trails is easy to read."

The driver grunted his assent.

Reed asked to be dropped about a quarter mile from where three roads met, way out in the country, in fading light. He took the fire trail, hopped over the No Trespassing chain hanging limply across the entry and trudged the mile or so deeper into the back country. After the first hundred yards, the lane became merely two parallel strips of dirt flecked with gravel, taking him steeply uphill into the forest.

When he reached the camp, he dropped his gear with relief. From his mountainside clearing he could see down across the familiar slender glen that meandered with the stream that ran through it. From his grandstand, he took it all in as the sun began to dip below the steep hills opposite him.

The camp was just as he'd remembered it, a small, wood cabin with plank sides, and one small window—just one room, with a roof that extended to protect a bare patch of ground as though the cabin had a porch. He'd spent a good many hours sitting there on a folding chair, watching the birds and small creatures. There was an outdoor privy round the left side and to the back. There was no lock on the door of the cabin.

He lit his lantern and shone it cautiously through the doorway. There was the folding chair, the fireplace, the wood frame cot. As he opened the bedroll, he remembered, too late, that water had to be fetched from the stream below. He'd get some in the morning. What he wanted more than anything right now was a beer.

As his eyes adjusted, he made out little bars of Irish Spring soap broken up and stuffed in the corners around the cabin. He smiled. It was something they'd been doing since he was boy to keep animals out. He'd done the same thing at his Beaver Island cabin. The smile still on his face, he marveled that no one had found a better deterrent. Reed took the chair outside, sat down and opened one of the canned stews he'd bought. He ate it cold out of the can with his fingers as he watched the vestiges of light turn to purple shadow and slip away behind the hills.

* * *

Imogen walked into the cold viewing room in the morgue, where Duncan's body lay on a metal table. Vega hung back at the door, waited for Imogen to return. An orderly drew the sheet down so she could see his face. The headshot had entered through his forehead. Fortunately for Imogen, the worst part—the exit wound—was at the back of his head, out of sight. Staring at him, she felt she was seeing someone else. The skin looked different. Like a creepy CGI likeness, the shape of the eyes and nose was not quite right. She struggled with the knowledge that it was not he when it was; that it was him when it was not.

She reached out and caressed his cheek. It was cold, the skin hard and rubbery. She brushed some hair away from his face, as if it mattered. He didn't, as some people claim of the dead, look as though he was sleeping. Duncan could never sleep on his back without snoring.

The memory felled her. She felt a rush of heat within her as she thought of all the wonderful, troublesome, noisome things associated with a man, this man: strength and tenderness, intelligence and frivolity, cultivation and vulgarity; pig-headed beauty, amiable vitality, beguiling warmth. All gone. She felt her legs losing strength, placed her hand on his arm for support. Her hand met the same alien, engorged rubber-dummy counterfeit of life.

She was suddenly furious. This body wasn't him. Not really. Duncan was gone, and he'd left behind this lump to be tidied up. His body, his real estate, his research; and his guilt—the crazy plan to revenge Matthew, which was somehow now a burden on *her* conscience. She almost shrieked, "Fuck you!" at the body, but she felt her strength and her wits returning, felt the need to hold onto the warmth and fondness for their brief life together. Vega had told her how it happened, and she was still shaking with anger, not at the agents who had killed him, but at Calder for being so stupid. She shielded her bitterness and rancor from Amanda as she turned. Vega hugged her again.

Imogen felt herself melting into Amanda, needing her friend's strength; felt the helplessness of the moment. If Duncan was dead, her lease on life had run out. There he was, killed in some incomprehensible way on *her* business. And yet, Reed was still out there, the Illinois murderers were still out there, the Senate would vote soon to confirm Drew Eliot as the new Attorney General, and something was planned for April 20, just five days away.

"All right," Imogen said as she withdrew from Amanda, though she kept a hand on her shoulder for stability. "I know he wanted to be cremated, so I'll..." Here she faltered. "You've probably got a cover story about the arrest for the news media—drug bust?"

"Exactly. Executed by the police, not us."

"So, we can't announce a memorial for Duncan?"

"No, I'm sorry. We need to keep this quiet until we're ready to make our move. I'll put in a call to the Poli-Sci department, tell them he's helping the Justice Department with our investigation and won't be available for the next two weeks."

Imogen nodded. It was surreal.

"Gen, I've talked with Weir. Obviously, under any normal circumstances, you'd be given leave to—you know, put your life back together—but *if* we can re-establish contact with Reed, we need you."

"Yes. Of course."

"You're the only one he trusts."

"Yes."

Though she thought a motel room would be better, Vega agreed to drop Imogen at the door to Duncan's apartment building above the Pike Place Market. Imogen climbed out of the SUV and opened the back door, lugging her suitcase and the box containing Calder's effects. Vega came to the front door too.

"I talked with Weir while you were on the phone making arrangements," she said. "There's one last thing. Duncan left a note for you. It was in his pants pocket when he died." Vega pulled the out the letter. "We're holding the original as evidence," she added apologetically.

Imogen stared at the folded sheet of paper. A photocopy.

"Why don't I come upstairs for a minute?" said Vega.

Imogen put a hand on Vega's shoulder again. "I'll be OK."

Upstairs, she found a half-bottle of Pinot Gris in the door of the fridge. She poured a tall glass and went to stand at her post by the French doors. It was surreal to be there, and she couldn't shake the feeling that he would be home any minute.

Though it was chilly, she opened the doors to let some air in. She breathed deeply the cold, salty breeze. This wasn't the last time she'd ever be in the apartment, but it was certainly one of the last. Look and remember.

Remember Duncan walking around naked after a shower. "No one can see in," he had protested; she could see his strong, beautiful thighs, trim hips, see the muscles moving in his shoulders as he cavorted. She could see the scars where he'd been shot before.

She swore she could feel his arms encircle her from behind as he would in the mornings when she stood there drinking coffee. She saw him stretched out on their bed with rare winter sunlight pouring over him, not small as in the morgue, but like a man, who took up too much damned space in the bed.

She saw him unpacking groceries they'd picked up together at the Market. He loved French bread, and she could see him cracking the end off a baguette and breathing in its scent, enraptured, before popping it into his mouth: so characteristic, so endearing. Such a banal thing really, but *him*. It was all real, and it was all gone.

She poured the rest of the wine into her glass and retrieved the letter before sitting down on what had been her side of the couch. It read:

Dearest Imogen,

If you're reading this, I'm dead, or in prison, and they won't let you see me. Either one is terrible to consider because each closes me off from you. I love you, and I want so much to be with you always. My heart breaks as I write this, thinking of not being with you.

Why have I done this then?

I've come to see that there can be no reckoning. Even if we're successful in arresting the conspirators, this is too big, too much for a jaded, cynical electorate to encompass, much less prosecute effectively. Assassins, like the ones who murdered Matthew, might very well go free in order to get at the top men.

These men are powerful and canny. There's lots of plausible deniability between them and the deeds with which they should be charged. They might wriggle off the hook completely. And then they'd be free to harden their defenses and further solidify their power. And the assassins, who've killed 20 or more people—Matthew included—would have been given immunity for nothing.

I need to do what I can, to strike the blow where I can.

I died the day Matthew was murdered. But you brought me back. You gave me back my life. I will love you always. You know that.

Duncan

Please make sure the FBI knows that Rich Lamberti knows nothing about any this.

Imogen was sobbing. "Always?" she asked aloud. "What the fuck does that even mean?" The letter had more of Duncan in it than the body she had seen earlier—right down to the meticulous, architecture-plan handwriting. She could hear his voice in her head as she read along.

Clutching the letter to her chest, she rolled herself into the blanket that Duncan had folded and draped in his precise way across the back of the couch. She lay sideways along it, her head resting on one of the armrests. Outside, past Alki Point, the sun dipped behind the Olympic Mountains, painting the snowy peaks first orange, then red and finally purple.

30

Over the past few days, via phone, but usually in person, Salter had met with more Cabinet Secretaries and trusted administrators in more out of the way spots across D.C. and suburban Maryland than he'd ever visited before. Tweedledum and Tweedledim continued to note in their reports that he seemed to drink an awful lot at work. Quantrelle was worried that he no longer had the manpower for individual, round-the-clock surveillance of their targets and lamented the necessity of killing more of his own to secure the safety of the final steps.

Even more alarming, for him, the Postman seemed to be growing impatient. For years he had kept proceedings at arm's length, but now he was calling regularly. He seemed obsessed with killing Reed. Certainly, it was necessary, but where before the Postman had issued an order and expected it to be carried out, now he checked in, asked for status updates, as if he could *will* the thing to happen.

Salter was hearing much the same anxieties from other Secretaries, bypassed by their own staff: the same constrained options and fears; the same lack of trust even in one another; the same dismal lack of hard evidence. And the message was the same. Everything was pointing to a wholesale remaking of the government with only ideologically sound men in it. And it was a tight circle, radius about six feet from the President. Quantrelle had thus far ensured that there were no leaks regarding what was happening—whatever it was.

And whatever it was, Hugh couldn't shake the idea that it looked like early maneuvering for a bureaucratic coup. But why do it at all? Why make these clandestine preparations when you had both houses of Congress and the presidency?

He met the Vice President, his wife and the omnipresent Georgia Desmond at One Observatory Circle, itself a group with a tight radius, representing yet another in a series of closed sets in a shocking Venn Diagram. Ostensibly for a chat about the VP-at-home puff piece, Desmond and the Carr's sat down casually with Salter in the Library sitting room.

"Presumably, the AG confirmation vote in the Senate will happen this week," David Carr was saying, "and the Speaker of the House has just announced an invitation for the president to give an address to a joint session on the 20th."

"Yes, I've heard that, too," said Salter.

"Do you think it's to announce Eliot? Seems like overkill...unless Eliot has some blockbuster intel?" asked Susan Carr.

"Or is it to announce Eliot's new direction?" Georgia wondered.

"The Press Secretary, Marek, has been notably absent. There hasn't been a briefing in almost a week," said Salter.

"And Quantrelle's been away from the White House a lot, too," the Vice President chimed in. "As near as I can tell, there haven't been any of those back-channel meetings."

"How are you coming with the Cabinet interviews?" asked the Vice President.

"I'm still working on it. People seem unsettled. Maybe even scared."

"Do you think this address is when they'll announce the new house cleaning in the various cabinet departments," asked Carr.

"Christ, it could be anything," Salter sighed.

Across town, President Moore, Chief of Staff Quantrelle and Press Secretary Marek were sitting around the coffee table in the Oval Office.

"Sir, how much of this do you really want to know?" Quantrelle asked.

"Everything."

"Sir," Marek began, "we know this is not your favored course of action..."

"Putting it mildly," Moore observed.

"But it clears the board for everything we want to accomplish, and it cuts our opponents off at the knees," Marek declared.

"I'm ready," said Moore. "I've registered my concerns, but I'm all in, and I need to know what's going on in order to be effective." He fixed each in turn with what he hoped conveyed a manful, committed gaze.

If Alec had been in charge, he thought, and not Quantrelle, he could have at least confided his misgivings and frustrations to someone likely to hear and understand them. Now, he had no one. He had heard of the "watchful doctrine" initiated among the foot soldiers. Any mistake, registering of doubt or flagging of enthusiasm was to be reported.

He had come to realize it applied to everyone—including himself; that fear and mistrust was how rank-and-file was kept in line. Was that what he was—just another grunt soldier in someone else's war?

The West Wing, and the Oval Office in particular, had previously been a place for frank discussion. While the expectation was that any strategy or policy forged there would receive robust endorsement when it became public, regardless of how an individual might feel, the need and allowance for reasoned, conscientious dissent was understood. But now, if he'd had anyone to speak or commiserate with, he would say that having agreed to the Postman's terms, he felt he had "invited the vampire in."

Was he Renfield then, Dracula's lunatic acolyte? The suggestion was apt, he allowed, if revolting. The coup, for that was the Postman's plan, would go forward with him or without him. Better, he decided, that it go forward with him in charge, where he might mitigate some the worst excesses. But to what degree was he really in charge at all?

Moore needed to know the details, because there was the possibility, however remote, that he had made himself surplus to requirements and would also be jettisoned. He wanted to know details for his safety, and so that he could watch for any deviation meant to bring harm directly to him.

"So," Moore began, "a three-pronged attack, beginning at 7:45pm on Thursday, April 20."

"Yes, sir," said Quantrelle. "An attack using Novichok 5. It will be dispersed in both its dry and ethyl forms. In the Capitol, the nerve agent will be activated at 7:45pm, just as you and the new Attorney General arrive—but *before* either of you have stepped out of the car.

"In New York, beginning at 7:55pm our operatives will smear it on the handrails and seating areas of the PATH train that leaves Exchange Place in Jersey City, bound for World Trade Center. When they get off at WTC, one will carry a disbursal bomb in a fast food drink cup. When they're at a safe distance, they'll detonate—"

"—How much of an explosion can you get from something that size?" Moore asked incredulously.

"Not much at all. That's not the point. The point is to disperse the dust particles of Novichok into the air near one of the vents. Inhaling a single speck of it will kill a man in less than a minute."

"Jesus," Moore whispered. "Aren't you worried our guys will kill themselves?"

"No. They've been trained. But we *will* use that deadly aspect to implicate a Lebanese exchange student we have our eye on."

"We're working with terrorists?" Moore asked.

"No. He's just a patsy, exactly what he claims to be—a young guy studying engineering. Chemical engineering. But his body—killed by the nerve agent—will be found near Wall Street, as though he was part of the plot."

"What else?" said Moore.

"At 4:55 Pacific time, our agents will release an airburst from the Dumbarton Bridge in the South Bay. The dust will carry a long way on the prevailing winds—to Palo Alto, San Jose and on into the Santa Clara Valley.

"So, beginning at 7:45, the threat realized, the Secret Service will whisk you away. Reports of the other attacks will be coming through by then, and you'll be taken to a secure location. I have both of your speeches ready, sir. The one you'll never give to the Joint Session, and the one you *will* read on television and radio later that night when you assume emergency powers and designate your new AG as the sharp end of the spear.

"There will be chaos, and it will continue for days. The dry version of the nerve agent stays active for days or weeks, even when it's wet."

* * *

Vega sat on the edge of her motel bed in Seattle, massaging her eyes. She had not slept well. Across town, Imogen cried bitterly in the kitchen of Duncan's apartment. Slowly, deliberately, she put the second coffee cup back into the cupboard from which she'd taken it by reflex.

A couple of hours before, on his hilltop in West Virginia, Reed had awoken with the scent of dawn, shivering in a cold sweat, thinking for a moment he was back on Beaver Island with the network closing in. And in D.C., Nettie and Abel Gardiner too were up at first light on April 17, preparing to present their findings to Don Weir. As soon as he arrived, Nettie rolled a conspiracy board into place behind the table.

"What can we prove about the payment structure of the dark network?" Gardiner asked Weir.

"You tell me," said Weir. He took off his FBI ball cap and placed it on his knee.

"Until now," Gardiner began, "not much, but the information from Brandenberg was like the key to an encrypted file. We know account numbers now, and we're starting to be able to match accounts and payments to individuals. We're also getting rapid compliance on the lifting

247

orders we issued. That fills in the gaps, and we have information right up to the present."

"Proceed," said Weir.

The conspiracy board could revolve, one side for Gardiner and his money trail through the PAC's and the offshore banks they used; the other for Nettie to show laundered extra-curricular payments from those banks to clandestine members and groups. As he began talking, Gardiner would push some papers toward Weir and then back away to show him where those were connecting on his side of the board. The network of payments was dizzying, but they'd been able to untangle much of it.

Gardiner concluded by saying, "Not only can we demonstrate coordination between all of them—and they went to great lengths to hide it—but with this bank info we can also prove coordination between the PACs and then-candidate Moore. I still have some areas for follow-up—who these two large payments are to, for a start, and for what. It's a million dollars each, and it settles on March 10."

"The day President Redmond died," said Weir.

"Yes," said Gardiner. "Those two payments don't go to anyone currently known to us. The date makes it significant, and after this briefing I'll focus on them."

Nettie Sartain began: "Not only can we see money movement on the otherwise legitimate campaign to elect the Christopher-Moore ticket that Abel just described, but money's cycling into the charitable orgs and out to the PACs and IEO's for decidedly *un*campaign-like activities.

"In fact, in a number of cases, we can match dummy payment records meant to conceal real payments to operatives we now have in custody." She tapped one of the sheets and then pointed at her board. "Abel's work on the gift card transactions and their clearances through offshore banks line up perfectly with payments to operatives for work they've done, like murdering Electors. There's also a strange back-and-forth of payments from and to Flintlock Industries, the murder delivery airline."

"Jeez," Weir said under his breath. Then, "This is excellent. It looks like we can charge Quantrelle and quite a few others. Is he the top man? You haven't told me who's pulling the strings."

"We can guess," said Nettie, "but we can't say for sure. I need more time on this last part."

"So," Weir began, "if we arrest Quantrelle, which we certainly can, and he doesn't roll over—he'd certainly be thinking about what happened to Alec Nash," he allowed "...if we get nothing more from him, we're left with whoever pulls the strings still in charge." He paused a moment to reflect. "What do you need more time for?"

"Imogen has impressed upon me the need to stop this once and for all. Each time we've thought we stopped them, we only slowed them down. If the leaders are left out there, they'll just fold up shop and open up somewhere else."

"OK," said Weir.

"I've kind of taken a page out of Imogen's book," Nettie continued, "and I've begun a network-link analysis. At first, it appears to point in multiple directions, but there's definitely a center of gravity to all this. It's a bit like when astronomers postulated the presence of Pluto based on—"

"—I don't give a shit about Pluto!" Weir hissed. "We want to understand who or what's at the *center* of all this."

"Yes, sir. If I may try again: the laundering and the payments have been orchestrated to appear random, but Imogen and I don't think they are. I'm still in the hunch stage, sir, but I reckon there's a purpose behind the way they avoid certain organizations—one in particular, the Fourmile Creek PAC, which wasn't even on our radar. Money comes out of it—a lot of money—to fund the other organizations, but where the others have money coming in and going out from each other, nothing cycles back through Fourmile Creek. Everything swirls *around* Fourmile, but it doesn't interact. There's some kind of quarantine. It's being protected."

"What do we know about Fourmile Creek? And aren't there hundreds of PAC's that give money without getting it back?" asked Weir.

"No, sir, there aren't. That's why it stands out. True, there are other PAC's and even individuals who give one-off payments to any of our targeted PAC's, but there's only one with a steady stream of payments to them all—Fourmile. I've got our analysts working on it right now."

"You haven't said anything about April 20. Is there anything pointing to what might be happening?"

"No, sir. I'm sorry. Like a lot of the investigation, we've been going backward trying to identify who's doing what and tying people to acts. We're much closer, but we still don't have the full picture."

"Are you recommending that we leave everyone out there for now in place?"

"If you're asking my opinion, sir, then yes."

* * *

"They missed him by minutes," Quantrelle was telling the President. "Somehow, Reed knew they were coming."

"How could he know?" Moore asked.

Quantrelle and Marek sat on the couches around the coffee table in the Oval Office while Moore paced the room.

"Unknown," said Marek. "But if we can keep to schedule, it won't matter soon."

Moore nodded, but he didn't look confident. "What does this do to our overall plan if they can't get him?"

"It's not ideal. But it makes the plan even more important because it's the only way for us to be in charge of information. Once we're firmly on top, if Reed's still out there, we can either quash his information, discredit it..." Quantrelle's phone rang. He didn't need Moore's permission to answer. "Yes?"

"Reed's new phone number?" said Tweedledim at the other end. "We think we've isolated it?"

"Where is he?" Quantrelle asked quickly.

"We don't know, but we have an idea which way he was going when he turned it off."

"Where?"

"He was heading due south through Kentucky. But at Lexington, he turned east and the phone went off."

Quantrelle thought for a moment. His face radiated smug satisfaction—all eyes on him—the fulcrum of the action in the White House and the nation. He leaned back on the couch and tossed his head back, the man in charge. "All right," he said, "so it's probable he is or was on a bus. Do you have a map in front of you?"

"Yeah."

"What route do you think he was on? What *Interstate* route?"

"It looks like I-64, I think?"

By this time, Quantrelle had pulled out his smartphone and was looking at a map, too. His thumb scrolled along I-64. He stopped and smiled. "Good work," he said to Dum, and snapped the phone shut.

"Roanoke," he said to Moore and Marek. "That's where he's from. *That's* where he's going." He opened the phone again. He was about to dial when he paused and looked at his audience. "These things are untraceable," he said, indicating the phone. "Even so, I normally wouldn't make a call from the Oval Office, but time's of the essence, I think you can agree"—and without waiting for assent, he called the leader of his Illinois team and dispatched them to Roanoke, Virginia. Not long left now for Reed.

* * *

The Tweedles were using snooping technology similar to the kit that Trey Kelly and Imogen had used so successfully to identify and bring down the first of the operatives by tracking their movements and their history from the phones they carried, and for once the government's tools were more comprehensive and powerful. At the FBI's hiding-in-plain-sight IT office, Trey had also been busy, and he was grateful finally to have something to contribute.

First, he had isolated the two Seattle operatives and had been able to trace their movements backward in time, confirming their presence at the sites of four and possibly a fifth murder. The history played out a little like a film of various colored phone icons and their trajectories across a landscape. He immediately sent links of this timeline map to Vega and Weir.

He had also been monitoring Reed's signal, which turned on and off erratically, but he'd been able to reckon that his base was in the Pendleton neighborhood along Orchard Street in Cincinnati. He sent that information to Vega and Weir. Before the FBI could move on Orchard Street, however, the dark network had tried to grab him first. Reed got away, and Trey identified one of the phone signals issuing from there as having no name or owner, a clear sign.

Whoever it was made a 20-second call to a phone, also unidentified, at a shipping warehouse in Springfield, Virginia, about ten miles from D.C. Kelly flagged them both and sent Weir a warrant request for a wiretap so they could listen in when either made another call.

The warrant had come through early that morning, just in time for Trey to record a call from a new number. Trey gasped as he zoomed in on the location. The caller was inside the White House. Trey felt a chill as it sank in that he had proof—proof—that someone at the White House was involved in a nationwide conspiracy of murder and treason.

As he listened, he was surprised that the new number, a young person with a habit of ending his sentences with a rising intonation as though asking a question, didn't use the plain-language code he'd grown accustomed to hearing, and was using Reed's real name. He flagged the uptalker's new number and made a note to ask Weir for another warrant. But he barely had time to send the request before the White House caller reached out to the Cincinnati-based number.

Though he didn't know it was he, Trey heard Quantrelle abandon his sonorous, official tone in favor of a brash, martial air: "Go immediately to Roanoke, Virginia. Find target Cooper. Immediately. Roanoke and find Cooper. This takes absolute priority. I'm with Chandler and Tucker now. Cooper's going to ground where he feels safe—first

252

Cincinnati, now Roanoke. I'll pass on any new intel as it becomes available. Your meeting orders stand. Any questions?"

"No, sir."

In the Oval Office, Quantrelle had snapped the phone shut with a flourish and nodded confidently at Moore and Marek. Perhaps they were impressed; perhaps they thought he'd seen too many B-movies; they didn't say. Their futures might depend upon him.

In a motel just outside Frankfort, Brandt closed his phone and sighed. He missed "Coop," who was sharp and all business, not a puffed-up buffoon like whoever this new person was. And what kind of code name was "Bannister?" It was a damn shame to have to kill Coop. But maybe, if he bided his time, the call to "have a meeting" with Bannister would come through from someone higher up. He'd look forward to that.

At IT, Trey stopped recording when they hung up, and sat frozen for a moment, staring at the map on his screen, hardly believing. Not only was someone at the White House clearly involved, but that person had just given the order to commit another murder.

* * *

In Seattle, Vega closed the door to the interview room where Cardoso sat handcuffed to the table, still barefoot. Agent Cleary stood in a corner, stony-faced and erect.

"Well, you're into some serious shit, Dan," she said. "Where the fuck did you get the recipe for Novichok nerve gas? You've got enough of that stuff to kill half a city!"

"You've got no idea who you're dealing with. And soon enough"—here he raised his shackled hands—"you'll be the one sitting here."

"You're talking about your plans for April 20?"

"Fuck you!"

"Why don't you tell me what's going to happen? I can see you want to. How you're going to destroy us, put us in our place. And what do you get? Money?"

"We get our country back," he spat.

"After the 20th? What happens then? Clearly, it can't be stopped. Why not let us in on the full shock and awe?"

"You'll be begging to go back to wherever you came from."

"Takoma Park, Maryland?"

Behind Cardoso, Agent Cleary cracked a smile.

"You think you're funny," said Cardoso. "But that's not why I'm laughing at you. I want a lawyer."

Imogen and Agent Reyes were also having difficulty with Janssen in the adjoining interview room: the chapter members she and Vega had captured previously had been mercenaries, keen for a deal. Not so, Janssen and his compatriot, Dan Cardoso. They were nihilist, all-or-nothing true believers, it seemed. Ready to go down with the ship. It was hard for Imogen to believe, but they seemed to welcome their coming suffering.

"You can't stop it," Janssen scoffed. "You don't know the half of what's going on. You should be worrying about yourselves." He glanced backwards at Reyes, who stood in the corner, arms crossed in front staring straight ahead.

Imogen looked across the table at Cardoso, so smug, so cocksure. She wanted to kill him. The world would be a better place. She imagined a bullet wound in *his* head, and thought how fitting it would be, like for like. For one long minute she sat stone-faced, silent, allowing the rage to dissipate.

This was a new puzzle. Janssen wouldn't respond to threats, didn't yet see the value in making a deal, wasn't interested in self-preservation. What *was* he interested in preserving and protecting, she asked herself?

He had a smirking, superior air, as though he saw himself as one called out, a noble hero. Where he saw himself as unique, part of some honorable brotherhood, she saw only one more expendable toady functionary. But that didn't help.

If she wanted leverage, she'd have to threaten the very thing he valued. What was it?

"I wonder if that's accurate Eric," she said meditatively, her tone professorial, as though a student had made a wild claim in a classroom discussion. "The 'not even knowing half part,' I mean."

"It's an expression, you stupid bitch. It means you don't know shit."

Imogen nodded equably. "You're part of the Seattle 'chapter,' which is what I think you call your terrorist cells. How do we come to know that they're called that, I wonder?"

"Some weakling blabbed what little he knew."

"A weakling, yes. A weak link. Not like you, of course."

"Nothing like me," he hissed.

"So," said Vega to Dan Cardoso in the other interview room, "about that attorney"—she drew a sheet of paper from her file and put it on the table between them—"if you want an attorney, I will let you contact one, or one may be provided for you, as we always say. But right now, I've got a lot of leeway here." She drew the paper back toward her slightly.

Cardoso looked flatly ahead, not meeting her gaze.

"But, if you call a lawyer, once we take that step, it's suddenly public. You can count on me to make it known that you've helped us with our investigations...whether you have or not. The Postman might be very anxious to send someone to have a *meeting* with you," she added threateningly. "Or," she said, sliding the paper back, "we take you into protective custody and you waive your right to counsel."

Across the hall, Imogen held to her professorial, Socratic exploration: "But if you're meant for greater things, as you should be, Eric—and for greater reward in whatever it is that's to come, as befits your considerable talents—how does it feel to know you've been undone by weaklings?"

Janssen stared straight ahead.

"Yes," she continued, "the half we know came because there were weak links in your network. They made their deals, and you'll pay for them. We eliminated the D.C. chapter, we turned the Boston chapter, and we're in negotiations with Frank Reed—Mr. Cooper, as you know him. In fact, it was he who gave you two up. It's unraveling, Eric. The Flintlock pilots are now working as FBI informants."

"I can't help what other people do," he said.

"No. No, I don't expect you can. That's a credit to you and your mission-focus. I admire that. I do. But your Mr. Cooper came to *us* because your friends in high places had Mr. Fisher murdered in his jail cell. He and Cooper built the network, didn't they? They recruited you and many others. But it turns out that they're both expendable. If your friends in high places think those two are disposable, whatever must they think of you?"

"You don't understand," he said bleakly.

"I'd like to," she said earnestly. "Because while admittedly I only know the half of it, even I can see that everything points to your high-placed friends letting you hang as a terrorist after doing whatever it is you have planned. It's true now, but it was true even before we arrested you. I'm sure that's becoming clear to you."

Janssen leaned back in his chair.

"It pisses me off," she confided. "They've relied on your stealth, your smarts, your professionalism. You've done everything right—everything they asked of you and more. And they're hoping you'll keep playing the good-soldier sap so they can pin it all on you. You'll be disgraced, reviled. And if you live, they'll pick a time to kill you."

She pushed a piece of paper toward him. "We haven't questioned you yet, by the way. If you sign this, waive your right to counsel and agree to be a cooperating witness, we can take you into protective custody and focus on sentencing recommendations."

* * *

256

Weir had a decision to make. Based on their traces, and what they had heard from their phone taps, Reed seemed to have gone to ground in Roanoke, Virginia. There was a field office in Richmond, just under an hour away, but Agents Guthrie and Davies had been part of the Faithless Elector Task Force from the beginning, and Weir was uneasy about widening the scope of those "read in" to what the task force was doing.

Davies was in Cincinnati—two hours from Roanoke— twice the time it would take a Richmond team to arrive. Guthrie was still in D.C. Keeping things within the family seemed the more prudent way forward, even if he lost some of the timeliness. He sent Davies directly from Cincinnati. Trager and Vega would turn over their interviews to Cleary and Reyes—good men he trusted—and travel back to babysit Reed, if and when he re-established contact. Guthrie would meet Vega and Imogen at Dulles and go from there to Roanoke. Nettie Sartain and Abel Gardiner would continue their work untangling the payment structure. Weir set off to brief his superiors on the task force's progress.

From deep in The Pit at Bus Rentals, Trey watched his monitor as the signal representing the Illinois chapter painted a snaking pink line across Kentucky and West Virginia. They were keeping off the Interstates and using only back roads and state routes, a necessary choice, but one that would add hours to their journey through the hills. It was a gamble. Though both the dark network goons and the FBI were converging on Roanoke, neither group was certain that Reed was in the area. Neither would have anything to do there until he turned on his phone again and made contact. Though they didn't know it, they passed within ten miles of his hideout as they slithered across the country.

Trey, studying the movement on his screen, wondered how it would all end. Here was a convergence: each side needed Frank Reed. What made the gamble so dangerous was that in this game of cat-and-mouse, the FBI couldn't arrest— or even let on they were following—the assassins until they made some kind of move. The whole scenario had to be left to play out. The Bureau needed clear confirmation that the group they were now tracking and the Illinois chapter were one and the same. Though Trey Kelly didn't know all the details, it was clear that without Reed, the FBI would have only the soldiers and none of the generals. The whole power structure would remain intact.

Weir's briefing and presentation of the evidence were accepted, his plan (such as it was) approved. He was ordered to give daily briefings to the FBI Director. The only development the following day was that both FBI teams, and the assassins had arrived in Roanoke well after dark. He noted that it was a dangerous moment, and his team would have to be careful not to trip over the bad guys as they felt around for clues to Reed's whereabouts.

As Weir continued to direct the investigation and wait for word of any progress, one moment in his presentation of the evidence to the FBI Director stuck with him. As the Director was turning over the evidence in the file, he had paused over a copy of Calder's note to Imogen about why he'd done what he did. He took a long time reading it. "...too big for a jaded, cynical electorate to encompass, much less prosecute effectively," the director read aloud. When he finished reading the whole letter, he'd looked at his deputy and said of Calder, "Poor bastard probably wasn't far off the mark, was he?"

The following morning, with still no sign or signal from Reed, the Senate leader filed for cloture on the hearings regarding Senator Eliot's confirmation as Attorney General, clearing the way for a vote. As he was a Senate colleague of long-standing, and his party held the majority, there was no doubt that the votes existed to confirm and install Eliot at the Justice Department. The hearings themselves had been embarrassingly perfunctory for the same reason. The confirmation vote was set for Thursday morning, April 20. It was the quickest confirmation in history. Within hours after that, hand-picked Justice officials could get to work exposing the evidence and leads the Bureau had gathered on the most sinister conspiracy in the country's history.

31

Reed's second morning at the hunting camp dawned brightly. As the sun swept the shadows from his little hollow, he walked down to fetch some water. He filled his canteen and a jug from the cabin. Then he lay face down on a thick tree root at the edge of the stream and drank from it using only his cupped hands. He thrilled to its coldness as he drank deeply.

He turned and sat up, looking back toward the camp. It was quiet, wholesome and inviting, he thought. And it was a mirage. He wasn't safe at all. He'd never be safe until he finished what he'd begun. Could he really trust Trager and her crew? The Illinois mob was onto him. Was it because they'd cracked the FBI, or were they tracking him through his phone now?

Either way, as soon as he made contact with the FBI, he'd have both to contend with. He would have to assume they were tracking his phone. Whoever he called at the FBI would immediately be flagged and tracked, too. He had worked hard to help Trager mask her movements from the network's snoopers. He decided he would contact Weir's landline.

He'd spent the previous day familiarizing himself with the deer paths running across his side of the mountain. It would be folly for Brandt and his Illinois irregulars to come at night, but he traveled the deer paths again, to fix them in his mind so that he could navigate even in the dark. He would have the advantage, daylight or darkness, but they'd be better armed. And he'd have to be careful not to kill any FBI agents who might arrive to assist him.

As he contemplated the battle to come from his high redoubt, he considered the best place to set himself to defend against Brandt and his men. It would be foolhardy to stay near the cabin, he realized. There was only the one window in front, so he could be encircled before he saw anything.

He tried to think like his potential assassins. They wouldn't come running at the first signal. They'd review maps, get a sense of the terrain before venturing out. They would know that he wouldn't stay near the cabin, and that he'd be likely to take to higher ground. He envisaged them entering the fire trail, driving in a hundred yards or so until they reached tree cover, and then getting out of their vehicle to fan out across the mountain. They'd be wary of their approaches, in constant contact with one another via radio or phone, though phones didn't always work up here in the hills.

Reed skirted through the brush along one of the deer paths to the side of the mountain facing the main road. From his vantage, he traced where and how Brandt's men would come at him. He went back to the cabin and turned on his phone, calling Weir's office.

"It's Reed," he said into the phone when Don Weir picked up. "I expect you're tracing this signal. Come and get me."

"Frank—" he began, but the line went dead.

Reed left the phone on, placing it on the battered table in front of the fireplace, gathered his dossiers and his gun and prepared to take up his position.

Trey Kelly called Vega and relayed the coordinates. Vega called Agents Davies and Guthrie into the motel room. They arrived just as Weir called. Vega put him on speaker.

"This will be hard," he said to the gathered agents, "but you're going to have to let the Illinois group commit before making your move. We've been successful this far because we haven't let on about what we know. And we need to keep doing that. If we arrive moments after these assassins, it'll be because we were there to get Reed, not because we're on to them. Second, we only have eyes on the Illinois group. We can't be a hundred percent sure whether they're the only team on this. There may be others we don't know about out there, too."

"Understood, sir," said Vega.

"Although Reed's a fugitive," he continued, "hostage rescue protocol applies. No mistakes, gentlemen...ladies. No unnecessary risks. Good luck!"

Imogen watched as Guthrie, Davies and Vega pulled on their vests and checked their weapons. She blanched at the sight of the weaponry—shotguns, sniper rifle, semi-automatics. Imogen carried only a pistol. Vega threw a vest at her, along with a box of bullets. "Get yourself right," she said. Davies and Guthrie, the armor cinched to their bodies, began loading their rifles.

Half a mile down the road in another motel room, Brandt's compatriots donned armor and loaded guns while Brandt sat crouched over his laptop zooming in and out on a topographical map of the area surrounding the coordinates from where Coop's signal had issued.

"He doesn't know we're coming," began Brandt, "but if I know him, he's ready for anything. Check this out." He turned his laptop around for them to see. "We'll come in here," he said, pointing at the fire trail leading to Reed's camp. "But we'll leave the truck here." He pointed at another fire trail on the opposite side of the main road, leading the opposite direction from the camp. "And we'll cross the road and come at his cabin or whatever it is, on foot. We'll spread out from here."

Once again, he zoomed in and pointed at the screen. "And we'll come at him from over the top of the mountain. We'll begin to converge as soon as we're at the top. No mistakes, boys. You see him, you take him down. Don't hesitate 'cause it's Coop. He won't just because it's you.

"The FBI's on its way, too. They'll be scrambling to get here, so we're working on a time limit. The nearest field office is in Richmond, which looks to be about three hours away from Reed's site. Even if they use helicopters, we've got the jump on them.

"Once we're in position and drawing down on Coop's cabin, I'm going to signal one of you to hold back and protect our exit in case the Feds arrive early. Leaving the truck hidden in the trees away from where he is might give us a chance to get away, since they won't know right away that we're there. Also: our guys are monitoring the redhead's phone. If she moves, we'll know about it."

"What if *he's* not there?" one of them asked.

"They tell me his signal hasn't moved since he made the call," said Brandt. "But if he isn't with his phone, we'll deal with that, too. We have to be in full communication at all times."

"I kinda hate having to kill Coop like this," said the first.

"You know," said Brandt, clicking a magazine into his rifle, "it's sort of Zen in a way. Coop will get to appreciate just how well he trained us as he dies."

"How is that Zen?"

"Zen philosophy enjoins us to find the beauty in everything—even the tiger leaping toward you to kill you."

"Let's get this done," said the other impatiently as he finished stuffing a loaded shotgun and two semi-automatic rifles into a long duffel bag. He zipped it shut.

"They're on the move," Trey relayed to Vega. "It looks like they're going to drive right past your motel on their way. I say you wait a moment. I'll be able to watch them onscreen and you can tail them at a safe distance."

The black truck carrying the assassins roared out of town toward Princeton, a two-hour drive. Imogen and Vega, together with Guthrie and Davies, sat in their black SUV in the parking lot of the motel on the outskirts of Roanoke, waiting for the go-ahead.

When Trey, watching their progress, relayed that Brandt and his crew were ten miles out of town, Vega pulled onto the road. In D.C., Trey watched onscreen as the dark network's pink line wound rapidly through the mountains and valleys of western Virginia and southern West Virginia, followed close behind by the blue trace of Vega's crew.

Brandt and his crew arrived at the wide clearing below Reed's camp, the sun still high in the sky. A chill breeze flowed through the trees. Except for the low growl of the engine, the area was tranquil, quiet, the crowding trees seeming to muffle everything: they certainly wouldn't have to worry about witnesses.

"They've arrived," Trey said to Vega over her headset.

Vega relayed the information to the rest of the car.

"You're about eight or ten minutes out," he said.

Vega nodded and pressed hard on the accelerator. "ETA *five* minutes," she announced to the car. The trees whipped by. In the front passenger seat, Guthrie flexed and then tightened his grip on a rifle. In the back, Davies inhaled deeply and then exhaled slowly, like someone managing pain. Imogen checked the tension on her seatbelt and returned to staring at the pistol resting in her lap.

Six miles ahead of them, Brandt cut back across the blacktop and reversed down a fire trail on the opposite side for about 50 yards until he reached a dip in the road and the beginning of the thick tree line, a spot where the truck would be hidden from the road. "Here we go," he said quietly. They jumped out and moved behind the truck. Brandt threw the duffel holding the firearms on the ground. They crouched around the duffel bag, each grabbing a rifle.

Across the road, just inside the line of Hickory, Oak and Maple, Reed was waiting, evenly breathing the fragrance of the Teaberry that spread across the ground to his left. He crouched behind a low rock outcropping of sandstone. Here in late April, the trees had leafed out, providing some cover, but he wished it had been high summer, when cover would be at its best. Still, he thought, in a moment all three of his recruits would be dead and they'd have never seen it coming.

He had bet they would pull up to the tree line on his side of the blacktop road before getting out, and he would be in position to pick them off easily as they got out of the truck to prepare for the assault. He felt his chest tightening as he watched the truck head to the opposite side of the main road and reverse down the fire trail there. He had to admit it made sense. He wished he'd thought of it. Still, they'd be expecting to find him on the opposite side of the hill now at his back.

With only a handgun, he didn't fancy his chances of picking them off where they gathered their gear. For one, the truck mostly obscured them. Secondly, they were more than a hundred yards away, across the near clear-cut scrub field, the blacktop road dividing the field, and then more scrub up to the tree line opposite him. He could make out that they were wearing body armor, which would make stopping them all the more difficult. He would have to wait for them to get closer.

Gathering their weapons and checking their gear took less than a minute. The assassins sprinted out from behind the truck, broke wide of each other and then slowed to a fast jog as they moved toward Reed's position, a classic, flanking attack. He had trained them well.

Brandt stayed in the center, trotting along the dirt road, flanked by his two colleagues, each about twenty yards to either side of him, moving across the scrub field, Alan Stanek on the left and Mike Balog on the right. Sun shone dully off their weapons, carried at the ready.

Brandt was advancing quickly. The scrub was hindering the other two with its tree stumps, saplings and briars. Reed smiled. Their first mistake. He knew the terrain better than they. Both men quickly returned to the edges of the fire lane and sprinted to catch up with Brandt.

Reed steeled himself. Brandt had a clear run along the dirt road, but the other two would be slowed when they came to the wide, deep drainage ditch that ran along either side of the main road. He settled himself, exhaling quietly to calm his nerves and steady his hand.

Balog, approaching on the right was now slightly ahead of the other two. Reed decided to take him out first as he crossed the irrigation ditch. Then, as Stanek did so, he'd kill him. Finally, he'd go for Brandt, who had no cover.

The ditch did not slow Balog on the right. He leapt over it. Reed fired anyway, hitting him in the face. Balog recoiled as if he'd run into clothesline. He lay motionless on his back upside down in the ditch. As Reed took aim again, Stanek threw himself headlong into the ditch, while Brandt moved sideways and took cover near his dead compatriot. Reed's second shot missed, and he fired again.

Brandt crouched in the drainage ditch, eye-level with the road. He'd roughly marked Reed's shooting position with the first shot, and the second and third shots confirmed it. Lying in the ditch, he aimed and began firing rapidly. The remaining assassin, Stanek, also well concealed, began firing too, shredding tree branches and bushes around the spot where the shots had come from. Reed, flat on his stomach, scooted himself backward and behind a larger outcrop of rock. The bullets were alarmingly on-frame, but because of their low shooting positions, the assassins were firing high.

He could just make out the tops of their heads on the opposite side of the road. Still some sixty yards away and with a headshot his only real option, he didn't trust his aim on a moving target with only the handgun. Just then, Brandt started firing rapidly and the trees above Reed exploded in flying debris. His compatriot jumped out of the ditch.

Reed, pinned under the withering fire from Brandt, squeezed off two poorly aimed shots at Stanek as he ran across the road and leapt into the ditch on the near side. Once again secure, Stanek now provided cover fire for Brandt, who also moved into position on the near side of the road.

As soon as they reached the safety of the nearer ditch, Reed saw them both moving wide apart, trying to outflank him. He could just glean the tops of their heads as they scurried along the bottom of the ditch and took up new positions. At any moment, they'd be far enough apart for one to give covering fire while the other advanced on his flank.

He backed up further, now inching up the mountainside. He would need high ground in order to counteract their flanking, and he looked to move to his second fallback position. As Reed rose into a low crouch to retreat, Brandt started firing again. He had anticipated this move, and his aim was superb. Bullets cut through leaves and branches inches above Reed's head, and he flattened himself to the ground.

Reed made it into a small depression behind more rocks and a stubby juniper tree, from where he could just make out Stanek sprinting across the scrub for the tree line on his left. The half-stumps forced him to run a crazed, weaving pattern. Reed fired on him, but didn't pierce the flak jacket. Reed heard him crash into the trees barely forty yards away, heard him reloading. Reed felt sick: now that the first assassin was inside the trees, and with a steep hillside at his back, there were only a few moves to checkmate. Reed could see that Stanek on the left would fire on him as Brandt also ran for the trees. Once they were both in the trees with him, they would have him between them.

Just as he feared, shots came from his left, pinning him down. Brandt was hoisting himself out of the ditch to run for the trees when a black SUV came roaring up the road and screeched to a halt. All four doors flew open. Vega was first out, and she began firing at Brandt as he ran, catching him twice in the back, to little visible effect. He staggered with the force of the bullets hitting his vest but continued weaving rapidly toward the trees. Vega aimed higher, hoping for a headshot, but she missed.

Agent Guthrie had leapt out of the passenger seat and had immediately taken up a position behind the massive hood. He was leaning over it, firing on Stanek, who retreated into the trees. Davies sprinted to the side of the road and dropped into the ditch that Brandt had just vacated, his gun trained on the area where Brandt had disappeared into the trees.

Imogen crouched and ran to the other side of the road where she hopped into the ditch there and found Balog's pitiful remains. His face was obliterated. Blood and bits of his head had become sticky as they spread across the dirt. She shuddered as she thought of the last time she had seen Duncan. A turkey buzzard circled high above, presumably waiting for the commotion to die down.

Vega left her position behind the SUV's door and joined Davies at the far side of the road.

Reed was grateful for their arrival, but his feeling of relief didn't last. Brandt was still moving into position. He knew they would continue their pincer move, take him out, and then take on the FBI. With the trees covering them, they could change position quickly, and the FBI would be wary of catching their potential star witness in friendly fire.

Reed saw Brandt move in among the trees and began firing at him. Guthrie was ready and began firing into the trees, pinning Brandt down. Reed moved slightly to get a better angle, taking care he was still out of sight of the other assassin and rained fire toward Brandt. He caught motion from Stanek in his peripheral vision and began shooting toward that, indicating where the FBI should be aiming. Davies, still behind the truck, took the hint and started shooting at Stanek.

With that covering fire, Imogen jumped out of the ditch she shared with the dead man and ran quickly to the opposite side of the road where she took cover in the ditch.

Davies's two shots hit Stanek in the side of the head, killing him instantly; but the pause in fire from Reed emboldened Brandt to move into position for a clear shot at Reed.

Vega and Guthrie were at the ready, but couldn't tell whether the slight movement they were seeing behind the trees was Brandt or Reed. Imogen, thirty yards to their right, had a better vantage point, and she could make out Brandt, closing in on Reed's position. She couldn't see Reed, but she could guess where he was.

Imogen lay flat on the edge of her ditch, sighted Brandt and fired three times in rapid succession, catching him in the head and neck. He fell, and a moment later, Davies and Guthrie were surging up the fire lane. Imogen and Vega stood up to cover them.

Five yards short of the trees, both men fell to a knee, their rifles taking aim at the dead assassin nearest them. Guthrie signaled clear. Davies signaled clear. Vega and Imogen ran up behind and stopped even with them. Vega signaled to Imogen to turn around and guard their exit.

"OK, Frank," Imogen heard Vega say behind her. "Anyone else here we should know about?"

"No," said a voice from the trees. "It was just three."

"Throw your weapon out here on the ground and walk slowly toward me...hands clasped on top of your head." She signaled to Davies and Guthrie to check on the assassins. They were both dead. Each agent retrieved a cell phone from the body.

Vega called Weir. A team from Richmond was on its way. They had left the moment the FBI had fixed Reed's position but were still more than an hour away. Vega and her team waited to turn over the crime scene.

Guthrie and Davies moved the SUV off the road, parking it at the side so as to hide the body of the assassin with no face, killed in the first ditch. The others were still hidden in among the trees.

"Yeah," Vega was saying to Weir on the phone, "it was fucking Hatfield's and McCoy's out here. Reed dropped one of them—" she gave a whistling sound—"Balog I think. It's hard to make a positive ID. They'd started advancing on him right before we arrived on the scene. Davies caught Stanek." She paused to listen. "Reed gave me their names. And Imogen took out Brandt, their leader. She's fine. She's in the car going over the dossiers with Reed right now."

Vega listened as Weir filled her in on Cardoso and Janssen's testimony. Her eyes grew wide as he told her that April 20th was the date for an attack made to look like a terrorist action. Cardoso and Janssen's part was to disperse the Novichok A-234 in dust form into the air above the Dumbarton Bridge in south San Francisco Bay. In light of the extremely sensitive nature of this final step, their handlers had told them to turn off their phones beginning on the 19th, so there would be no way to track them. They were to meet a Flintlock pilot—Rosewood, though they didn't know his name—at Boeing Field on the 20th. He wouldn't know where they were going until they told him the destination.

"We've gone over their houses, and what they've told us checks out. We've found maps of the South Bay, notes about police in the area. Stuffed inside a book on one of the shelves—the *Fountainhead*!—we found confirmation of a rental van and a car.

"But," Weir concluded, "they have no idea what the other parts of the plan look like. They only know that they're supposed to do the job and then wait for their handlers to make contact, a week or more later."

Vega was dismayed. "Fuck," she said finally. "And we just killed the three guys who could've given us more of the picture."

High in the piercing blue sky, the turkey buzzard had been joined by two others. Vega studied them for a moment, wondering idly whether the sound of gunshots drew them, or whether they could smell death even that high up. "I'll see what Reed can give us on the attack," she said and hung up.

In his West Wing office, door closed, Clayton Quantrelle was waiting for news on the capture of Reed. Moore was agitated and had already contacted him once to ask "what the fuck is going on?" Marek had stuck his head in, too. It had been fifteen minutes now since their team had arrived on the scene, according to Tweedledim. Phone signals, and therefore their tracking, were spotty at best in the hills, so Dim and Dum were having difficulty distinguishing movement toward the target. Quantrelle drew a deep breath to calm himself, but it didn't help. He needed only two words to know that all was well, and that the final phase had begun. "Just say the Goddamn words," he said aloud.

* * *

Vega and Imogen sat to either side of Frank Reed across the wide backseat of the SUV. Imogen was stunned when she heard the plans for the April 20 attack. Reed was seething. It wasn't what he had signed up for. He'd argued against it. It was an offense to his notion of a noble struggle, of the crucial distinction between soldiers and civilians. The Postman and his crew meant to blur every line, burn everything down.

270

"We've been behind at every step of this investigation," Imogen lamented to Amanda. "It *feels* like we might be out front now; that we know the next moves, but I'm not sure."

"No," said Reed, still staring angrily out the window, "this is his endgame."

"I guess what I mean is," Imogen continued, "how do we know there's not something more to this? Since we're talking chess and endgames here, the best gambits disguise their intent. Do we really know all the pieces involved?"

"Look," Reed began, "ever since they captured your queen by killing President Redmond, you've been on the back foot. You're caught in a series of forced moves, marching you backward toward checkmate. The appointment of Eliot as Attorney General is the final gambit of that attack. When he's in position, you'll have no more room to operate— checkmate." Reed looked at his watch. "They'll be waiting for confirmation," he said.

"We can't text?"

"Absolutely not," Reed responded. "A dead giveaway. Have one of your agents call it in," Reed offered. "A male voice. All he has to say is 'meeting concluded.' I think."

"You *think*?" demanded Vega.

"That was the training. *If* they haven't changed it, that's it. They're supposed to call it in, say 'meeting concluded' and hang up."

Vega stared out of the car window. "And if we're wrong, we've just put them on alert."

"If we don't call in pretending to be them, they'll definitely know it was a failure," Imogen began, "which may lead the network to do something we have no inkling of. Calling it in the way Frank describes has at least a chance of keeping them on track."

"And we don't fully know what the track is," said Vega. She opened the truck door and asked Davies to come over.

"Amanda, there's a lot here," said Imogen, indicating the files Reed had given her. "He says, there's more in a safe deposit box Alec Nash held under an alias at a bank in West Concord, Mass. Even if we blow it by calling in, pretending the mission was successful, we might have enough to catch the Postman, too."

Quantrelle jumped as the flip phone on his desk buzzed into life.

"This is Bannister," he said, giving his codename.

"Meeting concluded," said Davies. And he hung up.

In D.C., Trey recorded the message from Davies posing as the dead man, Brandt. As he was logging the details, Quantrelle himself made a call: "Yes?" said a new voice. "Cooper meeting concluded, sir," said Quantrelle. He rang off and immediately dialed yet another number.

"Is this good news?" asked a voice with a pleasant Southern drawl.

Trey dutifully logged the number.

"Cooper meeting concluded," said Quantrelle and then went to tell President Moore and Marek.

Trey relayed to Weir and Vega that the message appeared to have been accepted, and they had two new targets. The first had been in downtown Pittsburgh, the second, in Washington D.C. Unfortunately, both call recipients had immediately turned their phones off.

Weir contacted a trusted friend at the FBI Field Office in Springfield, Illinois, giving her the names and last known addresses of the three-members of the Illinois chapter. He sent the warrants and authorizations and he spelled out the need for conducting the investigation quietly, with the smallest possible squad she could manage. Then he headed upstairs to make his report.

Outside a boardroom in Pittsburgh, Rufus Hessel pulled the SIM card out of his flip phone and dropped it in the trash.

At Headquarters, Weir sat with the Deputy Director and the FBI Director around the Deputy Attorney General's desk, waiting for him to finish turning over the hastily prepared papers. Though the moment clearly needed quick and decisive action, it also needed careful thought. He reviewed the documents a second time, dealing them out in front of himself as he looked at each conspirator and the evidence against him. The Deputy lingered over an affidavit from the Secret Service attesting that President Moore and Press Secretary Marek had been the only ones in the Oval Office at the time Quantrelle had called from the White House and sent the Illinois chapter to kill Reed.

"When will you have the second set of dossiers?" the Deputy asked.

"We received the warrant just over an hour ago, and my people are on their way now."

The FBI had dispatched two small jets to Roanoke airport. Davies and Guthrie escorted Reed to the secret detention center just outside D.C., while Vega and Imogen flew to Logan Airport in Boston. They would rendezvous there with Nettie Sartain, who carried the court order to open the safe deposit box, and then travel together to West Concord to retrieve the Nash dossiers.

In Pittsburgh, his meeting finished, Hessel asked one of the junior executives whether he could borrow his phone to make a call. His was acting up, he said.

"Maybe we should buy the company," the junior exec joked as he handed over his phone. "We'd show them how it's done!"

"Yes," said Hessel. "There's a good idea in that." He walked toward the back of the room. "I won't be a moment," he said, indicating that he should be left alone. The junior executive retreated obsequiously from the room.

"Do you recognize my voice?" Hessel asked into the phone. "You're watching the bank in Massachusetts? Good."

32

Vega, Imogen and Nettie Sartain met at Logan Airport. Nettie handed Vega the paperwork and warrants for the bank manager. As a courtesy, they had phoned ahead to tell the bank to expect them in mid-afternoon.

"You have no idea how great it is to be out of that office," beamed Sartain as she hopped into the back seat for the 40-minute drive to West Concord.

"I've been thinking about what Reed said," Imogen said as they rolled by a historic marker for Lexington Common, "about checkmate. It makes sense. Each reaction, each move by us just backs us into a corner."

"We have a ton of evidence," said Nettie.

"But who'll get to see it if Eliot takes control of the investigation?" said Vega, eyes on the road.

"Of course," said Imogen. "We could leak it, keep working on it…but presumably they know that it won't be enough for them to quash the investigation, and they already have plans to delegitimize us and our work…and to introduce a counter-narrative. So, while they throw sand in everyone's eyes and Congress dithers—"

"—This is not helping 'Gen," said Vega.

"All I'm saying, I guess, is that we need to formulate—"

"—this isn't a game, 'Gen!" Vega snapped. "We can't do some castling move or whatever, and we sure as fuck can't march a pawn down to the other end and get one of our pieces back. What's gone is…" she winced inwardly.

"I know," said Imogen quietly.

The bank was located in a strip mall on the outskirts, and Vega, Imogen and Nettie snaked slowly through the parking lot. From across the sparsely parked lot, in front of a pizza parlor at the far corner, a man sitting in a silver Toyota Camry watched through binoculars as the three went inside. He spoke into his radio. A moment later, another car, this one a dark blue, well-used Honda Accord swept through the lot and took up a position in the painted aisle across from the agents' rental car. There was one man in the front seat and two in the back. The car parked, and they each lay down across the seats out of sight, the engine idling.

In the bank, Vega attended to the paperwork about the warrant while Nettie and Imogen leafed through the contents of Nash's safe deposit box. A quick glance suggested it was genuine, and that it held dates and plans. They were able to tell from the bank's logs that the deposit box hadn't been accessed since early January. They closed up the notebooks and placed them in a large FBI lock bag. As they left through the glass double-doors, Nettie carried the bag with the dossiers across her shoulder. Imogen was directly behind her and Vega to her left. As they crossed the sidewalk, Vega broke into a jog toward the car.

At that moment, the blue Honda lurched into gear, wheels screeching as it tore straight across the asphalt towards Vega's car. Vega had just opened the door and was unlocking the others when the Honda smashed into it. The force of the crash knocked her backward over a car parked next to her. Despite the shock and the momentary terror, and despite the crack her shoulder suffered as she landed, she was back on her feet in seconds.

The three men from the Honda were now firing and beginning to advance. Two shots hit Nettie. She cried out as she twisted and fell to the ground. Behind the gunmen, the Camry sped across the lot toward the scene. Behind the parked car, Vega began firing, driving the gunmen back behind the cover of their open car doors. Imogen scooped Nettie under the arms and dragged her behind their rental car, a wide trail of blood marking her movement.

No time for a medical assessment. Imogen stood up and began firing back. She ducked down for a moment and glanced at Nettie, who was conscious but bleeding heavily. One wound was a graze to the arm, the other into her abdomen. Nettie pressed with all her might on the stomach wound to stanch the blood.

An all-too familiar feeling of weightlessness flowed through Imogen. But amid the numbness and vertigo, there was clarity. The gunmen were firing wildly but the sound barely registered with her. She was about to stand and return fire, when she noticed that she could see the feet of one of the assassins behind the open car door. She crouched down and fired, hitting him in the foot and again in the other ankle. As he hit the ground, screaming, she shot him in the head. Now, she rose and began firing on the remaining two gunmen, each taking shelter behind an open door on the passenger side. The driver's side door was still open, and she began moving to her right, to get an angle on them through the car.

Vega saw what she was doing and began moving wide left around the car she'd tumbled over. She sighted one of the gunmen through the gap between the door and the wing window and fired. He recoiled against the car as the bullet hit him. As she continued moving, now even with him, her second bullet hit him square in the center of his chest. The third gunman, still covered behind the rear passenger door, cowered. He crouched to duck away from Imogen's fire. With his attention momentarily elsewhere, Vega continued to move wide and shot him twice, in the chest and head. The Camry, blazing across the blacktop was almost on top of them. Vega turned and fired on it as Imogen rose and ran next to the battered Honda where she also began firing at the Camry.

The Camry was meant to be the getaway car, once the Honda had rammed the agents' rental car. But with no one left to get away, the driver of the Camry cut the wheel sideways and sped for the highway. Imogen and Vega gave chase on foot, firing into the back of the car as it receded. As it pulled onto the highway, Vega stopped running and called into her radio for police and an Emergency Medical Response team. She gave the description and partial license number of the Camry.

Imogen, meanwhile, had turned to run back for Nettie.

She was losing consciousness. Thick blood spread across the asphalt. Imogen unzipped Nettie's coat and pressed hard on the spot where Nettie had been trying to stanch the flow. "Hang on, sweetie," she said. She looked round to double-check that their attackers were dead. In the distance, she could hear sirens approaching. "They're coming. Hang on!"

Imogen's heart was breaking, her mind reeling. How many more? she wondered. She was assaulted by memories of that first gun battle in the stairwell. Had that only been four months ago? There, too, thick blood had spattered and pooled. There, too, people she knew and loved were dying, eyes staring in mute terror even as they grew dim; lips pale and chalky, skin ashen. She saw Duncan dead on a slab. "Stay with me, Nettie," she heard her own voice saying, far off.

She pressed harder on the wounds, growing frantic as Nettie's aspect, her deep, inquisitive eyes, turned inward. With the light seeming to drift further and further from Nettie's face, Imogen shuddered. She wanted to comfort her young comrade, give some sign of affection, but she dared not take her hands away from their work. Blood was welling up around her fingers where she applied pressure, though it did seem to be slowing. Imogen wondered whether it slowed because what she was doing was working, or because there was so little blood left in her friend, so little heartbeat.

As Nettie fought to stay awake, Imogen fought back tears of despair. Three dead in this parking lot and Nettie in this desperate state? What was it all for? Duncan had been right. That son-of-bitch Reed would be offered some deal for co-operating, not reaping the full vengeance for his crimes. Was that justice? Would the documents in Nettie's bag, now smeared and sticky with blood get them closer to the Postman?

And was that enough of a win? Enough that the listing ship of state should make it back to harbor in a state unfit to sail? Matthew had been the first to die, trying to bring truth to light. Duncan had died, trying to effect some true reckoning. Now Nettie? Her heart ached for all of them; her fingers were numb with holding back the swelling blood. Worse, now it might not even be the qualified win she dreaded. The driver of the getaway car had surely alerted the Postman and the plans for April 20 might be aborted.

* * *

On his private jet back from Pittsburgh, Hessel sat brooding over the death of three of his palace guard in Massachusetts. He stared at a SIM card in his hand. He was debating whether to use it in the phone on the table in front of him. How had they tumbled to Alec's safe deposit box? Had he talked before he died? Had the FBI known about the alias, but it had taken them this long to trace the location?

If he called that weak-kneed idiot, Quantrelle and told him what had happened, he'd want to abort or would panic into doing something stupid. But there was no way to contact any of them, he reflected. Reed's erasure meant that everything was "go." The operatives and the command structure had been told to go dark and follow their standing orders. The juggernaut was in gear and must be allowed to run its course or they themselves would be sacrificed under it.

The dossiers were in the hands of the FBI, and there was no telling what damaging information they held. The only course to safety—and victory—was the one they'd already charted. He put the SIM card back in his pocket.

* * *

Just after 10:30pm the Springfield office Special Agent forwarded her findings to Don Weir from the searches she and her team had conducted. They had found the components for Novichok-5 in Brandt's home, both the A-232 dust and A-234 liquid ready for mixing, along with a small explosive device. There were also surveillance notes on a young exchange student living in Weehawken, New Jersey. The

278

Special Agent in Charge said she couldn't be sure at this stage whether he was a co-conspirator or a target of some kind.

Based on maps and notes they had collected, it seemed Brandt's compatriots had been instructed to attack the PATH station and World Trade Center, and Brandt himself was to deliver the Novichok A-234 to the Capitol ahead of the Joint Session. He had a gallery pass issued by the Press Secretary, Anthony Marek.

* * *

At 6:30 the following morning, April 20, with the sun just barely up, a pair of black SUVs rolled to a stop in front of the porch at Number One Observatory Circle. A chill April wind stirred the trees surrounding the house, sending leftover dead leaves skittering and tumbling across the semi-circular drive. The black trucks carrying the FBI Director, the lead US Attorney and the Deputy Attorney General stopped in front of the porch.

Vice-President David Carr met them at the door, and they walked briskly through to the Garden Room, gaily-accented scene of much *sub rosa* activity over the past weeks. The Deputy Attorney General handed Carr a summary of the investigation and charges to be brought and asked him to read through it. "I have the full report here," he said, indicating the briefcase the FBI Director held, "if you'd prefer, or if you have any questions about the summary, sir."

"I may," said Carr. "And I'll certainly want to look it over after I've digested the summary."

"Of course, Mr. Vice President."

Carr sat down on the settee, and gestured toward the chairs arranged around the coffee table, indicating they should seat themselves. He took his time reading the summary. Though his face betrayed some dismay—astonishment even—he did not appear surprised by what he read. Finally, he closed the folder and looked up. "So basically everyone," he said. "I assume you've looked at my background, my comings-and-goings; my campaign financing. Clandestine meetings since January, too?"

"We have, sir," said the Deputy.

"Do you think I'm involved with all this?" Carr asked, gesturing at the file on the table.

"No, sir. That's not why we're here." The US Attorney paused and looked at his gathered colleagues. Finally, he said: "Sir, you're going to have to make what may be your most difficult presidential decision before you're even president."

* * *

At 10:30am, President Moore received the news that Drew Eliot had been confirmed as Attorney General. At 11:15, the new Attorney General by his side, Moore held a brief press conference, touching upon the need for a new direction, and how Eliot had been given a wide-ranging brief to delve into the causes and forces behind the Faithless Elector plot and the Interregnum. He turned the conference over to Eliot and promptly left.

Quantrelle slipped out after him. "Sir!" he hissed. He quickly looked around for anyone within earshot. "I know it's nerve-wracking, but we've got to hold it together. After tonight, there won't be anyone who can stop us, no one who can touch us. We'll pull all the strings. It'll all be over."

Moore stared back at him. That was what worried him. They were doing away with everyone, severing every link that could implicate them. Why not him, too? But he said nothing.

"Sir, you need to project confidence. If you can't do that, you need to stay out of the public eye until the time is right. Can I count on you?"

"Of course," said Moore and turned to walk away.

Satisfied his message had been heard, Quantrelle returned to the press conference. Had he been less keen to get back, he'd have noticed Moore was trembling, sure that he would soon be killed.

Weir was heading a crash meeting in what was becoming his home-away-from-home, Imogen's office. She broke from her research as Weir, Vega, Davies and Guthrie filed in, seating themselves amid the heaps of paper.

"Eliot will be meeting with the Director over at Headquarters any moment now," Weir began, checking his watch. "In light of what's going on and Eliot's likely involvement in the conspiracy, I've asked the Director to stall. And he has agreed. Amanda, the Director has the 30-day review document from you, dated just over a month ago—3/13, which is what he'll give to the new AG. All it states is that you went to Fairmont, Nebraska, following a tenuous lead. He will state that he has called in all files for review, but that they won't be ready until tomorrow. After which none of this matters. Agent Sartain, if you haven't heard already, is still listed as critical, and her doctors are looking to stabilize her. They are, they say, hopeful.

"Someone in the conspiracy," he continued, "must know we have Alec Nash's dossier. Imogen, I want you to pick up where Nettie left off."

Imogen nodded, her thoughts a tangled nest of emotions.

"Sir," said Vega, "there's been no chatter along any of the lines we're watching."

"We have to assume they think it's all still on," said Imogen. "Going dark and flying under the radar was supposed to be their strength, but it makes them blind...which is our strength."

"We'll let this play out," said Weir cautiously. "We've neutralized the actual threat to life...so far as we know. I've taken Special Agent Allen Bennett into confidence about all this. He's known to your old boss, Imogen; and he led the team that responded to the shooting in the parking garage under the Eisenhower Building," he relayed for the benefit of the others. "I trust him...or I should say: I trust the people who trust him. We're taking a big gamble, and I don't want any of the agencies working at potentially lethal cross-purposes."

Back in the Oval Office that afternoon, Moore wanted to go over things one more time. "I want to be clear so there are no mistakes," he was saying.

"Yes, of course, sir," Quantrelle was saying indulgently.

Moore caught his tone and was not reassured.

"The speech is scheduled to start at 8:07pm," Quantrelle began patiently. "People will begin arriving at the Capitol in numbers by 6 or 6:15 tonight. Our man will arrive some time around then."

"How will you know he's there?"

"We won't—by design. But, I assure you, Mr. President, everything so far hasn't necessarily gone smoothly, but it *has* always fallen into place. So will this."

Moore grunted, decidedly unassured.

"You will leave the White House in your motorcade at 7:35," Quantrelle went blithely on, "slated to arrive at the Capitol at 7:50pm. But you will not get out of the car, because en route, at 7:45, our man in the gallery will activate and release the nerve agent. All hell will break loose."

"At 7:45....*Before* I arrive."

Quantrelle, with elaborate patience said, "Correct, sir."

"Then what?"

"As soon as the attack starts in the Capitol, the men in New York and in San Francisco will begin theirs. They will activate and release their nerve agent. It'll seem that the country is under attack...Again, by design. The Secret Service will respond accordingly and take you away to a secure location."

"What if it doesn't happen that way?" Moore asked quickly. "What if your man in the gallery can't do it for some reason?"

"We've thought of that, and as I've explained earlier, you will go ahead with the first speech I wrote. You'll give it, and we'll regroup back here. It's already loaded on the TelePrompTer."

"What if he releases it late? While we're there?"

"He won't."

"*How* do you know?" asked Moore, his voice pitched somewhere just below hysteria.

Quantrelle sighed deeply. "Honestly, sir, what would be the point then?"

Beleaguered, exhausted and frightened, Moore stared straight ahead. "...right. Of course."

Moore tried to rest ahead of the speech, stretched out on a couch in the Oval Office. But he could not relax. His mind kept going over scenarios in which he was eliminated. He feverishly reviewed each moment, tried to envision the threats, saw himself, and others around him, dying by nerve gas, writhing on the floor, bodies contorted by seizure, frothing at the mouth.

Just after 5:30, Attorney General Eliot arrived in the Oval Office. He clapped his hands together and rubbed them together briskly, eager to get to work. "It's better than we could've hoped," he said cheerfully of his meeting with the FBI Director. "They've got nothing. Total disarray. After tonight, we can either bend the Assistant AG to our will, or replace him. And with the way they've botched the Faithless Elector and Interregnum investigations—thank God!"— (here he nudged a grinning Quantrelle in the ribs)—"we can remove the FBI Director at will."

The Attorney General caught sight of Moore, haggard and distant. He clapped him on the shoulder. "It'll all be over soon, son!" He flashed a jovial grin.

Moore nodded, tried to muster a brave smile. True, it might all work out just as planned.

"We'll just stick to the script," Eliot added.

Weir had taken the step of inviting prosecutors from the US Attorney's Office to sit with Imogen and Gardiner and prepare the indictments. They had been working non-stop since the meeting in her office broke up. The Nash files, taken together with Reed's and their own digging brought the whole

283

criminal enterprise into sharp focus, confirming many things they had suspected and revealing new ones. The two federal prosecutors were frantically reviewing evidence and compiling the indictments.

There had been two sets of notebooks in Nash's safe deposit box, one green, and the other red. In the green books was a key to the work names of those involved, and Gardiner was able to align what had been educated guesswork with what was really going on, who was being paid, how and for what. The first notebook also contained dates, and in some cases compromising evidence; meetings, agreements and summaries of clandestine activities and the names of those involved, including the murders of Electors after the general election. It also held the outline for the false terrorist attack. Imogen and Gardiner duly handed it over for the federal prosecutors to place into ever-growing piles. Most damning, the last entry date was in early January, a week before Alec Nash was arrested. The plans had been in place from the very beginning.

After dealing with the subtlety of Reed-Nash tradecraft, the money laundering and payment schemes authored by Quantrelle and his minions, and duly noted by Nash for the files, were comparatively, dismayingly ill-conceived and transparent. The doctors, Menlo and Somers, were code-named Edison and Winters on the payment grid. Here was the damning family evidence used to bend the two doctors, as well as the payment arrangements.

The payments lined up perfectly with the two, separate, million dollar deposits Gardiner had flagged just two days earlier. Here, too, Imogen noted as she passed it over to the prosecutors, was the plan to kill off "Edison" and "Winters" as soon as the dark network had seized power. There in the notes, all in Nash's neat hand, were the plans to make it appear that the FBI had done the killing, part of a Deep State, false flag operation. It was unclear from the notebooks whether he had authored that plan, or merely taken dictation.

Where the green notebooks read like a "burn notice," the red books held a subtler narrative. Here, finally, was the top man, Rufus Hessel, the key donor associated with Fourmile Creek PAC, but he was not called "Postman" anywhere in the notes. Alec Nash had detailed notes about meeting Hessel for the first time on May 11, 2012 in Chicago, and their discussion about "a new kind of campaign." Hardly damning stuff. They had not met often, if the red books were an accurate guide, and their language was infuriatingly opaque.

It became clear that rather than a tell-all about him—and far from pointing the finger at Hessel/Postman—Nash may have conceived of this red book as a means of defeating and deflecting investigation of him or the Postman, introducing a shadow of doubt. With one, he could burn everyone below him in the network, notably Quantrelle who ended up succeeding him; with the other, he could note seemingly innocent meetings, discussions and transactions. Hessel's PAC, Fourmile Creek, Gardiner noted gloomily, was mentioned only in passing, nor could he find anything but payments from Fourmile Creek to other PAC's like Sovereign, V^3 and Opportunity Initiative, to be used, "in support of like-minded organizations and institutions engaged in important work."

Nash had equally somnolent follow-up notes about the meeting to use Flintlock Air as their personal, chartered murder-delivery service, noting that they would "work with our partners there to deliver our service personnel where they are needed and can give the best support efficiently and with a minimum of oversight."

As the morning became late afternoon, the federal prosecutors paused in their collating to point out what Imogen already knew—that absent any further corroboration, bland notes to the files by a known murderous criminal like Alec Nash, who could not give testimony or be cross-examined, was hardly a smoking gun. It would not be enough to convict someone with such deep pockets and deep political connections. "And this Frank Reed you're interviewing right now...he never met Hessel," said one of the prosecutors, "so he can't testify about that."

He sighed deeply. "On the face of it, looking at what's here, the best we can do at the moment is to designate Hessel an unindicted co-conspirator and hope to come back on him later."

Imogen shook her head. "There won't be a later."

"Well," said the other prosecutor, "we do have a lot on Quantrelle and Marek. They scrubbed the money, they funneled it, and you have the wiretaps confirming them ordering murder. You have the testimony from the various cells...they're going down for a very long time. If they can be flipped, you've got something." He searched through one of the piles in front of him and pulled out the brief transcript of Quantrelle relaying the information he'd been fed about Reed's murder to an unidentified cell number. "Quantrelle knows something about Hessel. Marek probably knows it too."

Imogen nodded. It was the best they could hope for, but she seethed with rage, thought again of Duncan, dead; of Nettie, clinging to life. There had to be a reckoning.

33

The motorcade for the Capitol left the White House at precisely 7:35pm that night. President Moore checked his watch twice. As the car left the gates, he panicked. "Where's Eliot?" he asked Quantrelle who was seated facing him.

"He's the designated survivor," Quantrelle quipped.

Moore looked ashen.

"Sorry, sir, that was a detail I didn't think to tell you."

"Jesus," Moore whispered.

"It's not a big deal. The whole Senate, House, Supreme Court and Cabinet will be present. As he's the newest senior Cabinet member, it seemed appropriate—and easy—not to invite him, and to make him the designated survivor." Here he cast a glance over his shoulder at the Secret Service agent seated in the front seat. "Since this speech is about the investigations and his role in it," Quantrelle went on for the benefit of the Secret Service, "and you've already told him everything you'll tell the nation, it makes sense that he be the one who stays behind."

Something in Moore's face troubled him, and he continued. "It's a formality, sir." He leaned in closely and murmured, "Usually." He leaned back into the soft leather with a smug grin.

Moore looked at his watch.

Federal prosecutors had prepared indictments against Quantrelle, Marek, the new Attorney General and President Moore himself on murder, criminal conspiracy, vote-rigging, wire fraud, lying to Congress and a host of other charges. Adding weight to the evidence they had garnered, there was now Grand Jury testimony from Frank Reed tying Attorney General Eliot to many of the deeds for which the FBI had earlier failed to find enough evidence. Agents in Omaha were ready to arrest the CEO of Flintlock Industries and its Director of Flight Operations, Allen Jardine.

The plan was to move after Moore's speech to Congress. David Carr was to escort the President out of the Chamber after the speech, and the FBI would confront Moore and his coterie in the Speaker's Lobby just behind the Rostrum.

Though the evidence was currently slim against Rufus Hessel as the Postman, Weir and Dyer had issued an arrest warrant, to be served on him at his residence outside Wichita by agents from the Oklahoma City Field Office. It might be useful to shake the tree a bit by bringing him in. In Moore, Quantrelle, Marek and Eliot, the FBI had four possible chances that one of them would provide testimony. It was even possible that the Flintlock executives would be eager for a deal, and that they might have something to trade. "It'd be nice to have him in pocket," Weir said to the Deputy, "if we do get something more." The Deputy had agreed.

As the president's car glided toward the Capitol, the Special Agent in the front seat of the president's car spoke quietly into the microphone in his sleeve. Moore perked up.

Quantrelle turned to look over his shoulder at the front seat. "Everything all right?" he asked the agent.

"Yes, sir," he replied. "Just giving the Capitol team a status report. They're on full alert for your arrival."

Now Quantrelle glanced at his watch—7:47. He leaned toward the president. "We go forward no matter what!" he hissed, trying to sound confident.

The convoy arrived at the Capitol. Both Quantrelle and Moore checked their watches again. Moore walked slowly.

"Sir," Quantrelle whispered urgently, taking him by the elbow and propelling him forward, "even if it doesn't happen here, you have to be giving the speech when the other events occur. It all depends on you. We can still use them to our advantage."

Moore was sweating, his breath labored and rapid, very near hyperventilating. He walked tentatively toward the Chamber doors.

In his study, in front of his banks of televisions, Rufus Hessel glanced at the time, looked at the televisions, all the channels waiting for the President to make his entrance. He tamped down his fury and occupied a growing sense of worry by working on his prized Thunderer. Well, maybe the House attack had been a tall order, he allowed, but there would be utter chaos when the New York and San Francisco attacks started. On his television, Moore stood outside the Chamber.

Moore felt dizzy. Quantrelle and Marek left him and scurried toward one of the nearby offices to watch proceedings on television.

Seeing them run away was the final straw for Moore. He would be part of the carnage, he felt sure. Eliot would be put in charge—the sole survivor—and the whole thing would play out just as Hessel and his minions had planned—without him. "When the doors open," he thought, "that's the signal."

The Sergeant at Arms threw open the doors to the Chamber: "Mister Speaker, the President of the United States!"

The Chamber erupted into applause. Moore froze.

The Sergeant at Arms walked a few paces into the Chamber, stood to one side, and made way for the president. He looked back. Moore wasn't moving. The Sergeant at Arms looked between the Rostrum and the President and back again. Not sure what else to do, he walked tentatively back toward the president, this time stopping and gesturing for him to enter. Quantrelle and Marek, having only just arrived at a nearby office, saw the president's anguished face on television and began racing back toward the door to the Chamber.

Inside, the gathered dignitaries and guests were wondering what was causing the delay. People craned their necks toward the door. David Carr, sitting next to the Speaker on the Rostrum, had a clear view of what was happening, and he realized why. The Vice President stood up from the Rostrum and moved down the aisle toward the Sergeant at Arms and the President.

On all eight television screens in the Postman's study the cameras zoomed in on Moore, stiff as the Statuary Hall figures he had passed between moments before. His face was pained, sallow and glistening. Was it a heart attack? one anchor was asking; it could be a stroke another opined. Any further conjecture on their part was drowned out by the Postman howling with anger as he brandished his gun. "You're dead now, you little fuck!"

In the Speaker's Lobby, the hallway behind the Chamber, Weir, Vega and Trager were alerted. They took off at a sprint through the perimeter hallways around the Chamber to the doors. Agents were converging from all sides, but Carr arrived at the President first.

"Mr. President," he said. "I think I can help. Let's get away from here. Follow me, sir." He took Moore forcefully by the arm and led him to the Congressional Cloakroom. Moore allowed himself to be led. Agents Davies and Guthrie, who had been on their way to arrest Quantrelle and Marek rushed up behind the two as they hurried back to the President.

Davies grabbed Quantrelle at the elbow, his powerful fingers digging into it so hard Quantrelle's hand shot with pain. "Clayton Quantrelle, you're under arrest for vote tampering, criminal conspiracy and murder. Walk!" Quantrelle's face flushed, words would not come. Guthrie had hold of Marek and bent his arm backward. Marek acquiesced.

By this point, the reporters on site, normally respectful and restrained at such solemn occasions were coursing through the halls. At a signal from Special Agent Bennett, the Secret Service and Capitol Police sealed access to the hallway leading to the doors to the Chamber. Cameramen lifted cameras above their heads, shooting blindly.

On the Postman's eight screens, there was nothing from the New York or San Francisco channels about a nerve gas attack—only pictures of the chaos in and outside the House Chamber, where those in attendance were very much alive, and like the nation they represented, anxious for information.

He stalked back and forth in front of the screens, molten with rage. The images onscreen were a jumble, as studio video editors cut back and forth between jittery, blindly-pointed camera shots and reporters tried to figure out what was happening. Blind was how he felt: he'd made sure there were no communications in the days leading up to the planned attack, no trail that could lead back to any of them, least of all him. But now he had no way of finding out what was really going on.

He stopped pacing when he caught sight of Imogen on screen, her red hair standing out amid a sea of FBI agents clustered around Moore as he was bundled into the Congressional Cloakroom. "That fucking cunt!" he raged, impotently brandishing the gun. On screen, she turned, looking for something, and the camera caught her fully.

"Th..That—" one of the anchors stammered, "that's FBI agent Imogen Trager. We've been speculating that President Moore may be in physical distress, but this could mean...It was she who lead the team that uncovered the Faithless Elector plot back in December...she was also part of the team, together with then-representative David Carr, that cracked the conspiracy during the Interregnum. The chaos we're seeing right now could be something else entirely, something more sinister than a medical emergency."

"I should've killed you myself!" the Postman spewed at the screen, brandishing the gun.

His phone rang just as one of the screens abruptly switched from a national news channel to images of a CCTV boundary alert. He picked up the phone, still holding the Thunderer in his right hand.

"Sir," said the leader of his security detail over the phone, "the FBI's here!" On the CCTV feed, FBI agents in riot gear were preparing to enter the compound.

They wouldn't fucking dare, he thought.

On screen, he watched powerlessly as the gate guard was handcuffed and disarmed and agents swarmed along the driveway. "Fucking impudence!" he stormed.

The house was alive with sound. He heard his security personnel rumbling through the hallways to take up positions. They'd been selected for their military background and dogged loyalty. Which suddenly seemed like a liability. Still holding the phone and the gun, he walked into the House's main hallway. Security, unheeding, bustled by him. "Do not fire!" he was shouting into the phone, shouting at armed guards as they hustled through the halls, at anyone who would listen. And no one did. He'd have to handle this himself.

But one of his security detail did shoot, and the FBI tactical team surged toward the house, returning fire. The power went out, and emergency lighting flooded the interior. The Postman began making his way to the front door.

In the Congressional Cloakroom, Moore, Quantrelle and Marek were backed against the walls, faced by David Carr, Imogen Trager, Amanda Vega, Agents Davies and Guthrie, Don Weir and the head of the Secret Service detail, Alan Bennett. They quickly separated them—Vega and Weir taking Quantrelle, Davies and Guthrie with Marek; David Carr and Imogen took President Moore aside.

"It's over, Bob," Carr was saying to the President. "You knew about and participated in a conspiracy to steal the Presidency. On your orders, or with your knowledge, your co-conspirators, led by Rufus Hessel, a.k.a. the Postman, murdered Electors—innocent people!—as well as people within your own criminal enterprise."

At the other side of the room, Davies was reading Marek his rights and handcuffing him.

"But I didn't do anything!" Marek whined, facing the wall, his hands behind his back. "I did what they told me."

"Who's 'they?'" asked Davies. "Be specific. You don't have as much to trade as your boss. You're the Johnny-come-lately in this, but we'll still be charging you with murder, attempted murder, conspiracy, vote-rigging, misappropriation of funds..."

Still further down the room, Quantrelle, his face flush, was saying to Weir: "I refuse to speak without my attorney present," said Quantrelle.

At the far end of the room, Carr was saying to Moore: "If you agree to supply testimony and resign, I will issue a Presidential pardon to you as one of my first official acts." He looked at Imogen, who nodded her agreement.

In their corner of the Cloakroom, Weir looked round the room and then back at Quantrelle. "I'd see if I could get your attorney here in a hurry, because by the look of things, I think it's gonna be a race to the finish to see who can give up more and get some sliver of a deal. And we're the least of your worries," Weir added. "Remember how well—and complete-ly—you all took care of Alec Nash."

In Kansas, Hessel's massive frame lumbered through the smoky emergency lighting toward the front door. He would put a stop to this ridiculous and insulting government overreach. Over the melee, he was screaming into the phone, trying to get his security chief to stand down his men, to no avail. Arriving in the front hallway, he turned and fired two shots from the Thunderer into the ceiling to get their attention.

He was about to yell, "Stand down!" again when the FBI fired through the windows. Concussion grenades and tear gas detonated on the first and second floors. In the next moment, the FBI crashed through the front door. The Postman, reeling, stunned, still holding his pistol, turned. The second agent through the door saw him, saw the gun and fired three shots, killing him instantly.

In the Congressional Cloakroom, Weir's phone rang. Recognizing the number of the Special Agent from Oklahoma City, he stepped back and took the call. He nodded as he listened. The room fell silent, all eyes on him. Vega, closest to him, heard him murmur, "And your squad? Any injuries?" He hung up and pointed at Quantrelle and Marek. "Get them out of here." He paused and then added, "Take them right past the cameras, handcuffed. But put some body armor on them first."

Weir turned and walked over to David Carr. After a brief discussion, Carr walked back to Moore and Imogen. "Will you resign, Bob?"

"Fuck you!" said Moore.

"Bob," Carr began, "you've seen the evidence against you. The Presidency can't protect you. The cameras are right outside. Tomorrow, the nation will hear about the conspiracy, about the murder of President Redmond, the succinylcholine. And about your part in it. Tomorrow, I bet we'll have testimony from those two," he said, indicating Marek and Quantrelle, now being bundled out the door, "and it will only get worse for you...and the nation.

"I'd like to believe you didn't know everything they were planning. I'd like to think that your panic at the door represented your final, full understanding that you weren't in charge. That you never had been the chief executive, and you never would be. I don't believe *this* is what you wanted. It's over. Finally, do the right thing."

34

Arrangements were hastily made and Moore and Carr arrived together at the door to the Chamber for a second time. This time, Moore's reluctance was understandable. He strode to the rostrum amidst mausoleum silence. The Speaker seemed uneasy about shaking his hand as Moore stood at the podium, and though he did so, he did it with elaborate reticence.

Moore resigned. In his brief speech he admitted no guilt, only cited the pending charges against his closest advisors, the wide scope of the investigation. He said that in that light, his Presidency had become untenable. With that, former President Moore walked slowly through the door leading to the Speaker's Lobby, where he was met again by Weir and Trager, to be taken into protective custody. Inside the Chamber, Vice President David Carr joined the Speaker, Senate President pro tempore, the Senate Majority Leader and the Chief Justice on the Rostrum.

From the Rostrum, he took the oath of office and addressed the nation:

"Mister Speaker, Mr. President, my fellow Americans, our perilous journey, our Constitutional nightmare ends tonight! All known conspirators have been caught. In the days and weeks to come, working with government leaders, the Justice Department and others, we will reveal the full scope of the conspirators' aims, deeds and plans. We will reveal the identities and roles of *all* the conspirators—dead or alive—so that government, as it was intended to function, may flourish again.

"No Constitution," he continued, "other than that of the United States could have withstood the brazen, cynical and coordinated attack made upon its—upon *our*—integrity. Yet here we are! Bloodied, but unbowed. Our nation, its laws, and our Constitution have been sorely tested, and we will all look to the leaders of both parties to come together...."

Throughout the night and next day, FBI agents moved on their arrest targets across Washington D.C., Maryland and Northern Virginia. They swept into the truck bay in Springfield, Virginia, arresting Tweedledum and 'Dim and impounding their equipment. At Bethesda Naval Hospital and at his private practice in Chevy Chase, doctors Menlo and Somers were taken into custody, charged with the murder of President Redmond. Clayton Quantrelle's home was raided, as was Marek's. In Nebraska, agents moved on the CEO of Flintlock Industries and its Director of Flight Operations, Allen Jardine, seizing documents.

In Kansas, the FBI began piecing together what they could from the wreck of Rufus Hessel's estate. The CIA and NSA were now involved, too, as there were grave questions about how the dark network had come by Novichok-5 and whether foreign actors were involved.

Further agents in far-flung Resident Agencies and Field Offices were detailed to begin a full review of files on the murdered Electors with special instructions to look for mistakes, missteps or collusion either by local or federal enforcement in the initial collection and presentation of evidence. At the offices of the Sovereign Caucus, Opportunity Initiative, Forefathers Institute, Fourmile Creek and V^3, agents arrived with court orders seizing records, computers and servers. The directors were brought in for questioning. As details of the conspiracy became widely known, campaign managers for politicians on either side of the aisle began frantically combing through their donor lists and returning PAC money, some of it not from any of the involved PAC's— better safe than culpable.

Three days later, President Carr gave a speech on the South Lawn. The White House and grounds were resplendent in spring, the sun dazzling on the white sandstone. Carr began by noting the beautiful, sunny day, adding, "As Justice Brandeis once said—and I heartily agree—'sunlight is the best disinfectant.'"

After brief remarks, he turned the discussion over to the acting Attorney General, formerly the Deputy AG, who detailed the criminal-electoral conspiracy and the Justice Department's case against the perpetrators; how it was constructed, how it was funded, and what it had done. And he named names: billionaire Rufus Hessel, the Postman whose cash and dark vision had brought this hell and night to the nation; Alec Nash and Frank Reed, who first built and then brought that monstrous birth to light; Clayton Quantrelle, Anthony Marek and Attorney-General-for-a-day, Drew Eliot, who took up the final stage of that plan, bringing the nation closer to destruction than at any time since the Civil War. He also named former President Robert Moore.

The Deputy described in detail the Byzantine tangle the FBI worked so hard to unravel: Hessel had provided the money and ultimate vision—a nation ruled by kleptocrats, a democracy in name only. Nash and Reed had supplied the means to fulfill that dark vision, imagining and erecting the structure.

He detailed the nature and organization of the so-called "chapters," the terrorist cells, the murders they had committed. He discussed Flintlock Industries (whose executive board was now cooperating with investigators), and their murder-delivery service. He noted with deep regret that some of what had happened would not have stayed hidden had there not been complicity within the Bureau itself, naming retired Special Agent Andrew Colls and Thomas Kurtz.

Aware of how straightforward it seemed now in the sunshine, the Deputy pointed out it had only been chance and the sacrifice of true patriots with the wit and imagination to understand what it portended that had peeled back a corner of the conspiracy exposing some of its workings.

The Faithless Elector Task Force was singled out for commendation: Don Weir, Amanda Vega, Imogen Trager, and Nettie Sartain (who was given special dispensation from her doctor to attend, though she still looked ashen and weak); along with Agents Gus Davies and Ron Guthrie, and Rawley Sims of the FAA. They stood to the Deputy's left, ramrod straight and squinting in the sunlight.

Special Agent in Charge, Amanda Vega, spoke of individual citizens who had helped in the investigation. Imogen came forward and noted the sacrifice of countless other Americans. She barely got through her remarks. She had lived with fear for so long, the sudden lifting of constraint brought all that she'd pushed aside crashing in on her.

Even in fear, she had dared to look forward to a moment like this sunny day on the South Lawn. This recognition was what she had wanted. But when she had looked forward, Duncan was always there. The promise in his final note that he would "always love her," was false, she saw bitterly. "Always" meant now and forever: present and future tense. He and his love were gone. They had no future, only a past.

Images of him assailed her—alive and vital one moment, dead on a slab the next. Why had he chosen no future? She had certainly worried fitfully about what the end of the investigation would look like, but she had somehow always trusted that a reckoning would come. Now it had, and she was bereft and alone as she'd never been before.

The press conference ended, and Imogen realized she was walking slowly, automatically shaking people's hands. Amanda gave her a hug. Nettie was looking at her strangely. She still had to go back to the Northwest and cremate Duncan, still had to attend the memorial his department would likely have. What future was that, making plans for someone who would never have one?

Someone was talking to her. It was the new Chief of Staff, Georgia Desmond.

"Sorry," said Imogen, blinking, "I didn't hear…"

"I asked if you'd come into the Oval Office now for a photo and brief discussion with President Carr," said Desmond. "Hugh Salter will be there, too. I think he'd like a word."

REVIEWS are the lifeblood of authors and books. Consider letting James and others know what you think, on Amazon and/or Goodreads

James McCrone has a Master of Fine Arts degree from the University of Washington, in Seattle. He's a member of Crime Writers of America (NY Chapter), Sisters in Crime (DE-Valley Chapter), International Association of Crime Writers, Philadelphia Dramatists Center and International Thriller Writers.

James's work explores characters pitted against forces larger than themselves. Both on an off the page, he's fascinated with politics and issues of social responsibility and justice.

A Pacific Northwest native, he now lives in Philadelphia with his wife and three children.

Follow James on Twitter at: '@jamesmccrone4'

Praise for *Faithless Elector* and *Dark Network*!

You can find the other Imogen Trager novels *Faithless Elector* and *Dark Network* online at Bookshop.org, Amazon, at Barnes & Noble and at your local independent bookstore. Watch for *Bastard Verdict*, coming next!

Publishers Weekly calls *Faithless Elector* "A fast-moving topical thriller." Its "surprising twists add up to a highly suspenseful read."

"A gripping and intelligently executed political drama."
                                              -Kirkus Reviews

"The pleasure of *Faithless Elector* lies not just its smooth evocative prose, but in the author's justified confidence that good writing can make chases through recognizable locales sufficiently exciting without a Navy SEAL or a terrorist plot."
        -Lauren Kiefer, *Plattsburgh Press-Republican*

"Gripping and unpredictable, **Dark Network** could not have appeared at a better time...highly recommended for political thriller readers and mystery fans alike."
        -D. Donovan, Sr. Reviewer, *Midwest Book Review*

"Baldacci and Meltzer fans will appreciate the plot's twists and the easy-to-empathize-with lead. McCrone's second political thriller featuring FBI agent Imogen Trager builds on the dramatic tension of its predecessor, 2016's *Faithless Elector*..."—*Publishers Weekly*

"[McCrone] yet again deftly delivers a combination of stirring action and remarkably intricate plot entanglements," and "skillfully depicts a country pushed to the brink...A rousing and provocative political thriller..."—*Kirkus Review*

CPSIA information can be obtained
at www.ICGtesting.com
Printed in the USA
BVHW041055051020
590305BV00012B/995